ELDER AFFAIRS

SILENCED

E. HOWARD JONES

ELLIOT FICTION
ST. MARKS, FL 32355 USA

ELLIOT FICTION

Elder Affairs — Silenced
Copyright © 2005 E. Howard Jones

Requests for information should be addressed to:
Elliot Fiction, P. O. Box 277, St. Marks, Florida 32355
sales@elliotfiction.com

http://elliotfiction.com

Library of Congress Control Number: 2005936005

ISBN-13: 978-0-9774407-0-2
ISBN-10: 0-9774407-0-2

This book is printed on acid-free paper.

- "As soon as I read the first chapter I knew I would enjoy the book."
- "I usually read a book like this in two weeks. I read this in one and half days."

> Millard Noblin
> Realtor
> Board of Directors,
> Tallahassee Memorial Hospital

- "I've never read or seen a book like this. It's about us. It's better than great."

> Beverly Moore
> Retired Florida Teacher

- "I found my heart racing, trying to get the characters through the situations."
- "This book takes on a life of its own and pulls you along."

> Leon Cassels
> Executive Vice President
> Florida Chamber of Commerce

- "I thought it was going to be about nursing homes, it wasn't."
- "A lot of mystery, suspense."
- "It was entertaining. I loved it."

> Bonnie Kidd
> Administrative Assistant
> Attorney General's Office

- "As you follow Arthur and his friends through their experiences in the retirement home, your anxiety elevates, wondering if this could ever happen to you!"

   Wayne NeSmith
   President
   Florida Hospital Association

- "This book takes the reader on an emotional roller coaster from anticipation to anxiety and anger, to humor, joy, and surprise. It was a great ride!"

   Joyce NeSmith
   Homemaker and Mother

- "The unique topic of this book will peak the interest of young and old alike. Once you pick it up it holds you spellbound until the last page."

   Donna Callaway
   Member, Florida State Board of Education

ACKNOWLEDGEMENTS

I would like to thank the many people who helped make this book a reality.

First, to my editor, Liz Jameson, who always had a kind word and was a constant encourager. Rhonda Harvey, who supplied me with vital information about the effects of different medicines. And of course those individuals already mentioned in the Reader's Responses, for their time, input, encouragement, and opinions. To the others who offered their expertise in legal and other aspects and helped shape this book.

To my daughters, who sacrificed their evenings and weekends with their dad.

To my mom and dad, who have always supported me in my endeavors.

And to my wife, who tolerated my many temperaments over the last five years that I have been writing.

Especially, to God, without whom this book would have been impossible.

CHAPTER ONE

The fireball vanished as the windows and doors rattled. Arthur's body catapulted away from the stove as if a wet towel had been flung onto the floor. He landed sprawled on his back, dazed, staring at the swirling ceiling. He could hear his daughter's voice warning once more, "Dad—you're going to kill yourself. You're becoming careless in your old age." And how could he argue with her? This was the fourth apparent accident he'd suffered in the past few weeks—and she would be sure to mention that fact, too.

Grayish smoke continued seeping from the oven; the once fragrant smells of oranges and grapefruits were now overpowered with the odor of acrid burned grease. The whites of Arthur's eyes glared in shock from behind a mask of soot. His waning gray hairline was now singed and blackened. Tools lay scattered across the kitchen floor. His chest rapidly rose and fell; each breath resulted in a hacking cough. His eyes teared as they tried to diminish the burning sensation. The smoke detector's screeching alarm compounded his already throbbing head.

He struggled to his feet, and blindly probed for the telephone. Finding it, he quickly lifted the receiver hoping to prevent the home's monitoring system from dialing the fire department. "Oh no! I'm too late," he exhaled and hung his head in regret.

His coughs echoed off the walls, and his eyes continued to burn as he fumbled behind the stove for the gas valve. He found it and stopped the flow of gas. Still coughing, he rose from behind the stove; his hands cupped his mouth. He staggered out the back door and landed in the lush grass. The world outside was blurred. He clawed at his face, trying to clear the soot from his eyes. His vision slowly cleared as the fresh breeze helped to flush the fumes and ash. Knowing the emergency vehicles would be arriving, he shuffled around the house to meet them.

A widower at sixty-seven, Arthur lived in West Palm Beach, Florida. He had retired seven years earlier as the owner of a lucrative heating and air-conditioning business. His expansive Key West style home graced an acre of Saint Augustine grass. Queen palms stretched skyward above the yard with their graceful limbs sweeping the turf. An unusually large sea grape tree sprawled into the salty air; it provided the perfect cover to enjoy the view of the wildlife and passing yachts. The backyard eased into the brackish waters of the Intracoastal Waterway, creating a normally languid landscape. But today was anything but tranquil.

Arthur was confused by the unexplainable mishaps during the previous weeks. *Why am I having one disaster after another?* Up until two weeks ago he had been active and accident free. He sat in the front yard under the shadow of the gumbo limbo, leaning against the reddish-silver bark.

Looking at the purple lantana, the firebush, and the penta—a bush with small clusters of individual red trumpet shaped flowers blooming around the tree—he remembered when Laura had planted and nurtured them. The hummingbirds were her favorite birds, and she had researched and found different plants that would attract them and yet survive the salt air and water. She had planted them all around the yard, every variety imaginable.

She had been his wife for forty-seven years. Last year she had succumbed to brain cancer. He wondered if she were still alive today if he would be having these accidents.

Sirens softly wailed off in the distance. Arthur knew from experience that they were approximately twenty seconds away. Taking a deep breath, he reflected back on one of the previous emergencies.

Two Saturdays earlier, in the afternoon, he had taken his seventeen-foot Proline, center-console, fishing. He had fished for only a short time before the temperature rose to ninety-one degrees. Hot, having caught nothing, and feeling woozy, Arthur had headed home. The breeze in his face was a welcome relief over the heat, but the beauty of the Intracoastal blurred and spun. As he stood to maneuver the craft up to the water's edge, the boat's backwash-wake jostled the craft. Arthur stumbled and jabbed the throttle forward. The outboard engine whined. Arthur staggered backward momentarily, but within a second the boat stopped on dry land and he found himself flying across the bow's railing, tumbling to an abrupt stop, on the sparse, sharp grass.

The raspberry marks were a painful reminder of what grass does to skin, he thought as he rubbed his elbows. He was thankful that a neighbor had witnessed the accident and called 9-1-1. Sam and Vicky, the paramedics had found him unconscious. They quickly checked Arthur's vitals and found all to be within acceptable limits. As they were lifting him onto the stretcher, Arthur's eyes opened and he sat up. Neither Sam nor Vicky could explain how he miraculously awoke.

Knowing the heat had never bothered him before, he wondered why all of a sudden it had caused this unexplainable symptom. If he had not lost his balance so easily, the accident would not have happened.

The sirens blared as the emergency vehicles raced down River Drive. Arthur's reflections were abruptly interrupted.

He dreaded having to greet the rescue men and women again. Mustering up courage, he reluctantly made his way to the sidewalk, where he waited for them to arrive.

Plugging his ears with his fingers, Arthur watched as a fire truck shuddered to a stop at the edge of his yard. The driver disengaged the obnoxious sirens but allowed the flashing red and white lights to continue. Observing Arthur's sooted face and singed facial hair, he grasped for his radio and depressed the mic's button. "This is engine five requesting an ambulance at 1760 River Drive."

Firemen leaped from their truck and raced around, grabbing hoses, axes, and oxygen tanks. Arthur hurried up to them and yelled, "It's okay fellows. There's no fire. Something went wrong with the gas stove. I turned off the valve before leaving the house."

Light smoke drifted from an opened window and through the front screen door.

"Step aside, Mr. McCullen," said one fireman, as he pulled his breathing apparatus over his mouth and dashed for the front door, dragging his fire hose. Two more dashed inside, one carrying an ax in his right hand, the other draping a fire hose across his shoulders and leaning forward as he disappeared into the house.

Closing his eyes, Arthur tried to imagine what could have caused a gas leak. The stove was relatively new, just a few years old. With all the safety features the salesman had promoted, why hadn't any of the automatic shut-off valves worked?

Neighbors rushed outside while others stood at their picture windows investigating what their neighbor had done this time. Soon another siren was heard in the distance.

Arthur reflected on the catastrophe that had occurred a week and half before. Sometime after breakfast and after taking his Ginkgo Biloba—a vitamin supplement that he began taking to improve his memory when he kept forgetting where he put his keys—he had gone to the garage and climbed behind the driver's seat of his Cadillac Deville to go shopping. He thought he had shifted into reverse. With the garage door up and his vision focused in the rearview mirror, he pressed the gas. His body lunged backward as the tires barked. Before he could press the brakes, the vehicle had crashed through the wall and his body had recoiled off the steering wheel. The front bumper stopped inside

10

the utility room and Arthur sat motionless, dazed to his surroundings. Perplexed, he focused on the fluorescent-orange needle. It pointed to "D." He could not believe how bad his eye-hand coordination was. *How did that happen?*

Again, Arthur's reflections were interrupted, as the boxy ambulance pulled into his driveway. Adding to his embarrassment was his recognition of the two paramedics.

"I'm okay Sam. Honest Vicky, I'm not burned. It's only soot," Arthur implored.

Having met Arthur three times during the last few weeks, they knew him personally. "Please be seated on the ground, Mr. McCullen and let us be the judges of your injuries."

Arthur's blood pressure was normal. His heart beat was the same as the previous days—high, but within acceptable ranges. They knew the elevated heart rate was due to the trauma. There was nothing wrong with him except a dirty face and singed hair.

"You're okay, Mr. McCullen. Will we see you tomorrow?" Sam inquired.

"No sir. I'm sorry that you had to come today for another minor problem."

As the two paramedics closed the ambulance's doors, they both broke out laughing. "Did you see his face?" Sam continued to laugh.

Vicky could not stop snickering, either. "It was hard not to laugh, when I looked at him. I wanted to call a veterinarian to get that raccoon off his shoulders."

They continued to chuckle, as they drove away.

The three firemen ambled back out the front door. The captain marched over to where Arthur was sitting, "Mr. McCullen, your house sustained minor smoke damage. Come by the station later today and pick up the fire report. Your insurance company will want a copy. You've got to be more careful. One of these times you're going to hurt yourself severely."

11

Feeling miserable at being reprimanded like a child, Arthur's head hung low. "Sorry sir, I'll be more careful." *How am I going to explain this one to Shelly?*

"Good, I don't want to respond to any more emergencies at your house."

The black boots disappeared and soon a loud hiss sounded, the airbrake released, and the last fire truck pulled away from Arthur's house.

Arthur remained motionless on the front lawn, watching a bug cross from one blade of grass to the next, not stopping to mock the neighborhood troublemaker. He hoped all the neighbors would soon disperse. With the frequency of the emergency response vehicles visiting his house, he dreaded seeing his neighbors. Their laughing and taunting eyes were more than he could face.

Across the street George Willis backed away from the large picture window. The other neighbors quietly retreated inside their houses.

Arthur raised his head looking around from one yard to the next. Alone and dejected, he slowly rose from the grass. His feet shuffled as he neared the front door. Arthur hesitated before opening it. How was he going to explain this latest accident to Shelly? *Something malfunctioned on the gas-stove. It could have happened to anyone. But why today?*

He swung open the door and slammed it against the wall. "Why me?" Arthur grunted, as he looked heavenward, stepping through the doorway.

After a quick shower and a change of clothes, Arthur fell into his recliner—his favorite seat, an overstuffed and oversized rocker— it teetered precariously. For a minute or two he stared at the cordless phone. *Pick it up; you've got to call her. She's going to find out sooner or later.* Arthur's eyes closed, hoping the smell and the sooted kitchen would all go away. *You might as well get it over with. Call her.*

"Maybe not!" Arthur shouted, as he leaped out of the recliner. His words echoed off the family room walls. *I've got to keep this from Shelly. She'll blame me for the accident. I didn't do anything wrong. I'll clean the kitchen. She'll never know.*

Arthur began whistling as he hurried from room to room, opening all the windows and the back door. A nice gentle breeze blew into the house. Arthur hoped the acrid smells would soon dissipate. At the kitchen sink, water sprayed from the faucet, splashing into a pan. Liquid soap spewed from the soap bottle. Iridescent bubbles rose from the pan sending fresh lemon scent airborne. As he continued whistling, Arthur grasped the kitchen sponge and swirled the suds.

Arthur began with the soot-coated wall above the sink and below the window. He was surprised at how well the wall was cleaning up. As he moved to the next wall, he weakened. The once jubilant whistle now tooted off-key and fizzled to a stop. As he moved to the third wall, he was exhausted. Arthur's chest labored with each breath inhaled; the mounting dread of Shelly's threats weighed heavier than this latest crisis. *Dad, you've got to move.*

Arthur turned; his attention was drawn to the oven door, which was protruding from the far wall. He pulled it out, leaving a large gouge. The door was slightly bent, and Arthur knew it would have to be replaced. Meanwhile, he could prop the door back in the opening, and try to hide the damage.

After a short rest, Arthur finished cleaning the remainder of the room. He stood back and inspected his work. The paint was definitely a shade or two darker, but no one would notice. Anyone who entered would, however, notice the hole that the oven door had left in the wall. He would have to find something to hide it from view until it could be patched.

Arthur sprayed air-freshener into each room. The April-fresh scent drifted through the house. *I'll get George to drive me to the fire department.* He smiled. *Shelly will never find out.*

CHAPTER TWO

Shelly returned to her desk and checked her voice mail. "Shelly, this is George Willis. A fire truck and ambulance just left your dad's house. The firemen and paramedics didn't stay long. Just thought you would like to know."

As Shelly rushed out of the office, she thought up excuses for showing up at her dad's. At forty-one she had gained fewer than five pounds since college, and at five-six, she still looked trim. Country music resonated inside the vehicle, but Shelly did not hear the words. Instead, she heard last night's conversation with her husband, Justin. "Shelly, you must admit that your dad can no longer stay at home by himself. He needs to live in some kind of assisted living facility, where he can be taken care of. If not, he's going to kill himself."

As she pulled into the driveway she saw that Arthur's house appeared normal, at least from the outside. *Thank Goodness. It must have been the monitoring system.* She was glad Mr. Willis was watching out for him. She couldn't let Arthur know. He'd throw a fit.

"Dad, I've come to take you to lunch," she said, as she pushed open the front door. Her noise twitched as she sniffed the air and smelled the fresh scent. She glanced around the entrance and everything appeared to be normal.

Arthur hurried from the kitchen. Their eyes locked momentarily. "Sure," he said, anything to get her out of the house.

"I need to use the bathroom before we go," she said, giving another excuse for her nosiness. Arthur stepped back and blocked her view of the kitchen.

As she made her way down the hall, she glanced into the bedrooms. Nothing appeared out of the ordinary. A breeze blew across the hall. *Dad never has his windows open.* She sensed something, but Arthur wasn't confessing.

Arthur watched Shelly as she approached and could tell she was looking for something. He wondered if he had used too much air freshener. "I've been cleaning," he said, as he steered her to the front door.

"I thought you just did that yesterday."

"I didn't finish."

Shelly still had doubts. "I'm thirsty," she said, in an attempt to check out the kitchen. He didn't seem to want her there.

"I'll get you a glass of water." Their eyes locked again for a brief second. He didn't want her snooping around the kitchen. He hurried to the cabinet and pulled out a glass.

Shelly sniffed twice, thinking she had just gotten a whiff of smoke. She glanced around the kitchen, as she stalled and drank her water. Against the far wall a large box sat on the floor. *Everything looks okay.* "Let's go eat."

Arthur breathed a sigh of relief. *I pulled it off.*

As Shelly passed the stove, she brushed against the oven door. It crashed to the floor. She gasped as the odor of burnt grease drifted from the oven.

"D-a-d!"

"I burned breakfast."

"What does that have to do with the broken oven door?"

Shelly wasn't moving until she got an answer.

Arthur knew she was not going to take this accident lightly. He thought if ever he was going to have a heart attack, now would be the perfect time. But not feeling any chest pains, he began to explain. "It wasn't my fault. The stove malfunctioned. When I went in the kitchen for breakfast this morning, I smelled gas. I searched the kitchen, and the odor seemed to be stronger near the oven. I got my tool box; the moment I opened the lid, a freakish spark ignited the gas fumes. The kitchen sustained minor smoke damage and I'm. . . ."

". . . Oh-my-gosh! You blew up the stove?"

"Calm down, Shelly, I didn't *blow* up the stove." Arthur's voice rose with agitation. "I told you it wasn't my fault. It malfunctioned. As you can see, the only damage is to the oven door." He wasn't about to admit that the door had blown across the room.

"Dad, you shouldn't have tried to work on it yourself; you should have called someone."

"Call someone! I've been working on these things all my life. You know that. Being in the heating and air conditioning business, I was certified to work on anything that was gas. I don't need a lecture. I need a ride down to the fire department to pick up the report. My insurance agent will need it and my car is still in the body shop."

Shelly shook her head in disbelief. "Yes, Dad, I'll drive you there." *What's he going to do next?*

Angered about Arthur's latest accident, Shelly gripped the steering wheel tightly as her wintergreen Chevrolet Suburban swerved, passing a slower driver. *How can he say it's not his fault? He never should have tried to fix a gas leak, especially the way he's been so forgetful and accident prone lately.*

She fought the thought of sending him to an assisted living facility—a place where he refused to live. As his only child, they had always had a special bond. From her early childhood she remembered how her dad had always been there for her during the good times and the bad times. She recalled memories of the times when just the two of them would stop after school and he would let her order two scoops of her favorite ice cream, chocolate-chip. Those were times when he had sacrificed to be with her instead of doing what he wanted to be doing or knew he should be doing—like the time when the family physician wanted to admit her into the hospital overnight so they could monitor her high fever. How she had cried, begging her dad not to take her. He reluctantly agreed with her, and had taken her home. How through the night he stayed by her side until the next morning when the fever broke. The sentimental times they had spent together left her feeling like a traitor, sending him off to be locked away like a criminal for life.

Neither spoke, but she could hear his warnings, "Shelly, you better not put me in an old-folks' home, because I'm not going." Fidgeting in her seat, she knew this would be the hardest decision of her life. She loved her dad and did not want to upset him. But just recently things had escalated to the point where something had to be done.

"Dad," she said, breaking the silence, "have you given any more thought to an assisted living facility?"

Arthur didn't acknowledge her.

At the fire station, the chief gave the report to Arthur. Shelly and Arthur thanked him and promised not to bother him again.

Afterward, the firemen stood around taking bets as to how many hours would pass before they would have to respond to another emergency at Mr. McCullen's house. None of the bets exceeded forty-eight hours.

Shelly grew more agitated as she braced herself in her bucket seat. Her knuckles whitened as she gripped the steering wheel; her tunnel vision narrowed on the traffic ahead. Arthur sat buckled in the front passenger's seat, with his hand massaging his growling stomach. He wished he was anywhere but here with Shelly. The ride seemed long, but he was glad she was not hounding him further about a nursing home. His stomach growled louder and Arthur clamped tighter, trying desperately to suppress its begging. He held his breath hoping Shelly would not hear its demands. He did not want to spend any more time with her than was necessary. Shelly's unspoken vibes were just as abominable as actual spoken words.

The Suburban slowed and suddenly turned right, into the parking lot of a fast food restaurant. "What are you doing?" Arthur demanded through his gritted teeth, his eyes rolled up in disbelief.

"Buying you lunch," she blared in frustration. The Suburban pulled into the drive-through lane, stopping behind one other car. She sat silently. She just wished her dad would at least go with her and check one out. There were great facilities within their community: individual private rooms and baths—kept clean by employees; a cafeteria—nutritious prepared food would mean no more cleaning or washing pots, pans, and dishes; people to interact with—card playing and dominos at night, something he dearly enjoyed; and planned outings—sight-seeing trips according to the season; arts and crafts. How could he refuse to live there? What was there not to like? With the added security for safety and not having to maintain a yard and a house, she thought he would have jumped at the opportunity. But how could she get him to have an open mind?

The vehicle pulled up to the order intercom and Shelly lowered her window. "Two grilled chicken sandwiches and two side salads."

"Anything else?"

Shelly looked at her dad. He sat staring ahead, not wanting much to eat. The less food, the quicker Shelly would leave. He knew she was bound to hound him any minute on moving and he wasn't having any part of it.

"No thank you, but could you put the order in two bags." Shelly turned, "Dad, I'm going to have to take mine to go. I've got to get back to the office." Shelly pulled around to the pay window. She fumbled through her pocketbook stopping briefly to look up at Arthur. He remained stiff, looking straight ahead. She knew now was not the time to bring up the assisted living facility, but later she would.

Arthur breathed a sigh of relief that she wouldn't be staying for lunch.

The Suburban's engine reverberated to silence in Arthur's driveway as Shelly pulled her key from the ignition, exhaled a long breath, and squelched her thoughts. "Come on Dad. I know you're hungry," her voice was back to her normal mellow tone. She grabbed his lunch, slid out of her seat, and closed the door.

Arthur scampered around the front of the car and up the sidewalk to his house, giving her less time to scold him.

Shelly forced her legs to move rapidly to keep up with him. "Dad, I've got to hurry."

Arthur's eyes brightened as he breathed, *thank goodness.*

Stepping up on the front porch, she continued, "This evening, I'll pick you up for dinner. Justin and I will be glad for you to join us." She was hoping to keep him from having another accident.

Arthur gritted his teeth. Justin was the last person he wanted to spend time with. He never liked Justin from the moment Shelly brought him home for the first time. *An arrogant wanna-be attorney.* "Now dear," his wife's memories echoed in his head, "We can't pick Shelly's boyfriends. We have to trust her and warmly accept anyone she brings home. Otherwise, she'll never come home again." Arthur knew she had been correct in her thinking, but now he was all alone to deal with Justin and he hated it.

"Can I just. . . ."

Shelly knew she couldn't allow him to object or he would have an excuse for refusing to come. ". . . If you'd like, you can also spend the night." A grin spread across her face. "Also, . . ."

". . . Uh, dinner will be fine," Arthur quickly answered. "Thanks very much," his half-hearted response died. Dinner was all Arthur was going to obligate himself. He opened the door, stepped squarely in the doorway, turned around and took the bag from Shelly, preventing her from stepping inside. "See you later," he said, knowing she was now off to work.

Shelly sucked in her stomach, squeezed past her dad, and hurried into the kitchen. "Dad, have a seat in your recliner and I'll bring you a glass of tea." Grabbing a glass from the cupboard above the sink, she stepped over to the refrigerator and began pouring tea. The amber liquid rose to an inch from the brim.

Arthur reluctantly did as he was instructed. He unwrapped his sandwich and began to eat. Shelly brought in the glass of tea and placed it on the end table beside the recliner. Grabbing the remote, she pressed the on button and began surfing the stations for something she knew he would watch.

Arthur grunted as he submitted to his daughter's requests, anything to get her to leave. *What will she demand next?*

Shelly, feeling the tension that was building, said nothing, but kept changing from one station to the next and finally stopped. There on the screen two cowboys sat on their horses, as the wind blew across their faces. Grasping the reins, each swirled a rope overhead with his other hand—westerns were Arthur's favorites.

"I've got to go," Shelly started walking toward the front door. Stopping and turning to look at Arthur, she continued. "And please Dad, take it easy the rest of the day. Don't start any projects and most of all, be careful and don't hurt yourself."

I'm not a child, Arthur thought sinking his teeth into the chicken. He waved at Shelly as if he agreed. She accepted his gesture. She shook her head and left the house, knowing she would find it difficult to concentrate on her work for the remainder of the day.

CHAPTER THREE

Arthur settled in his recliner, ate his salad and watched the movie. After a few more minutes, he recognized the main actors and remembered the plot. "With all the good westerns available, why this lousy one today?" He muttered as if the programmers were listening to him.

Picking up the remote, the TV blinked with each station scanned: Snowy pictures, news broadcasters, soap operas, and game-show stations all flashed on and off. Before long the TV was back on the same station that Shelly had chosen. "Oh brother, another boring day," Arthur grumbled, squirming in the recliner. Thirty minutes passed and his dissatisfaction intensified, as his patience thinned. Heavy-set actors lumbered across the open range impersonating cowboys. "Where are the real cowboys?" His question went unanswered.

The recliner shuddered with each twist and turn as he contemplated his to-do list: Patch the kitchen wall, clean the attic, clean the yard, and—he sighed heavily—clean the garage. As the cowboy cook clanged pots and pans, rallying the hungry cowboys to chow time, Arthur's what-to-do-list vanished. Arthur climbed out of the recliner and headed down the hallway to the bathroom.

Arthur stood in the bathroom and rinsed the soap off his hands. His gaze focused on the red trumpet creeper that his wife had planted outside the window years ago. Hovering above it was a metallic-green feathered hummingbird darting from one trumpet flower to the next. "Wow, a female," Arthur murmured and closed his eyes as he visualized Laura's whispery voice and reflected on her instructions about the red-throated-hummingbird—"ruby feathers on its throat, a male—white feathers on its throat, a female."

As her soft words faded, Arthur spoke, "Laura, I miss you so much." His closed eyelids fluttered as if she were standing before him, wrapped in her fluffy green cotton bathrobe. His face lit up at the phantasm.

Arthur drifted toward the window, mesmerized by Laura's appearance. His lips and nose brushed the glass pane. The cold sensation caused his eyes to open and Laura vanished.

He touched his lips as if the touch of the glass had been a kiss from Laura's lips. His eyes followed the hummingbird as it flew off to his left. Leaning his head to his right, he followed its flight and watched as it circled back. His heart throbbed, wondering if it had really been Laura coming to check on him disguised as a hummingbird.

Arthur's eyes squinted as the greenish feathers faded into the leaves of a storm damaged tamarind tree, leaning beside the driveway, drooping its shadow across the concrete. Staring into the leaning tree, he wished he had cut it down months ago when it first started leaning.

He shook his head and silently agreed that today was not the day to be cutting any trees down; he pushed himself away from the window. As he turned off the faucet and dried his hands on the towel, he saw the Gingko Biloba bottle sitting where a cup was intended to sit, on top of the toothbrush holder. He remembered that his routine of taking his vitamin after breakfast had been interrupted, and he had forgotten to take today's pill. As the single pill slid down his throat, Arthur wondered if he should start taking two capsules daily to prevent future accidents. Deciding against taking an additional pill, he placed the bottle back on the cup holder, and turned off the bathroom light.

The yard glowed radiantly as the sunlight warmed the air. With the outside visible through the window, Arthur was reminded of the to-do list and all that needed to be accomplished. "No," Arthur breathed, as if the outdoors had baited him, "no chores today. Shelly forbade me to start any projects." Arthur turned and hurried back to his recliner, fleeing from the beckoning outdoors.

Back in front of the television and watching chubby cowboys drive cattle to the auction, again he became bored. His mind drifted away from the movie and his thoughts returned outside to the leaning tamarind tree. *With the right cut into the trunk, it would easily fall away from the house and off the driveway.* In his mind he clearly placed the notch cut at a forty-five-degree angle from the house. Smiling, he pictured the tree falling to the ground just as planned.

An obnoxious car salesman's voice blared from the TV; the man stood beside a pickup truck banging on the hood. "Best deal in town." Head throbbing, tired of sitting in front of the TV, Arthur reached for the remote control, pointed it at the salesman and made him vanish. Instantly the annoying salesman's voice was gone, but Shelly's voice intruded and protested. *What are you doing?*

Arthur slumped back into the recliner and kicked up the leg rest as if Shelly were standing behind him. His hand numbly raised the remote and brought back the cowboys who were hollering and shooting into the air as they road into town. Arthur smiled, this was the only part of the movie he liked, celebration after a job successfully completed. The party moved inside the saloon. Drinks were poured and painted ladies clung to their cowboy heroes.

Arthur soon grew tired of watching cowboys chasing and seducing women. He kicked the leg rest under the recliner, turned the TV off, and covered his ears, trying to shut out Shelly's voice.

"I can't watch TV all day," he huffed into the air as if Shelly were listening. "Someone has to keep this place up." Shelly's demands were drowned out as his deep bass voice hummed off-key. His shoes slapped the floor with each step he took and he concentrated on the noise instead of listening to Shelly's nagging. Humming continued as each indoor job on the to-do list was investigated. As Arthur hummed a new melody, he stood looking out a front window, wondering if he should be out there working.

The shadows out on the front lawn insured a cool work environment. Arthur's attention was again drawn to the tamarind tree. From inside, it appeared to be much smaller than it was. He looked at his watch, and concluded that he could have it cut down and piled up at the front street before Shelly would be back to pick him up for dinner.

Stepping from the still-battered utility room into the garage, Shelly's faint pleas were thwarted as he mumbled, "there it is." He pushed the button, and the door rose, as he stepped over to his workbench and picked up the chainsaw. On his way out, he grabbed an extension cord off the floor—it was already plugged into a wall socket—and took long strides to the leaning tree.

He lay the chainsaw at its base, slid the plug into the extension cord, and then looked up, scanning the height of the tree. With a quick glance out in the yard to assure himself that nothing needed to be moved; he stepped from under the branches and looked up just to make sure no power lines were overhead. Seeing none, he began calculating where the notch should be positioned. His eyes burned as sweat seeped into them. Feeling a bit lightheaded, he closed his eyes for a moment. When he opened them he felt better. He raised the chainsaw into place.

"STO . . ."

The snarl of the chainsaw suppressed Shelly's silent warning. Wood chips scattered into the air as Arthur's hands vibrated. His teeth chattered, but a smile spread across his face.

The growl of the saw and its gnarling teeth chewing at the tree sent neighbors scurrying to their windows. What was Arthur doing this time?

George, the neighbor across the street, sensed disaster. Picking up his phone, he quickly pressed the numbers to Shelly's office.

"Your dad's outside with a chainsaw cutting down that leaning tree. Oh my-gosh, I hope he doesn't hurt himself!"

"Stop him, Mr. Willis!"

"I can't. He won't listen to me."

George's body filled the picture window; his wide-eyes watched his neighbor. "Oh what luck. The chain appears loose. He's pulling at it. Hurry Shelly, you've got to stop him before it's too late."

Exasperated, Shelly slammed the phone in its cradle as she vaulted from her high-backed leather chair. She worked only five minutes away, and hoped she would not be too late.

The engine roared and the tires spun as the Suburban pulled out of the parking lot. Moving from the right lane to the left on the four-lane street, she drove like a cop called to the scene of a crime. Shelly's body pressed heavily against the door as the vehicle swerved onto River Drive. The houses swooshed past as her heart raced, and she hoped there was still time to prevent a disaster. Approaching Arthur's house, Shelly pressed the brake and the vehicle rapidly decelerated. She grasped the steering wheel and turned into the driveway. Shelly saw her dad shuddering, clutching the chainsaw as chips flew around him. She breathed a sigh of relief seeing the tree still standing. As the Suburban stopped, she blasted the horn.

The chips stopped flying; Arthur looked up the driveway.

Cra–aaa–ck!

Arthur jerked his head skyward. Again lightheadedness overwhelmed him. The uncut portion of the tree-trunk creaked and moaned as gravity pulled. He teetered backward trying to keep his balance. Suddenly the trunk twisted, and changed the trajectory. He gasped and dropped the chainsaw. Shelly was in its path. "Back up," he yelled as his hands frantically motioned Shelly to hurry. "Move it, get out of the way, MOOOOVE!"

Swooooshh—CRAAASH.

The ground quaked as Arthur stumbled out of the tree's springing and slashing motions. The green Suburban was camouflaged instantly behind a veil of leaves.

Shelly hunched over at the wheel, quivering, wondering if she had died, as darkness swirled around her. Her lungs filled with short, raspy breaths. Time seemed to have stopped. Death couldn't be far away.

"SHELLY," Arthur's voice thundered. "Are you okay?" There was no answer.

Arthur grabbed the chainsaw and pulled the trigger. Its snarls cut the silence. Rays of light filtered into Shelly's window. Shelly's heart pounded with anger at her father. "DAD! DAD!" She screeched, but the pleadings were muffled inside her tomb, surrounded by the gnarling growls of the chainsaw. *Why didn't he listen to me?* Shelly fumed.

The resonating growls pounded at Shelly's nerves. Her hands covered her ears. Her eyes wide with fright strained to see through the leaves and branches. *He's not only a danger to himself but to others.* Shelly's frustration escalated. He can't live by himself!

The chainsaw slashed less than an inch away from her window and threatened to come inside at any second. Shelly screamed, "Dad stop! You're going to hurt me," her words barely audible.

With the rotating teeth slashing at her window, she became hysterical. Her fingers fumbled trying to free herself from the seatbelt. Her heart pounded and her chest heaved.

"Crack—Thud!" A large branch crashed, rocking the vehicle as the buckle released and her body sprang across the center console landing in the passenger's seat. The branch had dropped across the front windshield. Her hand lashed back toward the steering wheel, angrily jabbing the horn. "Dad," she yelled, "you're moving to an assisted living facility! I can't deal with this anymore!"

Startled by the blaring horn, Arthur's eyes narrowed and he stared into the branches. His pointer finger sprung away from the trigger. "Shelly!"

Pushing branches away from the vehicle Arthur could see Shelly's reddened face. Her slitted eyes spit fire, "I told you to stay inside!" He now wished that he had heeded her advice and taken a nap like the docile old man she wanted him to be.

With the danger of the chainsaw gone, she stopped jabbing the horn, scooted back into the driver's seat, and pushed against the door. Limbs did not give and the door did not budge. Shelly turned the ignition key backward and pressed her window button. The window eased down. The smell of wood chips and dusty leaves drifted inside. "Dad, don't do anything," she breathed heavily. "I'm calling 9-1-1." Reaching for her cell phone inside her pocketbook, her hands shook violently as she tried to press 9-1-1 in sequence. She tried again, but the phone flipped from her hand and landed on the floor.

Across the street, George held a cordless phone to his ear. "Hello. . . ."

"This is 9-1-1. What's your emergency?" the flat voice of the operator asked.

"A tree has just fallen across a vehicle at Arthur McCullen's house. His daughter is trapped inside," George hollered. "His address is. . . ."

"I know the address," she snapped, unable to suppress the aggravation in her voice.

CHAPTER FOUR

Arthur pulled the branches back and yelled, "Shelly, are you hurt?"

Shelly tried to take deep cleansing breaths; some of her anger subsided. She was determined to speak calmly, knowing anything spoken harshly would only have to be mended later.

"I'm . . ." her shoulders relaxed, her teeth unclenched as she answered, "fine."

Arthur continued to dig through the branches until he could see Shelly clearly. She appeared unhurt, but he knew that she was furious.

"I'll have you out of there in a minute," he bent down to grab the chainsaw.

"NO! . . ." Shelly blurted uncontrollably. Stopping and breathing, she regained control of herself, and continued, ". . . Wait for the emergency vehicles to arrive. I'm sure they're coming."

As her words fell silent, Shelly heard the sirens and reclined her seat trying to further calm herself. She was glad neither she nor her dad was hurt.

Arthur's head began to spin and his eyes once again blurred. He gritted his teeth and covered his ears as the flashing lights and blaring sirens stopped at his house, alerting his neighbors of another embarrassing mishap. He closed his eyes, hearing Shelly

31

shriek within his head, *I told you to stay inside and not to do anything. You almost killed me.* The hissing air-brakes interrupted Shelly's scolding. The blaring sirens shrieked their last warnings and fell silent.

"Mr. McCullen! What happened?" the chief's voice demanded, as he swung down from the cab and rushed over to Arthur.

Pushing his frustrations and dizziness aside, Arthur shouted, "Hurry, my daughter is buried under that tree."

Looking over at the fallen tree, a small amount of green paint from the Suburban could be seen.

"Step aside, sir." Then the chief turned to his men and began hollering instructions. "We have a lady trapped under that tree."

The red flashing lights darted accusingly, alerting all in the neighborhood as to who had caused the crisis. Arthur looked up and down the street. Neighbors hurried down their driveways; some already stood at the street's edge watching and pointing toward Arthur's yard. He cringed thinking of their laughter and jeers. Arthur backed away from the street until he could not see them anymore. His hands rubbed his eyes and forehead; the neighborhood swayed and swirled. Arthur sat down on the lawn under the protection of the shade. His head fell onto his knees and his eyes closed.

The firemen banged axes and chainsaws from the storage bins along the side of the fire truck. Their heavy boots thunder-clapped with each lunge taken. "Ma'am, we'll have you out shortly," a fireman yelled. The neighborhood's tranquility was once again shattered; pounding axes erupted and the louder gas-powered chainsaws sent wood-chips scattering.

The burned-gas fumes permeated inside. Shelly quickly rolled up her window as wood chips and grayish smoke filled the air.

"Fire truck five is requesting an ambulance," the chief transmitted over his handheld radio.

The fallen tree looked alive as limbs and branches shimmied and swayed. Leaves rustled softly as if waving their final farewell.

Hearing more sirens, neighbors' heads turned and they backed away from the roadway as they spotted the approaching ambulance.

"Oh no," one woman gasped, standing beside her elderly husband, "he's finally hurt someone." They both covered their ears as the lumbering ambulance zoomed past.

The siren fell silent as the ambulance pulled past the growing pile of limbs. Sam and Vicky leaped from its doors. Vicky turned and grabbed the medical bag from the ambulance's back doors while the chief met Sam. "There's one female victim trapped; we'll have her freed shortly."

Vicky rushed up to Sam and the chief. "Is it Arthur again?"

"No," the chief said shaking his head. "It's his daughter."

Shelly sat patiently waiting inside. She looked in the rearview mirror, and saw that the limbs and branches that once covered the rear of the Suburban were gone. Looking out her side window, only one large limb remained holding her prisoner. As the last limb was being lifted from her vehicle, something softy rapped on her side window. "Ma'am, unlock your doors." The fireman stood pulling at the door handle.

As the door opened, Shelly got a strong whiff of oil and gas. All chainsaws fell silent. Vicky maneuvered between the open door and Shelly. "Are you hurt?"

"No."

Vicky's eyes glanced up and down Shelly, looking for any blood or objects that might have penetrated her body. "She appears to be fine," she shouted over her shoulder.

Arthur watched as Vicky wrapped the blood pressure sleeve around Shelly's biceps. He was glad Shelly was not looking at him. Her faceless expression hid her thoughts. He dreaded what was lurking inside her mind. He had heard it many times lately, and again this accident was not his fault. *What is Shelly doing here anyway, and why did she pick then to pull into the driveway?*

The only medical concern Vicky had for Shelly was her elevated blood pressure. Vicky figured it would adjust once she calmed down. "You're free to go."

Shelly marched toward her dad with an angry scowl on her face. *Justin is right. Dad needs to live in an assisted living home.* "Dad!" she exhaled, realizing she was seconds away from initiating an arguing match. Calming, she continued, "Why didn't you stay inside like I asked? At your age you shouldn't be cutting down such a large tree. You're lucky again that you didn't kill yourself. You should be living at an assisted living facility. You're. . . ." Shelly froze having decided to postpone telling Arthur that he was moving. She could no longer handle his senility.

"Shelly, it's only a small accident. If you hadn't pulled into the driveway then, the tree would have fallen harmlessly to the ground. It wasn't my fault. And I'm not moving to some nursing home." He didn't mention his recurring dizziness and blurred vision to Shelly or the paramedics.

As the firemen were repacking their rescue equipment onto the fire truck, one of the firemen held out his hand for the others to pay up on their lost bet. He had guessed the nearest time of Arthur's latest accident, three hours and fifteen minutes.

The chief heard Shelly chastising Arthur and knew she would do a much better job of lecturing than he could. He motioned for the rescuers to head back to the firehouse.

Shelly knew this was not the time or place to argue with her dad about moving. Looking at her watch, she knew it was useless to go back to work. "Okay Dad, let's not talk about moving. Since I'm not going back to work and I'm here, why don't we ride on over to my house. I can start dinner and I won't have to come back and pick you up."

Arthur agreed and locked up his house. Walking to the Suburban, he saw that its front end remained under branches and leaves. The breeze had blown the smell of gas and oil away.

As Shelly backed up the Suburban, branches pulled away from the passenger's door allowing Arthur to open it and climb in. The vehicle backed into the street smoothly, having received only a few small dents and scratches, mostly on the roof.

As they rode down River Drive, Arthur and Shelly stared straight ahead. The tension was palpable and neither spoke. Shelly turned up the radio; Arthur laid his head on the headrest and shut his eyes.

Shelly began to tremble as she drove, wondering how she would get her dad to agree to move.

Once home, Shelly made Arthur comfortable in front of the TV, before she went upstairs to change from her work clothes into something comfortable.

In her walk-in closet, Shelly let her shoulders sag. The weight of the dilemma pressed heavily on her. She needed to talk to Justin. She reached for the cordless phone, wearily closed her eyes, and mechanically pressed his office phone number.

Shelly had met Justin Roble during college. He was studying law and she was in the school of business. They dated for nearly three years before Justin was able to persuade Shelly to marry him. They had not had any children. She did not want to bring children into the world with her rocky marriage. Her husband had turned out to be a big jerk most of the time and until he could show more responsibility, she refused to have any children.

"Justin," Shelly's voice stopped as she sniffled. Catching her breath she continued, "The rescue vehicles had to return to dad's house for a second time today. You're right, I'll have to put him into a facility, just like you've warned. He's not moving voluntarily."

"You can explain when I get home. I'll be there shortly. Don't worry. We'll get through this together okay. I love you."

Tears pooled in Shelly's eyes and began to roll down her cheeks.

"Shelly, you still there?"

"Yeah," she answered, feeling weak.

35

"You'll be okay. I'm on my way home now. Start cooking and you'll forget about your dad for a while. Good bye."

Shelly sat on the side of the bed, wiping at her tear-streaked cheeks, suppressing sniffles. Hurrying to the bathroom, she washed her face and rushed downstairs to the kitchen.

Arthur sat on the couch watching the news, his nose twitched as he smelled onions, bell peppers, butter, and beef aromas drift past. "Shelly, that smells great," he said, his mouth watering.

The front door creaked as Justin hollered, "I'm home."

Arthur winced. Justin was sure to say something about both accidents today. He hoped Justin would not stop and speak. Hearing a metal utensil scraping a pot, Justin stood inhaling, "Mmmmm! Beef stroganoff." Justin stepped from the foyer smiling. As he turned from the foyer into the hall, he saw Arthur sitting watching TV. His jaw tightened as he slipped into the kitchen and closed the door behind him. "What's your father doing here?"

"Shhhhh!" Her puffy eyes stared at him. "He might hear you. I've invited him for dinner."

Justin noticed Shelly's bloodshot eyes. "I saw scratches and dents on your car. Did your dad have something to do with that?"

Shelly turned as her eyes swelled and her chin quivered. She could not speak.

"Am I going to have to guess what happened?"

Shelly stirred the pot of green beans as steam rose. "Later," she whispered, her voice choking.

Justin stepped over to the stove and with her back to him, he wrapped his arms around her. "Okay, later," and kissed the back of her head. "I'm going to change." He released Shelly and left the kitchen.

Justin stepped back into the hallway, passing behind the couch where Arthur sat leaning forward staring at the news reporter.

"Hello Arthur," Justin's monotone voice came through his clenched teeth.

Arthur sat frozen in his seat, staring intently at the map of the Sahara Desert, as if the news of the heat wave would be affecting him. Arthur waved his right hand in acknowledgment, not looking up, unwilling to listen to Justin's propaganda about the virtues of nursing homes.

Justin hurried up the stairs to change clothes, anxious to hear about Arthur's latest catastrophe.

CHAPTER FIVE

"Dinner!" She shouted as she placed the sweet iced tea on the table alongside the salad plate. A red napkin covered the bread in the breadbasket. Steam rose from the beef stroganoff and green beans. The serving dishes were passed. No one spoke. Shelly and Arthur avoided eye contact with each other. Justin, however, looked back and forth between Shelly and Arthur. The suspense was gnawing at him.

"So," Justin's feigned cheerful voice pierced the kitchen's delicate air. "Tell me what happened." He glared at Shelly; he knew Arthur was not going to say much.

Shelly shook her head and then she looked up. Her angry eyes warned Justin to be quiet.

Justin sensed something terrible had happened. "Arthur! What happened today?" No one answered or looked up at Justin. "I'm the only one who doesn't know."

Arthur's cheeks puffed out. "Tell him Shelly," his voice was harsh and loud. He looked at Shelly who had buried her head into her hands. Turning to Justin he blared, "I blew up my kitchen and dropped a tree on Shelly's vehicle." His fork clanked into his plate as he pushed himself away from the table. "I want to go home. Now!" He marched out of the kitchen, down the hallway to the foyer, to the front door and swung it open with a bang. Arthur stepped outside off the front porch.

"Dad!" Shelly screamed as her chair slid backward and she jumped to her feet.

"JERK," she hissed in Justin's face. "Thanks for ruining dinner." Then she gave chase after her dad.

"I'm sorry," Justin's yell trailed after a deaf ear. "Thank goodness he's gone," he muttered as he inhaled his dinner.

When Shelly stepped out into the yard, she saw Arthur sitting in the front passenger's seat with his seatbelt buckled. She hurried around the car and slid behind the wheel. "Dad, I'm sorry that Justin ruined dinner. Do you want me to explain it to him by myself?"

"Please. He'll just ridicule me and I don't want to hear it from him. I just want to go home."

"Okay."

The engine roared to life and Shelly backed out.

After what seemed like an eternity of silent driving, she steered into Arthur's driveway and stopped. "Dad, call me if you need anything tomorrow. I want to help you."

"Thanks Shelly, but I'll be fine. Love you." Arthur opened the door and climbed out.

"I love you too, Dad," Shelly hollered as the door slammed closed.

Justin stepped out of the kitchen rubbing his forehead with his left hand. "Dang, blew up the kitchen," he murmured. Justin pictured a jagged hole protruding through the outside wall, ceiling falling across the counter tops. "Dropped a tree on Shelly's vehicle," that he could not imagine. Justin went upstairs hoping a shower would cool him off before Shelly got home.

Shelly locked the front door as she entered her house. Her anger toward Justin had subsided. She knew he would be curious as to what Arthur had done, and it was her fault for not taking a minute to explain before dinner. Before she went upstairs, she cleaned up the remnants of dinner.

As she stepped into their bedroom, Shelly saw Justin sitting propped up in bed reading a paperback novel. Hearing her step into the room, he lowered his book as he spoke. "I'm sorry for ruining dinner and causing your dad to leave."

Shelly held up her hand trying to stop him from speaking. "It's not *all* your fault. I should've told you before dinner. I know how it is when something happens; we want to know the full details right then. First, Dad had an explosion in his kitchen."

"I'm glad he's not hurt," Justin looked sincere.

Shelly sat down on the bed beside him. "The kitchen sustained only soot damage. And then, after telling him to stay inside and not to begin another project, he went outside with his chainsaw and began cutting down that tree that was leaning. . . ." Shelly lowered her head and stared at the carpet.

"Your dad *is* stubborn."

". . . George, his neighbor across the street, called warning me. When I pulled into the driveway, the tree fell on my car." Shelly's hands grasped her throbbing head, "I've got to put dad in a home before he hurts someone or himself. But he won't agree to go. What can I do?"

Justin put his arm around her, hugging her tightly. "Shelly, it's our only option. You know he can't live here with us; there would never be any peace in this house. If we hired someone to stay with him, there would still be accidents. If you can't keep him safe, they can't keep him safe. An assisted living facility is the only option left. Leave it all to me. I can handle this if you want me to. I know it's hard on adult children to put their parents into an institution, especially one as young as your dad. Honestly it's in his best interest."

"I know you're right, but it's still hard for me to admit that Dad needs help. He's always been strong and independent. I hope he'll forgive me."

"We're trying to look after his welfare. He'll forgive you Shelly, trust me. He'll end up enjoying the place. He'll have good hot meals cooked for him and will meet new friends, maybe even a lady friend. Besides, it's our only option."

Shelly chuckled softly. "With his crankiness, I bet they'll stay far away." The chuckle faded as her eyes drooped. Her facial muscles sagged. "I'm exhausted. I've had a long day." Shelly's shoulders slumped; her arms hung heavily by her side. She changed clothes, slipping her nightgown over her body, and fell into bed. "You're right; an assisted living facility is our only option," she said and turned away from Justin. For once he made sense.

Justin turned the lights off and eased under the covers beside her. He gave her a quick goodnight kiss and he settled into the bed lying on his stomach.

Still on her side, a tear slid out of the corner of her eye and down her nose. Shelly sniffled. Her hand brought up the top sheet to brush it away.

Justin rolled over on his side with Shelly and tightly held her in his arms. "It'll all work out fine. We don't want to admit that our parents need help. I'll help you—that's if you want me to help. You don't have to carry the load by yourself. I'll be right there beside you, all the way." She couldn't see his grin.

"Thanks," she whispered, fighting the tears. "I love you."

"I love you too." Justin gave a gentle squeeze and rolled over to his side of the bed.

Again Shelly rubbed her nose with the sheet, her eyelids moist, thinking; *moments like this I wish we had children. I wish Dad could have had the enjoyment of grandchildren.*

Justin rolled over on his back and looked at the clock, ten-thirty-five. Restless, after a few moments he turned on his side, his eyes wide open, his mind churning. Soon he lay on his back, again looked at the time, ten-forty-one. Justin eased from the bed not wanting to wake Shelly. He tiptoed to the room where he had his home office. Shutting the door, he clicked on the light, squinted, and groped for the path he knew well. As soon as his eyes adjusted, he searched the computer for the necessary documents. The lights were still glowing after midnight.

CHAPTER SIX

Shelly woke to birds chirping outside her window. Her leg muscles tightened as she rolled on her side. An arm stretched over to Justin's side, and her hand foraged across the empty sheet. "Justin?" her sleepy voice mumbled. Waiting for his response, she rubbed her eyes and stretched once more. Her eyes blurred as she strained to see the clock on the night stand. It was eight-thirty-two. *Oh,* her groggy mind recollected, *Justin's at work.* Slowly pushing herself up, her hand brushed against a single sheet of paper lying on the bed. She picked up the note and read:

Dear Shelly,
Have a wonderful day today. I've fixed breakfast. Sorry that I had to go to work and couldn't wait for you to wake up, but you'll find scrambled eggs, bacon, and toast waiting in the oven. I'll call you later this morning. Love, Justin

A smile spread across Shelly's face as she laid the note across her lap. Wrapped in her white terrycloth robe, she went to the kitchen to have her special breakfast.

As Shelly chewed the last piece of bacon, the phone rang.

"Good morning, Shelly. Did you find your breakfast satisfying?"

"I did. Thank you, but the best part of this breakfast is hearing your voice."

"I'm glad. I've finished drawing up the legal documents you'll need to sign. The documents will petition the court for your dad's guardianship. It's the only way to move him into an assisted living community against his will. If you'd like, you can stop by the office this morning."

"How about," she said looking at the clock on the wall, "thirty minutes?"

"Perfect. Just come on back to my office, I'll be waiting. Goodbye."

Remembering that she had an important meeting later that morning with her boss, Shelly rushed from the closet holding her white with black polka-dot blouse and a black skirt. Looking into the mirror, she brushed a wrinkle from the blouse. She splashed perfume behind her ears and rushed into the bathroom. The brush pulled relentlessly at the tangles in her shoulder-length, pecan-brown hair, the perm springing back the glistening swirls. Slipping on her black leather pumps, she gave herself a look of approval as she peered into the floor length mirror.

She grabbed her pocketbook from the foyer table, as she hurried out the front door.

On the ninth floor of the Hinson Building, Shelly made her way down the corridor. As she passed by Connie McDaniels—Justin's personal secretary—she gave a half-hearted smile and waved.

Connie's bright red lips curled in disgust. Everything about Shelly irritated her.

Shelly stopped outside Justin's open door. The office overlooked the Intracoastal Waterway. The room contained a large desk and a crimson-leather high back chair that swivelled. Behind the desk sat a bookcase with legal books piled and jammed tightly together. There were two smaller, leather client

46

chairs in front of his desk. A picture of a nineteenth century, two-story courthouse hung above them.

Shelly softly knocked on the open door.

Justin sat reclined in his chair with one hand behind his head, laughing, holding the phone to his ear.

"Is it okay for me to come in?" Shelly mouthed.

Justin motioned for her to have a seat in the first chair. "Two more minutes," he whispered while covering the phone's mouth piece.

"Good bye." Hanging up the phone, Justin grabbed the pile of papers from his desk and stepped around to the other side. "Shelly, these are the documents that must be signed." Justin inched his way past Shelly and plopped into the other client chair. He reached for a drawer pull, revealing a flat shelf used for signing papers, and placed the documents on it. From his coat's inside pocket, he retrieved a Mont Blanc pen. Shafts of light darted off the 10-karat gold-filled pen.

Shelly's hand trembled. Inhaling a deep breath, she thought, *Dad just doesn't want to admit he needs help. Men can't. Sign the papers. It's for his own good. One day he'll say thanks.* Breathing a slow sigh, the pen's tip quivered, and she scribbled— *Shelly M. Roble.* It looked nothing like her normal signature.

Watching her struggle, Justin tenderly touched Shelly's shoulder, giving a gentle squeeze of confidence, which seemed to give her the courage she needed. "Thanks," she said looking at him.

The next signature graced the line, *Shelly M. Roble.*

"Sign here," Justin said and pointed, "and here," he continued one document after the next.

The pen pressed heavier into the paper with each document signed. Her hand ached as she continued to scratch out her signatures. "There are lots of documents here. Why so many?"

"That's our legal system," he replied sarcastically. "Keep signing."

As she moved the pen across the last signature line, she wondered what her dad would have done if their lives were reversed and she was the one that needed help. She refused to consider. . . .

Justin looked at his clock on the wall; it was after ten. "Shelly, your appointment is in twenty minutes. You'd better hurry," he nudged her.

"Oh!" she said looking at her watch, "You're right."

Shelly scooped up her pocketbook and stood. "Goodbye dear," she said kissing his lips and hurriedly stepped into the hallway.

"You've done what's best for your dad," Justin spoke, following Shelly. "Try and have a good day and stop worrying. You're not the first to seek help for a parent."

Shelly disappeared and Justin stepped back inside his office to where the papers lay scattered. With a quick reshuffling, the papers were in order, in two distinct piles and neatly paper-clipped together.

Shelly sat in her car hunched over the steering wheel. *I hope I've made the right decision.* She looked at her watch—*ten-nineteen. Oh my gosh.* Sitting up and latching her seat belt, she slipped the key into the ignition and backed the car from the parking place. The tires hummed as the car rounded each turn inside the parking deck. She quickly braked for the lowered arm at the attendant's booth. Flashing her I.D., the gate opened and she was enmeshed in traffic.

Justin grinned as he picked up the phone, "Connie, I'll be out for a few hours. Take an extra long lunch on me."

CHAPTER SEVEN

Justin smirked, moving briskly, taking long strides, watching the courthouse growing larger. *Can't believe my luck. But that's what good friends are for.* Justin chuckled as he took two steps at a time rising to the entrance of the courthouse. Judge Blair had made an opening in his daily calendar and suggested a noon meeting. Walking into the judge's chamber, Justin understood the best way to get to a judge's ear was through his stomach.

"Come in Mr. Roble," the judge's deep voice beckoned.

"How about lunch, Judge? I'm buying."

"Where are we eating?"

Justin knew that Judge Blair couldn't resist a good meal. "How about the best steak in town. Ocean Atlantic Stockyard. Say we order two of their finest 24-oz. porterhouses." Facing a pound-and-a-half of tender juicy Angus meat, the judge wouldn't leave a bite of food. Justin knew how to bend the judge's ear. "Behind a stomach well fed, is a generous judge" was Justin's motto.

Outside the courthouse, Justin flagged down a taxi. As the taxi pulled into Ocean Atlantic Stockyard's parking lot, Justin was glad he was not riding up and down each aisle looking for a nonexistent parking space.

The ocean breeze blew in their faces as they eased their way past a line of waiting patrons and stepped up on the wooden wrap-around porch. Justin opened the door as the judge entered. As they approached the hostess's booth, a tall man wearing a black tie and sporting a black suede Stetson hat looked up. "How many?"

"Two, for Justin Roble." He stepped closer, within a foot of the man. Justin held out his crisp business card. The host's fingers tightly wrapped around the paper. Glancing down, an olive-green number fifty appeared in the corner.

"Ah, yes, Mr. Roble, I have your reservation."

The host looked at the seating arrangement. "This way please."

Picking up menus, he led the party of two back to a window seat, overlooking the Atlantic Ocean. "Will this do?"

"Yes, thanks," Justin answered as the judge slid into his seat.

A seductive, young blond wearing a tight, leather jumpsuit stood looking down at Justin and then to the other side of the table at Judge Blair. "What would you like?" Her melodious voice mesmerized her captive audience. She loved taunting men, only to watch their expression, as they yearned to order something not on the menu.

Justin looked at the judge, his eyes widening, his dimples showing behind a smile that suddenly appeared. The judge looked back, the tip of his tongue licked at his top lip slowly and then the bottom lip. Both wanted a taste of the golden tan beauty standing beside them.

". . . from the menu," she added after getting her customers over-heated and emotionally bothered. "Would you like to begin with a drink?"

"Drink," Judge Blair's deeper voice stammered. "Y-Yes please. What're you recommending?" His eyes traveled from her knees up to her shoulders, stopping at her dazzling blue eyes.

Her eyes darted momentarily into the depths of Judge Blair's, pricking his heart with an electrifying tingle. He sat motionless savoring the unaccustomed sensation.

Her head turned to Justin. Her chest bounced firmly. "Oh, I forgot to introduce myself. I'm Leah." Justin snapped his eyes up meeting her eyes momentarily; the candy-apple lips flashed, causing him to lower his view a few centimeters. Her lipstick shimmered warmly. Mesmerized, he watched the sparkles change as she suggested, "Sex-on-the-Beach."

"Really!" Justin blushed, turned away from Leah and gazed at Judge Blair.

"Sure. It's got Vodka, Cointreau, a sour and sweet orange liqueur, orange juice, and Passoa, a passion fruit juice."

"Sex-on-the-Beach," Judge Blair babbled louder than he intended. Those sitting at tables around him gave a cold glance his way. He never saw their scowls; he was captivated by her charm. "Passion, now that's what I want."

"Make that two," Justin barked. Neither realized the attention they were drawing toward themselves.

"Perfect." Leah turned smiling at those looking her way and hurried to the bar as the two leered after her. *I'll get a fat tip from that table. Charm. Charm. Charm. Men, they're so gullible.*

Justin and Judge Blair sat sipping their provocative drinks as Leah approached their table carrying two large stainless steel platters. After placing Justin's plate in front of him, Leah craftfully bumped Judge Blair's platter on the table; the slab of beef as if alive, stampeded down the steely surface. Leah's index-finger immediately pinned the steer to the surface. "Oh," she playfully bent over, looking Judge Blair eye to eye. "I'm sorry. I'll get you another steak."

The vodka flowing through the judge's veins had knocked the edge off his tongue.

"Aw, just a little sugar added." His eyelids raised slightly and he grinned. "I like my steaks that way."

"I try to please," Leah flashed a wink. "Enjoy." Each steak draped across the plate barely allowing enough room for a baked potato to rest on its edge. The steam carried the charbroil scent to their noses.

"Mmmm, that smells wonderful," the judge said.

"Chew carefully. It would be terrible if I had to perform the Heimlich procedure on either of you." She turned around and smiled, *What a line, that'll bring another buck or two.* Her leather pant legs swished with each passing. She had almost skipped away with delight while licking her fingers.

"Wow," Judge Blair dreamily exclaimed. "Does that procedure come with mouth to mouth?" Their boisterous laughter again brought the stares of those seated around them.

Savoring the juices from the steak, the guy-talk about Leah, and drinking another passion concoction, Justin smiled, knowing he could not have picked a better restaurant. Food dumping into the judge's stomach, alcohol flowing through his veins, and Leah frolicking somewhere in his mind, Justin was getting the buy of a lifetime. Arthur's legal needs could be discussed later back in the judge's office.

As their forks and knives rattled on the steel plates, empty except for the bone, Leah stepped to the head of the table. "Like dessert?"

Judge Blair chuckled, holding his stomach. "I don't . . ." his clenched jaw would not allow him to order the dessert that was on his mind. His eyes told of his desire.

". . . No-o-o, cherry delight with a pile of whipped cream?" she asked, her lips pressed together. "Mmmmm."

"Two please," Judge Blair ordered for Justin without asking.

Leah's leather cowgirl boots clicked as she spun and hurried into the kitchen. Judge Blair looked at Justin, "You did want cherry delight?"

"How could I say no?"

"Me too, and I bet we lick our plates clean."

Eating their desserts was a slow and painful chore as each bite overburdened their stomachs. Finally, their plates were clean, although neither was licked.

As Leah approached their table, Justin spoke before she could sweet-talk them into coffee or an after-dinner drink. He thought he'd be sick if he saw another plate of food or more liquid. "Here's my credit card." She reached for it smiling.

She wasn't gone more than a minute before she was back handing Justin the receipt.

"Judge, we've got to come back another day for lunch," he said as he scratched an illegible signature.

"Wow! You're a judge. If I ever need a judge, I'm asking for you," her eyelids fluttered as she spoke.

"Should I be expecting you?" Judge Blair chuckled. "Thanks for grabbing those two steaks. I've never had a better tasting slab of beef. You made it delightful." He pulled his hand from his pocket as he stood and pressed a folded bill into her hand. "Thanks again."

Leah's lips glimmered, showcasing her smile, as she thumbed the fifty.

Justin tossed a ten dollar bill on the table, not watching Judge Blair and Leah. He folded the ninety-eight dollar Visa receipt, and pressed it into his shirt pocket.

Stepping from the restaurant, Judge Blair gave a loose wave at Leah. She smiled and waved eagerly back. Remembering the name on the credit card, she snarled, "Justin's pathetic, can't afford a decent tip."

Justin couldn't wait to get back to the judge's chambers.

CHAPTER EIGHT

"Hey, thanks for the dinner. That was a blast," Judge Blair's words were muted by the smoldering cigar between his lips. Leaning back in his plush black leather swivel chair with his head tilted back, a billowing column of smog erupted. "Now, what can I do for you?"

Justin eased to the front of his chair, pulling his documents from the folder. "My father-in-law, Arthur McCullen, has become a danger to himself, his neighbors, and others. He needs constant supervision. He swears he'll never move into an assisted living facility. That's why I'm requesting your help. Judge, I know you can sympathize with me. You've gone through something similar yourself."

Chewing the butt of the cigar, the judge nodded his head and then pulled another drag from the smoldering Cuban.

"Sir, I'm requesting a quick hearing to ask the court to award my wife her father's guardianship. I need the quickest hearing date possible. The sooner Arthur's guardianship has been awarded, the easier life will be."

"I believe that can be arranged. In the meantime, I suggest that you contact Southern Retirement Community. It's one of the newest facilities in town, known for its safety records, and the staff is superb. Also the facility gives their residents large private rooms, the largest in town. And the cooks can cook. That's very important," he rubbed his bulging stomach. "Wouldn't you agree?"

"Definitely."

"If Leah was serving food down there, I'd be tempted to move in myself." A low rumble of laughter resonated across the room. "Your wife's dad will enjoy living there."

"Then, Southern Retirement Community is where Arthur McCullen needs to be. I'll call today. Shelly will be relieved to know a place like that exists where her dad will be safe."

A squeak emitted as the black leather chair sprung upright and Judge Blair's hands grabbed his weekly planner. "Let's see what I can do." The planner opened and the pages ruffled as his fingers turned pages one at a time, stopping at the next day's date. "Nope," his fingers finished sliding down the page and then the next page. Soon, his finger was moving through next week's dates. "This might work," his finger stopped. "How about next Monday at ten o'clock?"

"Sounds like a winner." Justin pulled out his palm pilot and quickly checked the date.

Holding up the documents, Justin asked, "Would you like to scan the request?"

"No, thanks," he replied looking at his watch. "I've an appointment in ten minutes. Hand the documents to my secretary, Gladys, as you're leaving. Oh, don't forget to call Southern Retirement Community. You won't be disappointed."

"Thanks for the time, Judge," Justin moved toward the door. "I owe you."

Justin handed the documents to the judge's secretary and then went to the second floor and filed the other papers with the court.

"We'll have the summons served tomorrow," the clerk informed Justin as he paid the fees.

"Thanks." Justin had one more task to complete. Walking from the courthouse, he whistled; his day was going perfectly.

Back in his office, Justin lazily looked out his office window, daydreaming with his legs propped up on the window sill, his head resting on the phone. "Hello." Justin's feet dropped to the floor, his mind now focused, "I'm Justin Roble, an attorney here in town. I'm looking for a place for my father-in-law and your facility was highly recommended by Judge Blair."

Justin leaned back listening half-heartedly to the marketing director's sales pitch. All he really cared to hear was if there was a vacant room for Arthur; he didn't want to waste time calling other facilities.

"The place sounds wonderful," Justin interrupted, as if he had been listening to the woman who had identified herself as Heather. He just couldn't get her to hush. His eyes rolled up, tired of listening to the in-depth details: from carpet colors; to wall paints and wallpaper; to strategically placed rooms for comfort and efficiency; to the ratios of staff, doctors, nurses, and assistants for all residents. Justin's knuckles were white; his fingers squeezed the phone, but the information kept spewing into his ear. "W-o-a-h, I get the picture." The redness in his face brightened. "I want my father-in-law to move in, but you haven't mentioned if there is a room for him. Is there?"

"Well, there is normally a waiting list, but since Judge Blair recommended you, we can most likely find you a room immediately." The director was elated with her perfect sales pitch. "When would you like to bring him?"

Remembering next Monday's appointment with the judge, he asked, "How about this time next Monday?"

"We'll be waiting."

"I'd like to come by today and pick up any informational brochures about the facility. It'll help showcase your facility to both my wife and her dad."

"I'll be expecting you."

CHAPTER NINE

The following day a sheriff's car pulled into Arthur's driveway. Standing on the front porch, the deputy rapped his knuckles on the door. Having overheard the scuttlebutt of Arthur's accidents, he could only wonder if he would walk into a crisis in progress. Concerned that he had not heard any response from inside, he peered through the picture window.

Inside, a game show blared from the television and steam rose from a coffee cup on the end table. Scenarios of past grotesque home emergencies where he had responded to 9-1-1 calls flashed potential visions: blood-covered bodies, amputated limbs, accidental gunshot blasts ripping through a person's body or head, the thoughts one after another sent chills up his spine. Shaking those memories from his mind, he pounded with the palm of his fist as he yelled, "Mr. McCullen. Are you all right?"

"Coming. Be right there."

The deputy breathed a long sigh of relief.

As the door swung open, Arthur's eyes bulged, his lower lip quivering as he gasped.

"I . . . I. . . . didn't call 9-1-1!"

"Mr. McCullen, I'm not responding to an emergency." He raised his left hand, holding the sealed envelope out for Arthur to grasp. "I'm here to serve you a summons from the court."

"Why? . . . What for?"

"I don't know. I just deliver documents for the court. You'll have to read it for yourself, or have your attorney read it."

Arthur ripped open the envelope. Unfolding the document, Arthur blurted, "A SUMMONS!" Now realizing what the deputy had been trying to explain, he cried, "What on earth for?"

The deputy stood shrugging his shoulders.

Taking another deep breath, he continued to read: *You are summoned to appear before the Honorable Judge Harrison T. Blair, on Monday morning at 10:00 A.M., in West Palm Beach County Courthouse, hearing room number 213.* Arthur's thoughts focused on Justin.

Looking at the deputy, Arthur blared, "Is this about me being committed to one of those nursing homes? If so, I won't go," his voice intensified.

"I don't know what that summons is for, sir. But, if you don't show up in court, I'll be back here charging you with contempt of court." His voice rose with authority, "I strongly suggest that you attend." When he had finished warning Arthur, the deputy departed.

Arthur's facial muscles tightened as he ground his teeth. The color of his skin was darkening. With a swoosh the door slammed, rattling the windows on the front of the house. The deputy shook his head never understanding why individuals responded that way over a simple summons. It wasn't like they were charged with a crime and could be sent off to prison.

Fuming, Arthur's fist tightened around the summons as he paced from one room to the next. "Justin, I bet he's responsible for this," he raged, stopping in the kitchen. Arthur boiled with contempt realizing how the legal system could be manipulated. He resented attorneys. Deep inside he knew the real reason for his hatred of lawyers—Shelly was married to Justin and that had forever colored his view. *How could anyone like or respect him?*

With a trembling hand, he reached for the cordless phone. His jittery finger pressed Shelly's work number and he plopped down at the kitchen table. Elbows on the table, his head was suspended between the empty hand and the telephone in the other hand, listening to the ringing. His heart pounded.

"Shelly," his head pulled up and he looked straight ahead speaking as if she were sitting across the table from him, "why am I being summoned to appear before a judge?" his voice was hot with anger and accusation.

As Shelly sat there, a heavy blanket of remorse overwhelmed her. She closed her eyelids as her heart almost stopped. Moisture swelled in the corner of each eye. This was the hardest decision she had ever made. She had practiced what to say for this moment, but she had not anticipated that her emotions would interfere. She recalled a vivid image of her dad standing at a daycare facility, unable to trust that stranger to care for his little daughter. He had held her hand tightly, and they both returned home smiling. Now her mouth was unable to form words, silence wavered between her lips. Clearing her throat a couple of times, she sadly sputtered, "D-Dad, I'll be there after w-work."

Hearing the grief-stricken words, Arthur's heart melted instantly for his daughter's love. She wasn't to be blamed. "Okay," he softly replied, his anger set aside for the moment.

Shelly's heart raced as she approached Arthur's front door. Words fled as she tried rehearsing what to say.

Arthur had heard the car door and stood at the front door, scowling. He had sat all day fuming about the summons. His melted heart now hardened and once again he was irate. As she stepped onto the front porch, Arthur's hand squeezed the door knob and yanked the door open. His scowl suddenly vaporized, his eyes and cheeks sagged, seeing wet streaks smeared from the corner of her eyes, down both sides of her nose, passing her mouth to her chin. He quickly wrapped his arms around her and gave a warm hug. "Thanks for coming."

Shelly's heart rate slowed in Arthur's embrace. Her voice cracked softly, "Dad, I love you. Everything will be all right," her arms limply tugged around his neck.

"Let's sit down," Arthur suggested, closing the door and walking into the family room with his right arm holding Shelly snugly.

Once both were comfortable on the couch, Arthur began. "What's this summons about?"

"Dad, I don't know what else to do and Justin has. . . ."

"I knew it," Arthur's voice raised. "Justin *is* behind this. Your husband's out to get my money. His work ethics stink, only working a few hours each day. He's not the successful attorney he misleads people into believing. I've asked around town and some say, 'He's nothing but a legal thief.' He lives an expensive lifestyle, beyond his means. No wonder you're in so much debt." Arthur had been trying to tell Shelly that Justin was no good from the moment of her engagement. Someday, he knew he would uncover who his son-in-law really was.

"Dad, please leave Justin out of this. He's only trying to help."

"I'm not asking for any help."

"Please Dad, just give me a chance to explain. I only want to do what's best for you. If I didn't love you, I wouldn't be here. You believe that you can continue to stay here and not be a danger to yourself. Well, you might be right, but I need someone who is independent to listen and give his unbiased opinion and that's where the judge comes in. If he agrees with you, then I'll stop pressuring you to move into an assisted living facility.'

"I've told you. I'm not moving to any nursing home."

"Dad, you say that you're capable of living by yourself. Then why fear telling your story to a judge? Surely you'll win and can stay here, but I need to hear it from someone other than you."

Arthur sat motionless for a couple of long seconds mulling over in his mind what Shelly had just said. It did make sense to him and then all this bickering would be over. "Okay. I'll meet with the judge and you'll see that I'm right."

Shelly breathed more easily as a small smile emerged on her face. Arthur sat smirking knowing that most judges were older men and would easily understand his point of view.

Stepping off Arthur's front porch, Shelly was relieved that the tension between them was gone. She bid him good-bye and headed home.

Maneuvering from the slower lane to the passing lane, she knew that Arthur couldn't continue living by himself. It just was not safe for him or his neighbors. Her stomach and head once again began to ache as she thought about the impending move and his verbal accusations.

She remembered what Patricia Lytton—a high school girlfriend and her best friend—recently told her. "Do you remember how mom and dad swore that I was out to steal their hard-earned money when I had them moved into an assisted living facility?" Shelly unconsciously nodded her head, agreeing. "And now both are glad to be living in such a wonderful place." A satisfied smile emerged as she exhaled, releasing all the tension from within. She envisioned the same for her dad. "They're still spending their money and I haven't gotten a penny."

The ride home became restful and Shelly noticed the palms blowing in the sea-breeze with seagulls gliding above the tree tops. Maybe the blue sky was an omen of good things to come.

Later that night, Shelly tossed in the bed, jostling Justin with every move. He could tell something was bothering her, but she had refused to confide in him. He clutched the top sheet at his waist, trying to stay calm. Suddenly the bed quaked with another of Shelly's rolls.

"I don't think those Gingko vitamins are helping Dad's memory. Maybe he should stop taking them," Shelly said finally turning and facing him.

"Wh . . . ," Justin gasped and quickly followed with a cough. His eyes were now wide open staring at the dimly lit ceiling. He lay motionless, hoping Shelly hadn't heard his shocked reaction. A couple of long slow breaths were exchanged as he contemplated how to respond.

"Maybe you're right. Maybe he should stop taking those supplements," he schemed. "Then the judge can really see how bad your dad's dementia is."

The bed remained perfectly still. Crickets chirped outside and an occasional thud could be heard as bugs flew into the window.

Shelly remained motionless as she sought an answer. But the magazine article proclaiming the study of Gingko supplements couldn't be wrong . . . they had to help him. . . . *How can I jeopardize his chance for staying home?*

"Maybe he should keep taking those supplements," she said as she rolled over onto her stomach.

Justin relaxed and soon they both were asleep.

During the next six days, Arthur kept to his daily routine. A good breakfast and lunch, followed by his daily walk; in the evening, after dinner, he watched TV, and then went to bed. Arthur didn't remember to take his Gingko Biloba all week. The days passed quickly without the fire department or any one else having to respond to an emergency at his house.

Afraid of doing anything that might cause another disaster, Arthur sat most of the day. His empty thoughts would be interrupted by Shelly's subconscious voice. "You deserve to enjoy your retirement years. Yard work will be a thing of the past. Housework, something you never enjoyed doing, will also be a thing of the past." Once in a while Arthur found himself beginning to agree that maybe he should slow down. He knew old age would eventually catch up, but was he one of the unfortunate to have it catch him in his late sixties? Must he slow down? What was happening to his body? Most of the time he felt fine and young inside. Arthur knew that if he didn't want to do yard work or housework, he could afford to hire someone to do both jobs; he had plenty of money in his savings. He envisioned the single room at the nursing home where he would spend the rest of his life, and every size imaginable was too small. *I'm not going.*

Chapter Ten

Early morning dew glistened off the blueish-green Saint Augustine grass. Inside Arthur's bedroom a few rays of sunlight scampered through the closed window blinds. Asleep, he squirmed from his stomach onto his back stiffening both legs. Abruptly the alarm clock buzzed, startling him. Eyes closed, he quickly reached for the night stand, mashing the off button and silencing the noise. Eyelids listlessly fluttered open; blurriness was overtaken by clarity.

"Six o'clock," his vocal cords struggled to life. As he stood and stretched beside the bed, the court summons lying on the dresser came into view. It was Monday, the day the judge would hear his arguments for him to continue living at home. He smiled, knowing the judge would rule in his favor.

Wrapped in a house robe, Arthur hurried down to the kitchen, poured water into the coffee maker, dipped out French roast and turned it on. Coffee began dripping into the pot and Arthur hurried outside, down the driveway, stopping at the newspaper lying at the edge of the driveway and grass.

Holding the newspaper under his arm, he stepped back into the kitchen smelling the aroma of fresh drip coffee. When he saw the once-sooted walls, he was glad the acrid odor had finally dissipated. A quick toss and the paper bounced on the kitchen table as he opened the refrigerator door. Eggs, bacon, butter and jelly were taken out and placed on the counter top. Arthur held his breath as one of the gas-stove's burners ignited. Although he had the stove professionally repaired last Friday, he remembered the previous explosion, and sweat formed across his forehead. Blue flames leaped above the stove top and he placed the frying pan on top of them. Soon two slices of bacon sizzled as he placed two slices of bread in the toaster. Arthur savored the additional aroma of bacon grease intertwining with the smell of coffee. He lifted the crispy bacon out of the frying pan and then he cracked two eggs and dropped them into the grease. His mouth watered anticipating the wonderful breakfast.

Both slices of toast sprang into the air and were quickly placed on the plate beside the bacon, leaving a perfect place for the eggs. As he began eating the hot food, his eyes scanned through the morning paper stopping to read only the major articles. In between eating and reading, he sipped coffee. It wasn't long before the food was gone, but Arthur continued to sip coffee and read the newspaper. An hour passed and then the second hour passed. As the last page of the newspaper was turned, his eyes caught the kitchen's wall-clock. The newspaper dropped out of Arthur's fingers, landed on the table, and the chair legs squeaked across the vinyl floor as Arthur gulped. "Nine o'clock!"

Arthur hurried down the hallway to the bedroom and grabbed the summons. "Whew, ten o'clock! That's plenty of time."

Before stepping into the shower he saw the bottle of Ginkgo Biloba. He realized that he hadn't remembered to take a pill for the last week, but knowing he'd need every bit of his memory working as he stood in front of the judge, he quickly swallowed a capsule. He sang a favorite song as he lathered soap all over his body.

The navy-blue pinstripe suit jacket hung elegantly off his shoulders and its pinstripe trousers graced his legs. The reflection in the full length mirror showed his polished patent black leather shoes and the suit made him appear younger, smarter and wiser. At nine-fifteen there was no way he was going to be late. With a savvy smile, he could not wait to see the judge's face while listening to Justin's tirades about his senility. The judge would have a good laugh.

Happily, Arthur scurried down the hallway, opened the front door and stepped outside. The fresh air and the sunlight caused him to smile. The penta, momentarily stopped him as the fragrance filled the air. Birds chirped and whistled cheerfully. Drawing a deep breath, Arthur closed the door and stepped off the front porch announcing softly, "What a wonderful day."

Hustling to the driveway, he marveled at the excellent work that had been done on the Deville and was extremely glad the body shop had finished repairing it. With workmen coming this week, the car would soon be parked back in the garage. Since he wanted to demonstrate his proficiency, he was driving to the courthouse. Shelly had offered, but he had refused. Opening the car door, his hand slipped into his pocket and stopped at the bottom seam. Arthur's heart skipped a couple of beats. "Huh, no keys," he gasped patting the other pocket.

Turning in a hurry, the car door slammed closed and he sprinted back to the front door. Half a smile remained, knowing there was plenty of time. Grabbing the door knob, and giving it a twist, the door knob did not turn. "Dang! It's locked." He did not panic—he and Laura had always kept a spare key in the backyard.

Several of Arthur's neighbors had heard a car door slam and had gone to their windows to investigate. When they saw Arthur scurry off the front porch, around the side of the house and disappear into the backyard, they watched with apprehension wondering if something tragic might happen.

George was sitting in his favorite old chair enjoying the morning sun and sipping tea. Having heard the car door close, he lowered his *Time* magazine into his lap. Arthur disappeared into his backyard. "Why's he running around the yard all dressed up?" he mumbled to an empty room. Knowing his neighbor rarely wore a suit, he considered alerting Shelly. He held his breath hoping Arthur would not create another catastrophe.

Arthur climbed the steps leading up to the back patio, crossed the deck to the flower pot beside the sliding glass door, and lifted it—no key. The small smile no longer graced his face, but sagging cheeks and an open mouth expressed concern. Hurrying from one flower pot to the next, he searched the other five flower pots on the wooden deck—nothing.

George's heart rate began to increase as Arthur failed to return from the backyard. He stepped over to the cordless phone and lifted its receiver. Back at the window with the phone in his hand, his fingers fidgeted with the numbers trying to convince himself to phone Shelly.

With ten o'clock rapidly approaching, Arthur had to do something. As he started to step off the patio, he remembered that Shelly and Justin had come over the other night. Justin had volunteered to sweep the patio, trying to make amends. Arthur squatted and duck-waddled along the patio's edge searching the dirt and grass for a bronze key. As he searched the deck's outer parameters, he realized the key could be anywhere.

George was dialing Shelly's number when Arthur dashed from around the corner of the house. Relieved to see Arthur wasn't hurt, he pressed the phone's off-button. Breathing more easily, he sat down, relaxed, but continued to keep an eye on Arthur, wondering what he was up to.

Arthur, breathing heavily, stopped at the bottom step as it appeared to slowly swirl to the right. Dizzy, he blinked trying to clear his vision. As things appeared normal again, he cautiously climbed the steps. As he stood on the porch, the door and door knob blurred into a haze. His head tilted to the right. Not knowing what was happening, he focused extra hard on the door and the haze cleared. Envisioning law officers breaking down doors with their shoulders, Arthur leveled his shoulder toward the door. Lunging forward, he quickly staggered backward as the door held firm. As he rubbed the stinging shoulder-muscle, the door swirled. "I've got to get that door open," he hissed aloud. He rubbed his eyes and the dizziness faded.

The neighbors watched Arthur repeatedly bounce off the door. They laughed each time. With each exertion he made, his thrust became weaker.

Arthur huffed and puffed, his head spinning more with each jar his body incurred as he rammed the door. Almost losing his balance, he leaned against the door, and bent over, resting his hands on his knees. *What's happening to me?* With time quickly passing and his appointment with the judge nearing, he had to think of something else. Otherwise that deputy would return and the judge might hold him in contempt. As he caught his breath, he remembered seeing an actor use his elbow to knock out a glass window and then unlock the door.

George watched as Arthur backed up to the front door, his right elbow nearing the glass. Sensing the next move Arthur was about to make, George leaped from his seat, grasped the phone with his left hand, and raced for the front door. As he opened the front door he yelled, "Arthur, don't do it."

CHAPTER ELEVEN

CRASH!!

George cringed as he heard the glass shatter. He only hoped that Arthur had not cut himself.

Scuttling down his front porch stoop and trudging down the driveway he saw Arthur standing on the front porch holding his elbow. Blood seeped from a slit in the jacket's elbow. He raised his cordless phone and pressed 9-1-1.

Arthur tried to stand up and reach through the broken window, but shards of jagged glass kept his hand from entering. Grasping his throbbing elbow with the other hand he noticed George rumbling across the street. Hoping George would drive him to the courthouse he tried to hurry to the street, but the spinning inside his head caused his path to snake somewhat.

"George," Arthur hollered as his vision blurred.

Assured that an ambulance was coming, he terminated the phone call. George, who was completely out of shape, wheezed loudly as he crossed the street. They met at the street's edge, George gasping for breath.

"Can you drive me to the courthouse?" Arthur begged.

Looking at Arthur's bloody elbow George asked, "How's your elbow?"

"I don't know!" he spoke as he looked down at the bloody hand compressing the elbow. Knowing he had to get to the courthouse he added, "It's not bad. Will you drive me to the courthouse, please?"

"Arthur, I've called 9-1-1," George replied, hating to tell him. "We best wait here and allow a paramedic to examine your elbow. Then, if you're all right, I'll drive you to the courthouse."

Dread began compressing Arthur's chest. Concerned over the appearance he'd now portray standing before the judge, he wondered how he would ever convince any judge he wasn't a danger to himself. "How many 9-1-1 calls does this make?" he could hear the judge ask. With blood on his hand, elbow, and jacket the judge might send him away for life. Arthur lowered his head and looked at his shoes. Once spotless, they were covered with grass, dirt, and blood that had dripped from his elbow. Sirens wailed louder and louder.

The siren and flashing red lights drew the neighbors outside once again, but this time they congregated together: *What happened?—Don't know—I saw George scurrying across the street with a phone to his ear—Look, there's Arthur—What's he holding?—Can't tell.* They began shuffling closer to investigate as the ambulance raced past.

Arthur cringed as Sam and Vicky got out of the ambulance.

George stepped aside as the two paramedics rushed to Arthur's side. Seeing blood, Vicky turned back to the ambulance grabbing a large bag containing her supplies.

"What happened, Mr. McCullen?" Sam quizzed.

Arthur never looked up. "I cut my elbow."

Sam gently touched Arthur's right elbow lifting it. With the blood oozing from the cut, he could not tell how bad it was. "Mr. McCullen, I'll need you to take off your jacket please."

Sam was helping slip the jacket off, when Arthur wobbled. "I feel dizzy." The spinning, flashing lights compounded the vertigo.

Vicky, hearing Arthur's comment, dropped the medic bag. She grabbed Arthur's waist and steadied him.

"Please sit down on the grass, Mr. McCullen." Sam feared his patient was close to passing out due to blood loss.

With the jacket off and the long sleeve shirt rolled up, Vicky dabbed gauze along one edge of the cut, exclaiming, "Oh goodness!" Sam's attention focused on the separating skin.

"Mr. McCullen, you have a nasty cut and it'll require stitches by your doctor. Or, you can allow us to take you to the hospital and someone there will stitch you up. Which would you prefer?" Vicky gently asked. Sam pulled out a bottle of peroxide and began pouring the cold liquid over and around the deep laceration.

Arthur's nose twitched sniffing the peroxide.

"That will have to wait until after my court appointment with the judge." He exclaimed, "I'm seven minutes late. George, please drive me to the courthouse," he pleaded in exasperation.

Sam held the roll of gauze in his fingers and began wrapping the elbow. Snugly, the gauze bandaged the sliced skin together, covering any oozing blood that continued to seep out.

"Sorry Mr. McCullen, but we can't allow you to go to the courthouse with that nasty gash. We'll have to transport you to the hospital," Sam said placing tape on the gauze holding it together. Vicky reached up and loosened Arthur's tie and unbuttoned the shirt's top button.

"But you don't understand, I have an appointment with the judge. I'm late. That deputy said I'd be held in contempt of court if I didn't show up. They'll arrest me!"

"Mr. McCullen, there's not a judge in this country who wouldn't understand your situation and reschedule today's hearing. Trust me. The judge will understand," Vicky countered.

Arthur let out a large whoosh and relaxed. "Okay, Vicky. I'll go to the hospital, but only because I trust you."

Sam stood, reached out for Arthur, and helped lift him off the ground and to the ambulance.

"Have a seat," Vicky patted the stretcher. "If you'd rather, you may lie down."

"No thank you. I'll sit," he said, but reconsidered as the wooziness returned. Sam steered the ambulance into the right-hand lane as George looked on. Red lights flashed as the siren remained silent and the ambulance passed the other neighbors grouped beside the street.

CHAPTER TWELVE

Downtown at the courthouse, in hearing room 213, Judge Blair sat at the head of a twenty-foot conference table. Looking down the right side, the first chair remained empty. The next four were occupied. On the left side of the table sat Shelly and then Justin.

"Allow me to introduce everyone while we wait for Mr. McCullen," Judge Blair began. "This lady beside me is Mrs. Roble, Mr. McCullen's daughter. She has requested this guardianship hearing." Shelly smiled pleasantly looking at each person sitting across the table from her. "Beside her is her husband, Mr. Roble, who happens to be an attorney." Justin nodded to all four strangers. "And the seat on the other side is for Mr. McCullen, when he arrives. Seated beside him is his court-appointed attorney, Mr. Hampton." Mr. Hampton sat stoically ascertaining Shelly's intentions. "The three remaining persons are the court-appointed committee who will give their assessments of Mr. McCullen. Dr. Ebert and Dr. Whaley are both physicians and Mr. Padilla is a lay person." The three leaned forward acknowledging the judge's introduction.

Judge Blair relaxed in his chair, leaned back, and glanced at his watch—it was ten after ten. "Mrs. Roble, do you know where your dad is?"

"No sir," she answered, wondering herself what could be keeping him.

"Would you like to give him a call?"

Opening her pocketbook, she pulled out her cell phone and dialed. Ring—Ring—Ring. She was glad he was not answering. "He's not home," she said meekly. "Hopefully he is just running behind."

"While we wait for Mr. McCullen, to use our time wisely, I'll ask Dr. Ebert, Dr. Whaley and Mr. Padilla to review Mr. McCullen's four accidents." Judge Blair handed the factual information to Mr. Hampton, who quickly read the report before handing it to Dr. Ebert.

Shelly fidgeted as she watched the second-hand sweep the dial on her watch. It was ten-seventeen. The air ducts softly whispered as cool air blew into the hearing room. Justin doodled with his pen swirling an ever enlarging black blob. Judge Blair sat hunched over the desk, hands propping up his head, reading *Yacht World*.

Turning the magazine's page, Judge Blair looked over at Shelly and asked. "How bad's your dad's senility?"

Shelly winced. "I don't know sir," her voice distressed.

"I can't wait forever," his voice asserted. "I have other hearings today."

Justin's pen stopped inking out an endless black line and looked up. "I apologize for Mr. McCullen's absence," he said with a delightful grin. "He could be anywhere, Your Honor."

Justin, sensing the perfect timing, hobbled his chair forward toward the table. Pulling out his yellow legal-pad, he turned the pages until Arthur's name appeared. "Your Honor," he continued almost a little too cheerfully, "Mr. McCullen's mind isn't like it once was. I've eluded to that in the guardianship papers that are before the court."

"I've reviewed the documents," the judge interjected.

"Perhaps we could begin this inquisition without Mr. McCullen." Justin held his breath hoping to proceed without any objections from the four seated across from him.

"Well," Judge Blair said, as he massaged both temples. "Mr. McCullen doesn't have to be present. I was allowing him the opportunity to respond to Mrs. Roble's guardianship request." His eyes glanced at Shelly.

She sat with her arms and legs crossed, quivering, wondering if sending Arthur to an assisted living facility against his wishes was honorable.

"Mrs. Roble, would you like to proceed?"

Thinking back on the previous emergencies when Arthur had almost killed himself, she slowly nodded her head. She knew he would have been here, but something must have happened. She only hoped he was all right.

"Mr. Roble, please begin," the judge said turning toward him.

The four men across the table sat straight up, listening attentively.

Justin slid to the front of his chair, as if he would stand before the judge in a courtroom, and then eased back in his seat. He was glad the judge hadn't told him to keep his seat.

After a quick glance at the legal pad he began. "Thank you, Your Honor. Mr. McCullen is now sixty-seven and his mind is not as sharp as it once was. We don't want to see him injuring himself or anyone else."

"Mr. Roble, I'm getting older and my mind's not as sharp as it was when I was younger, either. But, I sure hope that my children will not petition the courts to have my rights taken away from me and send me to an assisted living facility, without my permission."

"Yes sir, I hope not either, but for Mr. McCullen's safety he needs to reside someplace that has supervised personnel twenty-four hours a day; otherwise, he'll . . .."

". . . Judge Blair," the intercom echoed.

"Yes, Gladys."

Justin took a deep breath, angered by the interruption.

"Sir, there's an urgent phone call for you. It's Mr. McCullen; he says he's supposed to be meeting with you now."

Justin rolled his eyes as the others in the room perked up.

"I'll take it."

The three committee members propped their arms on the table, looking at the end of the table, as if Mr. McCullen had just entered.

Lifting the receiver, he answered. "Mr. McCullen. You were to be here at ten o'clock. Where are you?" Judge Blair's authoritative voice boomed. — "You're *where?* The hospital . . ." He hurriedly thumbed through the guardianship forms, and located the page explaining why the guardianship request was being sought. He pointed at the recorded accidents. "Mr. McCullen, why are you at the hospital? Are you hurt?"

Shelly sat motionless. Cupping her hands behind both ears, she listened attentively.

"You cut your elbow and need stitches! How bad's the cut?"

Dr. Whaley scribbled a note and then looked back at the judge.

Breathless, Shelly's jaw lowered. *If you'd committed your dad last week, this would never have happened.*

"The paramedics would not allow you to come to the courthouse for your hearing. . . . They did the right thing."

"I'm glad to hear you'll be fine. Yes sir, the court does take emergencies into consideration for . . . no, Mr. McCullen, I'll not hold you in contempt of court . . . yes, I'll excuse you from today's hearing."

Judge Blair looked at Shelly. "Now we know where your dad is. He's at the hospital. He tried to break the glass out of the front door with his elbow. A doctor will sew it up and then he'll be released."

Shelly exhaled; her tense eyes relaxed.

Justin's hand gently rubbed her shoulders. "Sending your dad to an assisted living facility is right; it's the only option you have," he cooed.

"I believe a decision can be made without Mr. McCullen being here," the judge spoke assuredly. Looking down the long table at the committee members, he continued. "With what you've read and heard today, can the three of you make a recommendation to this court as to Mr. McCullen's sate of mind?"

The three looked at each other and nodded their approval. "Yes, Your Honor," Dr. Ebert answered for the group. "If you'll give us a minute or two to discuss between ourselves, we'll give the court our opinion."

"Take your time," Judge Blair encouraged.

With their voices lowered, their discussion began.

"I believe ordinary people can have a string of bad luck, one accident after the next. But when a person uses his elbow to break a glass window, he's no longer capable of making sensible decisions," Mr. Padilla stated.

"Why didn't he throw a rock or a piece of wood through the window? It's much safer," Dr. Whaley asked while making an entry into his notes.

"Most people would not break a window out at all. They would simply walk to a neighbor's house and call a relative to bring over a house key. I know I would," Dr. Ebert stated. "I, for one, believe Mr. McCullen is a danger to himself. I'll recommend granting the guardianship request."

"I agree," added Mr. Padilla. "Otherwise Mrs. Roble just might be burying her dad soon."

"I wish all guardianship examinations were as easy as this one was today," Dr. Whaley remarked.

"I'll tell the judge the committee's decision," Dr. Ebert turned and looked down the table at the judge. All eyes focused on him as he cleared his throat. "Your Honor, the committee has unanimously reached a decision. We find Mr. McCullen to be incapacitated." He handed the guardianship documents to Mr. Hampton.

Shelly's heart skipped a beat and her breathing was labored. *They found dad incapacitated!* She had wanted to hear it, but the coldness with which the man had said it, sent chills up and down her body. It sounded as if her dad was doomed.

"Mr. Hampton, as Mr. McCullen's attorney, do you want to make any pleas on his behalf?" Judge Blair inquired.

"From what I've read and witnessed here this morning, I can't object to the committee's recommendation," and he pushed the guardianship papers in front of Judge Blair.

Pulling the documents closer to himself, he once again scanned Arthur's accidents. "Arthur doesn't need to be present for me to make my ruling. Previously, I had a hard time believing one person could be involved in so many accidents. Especially life threatening, as his have been. But after this morning hearing him calling from the hospital, having had yet another accident, I believe if I didn't grant guardianship today, I would be putting Mr. McCullen in grave danger. Seeing how he will not move voluntarily, I'll grant both the guardianship of Arthur and the guardianship of his property, as you have requested."

Shelly leaned forward. "Thank you, sir," she said with a confused heart.

Justin's eyes sparkled as he closed the yellow legal pad.

The judge propped himself on his elbows. "Have you contacted an assisted living community and arranged for Arthur to be accepted?"

"No," Shelly said with a dismal groan. "I wasn't sure it would be necessary."

The judge sent a daggering glance toward Justin. "Is Mr. McCullen living with the two of you? If I award guardianship today, he'll have to stay somewhere."

"Judge Blair, we have contacted an assisted living community and Mr. McCullen has been accepted," Justin interjected, looking at Shelly, "Southern Retirement Community."

Justin leaned over to Shelly and whispered, "I called after filing the guardianship request forms last week. I forgot to tell you."

The judge eased back in his leather chair smiling broadly. "He'll like it there. I've heard nothing but wonderful things about that place," he said enthusiastically.

The hearing room had grown stealthily quiet as Shelly tried to agree on Southern Retirement Community. She felt guilty for not checking the assisted living facility out.

Justin pulled his chair tightly beside Shelly. "Southern Retirement Community sounded wonderful. Try the place out and if you decide that it's not the right place for your dad, then move him to another home later. The judge has to know where Arthur's going to live."

Shelly nodded in understanding. "You're right," she whispered to Justin, rubbing her nose. "This is the hardest thing I've ever done," she said, her voice cracking.

Justin rubbed her shoulder. "Okay, and I'll notify Southern Retirement Community for you." Looking up at Judge Blair with a broad smile he said, "Shelly agrees that her dad will move into Southern Retirement Community."

"Shelly, you won't regret this decision," the judge said. Papers rustled as he began signing Arthur's guardianship documents. When he had finished, he looked up and added, "This hearing is concluded."

Shelly sat dumbfounded hearing those last words from the judge; they seemed so final. Her heart beat numbly. A dreaded suspicion hounded her: *Your life will never be the same.*

CHAPTER THIRTEEN

In the examination room, the smell of antiseptic lingered in the air. Arthur grimaced as the needle pierced the outer skin. "Ow."

"Hold still Mr. McCullen, I've almost finished stitching you back together," Dr. Hicks said, pulling the thread taunt. "One more stitch and we're finished." His white jacket hung loosely on his small frame.

Arthur gritted his teeth and his body tensed. "Okay."

The door swung open and a female nurse said, "He's in here."

Shelly and Justin stepped into the room as Dr. Hicks tied the final knot. Turning to look at the two newcomers, he motioned for them to come on over and said, "He's fine. It took fourteen stitches to close up the gash."

"I'm Shelly Roble, his daughter," she said. Then she turned and looked at Arthur. "Thank goodness you're okay, Dad."

Arthur sat looking at the stitches in his elbow; his teeth still clenched dreading the anticipated scorn.

"I'll bandage his elbow and then he's all yours," the doctor said while leaning over toward the cabinet drawer looking over the top of his bifocals for a roll of gauze. It took less than a minute and the elbow was nicely wrapped. "You're free to go, Mr. McCullen."

"Thanks, Doc."

Arthur began to stand, but the doctor instantly grabbed his shoulders and said, "Please sit down. You'll have to ride in a wheelchair."

Shelly turned her head knowing that he would never be allowed to return home again—only for a few minutes to pick up his belongings—then he would be taken to Southern Retirement Community.

"Why can't he walk to the car?" Justin asked.

"The paramedics reported that he was complaining of dizziness. They believe it was due to the loss of blood and his body hasn't had ample time to replace what was lost. We don't want him passing out and further hurting himself. Besides, hospital policy states he'll have to ride in a wheelchair," Dr. Hicks explained.

A young nursing assistant pushed a wheelchair into the room. She was a volunteer with a bright smile, eager to help. Her cheery presence caused Arthur to momentarily forget his dilemma and he, too, smiled.

"I'm Lizzy," her bubbly voice exclaimed. "I'm your driver for today." Her long straight jet-black hair swayed as she pushed the wheelchair next to Arthur and continued, "Climb in." Her smile never faltered.

Her youth permeated the room and Arthur did as instructed. She pulled down the foot rest and placed his feet aboard.

Justin led the way out of the room, followed by Lizzy and Arthur, with Shelly bringing up the rear.

"You're a great driver. Have you been driving wheelchairs long?" Arthur laughed as they turned a corner.

"Just a few months," she giggled. "Why, anyone can drive a wheelchair."

Shelly remained quiet as they passed from one corridor to the next, wondering how she would tell Arthur of Judge Blair's decision.

The outside door opened and the humid, stale garage air blasted Arthur in his face. Ahead he could see Justin's BMW

528i. "I wish you'd come home with me. I need someone like you to care for me," he chuckled.

"Aw, you don't need anyone to take care of you, Mr. McCullen. There ain't anything wrong with you," she said as they came up to the BMW.

Shelly cringed hearing Lizzy's declaration. He did look fine, but his mind was faltering. She assured herself she was doing the right thing.

Justin opened the back right-hand door and Lizzy helped Arthur out of the wheelchair. "Now you take care of yourself," she said as he eased into the back seat. "Have a wonderful afternoon," and she pulled the wheelchair backward. Arthur thanked her and then she was gone.

The two front doors closed and Justin cranked the car. The car backed out of the parking space. "Justin, would you please drive me to our house. I want to pick up my Suburban and then I'll drive Dad to his house."

"Sure," Justin replied, looking briefly in the rearview mirror at Arthur. He turned the steering wheel and rounded the spiral turns descending to the bottom of the parking garage.

Shelly fidgeted as she sat in the front seat, dreading when she would drop the judge's decision on her dad. Glad he was all right, she decided not to mention his latest accident.

Justin looked straight ahead having nothing to say, but grinning that everything had gone the way he'd hoped it would. *What a day!*

CHAPTER FOURTEEN

Shelly steered into Arthur's driveway—they had not spoken since they left the hospital. Arthur couldn't believe Shelly had not mentioned the latest accident. She had never remained silent over the other accidents. Something was wrong and he could feel it.

Shelly pulled at the door handle wondering when and where to break the news to Arthur about the judge's decision. She knew he'd be irate, but it wasn't her fault. *If he'd only allowed me to pick him up, he would have been at the hearing telling his story and not having stitches at a hospital. What was I supposed to do?*

The front door swung open and Shelly pulled out the key. Shards of glass lay scattered in the foyer. "I'll clean up this broken glass," she said, stepping gingerly across the floor. Drawing in a long breath she sighed, "Dad, we've got to talk."

Here she goes. Arthur shook his head not really wanting to, but he was ready to explain everything that had happened earlier this morning. "Okay. Why don't we go into. . . ?"

". . . the family room," Shelly interrupted. "It'll be more comfortable there and we can sit on the couch together."

With neither sitting comfortably, Shelly began, "Dad . . ."

". . . I can explain," Arthur blurted. "The time was passing quickly and . . ."

"Dad, you don't need to explain what happened this morning."

Arthur leaned back on the couch, looking perplexed.

"Dad, in the hearing this morning, a committee of three experts and your court-appointed lawyer . . ."

"Justin?" Arthur blurted as he scooted to the edge of the couch.

"No, Dad. Your attorney was Mr. Hampton. They all agreed you were incompetent and could no longer live by yourself. Then Judge Blair made his ruling and assigned me as your guardian."

"He did what? That no-good judge. He can't make a ruling without me there. I told you that I'M NOT GOING to live in a nursing home."

"Dad, please don't make it any worse than it is. It's not easy for me either." Shelly lowered her head, resting her chin on her chest. "I'm sorry, Dad." Her eyelids flittered as moisture gathered in her eyes. "Please give Southern Retirement Community a chance," she said sniffling. "You just might like it."

Arthur wondered if she was right. *Maybe life there would be easier. Maybe I won't have a to-do-list. Maybe I'll make new friends. These around here aren't much in the way of friends anyhow, but it won't be the same.* He fell back into the couch. "What if I give it a try and I don't like it?"

Shelly, sensing a little give on his part, breathed easier. "Well, we would have other options to consider later. One would be to interview other assisted living facilities . . ." she sat thinking, but was unable to conceive other options.

"I'll try it for a day or two but if I don't like it, I'm not staying. I'll expect you to get me out."

Shelly sensed it would not be as easy as her dad made it sound. "Sure, Dad." She hated the aspect that she might be misleading him. He had never misled her. "Let's get you cleaned up and pack your suitcase. Then we'll go somewhere for lunch."

Stepping over to the mirror, his eyes rolled up. Dried blood stains encrusted his right sleeve. He felt like having a shower, but he wasn't supposed to get the bandage wet. He decided to use a wash-cloth and wipe away the dried blood.

As they packed, Arthur opened a drawer and pulled out an unopened bottle of rum. When Shelly was not looking, he slipped it into the suitcase, beneath several pairs of pants. Pleased with himself, he hurried and piled some shirts on top and closed the suitcase.

Arthur stood in his bedroom, held his over-stuffed suitcase, and looked around the room. He envisioned Laura lying in their queen size bed. Turning to the closet he could see her pulling out an evening dress for their company's Christmas party a few years back, and he could hear her exclaim, *Arthur you look handsome tonight.* Arthur blinked and saw little Shelly in her nightgown come running into the bedroom, jumping into bed, snuggling under the sheets and blankets. Overwhelmed, he turned and hurried out from his bedroom. "Let's go," he demanded, lugging the suitcase down the hallway, banging it against the wall. His eyes blinked away the moisture pooling in the corners.

The sun beat down from overhead, and the temperature soared as Arthur stepped out into the yard and froze. He visualized Shelly running up the sidewalk, arms full of her toys, yelling, "Which room's mine?" Arthur shook his head trying to remove the thoughts of the family moving into their new home. That day, long ago, the sky had been blue and the air had been hot like today's. The image of a young Shelly vanished as he reached the Suburban.

Opening the back door, he threw the luggage in and slammed the door. He hurriedly climbed into the front seat, closed his eyes against his thoughts, and slammed the door closed. Each breath was a struggle as fleeing memories darted into his mind; each tried to vie for the short time remaining before he would ride off, never to be reminded of the sights again.

The engine roared to life and Shelly slipped the transmission into reverse. Looking over her shoulder, the car slowly crept backward. Her trembling foot muscles varied the pressure applied to the brake, causing it to shudder.

With his eyes still closed, Arthur's body shimmied with the irregular movement of the car transporting him into the past. Shelly, fifteen, sat in the driver's seat for the first time, having just obtained her restricted driver's license. She was unable to see clearly over the rear seat; the car lunged and stopped, lunged and stopped in reverse, inching its way to the street. The car had backed across the street and partially into George's yard. "Where you wanna go, Dad?" she had asked jubilantly in her teenage slang.

"Dad, where'd you like to eat? . . . Dad!"

"W-What?" he said jolting into reality.

"Dad, are you feeling okay?"

"As well as can be expected, I guess."

"Yeah, I know what you mean." The car remained in the middle of the road. "Where would you like to eat? My treat."

"Anywhere, I'm really not hungry."

Shelly sat motionless for a few seconds wondering where they should go. Suddenly a smile began to spread across her face. "How about some ice cream instead then?" The smile widened as she reminisced.

Arthur said nothing. He looked out the window at his house.

"Come on Dad, ice-cream always cheers us up. . . . Please!"

"Sure," he said bleakly focusing on the backyard and the Intracoastal Waterway. The water always seemed to calm him in the past. But now without the sounds of frogs croaking, fish snapping insects off the top of the water, and the smell of the waterway, the calming effect was gone. As the car moved down the street, Arthur could no longer see his house.

"What flavor of ice cream do you want?" Shelly asked Arthur as they paced slowly up to the old ice cream parlor. It was a community landmark. The original neon triple scooped ice cream cone sign stood in the same location that it had for more than sixty years. It was a wooden building painted white with two rooms—one for the customers and the other a large walk-in

90

freezer, keeping more than thirty different flavors of ice cream and sherbet.

As they stepped inside, a cold draft greeted their arrival. "Well Dad, I'm having our favorite. Two scoops of chocolate chip. Why don't you order the same thing, just like old times."

Arthur grunted, "Okay."

"Great! Two double scoops of chocolate chip, please."

Arthur heard his teenage daughter, gleefully ordering for both of them. Her frizzed hair matched that of a poodle. Her teeth sparkled from the braces.

"Dad, here's your chocolate chip ice cream."

Returning to the present, he blinked, focusing on Shelly. "Thanks." They found an empty table and sat by the window. "You know Shelly, I was just thinking about one of the times that you brought me here for ice cream. You always loved coming here. Most of the time when we came we just had a wonderful time, but a few times, like today, you tried buttering me up. I remember coming once when you wore braces. I believed we sat here or maybe at that other table. Anyway, you said, 'Dad, I'm growing up and I've been asked to go to a dance.'"

Shelly smiled, "I remember and you almost dropped your ice cream when I said Timmy Willis had asked me to go."

"Yeah, George's boy was all the time calling you after that. Too bad you didn't marry him—I liked him."

Shelly finished the top scoop and was licking the second. She was glad they were having a good time like years gone bye. She couldn't believe how the time had passed. Dad used to take care of her and now it was her turn to take care of him. She was letting him down by not taking him home with her.

Arthur had inhaled his ice cream like always. He wiped his hands on one tiny paper napkin and then another. Looking across the table at Shelly, he was glad that he had allowed her to go to the homecoming dance. "You know how time flies. Yesterday you were growing up and today you're all grown up. I guess I've done a good job."

They looked out the window as Shelly finished licking the ice cream, her tongue diving into the cone. She never ate the cone, claiming it was fattening.

"Thanks for my last memory," he said, stepping through the ice cream parlor's doorway.

Shelly wondered if there was any truth to his statement.

CHAPTER FIFTEEN

Southern Retirement Community was a few miles away, built on the west side of town. The ride seemed long, Arthur realized that Shelly was turning down the wrong streets, trying to make the most of the time she had with him and he was glad. He did not want to go and hoped he'd only be there a few days before she would become guilt ridden and change her mind. If she did take him home with her, he wouldn't bother either of them and especially not Justin.

The car slowed as the gated entrance way towered above the street. Sweeping brick encasements, one on either side of the drive accommodated an elaborate sign proclaiming, Southern Retirement Community. Arthur slumped in his seat, drawing what he feared to be the last free breath before being locked away. As the front of the car swung into the driveway, up ahead on the left a roof began to appear and to the right dense woods obscured the view of buildings from the street.

Once the car topped the rise, an enormous rambling stucco building materialized. Its glass entranceway glared, reflecting the sun's rays. Shelly drove up to the front of the building and parked in a reserved visitor-admittance space.

Arthur's breathing intensified. The place looked immense and impersonal. "I-I've changed my mind. I'm not going."

"Dad, you've got to go."

"Shelly! I don't like this place. Let's leave."

She sat numbed and exasperated. "Please Dad, they're expecting you. Please give them a try." Staring ahead, the front door swung open and a middle-age woman, dressed in a stylish suit stepped out into the sunlight.

Her gate was smooth and her track was irrefutable. Her eyes had locked on the Suburban and never glanced away.

Arthur, sensing she was coming for him, blurted, "Look who they sent to get me. A retired army nurse. I'm not getting out. I'm not going inside."

"Dad! She's not a retired army nurse. Look at her thin legs and arms. She wouldn't last five minutes out on a front line. And that smile is genuine. She couldn't kill anything that threatened her."

The woman stepped up beside Arthur's window and tapped. "Hello Arthur. I'm Dawn Weaver and I've been expecting you. Welcome!"

"You can't believe she's an army nurse. She doesn't sound like one. No barking of orders, just a kind hello and a warm welcome. Please be a gentleman and open your door to meet her."

His door opened slowly. "Hello," his voice sounded disgruntled as he stepped out of the vehicle.

Shelly raced around the front of the car to meet Dawn and hopefully prevent Arthur from climbing back in. She stepped up to him and eased the door closed. With her remote control, the doors locked.

Arthur heard the doors lock and shot a dirty look her way.

Shelly held out her hand, "I'm Shelly Roble, Arthur's daughter."

"Nice to meet you, Shelly." Dawn stepped up on the sidewalk. "Shall we go inside and check out your new home, Arthur?" she asked with a pleasant smile.

Shelly gave a gentle nudge for him to follow.

He reluctantly followed Dawn, ambling up the sidewalk and into the building. Arthur stopped and looked up at the large facade. Its stucco, painted a sandstone color, seemed cold and uninviting. Cool air buffeted his face as the door was pulled open. Goose bumps blistered his skin. *Don't go in. You'll never leave. Name one person who ever left a place like this.* He hesitated as Shelly pushed gently from behind. Arthur moved slowly across the threshold. *Shelly promised I could leave if I didn't like it.*

Inside, a twenty-foot ceiling dangled two Czechoslovakian chandeliers; their tear-drop prisms scattered brilliant red, blue, green, yellow, purple and orange colors throughout the fifty- by- thirty-foot room. Three lighted corridors led from the welcoming lobby. Arthur sensed that the glitz appeared to be deceiving. He wondered what life behind the walls was really like.

"This way," Dawn said, opening an office door. The administration office was a roomy office with a glass wall overlooking the lobby. "We'll get the paper work completed; it shouldn't take long and then I'll give you a tour." She led them over to a desk in the corner. "Please have a seat," she pointed to the two across the desk. She eased into a rolling secretary's chair and opened the middle drawer, lifting Arthur's file folder. She placed the open folder on the desk, with Arthur's admittance form on top. "Oh, this won't take long," she said picking up a business card. "Mr. Justin Roble, oh, your husband came by at lunch and filled out all the admittance forms." She laid the card back into the folder. "He said for me to call him if there was a problem. I don't see any."

Something nagged at Arthur. Justin had never done anything good for him so why the change today? He did not like Justin doing anything for him. He just didn't trust him, never had, and never would.

"Sign here Mrs. Roble," Dawn pointed to the signature line, and Shelly scrawled her signature shakily across the line.

". . . Now, let me show you both around." As they stepped out from the office back into the lobby, she said, "This beautiful room is used for more than just a lobby. It's used as a gathering place for residents to talk and watch television. We also use this room for parties, receptions, and dances." Turning to Arthur she continued, "Arthur, do you dance?"

Arthur thought the room was a little small to be dancing in. "I used to," he grumbled.

"Well maybe we can get you back dancing soon," she exclaimed with a smile. She turned down the corridor on the left. "This way. Down this hall is one of our cafeterias. This is where you'll be having your meals."

Arthur looked into an unlit room as he passed by. Inside were treadmills and exercise bicycles.

He hurried to catch up as they pushed the door open, and entered. Numerous round plastic tables dotted the cold tiled floor with six chairs circling each. An empty serving line and empty serving pans waited for the next meal. The smell of Clorox ascended from the spotless floor.

"Cafeteria food, yuck, I'd rather have a frozen dinner," Arthur mumbled under his breath.

She ushered them into a brightly lit room across the hallway. Tables, butted end to end, stretched the length of the room. Another door was at the far end of the long tables. A counter top ran the distance of the room with a sink for cleaning up in the middle. "This is the arts and crafts room. Here you'll have lots of interacting with other residents. You'll make a lot of friends." The walls held color paintings of previous projects. The smell of Elmer's glue permeated the room.

"Great," Arthur mumbled to himself. "These are similar activities I use to take Shelly to when she was a child." He had witnessed many arguments and kids fighting in supervised activities. *That's mine. Is not; I had that first. Didn't either; Give it back, or else. I'll tell—Smack—Teacher he hit me.* He never liked arts and crafts and was not good with creating things made from his hands. *Do senile folks act like kids?*

"This way." Dawn said returning out the same door and into the corridor. "We have one room left for us to view. It's your room, Arthur."

Shelly was anxious to see the room. She held her breath hoping that Arthur would like it. She had heard him mumble a few times, but so far, no real complaints.

Walking through the lobby, Dawn stopped. "Shelly, I noticed a suitcase in your car." She didn't want Arthur going back to the car. She had past experiences where others thought they were leaving and then she had to get them out of the car; that was a challenge. She was trying to avoid any unneeded anxiety.

"It is. Do I need to get it now?"

"No, if you'll give me your keys, I'll have someone get it and bring it to his room."

Shelly opened her pocketbook, pulled out her car keys and handed them to her.

"I'll be right back." She walked over to the window at the administrative office and handed the keys to the lady sitting at the front counter. "Have someone get Mr. McCullen's suitcase from that green Suburban outside and have it brought down to room fifteen."

Dawn stepped back to Arthur and Shelly. "This way, please."

As Arthur passed the middle corridor, he asked, "What's down there?"

"That's Ward B. That's where our non-risk residents live once they can no longer take care of themselves," she said. "This corridor is known as Ward A, this is where your room is located." They stepped into the corridor and halfway down the hallway Dawn stopped, turned to her right and grabbed the door knob. The number fifteen hung in the middle of the door. The door swung open and she flipped the light switch, illuminating a freshly painted room. "Arthur, do you like it?"

The strong paint fumes caused Arthur to sneeze, his eyes watered. The walls were painted white and there was a full size bed, its headboard up against the only window in the room with a night stand on the left-hand side. The bed appeared freshly made up. The comforter looked like one found in a top rated hotel. The carpet, low cut and blue, appeared new, but the smell of new carpet was missing. A little sitting area with one Lazy-boy recliner and a nineteen-inch TV was in the corner, behind the door. To the right of the bed was a dresser along the wall and the bathroom door. Arthur thought the room was adequate, but it definitely wasn't glitzy like the lobby.

A knock sounded from the door. "Mr. McCullen's suitcase," said the young man.

"Just set it inside the door. Thanks," Dawn replied. "Well Arthur, what do you think?"

"It's not home," Arthur blurted.

"Of course it's not, but it's cozy and quaint." Moving over to the thermostat she added, "You can set the temperature the same as you did at home. It's not home, but it's the next best thing. One day," she smiled, "you just might like it as well."

"Doubt it," he mumbled, so only Shelly could hear.

Shelly turned and gave him a smirk, questioning his remark.

Dawn could sense tension building as the two shared discerning looks at each other. "Arthur, what's your favorite drink?"

Arthur, not wanting to be here, wanted something that would make him forget where he was. "How about a couple of Heineken Beers?"

Shelly gave him another one of those cautioning stares, but did not say anything.

"Sorry Arthur, but we don't serve alcohol," Dawn said still smiling. "Name something else you'd like to drink?"

"Coke would be fine." He wished they would leave so he could make his own drink.

Shelly smiled and nodded her head at Arthur. "Thanks," she mouthed.

Dawn lifted the phone and dialed. "Hello, this is Dawn, would you send down some cookies, water and Coke to room fifteen. Thank you." She smiled looking at Arthur. "I bet you don't have room service at home."

Arthur shook his head. *I never needed it. The kitchen wasn't far away like here,* he wanted to reply, but bit his lip; he didn't want to receive another one of those unwelcome stares from Shelly.

It wasn't long before room service arrived with the snack.

"Hello," said a medium-height, older gray-haired lady, sticking her head in Arthur's room. "I'm Mabel and I live two doors down. You're new here, aren't you?" she asked looking at Arthur.

He nodded, "Yes ma'am."

Shelly gave him a stare and mouthed, "Tell her your name."

Arthur sighed, "I'm sorry, my name is Arthur," he said as he stepped over to meet her.

"We just returned from today's outing,' she said with a broad smile. "We went to the fisherman's pier and walked around. It was windy out there, but it was wonderful. I've got to go and get cleaned up for dinner. I'll see you there, Arthur."

"I'll look for you as well."

Mabel disappeared and a door could be heard closing down the hallway.

Dawn looked at her watch, "Oh my, I've got another appointment. Someone will come by and pick up this tray later. And Shelly, don't worry about your dad, we'll take very good care of him." She turned and smiled at Arthur. "He'll quickly fall in love with us and this wonderful place. We have lots of fun things planned, including going to many different places in our community. For instance, one day we may go to the mall. Another day we may go to the park. Well, those are only a few of the outside activities. The food here is superb, prepared by graduates from the local culinary schools. The hardest part of this adjustment period will be the first day or two when the two of you adjust to his new life. But trust me, everyone has these same kinds of feelings."

Arthur sat sipping his Coke, forcing a weak smile.

Shelly stood. "Dawn, thanks for spending time with us and thanks for your encouragement. We need it. Please take very good care of my dad."

"I promise he'll be well cared for," and Dawn stepped from the room, hurrying down the hallway.

Shelly turned to her dad, "Dad, I think it's time for me to leave. You need to unpack and go meet more of the residents." She hated leaving her dad in a strange place, but Dawn was right, these next few days were going to be hard for both of them, but just like when she went off to college, adjustments would quickly be made.

Arthur gritted his teeth. He wanted to speak his mind, but knew it would only cause Shelly to cry. Jaw clenched, he stood, "Yeah, you're probably right," something deep inside insisted he wouldn't be staying long.

"I'll see you tomorrow," she said. After a hug and a goodbye kiss on the cheek, Shelly walked down the hall and wondered how long it would take before Arthur would accept this place as home.

Walking outside, the wind blew in her face. The sun in the western sky continued to make the afternoon hot. *This is the worst day of my life.* Her head hung down. *He hates me. What have I done?*

Opening the door to her car, she tried to reassure herself that the decision made was best for both of them.

Shelly sat in the Suburban as it idled; her stomach and head ached. She wished that Arthur could have moved in with her. There was plenty of room in the house for him—two bedrooms unused—and most of the day no one home, but when he and Justin came together there wouldn't be any peace. She couldn't understand why the two couldn't get along.

But as she flipped through the scenarios in her mind, she knew if Arthur was alone during the day at her house, he'd end up hurting himself.

Finally, Shelly mustered enough strength to back out of the parking place. "I love you, Dad," she whispered through tears as she drove away.

CHAPTER SIXTEEN

Arthur plopped his suitcase on the bed, wondering what he would wear to dinner. *Did the residents dress up?* He wasn't putting on a coat and tie.

The bathroom light illuminated the room. A small room with a tub and shower, toilet, and sink. Arthur didn't like it. He felt cramped. A small mirror hung over the sink, no bigger than the sink itself. A clear plastic shower curtain hung from a chrome rod. The tiled floor caused a cold shiver to pass through him.

Back in the bedroom, Arthur pilfered his suitcase looking for something to wear. Before he wrinkled his clothes more, he placed his shirts and underclothes in the dresser and hung his pants in the four-foot wide by two-foot deep closet. As he held the bottle of rum in one hand, he reached for the lid, but then reconsidered, realizing someone might smell the rum on his breath at dinner. Instead, he looked for a place to hide the bottle and finally slipped it under a stack of shirts in the top drawer. *I'm definitely going to need this later.*

After another glance into the mirror, he decided what he had on was fine. As he closed the dresser drawer, a knock sounded on the door.

Who could that be, he wondered, hurrying to answer. Opening the door, he saw Mabel standing dressed in a casual flowered dress, reeking of perfume.

"Good evening, Arthur. I'm going to the cafeteria. Would you like to join me?"

Arthur was glad she had stopped and invited him, but hoped she wouldn't think that he was interested in her. She looked like she was a good ten to fifteen years older than he was. "Thanks," he began. "I just need to put my shoes on and then I'll be ready."

Mabel smiled.

"Thanks for waiting," he said.

Mabel's plump pear shape figure shuffled, struggling to keep up with Arthur. Hearing her heavy breathing, he slowed his strides.

Entering the lobby, the smell of lemon-garlic baked chicken and sweet potatoes permeated the air. Arthur took another deep breath through his nose; if the smell was an indication of how the food would taste, at least he would enjoy dinner tonight.

The double doors to the cafeteria had been propped open and Arthur allowed Mabel to enter first. She walked up to the short line of residents. "Hazel, I'd like for you to meet a new resident. This is Arthur."

He nodded. "Nice to meet you, Hazel." She, too, appeared to be well into her eighties.

The line moved up and Mabel pulled a tray off the stack and placed utensils on it. Arthur did the same. "I'll have a tossed salad with French dressing," she said sliding her tray on the tubular railing. Turning to Arthur, she continued. "You can order as much as you'd like. Try everything if you can. It's all superb."

"Tossed salad with blue-cheese dressing, please," Arthur said. The dressing was lumpy with large chunks of cheese, just the way he liked it.

"Hey Mabel," Emma said. "Wasn't the trip to the pier wonderful? I got some sun today."

"Yes Emma, it was fantastic. I'd like you to meet Arthur. This is his first day."

"Nice to meet you, Arthur," Emma said, winking at Mabel. It was hard to tell her age due to her scrawny figure and sagging skin.

"Stop that," Mabel mouthed.

"Hello Emma, it's nice to meet you," Arthur said rolling his eyes in disgust. He wasn't in the mood to meet people. He was hungry and wanted to eat.

After placing their apple pies on their trays, Mabel led Arthur over to a table with two elderly ladies. Arthur had hoped to sit at the table with one of the other three men in the room.

"Frances, would you mind if we join you?"

Frances shook her head, "Not at all." She was sitting in a wheelchair, sipping her drink through a flexible straw.

"Frances, this is Arthur. He just moved in today."

"He's cute," Frances said. "You can sit over here by me." What used to be her biceps draped on the wheelchair's armrest. Her over-sized dress hung loosely on her shoulders.

Arthur cringed at the offer and sat down beside Mabel. "Hi, Frances," he said, avoiding eye contact with her. With his fork, he stirred the salad dressing into the lettuce.

Allie sat smiling, waiting to be introduced. Unable to wait she blurted, "I'm Allie." She was trim and short, around five feet tall, she was somewhat attractive for her age, probably in her late seventies.

"Nice to meet you, Allie," Arthur tried sounding sincere, but he was tired of all the introductions. He hoped they wouldn't require him to name everyone after dinner.

Arthur chewed, savoring each bite of the lemon-garlic chicken. He couldn't believe how marvelous the food tasted. Arthur was stuffed after eating dessert. Next time he wouldn't order so much.

"Mabel, are you bringing Arthur to the dance tonight?" Frances looked inquisitively at her.

As Mabel shrugged her shoulders and looked at Arthur, a lady pranced up to the table and grinned, "Hi, I'm Lucy." She was slender from walking three miles every other day. Her hair, dyed black, was short and wavy.

"Go away, Lucy. He's . . ." Frances started.

Arthur was not going to allow any of these ladies to claim him. He stood and greeted her, "I'm Arthur."

Lucy smiled at him and then gave Frances a dirty smirk. "I'll see you around, maybe tonight," and again smiled at Arthur. Then before any more fuss from Frances, she left.

Still standing, Arthur felt it was time to leave before there was a tug-o-war over him. "Thanks Mabel for inviting me to dinner, and thank you ladies for sharing your table."

After pushing his chair under the table he grabbed his tray and looked for where to take it. "Arthur," Mabel said, "leave your tray on the table; they will remove it later."

"Arthur, there's a dance later tonight. Well, not really a dance, there's not many guys to dance with. It's mostly a social where music is played and there's always trays of finger-foods."

Arthur didn't want to go, but he could hear Shelly saying, *Dad, you've got to make an effort to like this place. What can it hurt?* "Well maybe for a little while."

"Great! We'll go just as friends."

He felt better hearing she had no intentions for him. Maybe she would be a better friend than he had at home.

Two hours later, Arthur and Mabel walked into the lobby as a waltz played. He was glad the noise level wasn't too loud. Mabel gave a quick wave at Emma and Hazel as she and Arthur made their way over to the table covered with a white cloth, laden with cheeses, crackers, dips, chips, and cut up vegetables. A large punch bowl was placed at the end of the table with a pink colored liquid and raspberry sherbet floating on top. Chit-chat bounced throughout the air.

Arthur wasn't hungry, but followed Mabel down the table as she picked and placed different cheeses and crackers on her plate. Before leaving the table, both picked up a cup of punch.

Frances spotted Arthur and pushed at the wheels, propelling herself over to him. "Arthur would you like to dance?"

Arthur looked at her in disbelief. How was she going to dance?

"Now Frances," Mabel began. "No one's dancing. Leave Arthur alone."

"Is he yours?" she snapped.

"I don't feel like dancing," Arthur interjected, hoping to prevent a cat fight.

Hazel had walked up behind Arthur and stood silently listening. "Oh, I'm sorry to hear that," she said. "I was hoping to be able to dance. It's been a long time since I've danced with someone capable of dancing."

Before Hazel had finished speaking, Allie had joined the congregating group.

Arthur looked from one end of the room to the other. He could not find another male present. He was beginning to understand why they did not participate. He didn't want to hurt Mabel's feelings, but if he was to continue to stay for the dance, he was going to need a stronger drink. "Mabel, I've got to go use the restroom. I'll be right back."

He hurriedly closed the bedroom door, pulled open the drawer concealing the bottle of rum, twisted the lid off and poured. The rum splashed into the pink punch. After taking a quick sip, he thought, *that's strong; that should last me until the dance is over.* Arthur buried the bottle back under the clothes, and before long he was standing beside a small table, its white linen now splotched with pink stains and cluttered with empty cups. He listened to Mabel telling Emma, Frances, and Allie about a grandchild.

When Mabel finished embellishing the story about her grandchild, she turned toward Arthur. "Have you tried the smoked cheese? It's delicious."

107

Arthur shook his head and before answering, Mabel held her plate up. "Try one of mine."

Not wanting to knock the plate from her hands, he put his cup down on the table to help support her plate as he picked up a slice of cheese. "Mmmmm, this is good," he said.

Lucy spotted Arthur through the crowd of ladies. She eased up behind Arthur, having seen him place his drink on the table; not having one of her own, she picked it up as Frances watched. Sipping, she mischievously grinned as she took one sip and then another.

"Put that back Lucy. It's not yours," Frances said, wanting to share Arthur's cup herself.

Everyone standing in the group turned to see what Frances was fuming about.

Lucy sipped again with a grin. "What's the problem Frances? He didn't offer you his cup!"

Arthur looked at her cup and then down where he'd placed his. It wasn't there. "Oh no," he gasped. "Give me my cup."

Lucy smiled and gulped down the punch. "Wow," she said, her eyes closed tightly and her lips puckered.

Arthur's eyes widened as Mabel watched him. "Don't let Lucy bother you Arthur. I'll get you another cup of punch."

Arthur watched as Lucy gave him a sensual smile. What should he do? He looked over at the tall, husky man standing by the front door and wondered what the staff would do if they discovered Lucy tipsy. He kept an eye on her.

After awhile, Lucy approached the group again. "Ar-thur how about dancing now?" she asked loudly.

He stood motionless, hearing the slight slur in her speech. *Did she have too much rum? I'm glad that it was only a small cup.* For the moment she seemed to stand upright and steady.

It was not long before Lucy stood on the empty dance floor, her hips and arms swaying to the music. Her eyes fixed on Arthur. "He's mine," she breathed heavily, "and watching me." A tingle ran up her back and she swirled around smiling. She stopped after completing a circle. Their eyes met. She motioned for Arthur to join her on the dance floor.

Arthur's jaw dropped. He was concerned about what the staff would say once they discovered Lucy had been drinking.

Lucy swayed to the beat of the music as she twisted her way over to the stereo.

Arthur covered his ears as the music blared from the speakers. Again he watched Lucy motion for him to step out on the dance floor.

"Lucy's been drinking alcohol," Arthur shouted to Mabel.

"What?" she hollered as someone turned down the music.

Lucy was still the only one out on the dance floor.

"Don't ask. Just help me," Arthur begged.

Mabel looked down at the empty cup and nodded. "Okay, but what do you want me to do?"

"Watch out," Frances exclaimed as she pushed backward, rolling her wheelchair away from Arthur, as Allie jumped out of the way.

Arthur caught Lucy in his arms as she stumbled into him. For a brief moment she squeezed him in a delightful hug.

"Ar-thur," she slurred, "let's dance?"

"Not now. Why don't we sit down for a little while?" He managed to get her back on her feet, but suddenly found himself being pulled out on the dance floor. Her hands were clammy, but she had a firm hold on him.

Mabel gulped. She looked at the man who was watching Lucy and Arthur on the dance floor.

"Stop her Mabel," Frances said jealously.

As Lucy swayed her hips, she unbuttoned the top button of her blouse. "I'm hot," her voice was barely audible over the music.

Arthur felt uncomfortable as he stood on the dance floor with Lucy moving around him. He noticed the man watching them, and was uneasy with his stares.

Lucy bumped into Arthur drawing his attention back to her. As he watched, he stiffened in horror. Lucy unbuttoned another button and wiped the perspiration off her face. Suddenly her white bra was exposed. His heart pounded as he feared the consequences. *She's drunk.* It was time to get her off the dance floor.

Lucy's fingers fumbled for the next button.

Arthur quivered and grabbed her hands and pulled her close to him, slowing their dance. As Lucy grinned, the rum assaulted him.

"Ar-thur," she slurred, her eyes fluttering. "Danc-ce-fas-s-ter."

Arthur grimaced and wondered what she would do next. He stumbled to his left as Lucy initiated the lead. She twisted and he followed in the tight spin. The room swirled. He tried placing his left foot out to overtake her lead. "Oowww," he moaned as she stepped on his foot. Limping, he followed her and they continued in their gyrations with her blouse fluttering and opening wider.

"Oh, it's so hot in here," she said as she pulled Arthur's hands down to her side. Her fingers grabbed at the hem of her skirt.

Suddenly, Arthur found his hands being drawn up to her breast. His hands were draped with her skirt. All eyes followed their every movement. Unwilling to look down, he tried shaking his hands free of the skirt, but with no luck.

"This way," Arthur demanded as he forcefully pulled her over toward the edge of the dance floor where Mabel stood motioning for him to come her way.

Lucy's head began to roll and her eyes fluttered as the ceiling spun.

Arthur grimaced as his sutured arm ached as he tried to support her weight.

Lucy knavishly grinned. "Hii . . . M-a-b," she sputtered.

Mabel coughed as she smelled the rum. She shot a glance toward the man who was now standing on his toes trying to see over the others who were looking toward Arthur and Lucy. She hoped he couldn't see that Lucy was drunk.

"Do you know which room is hers?" Arthur asked Mabel.

"I'm-not-finished-dancing." Lucy stuttered and leaned toward the center of the dance floor.

"You're finished." Arthur's grip tightened and he drew her tighter to himself. "Let's go to your room," he whispered into her ear.

Lucy giggled and leaned into him. She tried throwing her arms around him, but her hands slipped down to his waist. Her skirt shifted and fell back down below her knees. "O-key-do-key," and her eyes closed.

Arthur grimaced as he struggled to keep her standing. "Wake up," he groaned as he shook her.

All of a sudden, Lucy dropped from his arms on the floor. Arthur looked on in shock as she lay motionless.

The dreadful man moved the second Lucy hit the floor. "What happened?" he snarled, rushing over and dropping to the floor beside Lucy. With one whiff, the alcohol permeated his senses. "She's drunk!" Looking up at Arthur he continued, "You're new, aren't you?"

Arthur looked at the threatening man, realizing how big he was. A cold shiver swept through his body.

Mabel froze hearing the man's voice; she eased backward into the hallway until she was standing at her bedroom door. Opening it, she stepped quietly inside and shut the door.

"Y-Yes," Arthur answered as he looked for Mabel but couldn't find her.

"Where did she get the liquor?" His stare pierced deep into Arthur eyes. "She can't drink. The medicine that she's taking can't be mixed with alcohol."

Arthur said nothing. All those attending the dance social had gathered around and were staring.

"This is Otman, Lucy's drunk and passed out on the floor," he spoke into his hand-held radio. "I'll need a female nurse to put her in bed. She doesn't appear to be hurt. Just out cold," he spoke still looking Arthur squarely in his eyes.

With his radio back in his pocket, he drilled Arthur again. "Did you slip something into her drink?"

Arthur wasn't going to admit that the alcohol had come from him, especially not to this man. "No sir," his heart pounded. He needed to hurry to his room and get rid of the evidence.

Otman didn't believe Arthur's statement. "I'm going to keep an eye on you," he huffed with a stare boring into Arthur's eyes.

A cold shiver sent tingles across Arthur; he eased backward away from Otman. Turning, he hurried down the hallway to his room. As he shut his door, he could see Otman still attending to Lucy.

Standing beside the dresser, he quickly pulled open the drawer and rummaged through his clothes. His hands trembled as he lifted the bottle and hurried to the bathroom. As his heart pounded, he thought about pouring it out. The aroma reminded him of why he had brought it in the first place. Arthur wanted to take a swig, but did not. He was afraid that Otman would enter his room to question him further about Lucy and smell the rum. He looked at the bottle, but just couldn't bring himself to pour it out. After the evening that he had just had he was certain he would need it in the future. He returned it to it's hiding spot. He was not going to make a rash decision tonight.

Arthur turned off the light and crawled into bed. He lay motionless as if he were asleep, wishing he had never attempted to cut down that tamarind tree. He didn't like this place. All these old ladies fussing over him and the way that fellow, Otman, had looked at him still caused chills throughout his body. He wasn't staying. Tomorrow he'd call Shelly and demand she get him out.

The night seemed long and eerie. New sounds creaked and cracked inside his new bedroom, and out in the hallway. He envisioned his bed at home and wished he were in it.

Unable to sleep, Arthur rolled onto his back and reflected on the past unexplainable accidents: *That day fishing, what did Sam, the paramedic, mean when he said, "It was like I mysteriously awoke and was fine?" What caused that?* Arthur looked at his hands. *What happened the day I crashed the Cadillac into the utility room? How did my eye-hand coordination screw up so badly?* He stretched his legs under the top sheet as he thought about the leaning tree. *Why did I experience lightheadedness?* Arthur drew a long breath and gently rubbed his elbow. *What caused my dizziness today? If I hadn't been dizzy, I might not have cut my elbow. Am I losing my mind? I'm not old. Is it Dementia? Alzheimers? Has Father Time caught me? Am I in denial?*

CHAPTER SEVENTEEN

Shelly flipped from side to side in bed wondering how Arthur was. She felt bad for sending him to the assisted living facility against his wishes, but she didn't have a choice—he had to move for his own safety.

Shelly had finally fallen asleep when the phone rang.

"H-e-l-l-o," she said her eyes unable to focus.

"Shelly, I'm leaving! Come and get me. I don't like this place."

"Dad," she said looking at her clock. "It's six o'clock in the morning!"

Justin rolled away from her, pulling the pillow over his head.

"And I'm ready to go. My suitcase is packed. Come and get me!" Arthur had showered and dressed. His suitcase lay on the wrinkled up sheets, bulging with his clothes thrown hurriedly inside. A collar poked out where the suitcase's sides had closed.

"Dad! You've not been there for twenty-four hours. You can't possibly know whether you like the place or not. You've not given it a chance. Now go back to bed."

"Shelly, I've been here long enough. These old ladies are fighting over me. . . ."

". . . So what's wrong with that?"

"My-gosh, they're dancing fossils. There's not a one under eighty. Everything seems to have sagged or is falling. They're not my type if that's what you're implying. I'm not that old!"

"Dad, I'm going back to bed and so should you. I'm not coming to get you today. You promised to try that place for a few days. It's only been a few hours. Good-bye." The phone rattled in its cradle.

Arthur locked his suitcase, pulled it off the bed and abruptly slid it under the bed. Then he plopped into bed still dressed in his shoes and clothes.

As he tossed, he became angrier by the minute that Shelly had cut him off before he could tell her about the man that he'd had dealings with last night. He snatched up the phone and dialed.

"Shelly, last night at the dance a large man with hollow eyes stood watching me. Then a lady . . . Hello!" Arthur jabbed the phone back on the dresser. *I can't believe she hung up on me, again. . . . I'm leaving today.*

Arthur lay in bed watching the room brighten as the sun's rays began to flood in with warmth and cheer, but he was having none of it. His mind was deep in thought as to how he could get out of this place.

"Arthur . . . Arthur! Are you all right? I've been knocking on your door and you didn't answer," a sweet energetic voice spoke. As the door opened further, a young Latin American woman stepped into his room. Her skin was dark and smooth.

"I'm fine," he answered with a gruff voice. His nose twitched - *Shalimar.*

"I'm Annette Manuele."

Arthur watched her long black hair tossed one way and then the other as she stepped to the bed. Her dark eyes sparkled. *They think that charm will change my mind. Ha!*

"Good morning. I'm the activity coordinator." She smiled watching Arthur enjoying the freshness that her perfume brought into the paint-laden room. She extended her hand.

Arthur hesitated to stick out his hand, but did it anyway. "Nice to meet you," he said in a monotone voice.

Annette's smile didn't leave her face. "Come on Arthur," she said with a gentle tug. "Get up."

He didn't budge. He wasn't going anywhere except home.

Mabel, passing in the hallway, heard Annette's voice. She stuck her head inside the room, "Good morning."

Annette turned to see Mabel. "Good morning. I see you've met Arthur."

"Yes ma'am. Where are we going today?"

Arthur's ears perked up.

"I don't know. Why don't we ask Arthur where he'd like to go? Newcomers always get to choose," she turned back and looked at him.

Arthur's mind raced with excitement. He was getting out of here and they were going to take him. Pushing himself off the bed, he headed for the door. "Let's go."

Mabel stepped out of his way.

"Arthur, you've got to eat breakfast first. The bus isn't ready yet," said Annette.

He stopped in the doorway. *Good idea; I need time to plan.* "When is the bus leaving?"

Mabel smiled. "It'll take more than an hour for everyone to eat and get ready."

"That's right, Arthur, I'll make sure you're on the bus before it leaves." Annette assured.

"I'll keep an eye out for him," Mabel said. "I'll show him where we meet the bus."

"Thanks, Mabel. Would you like company eating breakfast?"

"Okay."

"I'll see both of you at the bus." Annette stepped out into the hallway and entered another room.

As they walked down the hall, Mabel whispered. "What happened last night after I left?"

"I don't know. I left in a hurry too."

"I'm glad you're okay." Mabel put a finger up to her lips. She then carefully looked up and down the hallway; not seeing anyone, she breathed a sigh of relief. Looking back at Arthur, she whispered, "That man beside you last night attending to Lucy, he gives me the creeps. You shouldn't trust him. I hear he's dangerous."

Arthur did not move, but looked at the warning in her eyes. Her pleasant good morning smile had been replaced with a stern face. His skin crawled up his back and his ears tingled. "I sensed that last night. Thanks."

Breakfast consisted of scrambled or poached eggs, bacon, sausage, toast, bagels, cereals—bran flakes, Total, oatmeal, anything except sugared cereals—grits, French toast and pancakes, and freshly cut fruit. Arthur had forgotten his promise last night at dinner. He had ordered it all, with the exception of the cereal. He was stuffed and laziness was setting in. The tasty food had also caused him to forget to plan where to go and how he would escape from the group.

"I'm going to get a cup of coffee. Would you like a cup or anything else to drink?" he asked Mabel.

"Coffee, black please."

"That's how I drink mine, unless it's too strong."

On his way to the coffee pot, he passed the table where Frances, Emma, and Allie sat. They all stared as he passed. He wondered if they knew that it was his alcohol last night that had caused Lucy to pass out.

As Arthur placed both cups of coffee on the table, he slumped in his seat, hiding from the stares of the women. Annette with her genuine smile stepped over to their table and sat down. "Well Arthur, have you decided where you'd like to go?"

He smirked. "How about 1760 River Drive?"

Annette's smile vanished. "I'm sorry, but I don't know where that is."

"My home," Arthur mumbled.

Annette smiled. She could see Arthur trying to hold back his smile. Then she laughed. "You got me Arthur. I can see we'll get along just fine."

Arthur's broadening smile assured Annette that he would adjust perfectly in his new home. "Okay, give me your second choice of where you'd like to go."

Rubbing his forehead for the answer, he grinned. "How about West Palm Beach Mall?" West Palm was an enormous mall and he could easily get lost there.

"That's where we'll go." Annette pushed herself away from the table and exited the cafeteria.

After breakfast, Mabel led Arthur to the front door and outside where the bus was idling at the end of the walkway. There, other residents stood in a line waiting for their turn to climb aboard. Annette stood at the door writing the names of all who entered. As he stood in line, he looked for Lucy and was glad that she was nowhere to be seen.

Arthur ducked his head entering the minibus. "Do you mind if we sit on the front seat?" Mabel asked Arthur. "I get motion sickness in the back."

"I don't mind," he replied as Mabel entered and sat by the window. The interior's crisp fabric and unstained carpet discharged a clean, new smell. A big picture windshield exposed the well-manicured grounds. Arthur was glad to sit in the front. An opportunity might present itself for him to escape.

Once everyone was seated, Annette stood at the front of the bus and cleared her throat. "Everyone, say hello to Arthur. He moved in yesterday."

"Hello Arthur!" their voices collectively announced.

"Arthur's asked if we can go to the mall and that's where Bishop is taking us."

A low murmur rose from the back of the bus.

Bishop Braswell was in his mid fortes, short, muscular with mostly dark black, crew-cut hair. He had been driving for the facility less than a month and was very courteous and always on time. A look in the rearview mirror revealed only two of the twenty seats were vacant. After seeing that everyone was seated, the bus' door closed. "Arthur, I'm glad you're coming with us today," he said, as the air brakes hissed and the bus began to move away from the curb.

The bus rolled to a stop in front of the mall's glass-paneled entrance. With its flashers blinking, vehicles maneuvered around the bus as residents slowly stepped down onto the concrete sidewalk. Once all were out of the bus, Annette motioned and said, "Follow me."

The group followed Annette through the glass doors and began meandering down the corridor. Passing a jewelry store, a large diamond sparkled from a solitary ring. Arthur stopped, the sparkle lured his memory to the day he had bought a similar diamond ring. Smiling, he imagined Laura sliding the large sparkling ring onto her slender ring finger. *Yes,* she exclaimed, accepting his proposal, her face glowing with excitement.

"Arthur, are you okay?" Annette gently asked, stepping beside him.

With a blink of an eye, Arthur was back in reality. "Yes," he said wishing the doctors had cured Laura, "I'm fine."

His eyes lingered on the diamond's sparkle, even as he stepped away. A deadening feeling lingered in his chest as he walked past other stores, unaware of their display of merchandise. Even the aroma of roast beef drifting into the corridor from the eatery didn't bring him into reality. His mind still focused on Laura's memory.

Beside the cell phone booth, a lady stood at the counter examining a new cell phone. Passing, he brushed against her unaware.

"Arthur!" yelled Annette.

His footsteps froze and his eyes focused on the spraying fountain he was about to stumble into.

"What's wrong?" Annette said, running up to him.

"Thanks for the warning. I was thinking about Laura, my wife who died last year, and how I wished she was still alive."

"I understand." She put her arm around his shoulders. "Do you need a moment here before we continue?"

"No." Arthur looked around to see the group gathered around him.

Mabel stepped up to him, "I'll be Arthur's buddy for today and watch out for him."

Arthur weakly smiled at her. "Thanks."

"I lost my husband thirteen years ago and I know how memories overwhelm a person from time to time." Mabel smiled. "It happens to all of us. You're not alone."

Arthur breathed a sigh of relief knowing that he was not any different.

Walking beside Mabel, they passed a shoe store with a display of tennis shoes piled on a table, and then Sears. In the doorway, a display of Oxford button-up shirts hung on a round rack. "Isn't that blue shirt nice?" Arthur said to Mabel.

"It surely is," she said, stepping over to the rack as the group ambled ahead.

Arthur lifted the deep midnight blue shirt from the rack. He carried it over to the cashier. "I'll take this shirt," and placed a credit card on the counter. Mabel stood anxiously beside him. She knew they should stay with the group, but she hoped the new shirt would cheer Arthur up.

The cashier rang up the shirt and swiped the card through the card-reader. . . . "I'm sorry, but this credit card is being rejected."

"What! How can that be?" he said.

"Arthur! Mabel!" Annette shrieked. "I thought I'd lost both of you."

"I'm just buying a shirt," said Arthur.

"We're not buying anything today," Annette explained. "Someone will have to bring you later." We're here to exercise and window-shop. You can't wander off by yourselves. I'll lose everyone if we don't stay together. Come on."

Mabel stepped over to Annette. "Sorry, but when I saw that blue shirt, it reminded me of Wilbur, my deceased husband, and I forgot about the group policy of staying together."

"No harm done. Let's go back to the group."

Arthur looked at his card wondering why it was rejected. "Stupid computers. They are always crashing."

Once back with the group, Arthur could understand why they had to stay together. It wouldn't take much for them all to become scattered.

After thirty minutes of walking they met Bishop in the food court in the center of the mall. There he had reserved five tables. Each table had four chairs and on top of each table were four identical sacks.

"Lunch," Annette announced as the group hurried to the tables.

Arthur and Mabel joined Hazel and Emma.

Hazel pulled out her sandwich, bag of chips, and a bottle of water. Pulling open her sandwich, she mumbled, "Turkey and ham," and pressed it back together. She nibbled at it.

Arthur and Mabel ate their sandwiches and chips without a complaint. With each bite taken he was lost in an imaginary escape, except when the ladies interrupted.

Emma wasn't hungry. She ate her chips and drank the water. After their forty minute lunch stop, Annette led them on their last lap around the mall.

Arthur shuffled along and followed behind Annette. Mabel walked beside him as the group ambled down the corridor. He no longer looked in the stores' windows or at his surroundings. Arthur's head hung down and watched the square tiles pass by. He had never been one to just window-shop or exercise at the mall. Where one went, they all had to go. No buying or shopping. Just walking from one end of the mall to the other. He sympathized with everyone who had groaned earlier, hearing that he had chosen the mall. *I don't live in an assisted living facility. I live in a nursing home. All nursing homes are the same. I'm not going back!* He breathed heavily, remembering why he'd chosen the mall in the first place. Lifting his head, he searched for the perfect means of escape.

Fresh coffee aromas drifted into the corridor. Arthur's nose twitched as he saw the Starbucks' coffee stand. Knowing he couldn't purchase a cup, Arthur hastily looked away and saw a small side corridor that separated two clothing shops. There, a sign pointed to the restrooms.

"Annette, I need to use the restroom. May I go?"

"We call restrooms the Magic Room. This prevents people from becoming embarrassed."

The Magic Room? That's ridiculous. That's something a child would say. Reluctant and feeling embarrassed, he asked, "May I use the Magic Room?"

"Okay, but come right back."

Annette took a few steps over to the pet shop. The group gathered to watch two buff-colored cocker spaniel puppies tugging on a rope.

Arthur hurried into the men's room. While inside he noticed other men coming and going freely. He wished he could do the same.

The soft flow of water cascading down his hands reminded him of a time when his family had been caught out in a rain shower. They were laughing as they darted around under the rain drops and splashed through water puddles.

The slamming of the bathroom door jolted Arthur from his memories.

Arthur finished drying his hands and stepped out into the corridor. He couldn't see Annette and the group. With a perfect opportunity for escape, he quickly looked behind him. There at the end of the corridor was a door. Above the door glowed the sign, EXIT. Arthur couldn't believe his luck. He imagined his freedom and how it awaited him on the other side. Arthur glanced back once more then bolted for the door.

As the door swung open, the alarm sounded. With the bright sunlight illuminating the door, Arthur could now read the sign attached to the face of the door. *Emergency use only. Alarm will sound.* Quickly glancing back into the corridor, he didn't see anyone racing his way. He turned loose of the door and vanished.

CHAPTER EIGHTEEN

Annette stood anxiously waiting for Arthur to return from the restroom and then heard the alarm bell sounding. At first she paid little attention. After about ten minutes she became concerned and walked to the men's restroom. She pushed the door open slightly and called, "Arthur, are you all right?"

There was no answer.

"Arthur, are you in here?" she asked more loudly.

Silence.

"Is anyone in here?"

Annette stepped inside and searched for Arthur. *Where is he?*

Panicked, she yelled, "ARTHUR!"

Unable to locate him, she notified the security department. After thoroughly searching the mall and not finding Arthur, she thanked the security employees for their help. When the other seniors were loaded, Annette instructed the bus driver to leave.

It didn't take Annette long to remember 1760 River Drive. Within ten minutes, the bus pulled to a stop.

Annette could only hope he was there.

George heard the mini-bus stop and hurried out to the street.

When she stepped off the bus, George hustled over to her, breathing heavily. "Are you looking for Arthur?"

"Yes, sir."

"I'm George, his neighbor. He's inside. I saw him go into his house thirty minutes ago. I tried calling his daughter, but she wasn't at work."

After thanking George, she hurried down the driveway and followed the sidewalk to the front door. When she reached for the door, to her surprise, it opened. She stepped inside and there on the couch, Arthur was slumped with his head buried between his legs.

Arthur felt sick that his Cadillac was not there.

Deep inside herself, she could feel Arthur's pain. She knew it was never easy for someone to move into a new environment. She stepped quietly over to the couch and sat down beside him.

"Arthur," she softly spoke, "are you okay?" Her arm slipped around his shoulder.

Arthur coughed and wiped his eyes with his sleeve. He shook his head. Reflecting back on the accidents that had caused him the loss of his freedom, he mumbled in outrage, "It's just not fair!"

Annette gently squeezed his arm, pulling him closer to herself. "Take your time Arthur. We have a few minutes before we need to leave."

Annette broke the silence as she rose, "Arthur it's time for us to go. I promise not to tell anyone back at Southern Retirement Community, nor any of your family members, about your little escapade today."

"Please, Arthur, we've got to be going now. Someone will begin to suspect that something happened if we're late arriving at Southern Retirement Community. I don't want to report your whereabouts. If they find out what you did today, they won't allow you to go next time."

Arthur stood up, his heart ached and he did not want to go. He dragged his feet as he followed Annette out the front door. Annette locked the door after Arthur stepped through the threshold. "Arthur, please give me the house key."

With his head hung forward, he pointed to the broken window. "I don't have a key."

Riding back to the facility, Annette sat beside Arthur. "Cheer up. It always takes time before anyone likes his new environment. Please smile when you get off the bus. You don't want the administrators to think you had a bad time."

Arthur forced a smile on his face and leaned back in his seat. Mabel, sitting behind him, gently patted him on his back. "You'll adjust. Just give it some time," she whispered.

"Put a little more effort into that smile and if anyone asks, tell them you had a wonderful time," Annette coached.

The ride back to Southern Retirement Community was quiet. Arthur thought about how his past symptoms related to his accidents: lightheadedness, dizziness, blurred vision, coordination problems. *It just doesn't make sense. What's wrong with me? Could it be a brain tumor? Laura had some of those same symptoms before she was diagnosed with inoperable brain cancer.*

When the bus pulled into the parking lot at Southern Retirement Community, Shelly was standing inside the front doors waiting to see her dad. Once he stepped from the bus, she ran up to him throwing her arms around him.

Hugging tightly, she asked, "Dad, where did you go? Did you have fun?"

Arthur turned to see Annette watching him. He returned the hug. "I don't like this place. Give me a couple of minutes and I'll grab my suitcase." *I'm glad it's still packed.*

"Dad," she exclaimed. "You promised to give . . ."

Arthur could see Annette's smile turning to a warning scowl. Sensing Shelly's unwillingness to take him out and not wanting to jeopardize his chances of escaping tomorrow, he interjected. ". . . Just teasing. I had a wonderful time at the mall." He looked over Shelly's shoulder at Annette. Her smile had returned. She pulled her fingers across her lips and then tossed the imaginary key away.

Arthur envisioned the next group outing and thought of his failed escape from the mall. *I need a better plan.*

Annette watched Arthur and hoped the smile on his face was authentic. She assumed within a few more days, Arthur would accept this as his new home.

"Well, tell me what you did at the mall?" Shelly inquired.

"It's not like when you and I used to go shopping at the mall. All we did was amble up and down the corridors. It was our daily exercise. We weren't allowed to buy anything, not even a cup of coffee." He shook his head in disbelief.

"Why not?" she asked.

"If we all went our separate ways, she'd never locate us. If I want to buy something, you'll have to take me."

"Just ask and I'll take you."

Trying to appear sincere about today's excursion, he continued. "Oh, I want you to meet someone." He turned around. "Annette, this is my daughter Shelly."

"Nice to meet you," Annette said, greeting her with a handshake.

"Thanks for taking a special interest in Dad."

"We had a wonderful time getting to know each other." Annette knew Arthur and Shelly needed some time together, in order to make the adjustment complete. Excusing herself, she departed.

"I like Annette," Shelly whispered.

"She's okay."

Mabel stepped off the bus, following the last person. "Hello. We're glad Arthur went with us today," she said, stepping past Shelly.

Shelly remembered seeing her yesterday, speaking to Arthur in his room. "Oh hello," she said, smiling, unable to remember her name.

Mabel hurried to catch up with the group.

"Arthur, what's her name?"

"That's Mabel. She's trying to help me become adjusted to this place. She's been very nice." He saw Shelly's eyes sparkle. "It's nothing like that," he sighed. "Are you staying for dinner?"

"Sure."

"Good, it's dinner time." Arthur led Shelly up the steps into the building and down to the cafeteria. With their trays of food, he found an empty table and sat down. After a few bites he began pleading. "Shelly, I'm not a danger to myself. I don't belong here. I've been trying to determine why each accident happened. I was trying to take my vitamins daily, especially that Ginkgo capsule for my memory. My mind's very alert. But somehow it seems that before some of my accidents I became dizzy and my vision blurred. I haven't been dizzy today and nothing happened. Maybe I had some kind of bug that was causing me to become dizzy and then my judgment would be impaired and. . . ."

"Dad," Shelly interrupted, wanting to change the subject of their conversation. "Give this place a few more days. You'll love it. It does have its pluses. For instance, you didn't have to cook today or do the dishes; you didn't have to work in the yard or around the house. So you didn't enjoy the mall because you weren't allowed to buy anything. When I was a teenager, my friends and I would go to the mall and hang out. We didn't buy anything, but we had a blast just getting out of the house and being with friends. You can do the same and when you'd like to buy something, call me and I'll take you to buy whatever you want."

"You might be right. I should start looking at life's positives; I'll try a little harder to like this place," he said, sipping his steaming coffee. He had his doubts.

Shelly sat holding her glass of iced tea feeling relieved. Wanting to keep the positive atmosphere she asked. "What does Annette have planned for tomorrow?"

Arthur shrugged his shoulders. "I haven't heard, but it won't matter, I'm going to have a good time wherever she takes us."

Shelly leaned back in her chair sipping her tea as the last bite of food was swallowed. She was encouraged that he was willing to give this place a fair chance.

Mabel stepped over to their table. "Arthur, if you haven't heard, tonight is game night. Tables will be set up in the lobby with different card games and board games. I enjoy playing Spades."

"I like card games. When Shelly lived at home, we'd spend hours playing cards. What time do the games begin?"

Shelly was glad to see him willing to interact with the others and play cards.

"In about an hour and Shelly if you'd like, we'd love for you to join us."

"Thanks, but I've got to get home. Maybe some other time," Shelly said looking at her watch. "I've got to leave." Scooting her chair away from the table she stood and Arthur did likewise.

"Mabel, I'll meet you in an hour. I want to tell Shelly goodbye."

Shelly watched Arthur step back inside as darkness shrouded the building. She was glad he had decided to give living here another chance. She didn't know what else to do with him.

Shelly made a detour on the way home. Pulling into her dad's driveway, she shut off the car. The empty house's windows secreted blackness. It didn't feel like home anymore. She shivered, remembering how the house looked similar after the passing of her mother. Eeriness swept over her body. What had she done by sending her dad away? She remembered hearing stories about people who gave up the will to live when they were moved against their wishes. Would he soon be dead? She cradled her head between her hands and slumped over the steering wheel.

Shelly's fears hounded her. *What if Dad really doesn't like where he is?* Chills swept across her body. *What if I'm wrong? Maybe I was in too big of a hurry to protect him.* She trembled. She did not know what to think.

With plenty of time before the games began, Arthur went back to his room and unpacked his suitcase, leaving the bottle of rum locked inside. After tidying up his room, he made his way to find Mabel.

The cards clattered on the square card table as Mabel shuffled the deck. Arthur sat across the table from her. They needed fifty-one more points and they would beat Frances and Allie who needed two-hundred and twenty-one points to win. Mabel cut the deck and dealt thirteen cards to each player.

A total of ten tables had been set up in the lobby. Eight tables were being utilized and Arthur was the only male playing cards. The room echoed with laughter and chatter.

"I'll take two tricks," Mabel called out.

Frances claimed she would take three tricks. Arthur held his breath as he announced four tricks that he wasn't sure he could accomplish and Allie laughed, "I doubt that. I'll take five tricks." With a maximum of thirteen tricks to be taken, they looked at each other wondering who had over bid.

Frances, who sat on Mabel's left, led off with her lowest club, two. Allie sneered as she lay down her lowest club, a jack, which was the largest card played. She pulled her trick in and led off with the ace of clubs. "Four more tricks," she giggled.

Two tables away, four older but boisterous ladies drew the attention of all in the room. "It's My Turn to Deal!—No, You Dealt Last Time!—Give Me The Cards!—I Don't Think So!"

Large shoes whacked the tile flooring as Otman raced to their table. "Ladies! You're too loud," his voice echoed throughout the lobby. "If you don't quiet down, you'll have to stop playing."

"And who'll make us?" one feeble lady snapped at the muscular, leathery-skinned man—darkened by excessive hours in the sun—with hair that hung in his eyes.

"Now Kathleen, don't start with me," he snarled.

Mabel laughed softly as she leaned across the table and whispered to Arthur. "Those ladies always do that. They get a kick out of antagonizing Mr. Otman."

Arthur wanted to smile, but had better sense.

Otman appeared to be in his early thirties, a large unattractive man. Just the sight of him was enough to make one cringe. He was someone no one wanted to cross.

The card game had progressed with Mabel collecting two tricks and Allie completing her five tricks as called. There was one round left and Frances had taken two tricks and Arthur had won only three. Everyone looked around at each other wondering who would take the last trick.

Arthur maintained his deadpan confidence; Frances struggled unsuccessfully to keep a poker face—she just knew she held the winning card.

Allie won the previous trick and started off by tossing the two of hearts on the table. Mabel dropped a seven of diamonds on the table. Frances glowed as she laid the ten of hearts on the table. Arthur smiled as he laid his card on the table. It was the two of spades. He won the last trick.

"You weren't kidding about playing cards, Arthur. You're good," Mabel congratulated, looking at her watch and yawning. "I'm tired. I think I'll turn in for the evening."

Arthur, not wanting to go to his room or to continue playing with the other ladies, stood as she did. "How about a walk outside for a few minutes? It's clear out; the stars should be brilliant."

Since it was only nine o'clock, she smiled and accepted. As they stepped to the front door, Otman stepped in front of the door. "And where might the two of you be going?" He towered five inches above Arthur. Bad breath blasted Arthur in the face.

Arthur's skin crawled as goose bumps raced up from his legs to the back of his neck, standing the tiny hairs on end. "Um—um, just outside to look at the stars. We won't be long."

"You two aren't going anywhere. The doors are locked to prevent people like you from wandering off and hurting yourselves," he said, staring into Arthur's eyes.

Arthur shuddered, anger rising. *What is that man's problem?*

They turned in a huff and walked away from the front door and into the corridor leading to their rooms. "That's strange. I don't recall the doors ever being locked before eleven o'clock," Mabel said, with a puzzled look in her eyes.

After saying good night, Mabel entered her room and Arthur retired to his.

With the moon high in the night sky and a light wind blowing, slithering shadows snaked along Arthur's walls and ceiling. With eyes wide open and lying on his back, he watched odd shaped shadows crawl away as new forms began their creepy squirm into his bedroom. One of the shadows looked like Otman. Watching the forms disappear, Arthur grinned imagining himself lurking in the shadows, slinking away unnoticed by anyone. His eye lids fluttered closed and he dreamed he was flying away like Superman.

CHAPTER NINETEEN

Early the next morning Shelly awoke to the ringing telephone and answered with a groggy voice.

"Pack your bags. You have a business meeting up in Chicago this afternoon. You'll be home tomorrow," Shelly's boss broadcasted loudly in her ear. "You have an e-ticket; don't forget your i.d."

Arthur stepped from the shower singing loudly, toweling off. Today was the day he'd escape, but without any decisive plans, he was resigned to winging it. As he rubbed the towel through his hair, the telephone rung. Wrapping the towel around his body, he stepped out into the room and around the bed to the telephone.

"Hello."

"Dad, I'm on my way to the airport for a nine-thirty-five flight to Chicago. I'll be back tomorrow and will come see you then. Please try accepting your new home. All the other residents seem to enjoy living there."

Arthur understood about unexpected business trips. He had made many in the years past, though not of such great distance. *You may come see me when you get back, but I won't be here,* he smirked as he hung up the phone.

After dressing, he hurried down to breakfast. With his tray of scrambled eggs, two slices of wheat toast, hash-browns, sausage, glass of milk, and cup of steaming coffee, Arthur found an empty table and sat down. Daydreaming—about running across the grass and disappearing into the woods—he nibbled on the crunchy toast and gazed outside at the swaying tree branches.

"Hi, Arthur!"

Startled, he turned his head; standing beside the table was Lucy. He held his breath wondering if she was going to confront him about the other night.

"Do you mind if I join you?" she asked looking cheerful. "I don't mean to intrude."

"Oh, I'm sorry. I was aah . . . sure you can join me." Arthur continued to hold his breath as he picked up his steaming coffee and sipped.

Lucy placed her tray on the table and slipped into a chair. "Thanks," she said with a smile. "Mabel isn't feeling well today and is sleeping in."

Feeling confident that she wasn't there to confront him about the alcohol, he relaxed. "I'm sorry to hear that. I hope it's nothing serious."

"I hope not too. I've called Jerry this morning; he's my son," she said with a proud smile, "and asked him to take me to the mall shopping. It's his day off." Lucy took a swallow of milk and continued, "I heard that you tried to buy a shirt yesterday at the mall. If you'd like, you can go with us and buy it. I'm sure he won't mind."

Arthur's blank expression quickly disappeared anticipating an opportunity for escape. "I'd love to go. What time do you expect him?"

"He'll be here around ten o'clock. We'll meet in the lobby," said Lucy smiling, scooping a spoon of Raisin Bran and milk.

The remaining food on Arthur's plate went untouched as his mind drifted off to the possibility of escape.

In the lobby, Arthur sat eagerly waiting for Lucy and Jerry. He'd been waiting for more than forty minutes not wanting to be left behind. A car eased up to the front curb and a tall, slender man wearing blue jeans and a yellow golf shirt emerged.

Excited, Arthur watched. The man opened the door, stepped inside and looked around. Not seeing the person he looked for, he walked to the corridor on the right and disappeared.

"Mom, are you ready to go?" The man's voice drifted out into the lobby.

Knowing the two would return at any moment, Arthur stood and waited, looking intently at the empty hall. He didn't wait long.

"Come on Arthur," Lucy shouted and he hurried over to them. "Jerry, this is Arthur."

The two shook hands. "Mom says you'd like to go with us," Jerry said.

Arthur nodded his head. "I don't want to inconvenience you," he said not meaning it.

"No problem. Let's go." Jerry stepped over to the glass window, looking into the administration's office. "I'm taking Mom and Arthur to the mall shopping. We'll be back after lunch," he said looking at the lady sitting behind the desk. He signed his mother and Arthur out and headed for the door, which he held open for Lucy and Arthur.

"Wait," the lady behind the glass enclosure hollered and ran out of the office to the front door. "Stop! Arthur can't go with you. His family hasn't signed a release for him to go off with other people."

Arthur's heart stopped. He couldn't believe he'd need permission from Shelly to leave.

Jerry looked at Arthur, "Sorry. Maybe next time."

Lucy sulked. She didn't need anything from the mall.

Arthur turned without saying a word and headed to his room. His lip seemed to drag the floor. Entering his room, he slammed the door and plopped down in the La-Z-Boy. It didn't feel as comfortable as the one at home.

Suddenly he jumped back on his feet. "The bus!"

Arthur ran out of his room almost falling over Frances rolling past his door. "Hey Frances. Have you seen Annette today?"

"Yes, she was heading into the fitness center."

"Thanks." Arthur hurried down the hallway.

The door was open to the fitness center. He could see Annette inside and dashed in. "Annette!" he said beaming, rushing to her side. "Where are we going today on the bus?"

"We're not taking the bus anywhere today. We have other activities planned."

"Oh . . ." Arthur groaned as he hung his head down and slumped over a treadmill's handrail. The walls seemed to close in on him. It didn't look like he was going anywhere today. He wondered if this was the last opportunity of the day. *How am I going to get away? I can't walk out the door.* His rosy cheeks turned pale.

"Don't look so disappointed. We've got a lot planned. Here, have today's activities list." She forced the sheet on him.

"Exercise!" he read aloud.

"And you're right on time," Annette exclaimed as Hazel and Emma stepped into the exercise room.

"Crafts! . . . Finger painting, wonderful," Arthur said, reading.

"It's wonderful therapy for your finger joints," Emma said.

"It helps my arthritis," joined Hazel, holding up her hands and wiggling her gnarled fingers.

Arthur looked at his activity sheet and read silently, not wanting to hear any more comments from the elderly ladies. *Lunch; Free time—watch a movie, read a book, visit with other residents, or rest; Dinner; Tonight—Bingo.*

"Everyone, find a treadmill and step up on it. Carefully increase your walking speed. I don't want any accidents. We're two-hundred and fifty-one days accident free," Julie shouted from the front of the room.

Hazel smiled at Arthur as she stepped up on the treadmill he was leaning against. "I always use this one," she said looking down on him. As the treadmill's belt jostled and she began walking, he grunted, "Fine," and walked over to another one.

Up on the treadmill, Arthur grumbled, contemplating the day's activities and cringed, "Recess? Finger painting? Movies?" His eyes rolled up and then down. *I've made the full circle of life. I'm back at the beginning.*

I shouldn't be here! Arthur's face was reddening with each step taken. With today's activities limited to the assisted living facility, he knew there was no escaping today. After twenty minutes and having walked one mile, he'd had enough. Feeling hopeless, he stepped off the treadmill and walked over to the wall where Emma was sitting. She had stopped walking a few minutes earlier.

"Exhausted, huh?" she asked, breathing heavily.

"No!" he snapped. "I'm not feeling good."

Emma didn't like the tone in his voice and slid down two seats away from him.

After more minutes passed, a bell rang up front. "Ok, our thirty minutes are up. It's time to switch rooms. Those from finger painting are waiting and it's your turn to paint," Julie instructed.

"Come on Arthur," Annette said watching him sulk.

He stood up and followed her from the room and across the hall. Stepping inside, his noise twitched, smelling the paint fumes. Walking to an empty table, he noticed the wet papers drying along the wall's counters. "Art!" he mumbled. "That's a waste of good paint," and he continued grumbling, crossing his arms.

Frances pushed forward in her wheelchair, rolling around the table where he sat. "I wanted to exercise with you, but my body refused. Do you mind if I join you?"

Yes, Arthur wanted to say, but he bit his tongue. He assumed she'd sit anyway and make his life more miserable. "I don't mind." He wished Mabel was feeling better. She'd tell Frances to move along.

A short woman, with a few gray hairs emerging from her black hair, stood beside him looking at her clipboard, glancing at the top page. "Arthur! Welcome to crafts. I'm Cindy," she said with a giant smile. "We'll have lots of fun today."

Arthur forced a smile in return. He wished he was anywhere other than sitting in this building. "Hi, Cindy."

"Here is the paint," she said, placing the bottles on his table.

Frances snatched two bottles off the table and squeezed. Paint spattered across her white page.

Dabs of paint pooled on Arthur's sheet. He grimaced at the cold paints, as he let his fingers slip across the page. The red, yellow, and blue paints slithered across one another, snaking into greens, oranges, purples, browns, and black. Arthur didn't notice the oozing color changes. Frances was constantly chattering. He'd closed his eyes trying to block out the noise. The last thing he wanted to hear about was her cats. His allergy to cats was mental, as well as physical.

"Arthur," the craft instructor exclaimed, placing a hand on his shoulder. "What a wonderful picture. Congratulations. Everyone, look at Arthur's beautiful picture."

His eyes opened, staring at the gooey blackened page, Arthur's formless work curved and zigzagged across the page and on the table. His apron was smeared with paint. "Ugh. What a mess," he moaned as paint dripped from his finger tips.

The clock above the sink indicated noon. Arthur was glad the thirty minutes were over and in a few minutes lunch would be served. Feeling humiliated at being treated like a child, he swore never to participate in crafts again. He was leaving with or without Shelly's help.

Water washed the gooey paint off Arthur's hands. He watched the colored water swirl and disappear down the drain. Grabbing a couple of paper towels, he hurried out into the hallway, separating himself from Frances.

Arthur stood looking down the corridor to his right. At the end were double doors. On the doors he read: Emergency Exit Only.

Alarm Will Sound if Door is Opened. He knew all about that from yesterday. He wouldn't get far.

With a renewed sense of urgency to leave, Arthur turned to his left and walked out into the lobby. His eyes focused on the double doors, wondering if now would be the appropriate time to walk out, when receptionists and other office staff were more interested in eating their lunch and not watching the front doors. He saw no one through the glass partition and his heart raced. He tried to slow his breathing, but instead it intensified. His knees shook with each quiet step taken toward the double doors. With two steps remaining, Arthur was not breathing. As he lifted his hand to open the door, a heavy-set receptionist rose from under the counter clasping a handful of disorganized papers. Her threatening eyes pierced his heart, draining the life from him. His hand fell limply to his side. Frozen, Arthur peered through the glass doors. "Nice sunny day," he said pretending to be interested in the weather.

Her mouth clenched and her eyes threatened serious consequences if he touched the door.

Arthur wanted to share some of his anger and leaned toward the doors, provoking the receptionist who dropped the papers on the desk as she reached for the phone. He turned around with an animated grin and walked to the cafeteria.

CHAPTER TWENTY

After lunch, Arthur lay on his bed resting, envisioning one brazen escape after another, knowing all along that it was an event for the movies. It would never work here, but it sure helped the time to pass. After many differing visions, Arthur grew restless. He got up and stepped into the hallway; he had to find some way to slip beyond the front doors.

As he entered the lobby, he saw purple and white streamers arching above. Curious about the festivity, he asked one woman standing on a ladder pulling another streamer. "What are the decorations for?" He couldn't imagine that they would have decorated for tonight's Bingo.

"It's one of the resident's birthday, she's one-hundred-years-old today," she answered, looking down at him.

With the staff working in the lobby, Arthur returned to his bedroom. He picked up the daily activity list and saw that no birthday party had been scheduled. Relieved that he didn't have to attend a party for a stranger, he lay down on the bed. Restless once more, he moved to the recliner for a brief moment and then, wrestling with the thought of spending another night, he began pacing from one side of the room to the other.

The walls squeezed Arthur from his room. The urge to escape moved him toward the fire escape door. Standing at the end of the hallway, he heard an imaginary alarm blaring as his hand reached for the door's release bar. To his left were double doors and a sign above it read: Ward C. Arthur had overheard in the cafeteria that demented people lived through those doors. He knew they were housed somewhere and didn't want to venture inside. Despondent, he turned and walked away. He watched as guests entered through the lobby's double doors, greeted by an employee.

The one-hundred-year-old, great-great-grand mother sat in a wheelchair with many guests around her talking. A little girl stood face to face with her. Arthur did not remember seeing the woman eating in the cafeteria or at any of the activities. He assumed she lived in Ward B.

Feeling unwelcome, Arthur returned to his room and dropped onto his bed, demoralized. Unable to envision another escape scenario, his mind drifted to the last wonderful birthday party his wife Laura had given him, only months before she died. People had drifted in and out of their house. Some were old friends and distant relatives he had not recognized. Only after a brief introduction did recognition return to him.

The birthday laughter bellowed through the hallways.

Arthur's imagination locked on his dad's brother, a favorite uncle he had not seen for decades.

POP – POP Two balloons touched a hot light bulb and exploded in the lobby.

The uncle's memories lingered as Arthur's birthday party disappeared. With his head nestled on the pillow, he wondered if his uncle were still alive today, would he be recognizable?

"That's it!" Arthur leaped off the bed, rushed into the bathroom and stood in front of the mirror. Brushing his hair to the side, he wondered whether the guests at the birthday party would accept him as their long lost uncle. After freshening up and rearranging his hair for the third time, Arthur closed his bedroom door.

Easing from the hallway into the lobby, Arthur smiled warmly as he casually joined the birthday crowd. Slowly, he made his way into the center of the crowd, hiding from the staff.

Above the birthday cake, a banner read, "Happy One Hundredth Birthday - Mom - Grandmom - Great Grandmom - Great Great Grandmom."

Looking around, Arthur estimated the birthday group had grown to more than one-hundred well wishers. He noticed most guests held a glass of punch or water, sipping as they talked. Needing to blend, Arthur inched his way toward the punch bowl, but his path suddenly disappeared. People pressed against him as they began singing happy birthday. Arthur joined in.

Cheers erupted as the one-hundred candle flames were extinguished. Cake was cut and placed on paper party plates with the first slice given to the birthday girl. Then teenage great-grandchildren eagerly served plates to all guests.

"This slice is for you, sir," a sandy-red haired teenage girl said.

Surprised, Arthur reached out his hand and took it, "Thank you."

The cream cheese and powdered sugar icing was Arthur's favorite. As he savored the creamy icing, he blended perfectly into the family's festivities. Looking around, he was dressed as well as most of the crowd. As the crowd mingled, talking with different relatives, Arthur soon found himself relaxed in the middle of the family members.

Arthur began speaking to any who would talk. None seemed to mind. Most seemed not to know who the next person was, especially the younger generation. He was having a blast.

Time passed and Arthur felt like he'd known this family forever.

As the line of well wishers spoke with the birthday girl and gave hugs, Arthur ambled forward. "Oh no!" Arthur gasped as he turned to find himself stuck in line and the next to offer congratulations. His first instinct was to step out of line, but fearing greater attention brought to himself by fleeing, he gritted his teeth and stepped up to the old lady.

"Happy one-hundredth birthday," he said as he bent over, giving her a hug.

The lady smiled as she had done with everyone before him.

Walking away, Arthur overheard, "Who was that?"

"Oh he's mother's brother's son-in-law, I guess." Smiling, he made his way to another couple and began conversing with them.

The afternoon was late and the birthday girl had thanked everyone for coming. A nurse wheeled the lady down the middle corridor, back through the double doors into Ward B.

The crowd of relatives slowly began leaving.

"The city bus just arrived," a voice was heard broadcasting from the front door.

Hugs and kisses were quickly exchanged. Stopping to receive a stranger's hug, Arthur noticed a baseball cap at his feet. After the tight embrace, he bent over and picked up the hat. Snuggling it on his head, he stood up. Flowing toward the double doors, hidden in the middle of the crowd, Arthur's racing heart stopped as he grimaced when a man accidentally stepped on his right foot.

"Excuse me Cuz´. Did I see you riding the bus here this afternoon?" The man had a scratchy voice and his thick bottle-lense glasses made his eyes appear as large as golf balls.

Arthur's toe throbbed. Without missing a beat, Arthur said, "Yes, you did. How about we sit together on the way back to town? We have a lot of catching up to do." His voice had taken on a southern drawl.

"Sure Cuz´."

The group tightened as they approached the double doors. Arthur crept along in the middle of the group, walking slouched over, looking at the floor. Obscured from the front desk, his heart pounded as he waited to exit the lobby.

The crowd stopped momentarily, but Arthur dared not look up, fearing an administrator would recognize him. He waited, expecting any moment that a hand would snatch him from the line. *Move along,* he whispered. Momentarily, the crowd started moving through the door and Arthur shuffled with them. As he got closer, his anxiety grew. His heart pounded, echoing in his ears. He couldn't breathe. Each step was laborious. Fresh air rushed past Arthur as he stood pinned in the mass of people stepping to the doors. Head down and heart pummeling, he stepped outside unnoticed.

Run, his inner voice hissed, *you're going to get caught.*

He fought the desire and stayed with the group. As the group reached the curb, they started disbursing. Cars were parked everywhere, many illegally blocking vehicles. They were on the sidewalk and in the manicured grass. A few people turned and walked to their left, where they had parked their vehicles. Some continued walking straight ahead to the front parking lot. Others stepped to the right, crowding the entrance to the city bus.

Arthur found himself unsure of which way he should go.

Suddenly a hand grabbed Arthur's shoulder. Freezing in his stance, his heart exploded into numbness. Standing ridged, his ears hissed and his hope evaporated.

"Come on Cuz´." Feeling Arthur's tense shoulder muscles, he remarked, "Cuz´, you're one nervous dude. Relax."

Arthur let out a large sigh, stepping toward the bus. In order to hide his shaking hands, he pushed them deep into his pockets.

As the line of birthday goers entered the bus, Arthur could see they were dropping change into the bus' change-box. Arthur's eyes rolled to the right in exasperation. Another obstacle stood in his way. He had assumed the bus had been hired and the fees had been prepaid.

His newly discovered cousin kept pushing Arthur toward the bus' door. Trapped in the middle of a group, he stepped up.

"Your money, sir?"

Arthur stood motionless on the step. The bus driver and all the unknown relatives behind him stared.

CHAPTER TWENTY-ONE

"Here's his money." Change fell into the box and Arthur was pushed past the bus driver by his unknown cousin.

"Thanks, I owe you."

"Don't mention it Cuz´. Sometimes I forget my money, too."

Arthur made his way to the back of the bus and found two seats. His good-natured cousin followed.

Sitting on the hard seat, Arthur sought answers to the new challenges that would inevitably arise. *Where am I going? How am I going to get money? What am I going to do for food? Who can I tru . . . ?*

"Hey Cuz´, where are you heading?"

Arthur could not believe his bad luck. This cousin-character wanted to talk.

"Well . . . ," Arthur stopped to think about where the international airport was, ". . . south of town. I need to pick up some supplies," Arthur said. Supplies, that sounded lame, he told himself.

"What kind of supplies?"

Arthur searched for an answer. His hands continued trembling as he folded them across his chest.

"Horse supplies?" The cousin began laughing. "Just kidding. I remember years ago when I was a kid, mom made me ride the bus into town to buy horse feed. Can you imagine the looks I got from other riders when I dragged that sack of feed down the aisle and into the seat with me? Ha, ha, ha. And that smell. People were sneezing. As I left, that bus driver told me never to bring horse feed onto his bus again. Ha, ha."

Arthur could not believe how this person could go on and on talking. Asking and answering his own questions. At least he didn't have to answer; instead his thoughts raced.

The idea of spending the night in his own bed was appealing, considering what he had slept on the two previous nights. The mattress was firmer than what he was accustomed to. Knowing his house would be the first place searched, he was determined that he would stick with his plan. He was flying out of town tonight. He drug his fingers through his hair as if he could pull the thoughts from his mind. *Money.* His fingers froze. All other questions pivoted around the need for money. *Without money, I won't get far.*

As the bus meandered through the streets of West Palm Beach, Arthur wondered when it would reach its maximum distance away from Southern Retirement Community. Only then would he exit, unless he saw the airport. He shuddered at the thought of being an indigent, but thankful he'd be free.

The bus' door closed and its air-brakes hissed, after allowing numerous riders off at the West Palm Beach Hilton Hotel. The bus pulled away from the curb and back into traffic.

Looking out the window, Arthur wondered how long before someone would discover him missing. He hoped to be off the bus by that time.

"Hey Cuz´, I apologize for not remembering who you are, but grandma's family is large. She had seven children. My dad Albert was the second child. How are you related?"

Arthur coughed, pretending to clear his throat. "I. . ." and he coughed again buying himself more time to think. ". . . the last . . . excuse me. Something's in my throat." Arthur wheezed and coughed again, trying to stall.

"Oh, you must be Louise's son! No wonder I don't remember you. She married your dad who was a professional soldier. What was he in . . . Oh yeah, I remember, the Army. You guys were lucky. Always moving overseas to another location. I wish I got to see the world like you."

Arthur was relieved to find out who he was impersonating. He squirmed in his seat searching for the most comfortable position. Another cough kept the man talking.

As the bus swayed, turning down a side street heading for the next hotel, Arthur watched children pumping their bicycles hard, trying their best to stay up with the bus. A couple of blocks away, children chased a kick ball through the grass, as another child ran around makeshift bases.

"You know," Arthur blurted, "all that traveling isn't always glamorous. Just as I made a good friend, Dad would get a new assignment and off we'd move. I hated leaving my friends behind. Most I never saw again. That's tough."

"I guess you're right. I never thought of that. I'm glad we didn't move like you."

Over the top of a house, Arthur saw a tree house high in the air. Memories of his young childhood had him building his first tree house. He could hear his mother hollering over the pounding hammers; *You boys be careful.*

Inhaling, Arthur closed his eyes and smelled freshly cut grass. He could not believe the details of life he'd forgotten.

The further the bus drove, the more relaxed Arthur became. He was free again.

"Cuz', where're you staying tonight?"

Another round of coughs developed. Arthur couldn't believe this guy.

"You need something to drink to wash that tickle down. I'll try not asking you any more questions for a while."

Outside the windows, businesses zoomed past, people hurriedly crossed the streets. Arthur wondered how much further the bus would go before it would turn around and head back.

"Hey Cuz', where'd you say you're going?"

Arthur looked out the window and recognized where he was.

Glancing at the man's wristwatch, Arthur realized he had better hurry to the bank before it closed for the day. "I've got to go to the bank. Remember, I don't have any money." Arthur could not wait until he got away from this man. He never stopped talking.

The bus pulled over to the curb and stopped. A block away was where he did his banking, the south-side branch. He hoped the man was not getting off here.

"Well, this is my stop. I'll talk with you soon. Goodbye."

Arthur was halfway down the aisle, when the scratchy voice stopped him. "Hey Cuz'. I've had a wonderful time hashing out old times together. If you don't have any plans for dinner tonight, why don't you come to my house? We can cook steaks and potatoes."

Remembering the food question had not been answered, Arthur reconsidered this new cousin's worth. He could put up with a lot of talking. It was better than living in a nursing home and maybe the man would drive him to the airport later. "That sounds wonderful. I haven't made plans for dinner and would be glad to eat with you. But, I do have a late flight to catch. Oh . . . I need your address. I'll catch a taxi."

"Cuz', better yet, we can ride together to my house. I'll walk with you to the bank. We can catch the next bus out to my house."

Arthur wondered if this man really had all of *his* mental faculties together. *How could a judge rule that I'm a danger to myself and society, but allow this nut to roam the streets freely? It's just not fair.* He steamed.

The two stepped off the bus and crossed the street. Arthur exhaled and then inhaled quickly. Holding his head high and smiling, he felt hopeful that no one at the nursing home had reported him missing.

"Cuz', slow down," the man gasped as he hurried to catch up.

The doors electronically swung open. Arthur stepped inside with his cousin a step behind.

"Good afternoon," the security guard greeted them as they entered the bank's lobby.

They both nodded at the guard.

"Cuz', I'll just stand over here and wait while you get your money."

Arthur stood in the lobby's center searching for Peggy. She was easy to spot with her red frizzy hair. He knew them all and they all knew him, but she was special. She'd give him the money. He was glad Shelly had gone off on business. She wouldn't have had time to close his banking account.

His favorite teller was Peggy. He smiled when he saw that no one was at her window. "Hi Peggy. I'd like to withdraw some money today." His voice was cheerful.

"Hi Arthur. I've not seen you in a few weeks. What's happening in your life?"

"Oh, nothing, I've just been around. I'd like to withdraw, say — ten thousand dollars, please?"

"Arthur!" she gasped. "It's too dangerous for you to carry that large sum of money. Why don't you use your credit card?"

Momentary silence. And then Arthur replied. "I'm going to buy a car in Palm Beach and the person won't take anything but cash."

"Okay, but be very careful. Don't trust anyone." After a momentary wait for Arthur to present his withdrawal form she asked, "Did you fill out a withdrawal request?"

Oh, not another obstacle, Arthur brooded. He wondered how many more obstacles stood between him and his money. Pretending to reach for his wallet, he stopped. "Uh," he gasped. His eyes opened wide and his jaw dropped. "Oh Peggy, I've left my wallet at home. Is there anyway that you could pull up my account so that I won't have to go home? You'll be closed by the time I come back."

"Sure Arthur, I can do that for you. One moment, please."

Peggy typed commands into the computer, then waited. She smiled at Arthur with her usual large, kind smile. "Want a lollipop?"

"No, thank you."

The computer screen printed bold letters, ACCESS DENIED.

Her smile disappeared; she re-typed the commands into the computer . . . ACCESS DENIED.

"I . . . ah . . . something's wrong." She rubbed her forehead. "Arthur, this computer's having problems today. Give me one minute and I'll ask my supervisor. I'll have your money shortly."

Peggy disappeared through a door. He hated computers. They never seemed to work when one's in a hurry. Just his luck.

Arthur turned to see if his so-called cousin was still waiting. He was talking to the security guard. It appeared the guard was tired of all the talk. Arthur smiled sympathetically.

Arthur turned back around and continued waiting. A woman walked up behind him forming a line. Soon he could sense her impatience and he started feeling embarrassed for tying up the teller this long. The woman turned and walked to another teller's line to wait. He wished Peggy would hurry.

Another minute passed, then a tall, young executive and a security guard met in the center of the lobby. They walked over to Peggy's counter.

A hand gently touched Arthur's shoulder. Thinking it was his cousin, he winced, waiting to hear his voice.

"Arthur, I'm Samuel Parker, a vice-president at this bank. I hear there's a problem trying to access your account. I think we can get to the bottom of the problem. Will you come with me please?"

Pleased to hear someone was going to straighten out the computer glitch, Arthur followed, although he had never met this vice-president.

With an escort on either side, Arthur followed their lead across the lobby, questions running through his mind. *Why does he have a guard with him?* A sickening feeling swelled in his stomach.

As Arthur stepped into the hallway, a hand grabbed his shoulder. The scratchy voice screeched, "Hey Cuz′, where you going?"

Arthur turned around, shrugged his shoulders, "I don't know."

"Excuse me sir, are you with Arthur?" Samuel Parker asked.

"Yes sir, he's . . . my . . . cousin." His eyes narrow looking at Arthur. He didn't recall any cousins from Louise's side of the family being named that. *Maybe he's going by a middle name.* He wished he'd remembered names better.

Samuel invited him to join them in his office. "There's a small banking glitch that needs to be worked out. Then the two of you may leave."

Breathing more easily, Arthur followed.

Inside the office, the door closed and the two were instructed to have a seat. "Mr. McCullen, your account has been closed and the balance is zero. Maybe you have another bank account I could pull the money from. Or maybe you changed banks."

"No sir, that's the only account I have. What do you mean, there's no money in the account? There was more than six-hundred thousand dollars in that account."

"Sir, that account was closed yesterday."

"Dang Cuz′, you've been robbed."

"Who closed my account?" Arthur shouted.

"Let me look; here it is, Justin Roble."

"What! How did Justin steal my money?" Arthur screamed.

"It appears he had your power-of-attorney."

"No way! Shelly my daughter has . . ." he slid down in his seat running his hands through his hair. He'd almost admitted that Shelly had his power-of-attorney. That would have thrown up a red flag. He couldn't believe he no longer had the right to withdraw his money. Pain spread across his body. His breathing slowed, as did his heart beat. His brain was numb.

Samuel, sensing a problem, needed to find Arthur's personal information. He typed the commands that took him to a different screen and found two phone numbers. The young man dialed the home number first. When no one answered the phone, he dialed the office phone number.

"Hello."

"Hello, this is Samuel Parker at West Palm Beach Bank . . ."

Arthur stopped rubbing his head and eavesdropped on the phone conversation.

". . . I have Arthur McCullen, sitting in my office trying to withdraw his money. But, the account has been closed. Do you know anything about it?"

Arthur's heart pummeled his ribs as he heard the questions. He'd been caught. He had to get out of the room and quick. Remembering his escape from the mall, he turned to the security man, and asked. "Excuse me sir. Can you tell me where the men's restroom is located?"

Samuel covered the mouth piece and looked at Tom and Mr. McCullen. "Tom, would you escort Mr. McCullen to the restroom and make sure he accompanies you back into my office when he's finished." He then returned to his call.

Rising from his chair, Arthur knew with the escort by his side, he'd have to plan his escape well. Perceiving one opportunity for escape, it was all that stood between freedom and a return trip to the nursing home.

Now past five o'clock, the bank's lobby was emptying. The cashiers who no longer had a customer thumbed their stacks of money, inattentive to Arthur's presence.

Coming out from the restroom, Arthur noticed that the bank's security cameras continued scanning the lobby. Looking across the lobby, two customers headed for the exit door. Outside the glass doors, crowds of people scurried past on the sidewalk. Arthur figured if he could time his dart for the door as the security guard politely opened it for departing customers, then he'd quickly become lost in the crowd.

The guard walked between him and the guard standing at the door. Arthur felt the nursing home's walls closing in on him.

These men were preventing him from bolting through the bank's doors.

The front door security guard smiled as he pulled the glass door opened for the two departing bank customers. Arthur's ears throbbed as his heart pounded the blood throughout his body. His ears rang and all noise was drowned out.

Following his instincts, Arthur thrust his left foot out. Tom stumbled but seemed to be catching his balance when Arthur shoved his hands out, knocking Tom down on the polished granite floor. The two were at the door as Arthur leaped over Tom.

Arthur sprinted to the door. The two customers stepped outside the bank building.

Lifting his head off the floor and catching his breath, Tom yelled, "Help! Stop that man."

Arthur felt the sea breeze brushing past his face and smelled the aroma of the salt in the air, as he stepped to the door. His heart pounded, his feet throbbed with each step taken. He stepped through the door and into the hurried crowd. "Ugh," Arthur groaned as two beefy hands grasped his collar. The shirt buttons bulged as Arthur was lifted back into the bank's lobby. Unable to move, Arthur hung limp as he was drug back to Samuel Parker's office. Tom's hand pressed firmly on Arthur's shoulder, securing him in the chair.

"Are you sure he is not my Cuz´?"

"We're sure. His name is Arthur McCullen and he is a resident of Southern Retirement Community."

"Well, he surely had me hoodwinked. I feel foolish. May I leave?"

Arthur hung his head down, feeling deceitful; he never even acknowledged his 'Cousin.'

Samuel nodded as he picked up the phone. "Hello, I'm Samuel Parker, vice-president at West Palm Beach Bank, South-side. I have Arthur McCullen in my office. My understanding is that he's a resident of yours."

Picturing Justin with his money, Arthur steamed and surged to flee. Tom's grip tightened, counteracting Arthur's attempt.

"Yes sir, I'll keep Arthur in my office until you arrive."

Waiting in the silence of the room, Arthur grimaced, knowing Justin now had his money. *I'd rather be homeless than live caged inside the walls of Southern Retirement Community.* Arthur imagined living in the woods. His dirty appearance would change his features forever and then no one would recognize him. He could stand on the street corners holding his sign, asking for money. They'd toss him some change and never know it was him. He chuckled. That just might be okay, he thought, resolved that he'd have to wait another day to escape.

Samuel read and marked documents as if no one was in the room. Tom's hand continued to immobilize Arthur. The more he thought about Justin taking his money the more he hated him.

The door clattered as it swung open. Startled, everyone's head snapped, turning to see who had burst in.

CHAPTER TWENTY-TWO

A bulky, long-haired man in his thirties entered.

"Excuse me. Is this Mr. Samuel Parker's office?" his voice boomed.

Arthur shuddered as he recognized him.

Mr. Parker stood, stepping around his desk. Looking up at the man, he held out his hand. "Yes, I'm Samuel Parker."

"I'm Mr. Otman. Sorry it took me so long, but the traffic is terrible. I'm here to pick up Mr. McCullen." Their hands met. Otman's hand engulfed Samuel's.

"I appreciate your detaining him until I could get here."

Tom quickly stepped aside.

Burly hands grasped Arthur and pulled him out of his seat.

"Thanks for the call. It won't happen again." Arthur's feet barely touched the floor as Otman led him down the hall. The sidewalk was now empty and the walk was quiet, but dreadful. Arthur saw the mini-bus parked by the curb. The doors opened as they approached.

As they climbed on the bus, Bishop, the driver, commented, "Yep. That's the one that ran away from the mall yesterday."

Arthur was firmly pressed down into a seat. His seat belt snapped and the loose end was jerked tight. "I don't expect any trouble from you," Otman said as he sat across from him.

The bus rolled to a stop in front of the double doors at Southern Retirement Community. The mini-bus swayed as Otman stood and stepped toward Arthur. "Get up!" With fingers clawing into his shoulders, again Arthur's feet barely touched the ground. Whisked off the bus and through the doors, Arthur was steered to the left of the lobby to a room beside the cafeteria which was always kept locked. Turning the key and opening the door, Otman heaved Arthur into the windowless, empty room. The room vibrated as the door slammed.

Looking at the hard floor, Arthur decided to stand for a while. He was glad Otman had left. That man just didn't seem right. The bright white walls glared as the single light refracted off them. The longer the silence, the more rapid his thoughts changed from Justin to Otman and back. He'd like to wring both their necks. After what seemed like more than an hour, he wondered if someone was punishing him and had placed him in solitude. With thoughts of spending the night locked up, he sat down. The vinyl flooring, cold and uncomfortable, didn't allow him any comfort. His back hurt leaning against the wall, his butt hurt, and his empty stomach ached. With the time well after six o'clock, he knew that dinner was being served and some had even finished eating. Fatigue began to set in from his long afternoon's partying and escape. Closing his eyes, he wished he could turn the light off.

Arthur flinched as the door knob rattled and the door swung open. There in the doorway was Otman and a nicely dressed administrator in a black suit. Stepping inside, Otman stooped to fit under the doorway. The other man followed. Arthur rubbed his eyes and yawned as he stood.

"Mr. McCullen, my name is Mr. Elsway. I'm one of the administrators here." He opened the file folder and pulled out Arthur's personal records. "Looking in your file, I see you have a history of trying to leave. To be exact, you've tried to walk away four times in two days."

Four times? Why's he lying? I've left twice: once from the mall and once today. Arthur stared at the man with contempt, his breath heavy.

"You obviously don't understand that you've been committed here under court jurisdiction. The judge ruled that you need twenty-four-hour supervision. It is my job to ensure you stay where the court system has placed you. Because of your tendency to walk away from our facility, we're required to move you to our high risk ward, Ward C. There you'll no longer be able to wander off."

"Those records are . . ." Otman slapped his burly hand over Arthur's mouth. He continued trying to make himself heard, but only a faint mumbling noise sounded.

Otman's other hand grasped Arthur's shirt and pressed him into the wall. "Shut up!"

The behemoth hand compressed Arthur's chest causing pain and laborious breathing. Unable to breathe, he gave up the fight but he remained irate. *Four times?* He assumed the other two possible times of escape must have been when he tried to step outside with Mabel and the receptionist today must have reported him trying to walk out the front door. *Wait till I tell Shelly. I'll show them. One more night and I'm out of here.*

"Mr. Otman, you know what to do. Please see to it." The administrator closed the file folder, turned and exited the room.

Removing the hand covering Arthur's mouth, Otman stuck his hand into his pocket and pulled out a foot-long, shiny object that snaked out from his pocket. Arthur's eyes widened as he focused on a small metal case that was attached. Having heard of shock treatments used at nursing homes or at least projected on television, Arthur feared the prospect of receiving jolts of electricity. His heart beat increased, wondering if the shock would be extremely painful, something like a dog received when it got too close to an invisible fence. He remembered hearing a neighbor's dog yelp when it tried to cross the line. He could only imagine how bad it must hurt.

"Mr. McCullen, you'll wear this leg anklet the rest of your life. We'll be able to assure both the judge and your family that you'll never wander away from our fine institution again. Stick out your left leg," his demanding voice boomed as his hand released Arthur's body.

Arthur hesitated and wheezed as air rushed into his lungs.

Otman didn't wait. With his free hand he wrenched Arthur's leg forward and wrapped the anklet around his leg. With a swift tug the metal cleat was permanently fastened.

Arthur smirked, knowing it was only a matter of time before he would figure a way to remove that anklet. But, even if he had to wait until Shelly picked him up tomorrow to remove the anklet, he didn't mind.

"Come on Mr. McCullen, follow me," Otman coarsely growled. With one meaty hand wrapped around Arthur's wrist, the other hand swung open the door.

Walking down the corridor of Ward A, Arthur passed his room and wondered what his new room would be like.

The double doors leading into Ward C creaked as they opened and Arthur froze. His nose twitched, whiffing an awful smell.

"What, you don't like the smell of antiseptics and bodily fluids? Don't worry. Everything is sterile here, unless you soil yourself." With a smirk, Otman's hand jerked Arthur into the room, sounding an alarm. Arthur froze once more.

"Come on," Otman snarled, trudging out from the hallway entrance. Arthur's arm felt like it was being pulled out of its socket. "You'll never wander off now. I hope you like it here." Otman's smirk grew more treacherous before stepping over to speak with one of the nurses.

"I doubt it," Arthur hissed.

"This way," Otman said, motioning to Arthur, "your room is down wing two." They passed a resident ambling in the wide hallway; she never noticed them. It was as if the two were invisible. A cold chill spread through Arthur as he realized the truth. These people really were clueless.

"Mr. McCullen, this is your room. You'll have your own room for now. But sometime in the near future, you'll get a roommate."

Arthur stopped in the hallway. "Mr. Otman, I was promised a private room. I don't expect to share this room with anyone."

"There are no private rooms available."

As he started to protest, an elderly woman brushed aside Otman and stepped over to Arthur. "Harry, is that you?" Arthur's hands cupped his ears, to block the high screeching voice.

"Bessy, this is Arthur, not Harry," Otman spat.

Arthur stepped inside his white-walled room to escape.

Bessy followed Arthur inside and pressed against his chest. "Harry, where have you been? I've been looking for you," her shrill voice backed Arthur into the wall. She grabbed his arm and began pulling as he pressed himself to the wall in resistance.

He shuddered at the touch and wondered how long Harry had been dead.

"Mr. McCullen, you'll have to excuse her," Otman said, prying her fingers off Arthur, releasing Bessy's grip. "She doesn't know where she is or who anyone is. She thinks every man is Harry."

"Get her out of my room!"

"Now Arthur, . . . you don't mind if I call you Arthur do you?"

Furious, Arthur stared at Otman.

"Well Arthur it is. Now you behave yourself or I *will* get one of these nurses to give you a sedative. Then, you'll behave yourself. And if the nurses can't handle you, I'll come back."

Otman ushered Bessy out of the room.

Arthur turned away and looked at his smaller room—white walls, vinyl-tiled floor, a twin bed, a mirror-less dresser, and no window. The room felt cold. Gritting his teeth, he knew he'd have to tolerate it for one night. After all, he wasn't staying. He stepped over to the dresser drawer and pulled open the top right drawer. There he found his clothes. He found the top left side drawer empty. Quickly checking the other drawers out, he realized the right side was his and the other side was for his future roommate.

Arthur wanted a drink. He rummaged through each drawer. Shirts, slacks, socks and underwear were turned upside down. He made a second sweep through each drawer, but the bottle of rum was nowhere to be found.

He stepped into the bathroom, wondering if it was private or shared with an adjoining room. He was relieved to find that while it was tiny, at least it was private. He could not imagine how the builder had crammed everything inside. Only an inch and a shower curtain separated the wheelchair accessible shower from the toilet.

With his stomach growling, it was time to find something to eat. Unsure of his surroundings and those who worked here, Arthur stepped into the deserted hallway. His arm and neck hairs stood on end as he crept down the hallway. *This place gives me the creeps*, he mumbled to himself as he passed a woman dressed in a nightgown.

"Hi. I'm Missy. You must be our new patient, Arthur." Arthur gasped. He didn't see the nurse coming. She had sneaked up on him. "We're informal down here and call everyone by their first name. May I help you?"

"Well, uh, I was wondering what time it is."

"It's a little after ten. We turn the lights down low at ten o'clock. You may go to bed or stay up later, if you prefer. We only ask that you don't disturb the other residents."

"I'm hungry. Can I get something to eat?"

"Not tonight. I'm sorry, you'll have to wait until breakfast."

"Oh!" Arthur thought about the piece of cake and punch he'd eaten at the birthday party this afternoon and was glad they'd offered him some. Continuing his stroll in the hallway, he stopped at the nursing desk. Straight ahead were the double doors he had walked through into Ward C. Looking around the lounge, he saw a television playing on the far wall with a few residents watching an old black and white movie.

Hungry, Arthur headed back to his room. He was glad Shelly would be back tomorrow. Once she saw how he'd been treated, she'd give the staff a piece of her mind and take him away from here.

Inside his room, he opened the dresser drawer and pulled out his pajamas and got ready for bed. After he brushed his teeth and shut off the lights, he climbed between the sheets. He heard an awful crackling. With one quick motion, Arthur was on his feet turning on the lights. He pulled back the bottom bed sheet. He couldn't believe someone had put a plastic mattress cover on his bed. He wasn't a bed wetter.

After refitting the bottom sheet, Arthur lay on his back in the bed. The mattress was hard and lumpy. Every time he moved to try repositioning the lumps under his back, the plastic crackled. Without a window to allow moonlight to filter inside, the room was darker than the first one had been. The only light that penetrated the room was coming from the hallway through the half-inch crack under the door. The sterile room gave no warmth; the air around him seemed cold. He knew it was going to be a long night. Unable to see a clock, he lay wondering how much longer until morning. *I don't know which is worst, finding out Justin took my money, or returning here.*

CHAPTER TWENTY-THREE

"Good—Morning—Harry!" Arthur's ears rang. He cringed as his eyes focused on Bessy's dark silhouette.

Smack. His lips recoiled behind his teeth. The slobbery kiss smeared across his ashen cheek. He instantly wiped it off.

"Bessy, this is Arthur's room. He's not Harry," Missy's soft voice explained. "Arthur, she thinks you are her husband. I'll try to keep her out."

Arthur coiled under his sheets, hiding from the gnarly-skinned woman. He could not imagine how old she was. He was determined to change his looks, hoping it would help fend off this demented woman.

"See you later Harry," Bessy called out as she was led from his room into the hall.

Peering from under the edge of the sheet, Arthur knew he wasn't crazy yet, but feared if he stayed here long, it would only be a matter of time before he'd lose it.

Lying in bed, he tried to go back to sleep, but all he could imagine was the old lady coming back into his room, thinking he was her Harry. "Get me out of here," he mumbled angrily. He remembered that today Shelly would be coming home from her business trip and she would take him from this ungodly place. Anxiously Arthur sprang from his bed and washed his face. He didn't dare take a shower with that crazy lady wandering in and out of his room. While brushing his hair, a nurse kindly announced, "Breakfast, Arthur."

Hunger pains thrashed inside his stomach from missing dinner last night. Arthur hurried out of his room. At the end of the hallway, he stopped. *Where's the cafeteria?* He watched as residents ambled from the three different hallways into the lounge area and stepped into a side room. He fell in behind an elderly man, having to slow his stride as the man shuffled along. Once inside the room, Arthur glanced around and could not find the serving counter. People sat at tables unconcerned as to what was transpiring. He must have entered the wrong room.

"Find a table and sit down," a woman's voice rumbled.

Arthur turned to see who was speaking and saw a lady staring at him. "I'm in the wrong room. I'm looking for the cafeteria."

"You've found it. I'm one of the dieticians here. Would you please sit."

Again, Arthur looked around the room for the serving line. "I haven't gotten my breakfast tray. Where is the line for food?"

"We'll bring the food to you once you're seated."

Not knowing anyone, he chose to sit alone at the end of a table. He couldn't believe he wouldn't be allowed to pick the food he wanted to eat. As soon as he sat, a dietician plopped a breakfast tray on the table.

Arthur gagged. "What's that?"

"That yellow pile is your eggs and sausage," she said.

"It looks like someone's already chewed up these eggs and spit them out."

"Ha, ha, ha. You're funny. The food's been pureed. We don't want anyone choking. You're lucky to still have your teeth; most of our residents don't."

"Thanks for explaining." He'd never seen any food that looked that awful, and didn't want to know what the rest of the food was. He was hungry and did not want to lose his appetite. The toast appeared normal, as did the apple sauce; the white pile smelled like grits, but the pureed mush didn't look anything like eggs and sausage. Hungry, he'd eat it fast.

An older gentleman sat beside him and a breakfast tray was placed in front of him. Arthur ignored the man while swallowing his food between gags. The texture was awful, but his stomach didn't care. He tried camouflaging the eggish substance on his toast. It didn't work. He gagged as he swallowed each bite.

The man beside him looked straight ahead and slurped each spoonful at his lips.

Arthur hoped he would die before his mind left him. He did not want to return and live in a place like this. This wasn't living. He tried blocking the slurping noise as he attempted to finish his meal.

Before he could complete breakfast, a man about his age shuffled past talking gibberish, while drool oozed off his lips. Arthur leaned into the table each time the man passed. He didn't want any saliva landing on him. *Why does he keep staring at me? If he wants this slop, he can have it. I've almost stomached all that I can eat.* Arthur cowered as the man made another pass. With each pass the man had slowed his pace. *What's with him?* As the man passed again, Arthur swallowed the last bite of food. He hoped the man would now stop ambling past.

After a minute, Arthur's stomach growled loudly. He looked at the plate of the man next to him. Toast was all that remained. A quick glance told Arthur that the man was finished eating. *Why doesn't he get up and leave?*

His cataract-covered eyes stared blankly ahead.

Arthur, still hungry, thought about helping himself to the man's toast. The man would never see the toast snatched, but Arthur asked anyway. "Excuse me sir. If you're not going to eat your toast, may I have it?"

The old man's eyes remained transfixed. His fingers slowly fumbled for his plate, rattling his fork. His hands stopped at the toast. Both slices crumbled as he grasped them. He slowly stuck out his hand toward Arthur.

"Thanks," Arthur said as he took the slices from the older gentleman.

"Arthur," the dietician's voice chastised as Arthur dropped the slices in his plate. "We do not allow sharing of food."

"But . . ."

"Now, Arthur. That's how germs are passed." The dietician picked up the two slices of toast and threw them directly in the trash can as she walked away.

The old gentleman pushed his tray away as he stood. Turning, he walked out of the cafeteria.

"Psst!"

Startled, Arthur's head spun around, his eyes narrowed on the odd man who had been ambling back and forth past him. While Arthur wasn't looking, the man had moved in and now sat across the table from him. Concerned, Arthur backed his chair away from the table.

The man looked Arthur in the eyes and whispered, "Are you crazy?"

Shocked, Arthur could not believe the man's question. The man's appearance had changed; his face no longer appeared wrinkled and twisted. Even his eyes were clearer, no longer glazed and there wasn't any drooling. Arthur stared at the man's changed appearance.

"No, but up to a minute ago, I would've said you were."

"Keep your voice down. My name's Walter Clemmons. The staff here thinks my mind's gone. I don't want them to believe otherwise."

"I'm Arthur McCullen."

Walter watched as a nurse stepped into the cafeteria carrying a plastic tray. His eyes followed her to the other side of the room. There he watched as she began handing bathroom-sized paper cups to those seated.

Leaning across on the table, Walter whispered, "Arthur, that nurse is passing out pills. Don't swallow any. The medication will keep you in a sedated state. The more medicine they give you, the worse you'll become."

"Here's your medicine, Walter," the stout nurse said.

Walter slowly reached out with a trembling hand; his face again twisted with wrinkles, and grabbed the paper cup. The three pills rattled as he drew the cup to him. Wrapping his hand around the water glass, Walter popped the pills into his mouth with his other hand. Then he raised his glass to his lips. With the glass resting on his lower lip, he stopped and gasped, filling his lungs with air. Slowly he began drinking as the nurse watched.

With a small wink at Arthur and half smile, he lowered the glass, tilting it on the table. Arthur looked in amazement into the glass. There, hidden from the nurse by Walter's hand, lay three pills at the bottom.

The nurse turned and gave Arthur his paper cup next. Looking in, only one pill lay in the bottom. He tilted the cup, allowing the pill to fall into his mouth. While picking up his glass of milk, he shifted the pill to the side of his mouth. Gulping the milk down, the nurse turned and handed the older woman two seats down her cup of medicine. Arthur coughed and the pill popped into his hand. He lowered his hand and slipped the gooey pill in his shoe.

Walter leaned forward and asked, "Are you coming to the morning craft class?"

"I don't want anything to do with crafts after yesterday's finger painting and being made to feel like a kid. I'll skip it. Thanks."

"You've got it wrong. It's a time you can have fun at their expense. Trust me. I'll show you. Anyway, there's nothing else to do here."

"My daughter, Shelly, is coming to get me today. She promised that if I didn't like this place, I could leave and I don't like it."

"Really!" Walter's eyes widened as he saw a nurse stepping their way. "Shh. Here comes trouble. Meet me at ten o'clock in the craft room," he said murmuring as his face drew up into contorted wrinkles and drool slid down his chin. Picking up Arthur's tray, Walter headed for the doorway.

"Give me the tray, Walter," the nurse said as he passed.

Walter pulled and twisted the tray as the nurse slowly wrestled it from him.

Arthur watched and wondered how crazy Walter really was. *Why does he act that way?*

A little before ten, Arthur changed his mind about going to the craft room. He wanted to talk with Walter again, and that seemed the best opportunity. *I guess I can tough out one more session of kindergarten.*

CHAPTER TWENTY-FOUR

At ten o'clock, Arthur followed two residents across the room to another door. The room looked identical to yesterday's craft room. Today, all the tables had been covered with white paper. There on the wall above the sink, hung his finger painting. He now knew where the far door led. He found a table and sat with his back to yesterday's art work.

Walter ambled into the room. Bumping tables as he passed, he made his way over to where Arthur sat. As he plopped down into his seat, he fell into the table ripping the paper loose and gave a quick smile as he mouthed the words, "Loosen up."

Cindy emerged from the back closet carrying a five gallon plastic bucket and a ream of white paper. She walked from one table to the next placing colored crayons, colored chalks, and sheets of paper on top of each table. Arthur watched and already regretted having come. This was worse than yesterday.

"Arthur," Walter whispered as Cindy was on the other side of the room. "When did you say your daughter's coming to get you?"

"She's flying into town today. I don't know exactly when, but she's coming," he whispered.

"I need help. I was put in here against my will."

"So was I," Arthur exclaimed with anger.

Walter cleared his throat loudly covering Arthur's outburst. "Shhhh," Walter warned. "Employees in Ward C don't tolerate people being loud. They claim it disturbs the other residents." Again he pretended to clear his throat.

Arthur sat with a puzzled look trying to figure what Walter meant.

"I don't have any relatives living here. I'm from Oregon and no one knows that I've been put in here. I'm not allowed to . . ." Walter's voice trailed quiet as Cindy stepped over to their table and placed the craft materials down. Without saying a word, she continued her handouts to the next table.

With Cindy a safe distance away, Walter continued. "I'm unable to get any outside help. Once you get out, call the police, a social worker, anyone who'll listen. Tell them that I'm being held against my will." Again he stopped whispering as she approached their table.

"Today we'll be drawing. Everyone take a sheet of paper and some crayons or chalk and start drawing your favorite animal."

Walter snatched up some paper and fumbled through the crayon pile. They tumbled and rolled across the table. A few rolled off the table, and landed on the floor. He shot Arthur a grin while mouthing, "Watch this," with a crayon clenched in his fist.

Arthur watched in disbelief.

The crayon whooshed back and forth across and around the paper. Black lines swirled around, crossing, zigzagging, faster and faster. The black blob grew bigger and bigger.

Arthur shook his head, wondering if Walter really was crazy. *Why did I let him talk me into coming to this stupid class?* That was the ugliest picture he'd ever seen, even worse than the finger painting hanging on the wall.

Walter hobbled his chair closer to Arthur and whispered. "Isn't this lovely?" he winked.

Arthur lied, nodding his head.

"Watch this," Walter continued. Holding the finished picture high in the air, he began waving it. "I'm done. I'm done. I've drawn my snake."

"That's a very pretty snake, Walter," Cindy complimented as she patted him on his back. Walter's tongue hung between his bottom teeth and lip, smiling. Turning, she drifted back down the rows of tables encouraging others.

"What do you think, Arthur?" Walter questioned, as Cindy walked away.

"She's no art buyer."

"Come on Arthur. That lady knows quality when she sees it. That's one of the best ink blobs she's ever seen. Why a psychiatrist doesn't have a better ink blob in all of his collection."

Arthur smiled. He decided to have a little fun while waiting for Shelly to arrive. "Watch and learn," he grinned at Walter and snatched up the black crayon.

Whooshing and slashing, the black crayon marred the white sheet of paper. The crayon snapped as it crossed the page. One half lay in the middle of black x's. The other was squeezed tightly in Arthur's hand. Surprised, he smiled and looked at Walter.

"He broke a crayon. Teacher . . . he broke a crayon," Walter yelled.

"Shhh . . ." Arthur begged. Walter was crazy and he regretted that he'd ever come. Now he was in trouble. *Where's Shelly?*

"I wanted to use that crayon. Teacher."

"Walter," Cindy cried, racing to his side. "It's okay. Here, use another color."

Walter smiled at the teacher and took the crayon. He began swirling it around the paper. Walter was as happy as a child.

Arthur sat stiffly in his seat, terrified at what she would do.

Cindy put her hands on Arthur's shoulders, as he cringed. "It's okay, Arthur. Crayons break all the time. Don't worry." She picked up both broken pieces to prevent someone from putting them into his mouth and choking. She tossed the broken pieces into the trash can. She hurried across the room to defuse another erupting problem.

Glaring, Arthur demanded, "Walter, why did you yell, telling the teacher I broke that crayon? You could have gotten me into trouble."

"Nah . . . don't you remember? Our minds are gone. We're crazy. We might as well have a little fun."

Arthur's anger subsided into a childish grin. "Oh . . . okay, It's my turn." Holding his paper up toward the light, he mumbled, "Wow! That's neat. I can't believe what I see."

Walter stopped drawing when he heard Arthur's utterances. He watched as Arthur slowly twisted the paper in the light.

"Walter, there's really a horse materializing from all the crazy lines."

"Let me look."

Walter grabbed the paper and held it into the light. Slowly he turned the sheet, anticipating the emerging horse.

"Give me back my paper!" Arthur screamed as he stood, "Teacher, he took my paper."

Walter froze motionless.

"All right. Sit down, Arthur. Am I going to have to separate the two of you?" Running over, she reached out and took the paper out of Walter's fingers. "Here Arthur. Walter only wanted to see your picture."

Walter sat shaking his head. What had possessed Arthur to respond like that? Had he taken that pill?

With the teacher pacing the room looking at the other pictures, Walter asked. "What was that about?"

"A little fun." Smiling, Arthur picked up another crayon and started a new picture.

After hearing that lunch was being served, Arthur and Walter jumped up. "Come on, it's going to take me awhile shuffling to get to the cafeteria," Walter said. His face was already twisted and his signature drool appearing. On their table lay broken crayons and shredded papers; colored scribbling had made its way through the paper covering the table, to the table's hard surface. Under their table, papers and whole crayons were scattered around.

Arthur looked in horror at what they'd done.

"Don't worry. I do it all the time. It gives Cindy something to do for the rest of the afternoon," Walter said shuffling away from the mess. "Go ahead, get us a table. I'll be there soon."

Arthur looked around the cafeteria for an empty table. Finding an end seat at a table unoccupied by others, Arthur sat. Soon, Walter joined him. They watched an old gentleman shuffle, placing his walking cane inches in front of each step. He stopped beside Walter and slowly pulled out the chair.

"Oh, I'm sorry. This chair is broken and this other seat is taken." The man turned and shuffled away to another table. "I wanted privacy so we can talk," Walter muttered. "I learned quickly; don't trust anyone."

After receiving their lunch trays, Arthur sat staring at the pureed brown lump.

"It tastes better than it looks," Walter said, after swallowing. "I think it's a peanut butter sandwich. I remember the first time I saw their food. I almost threw up. But after a while, you get used to it and the mush is kinda tasty, especially when you're hungry."

Arthur was glad he'd never have to get used to eating that food. Food wasn't supposed to look like that. He spooned a small bite and tasted. Walter was right; it tasted like peanut butter and grape jelly.

Walter swallowed something that tasted like a banana. "I think this is our fruit, creamy bananas."

"It's baby food!"

"No, it's lunch. You'd best eat. There's nothing to eat until dinner and it'll look similar." Walter swallowed another scoop of his sandwich. "What time do you think your daughter will get here?"

"I don't know. Sometime today. She's flying in from Chicago."

"Well, when you get out of here, please remember me and notify the authorities. I don't want to eat food like this the rest of my life," he said with a laugh.

"I won't forget you. No one deserves to live like this." Arthur sat nibbling at the spoonful of bananas. His crackers were long eaten. He wished Shelly could see what he was eating. She'd have a fit. Slowly his thoughts turned to her flight. He knew most business trips didn't return before the afternoon, especially ones from Chicago. He cringed at the thought of having to eat dinner here if she was on a late night flight. But her promise to see him today reassured him she wasn't on a late night flight.

"Arthur," Walter whispered, bringing him back from his thoughts. "Why is Shelly coming to get you? I mean, why did she put you in here to start with?"

"It sounds strange, but she didn't put me in here. It was my miserable son-in-law, Justin, an attorney, who convinced her I'd hurt myself or worse, kill myself. He put me in here and stole my money. The judge ruled in his favor and I wasn't even present at my hearing. I didn't get a fair day in court and that's how I got here. Shelly promised if I didn't like it here, she'd move me somewhere else. Do I look like I'm a threat to myself? Am I dangerous?"

"Absolutely not," Walter said his voice trailing off contemplating Arthur's statement. "I didn't get a fair day in court, either."

"Shhh," Arthur warned as people looked their way. "Keep it down. Remember?"

"I was also forced to come here against my wishes. I tell you the legal system is tainted with unscrupulous men and women. A rich man wanted my property and when I refused to sell to him, he built a false file against me and then showed it to the judge. Said I was a risk to myself and others. The judge ruled in his favor, probably was bought off somehow. He ruled that all my assets were to be sold and used to pay for me to live in this expensive place. I'm now in the custody of the state and no one is out there fighting for me. I've never been married and had no brothers or sisters. No one misses me. The first time I tried to escape from Ward A, the administration brought me down here and locked me away. Then they started pumping me full of all kinds of drugs—either to kill me or make me crazy. I'm stuck here without any help."

"You're right about the legal system." He held up two crossed fingers, and said, "They're like this. Judge Blair put me here without listening to a word from me."

Walter's eyes widened with disbelief. "Arthur, my judge's name was also Blair." The two immediately understood. "That's one crooked judge," they said almost in unison.

"You'd better finish eating before the food cop comes over and investigates," Walter warned Arthur. "We don't need to draw attention to ourselves."

"Harry!"

Walter jumped, banging his knees under the table.

Arthur's heart stopped as he spun to look at Bessy. "Oh no," he murmured, "not her!"

Bessy stood beside him smiling, easing between him and the empty chair. As she sat, she scooted the chair tightly beside Arthur.

"Bessy," Wendy, the kind dietician spoke. "Why don't you come with me?"

"See you in a little while, Harry," said Bessy. She stood and followed Wendy from the cafeteria.

"Ha! So you're the new Harry," Walter said.

"What do you mean?"

"Well every time another man arrives, she believes he's her husband. You'll be history as soon as somebody new moves in."

"I hope so; she gives me the creeps," and his body twitched.

"Better you than me."

Arthur looked back at his food, trying not to dwell on its appearance and quickly swallowed another mouthful. Soon his plate was empty.

"I'm completing my third month of incarceration, here at Southern Retirement Community. They've had me locked up in this section, Ward C, for almost the whole time. If I don't get out of here soon, I'll go crazy and fit in perfectly with the other residents."

"I know what you mean. I've been here only two days and am concerned about going loony-tunes myself."

"There's not much to do until dinner, no afternoon activities. Let's meet in the lounge. We can find a seat at the television and watch whatever's showing. It helps pass time."

As they left the cafeteria, Walter gasped and quickly stepped backward, knocking Arthur off balance.

Beep . . . beep . . . beep . . . the soft warning signal rolled by the door. Otman sat in the driver's seat, steering the white extended electric golf cart past the cafeteria. The wheels stealthily rolled across the tiled floor. "I don't like that man," Arthur breathed.

"Stay away from him; don't even look at him. He's dangerous," Walter warned.

Arthur's curiosity caused him to watch the cart roll down the first corridor. Half way down the corridor it stopped and Otman disappeared into a patient's room.

"What's he doing?" Arthur gasped.

"Someone's died and he's picking up the body. Come on, we don't want to be here when it returns. It gives me the creeps watching that cart hauling away someone. He treats most with little respect." Walter scurried to where the television was and sat down with wing one to his back. Arthur followed, but kept a watchful eye of the situation that was developing.

Beep . . . beep . . . beep . . . the white cart rolled toward the lounge. Walter stared at the television while Arthur continued to watch the cart. The back of the golf cart was draped with a white cloth with the curves that formed the shape of a body beneath the sheet. Double doors at the other end of the room that Arthur had never noticed before swung open and the golf cart disappeared through them.

"Walter!" Arthur blurted. "Where do those doors go?"

"To the awaiting hearse."

"It gave me chills watching," Arthur said.

"That's one reason I don't look. Otman generally picks up the bodies. Especially those who are troublemakers. For example, Bill, who gave Otman a hard time, suddenly died last week. I saw Otman dragging his body from the room and then drop it into that cart. Whatever you do, don't make him mad."

Arthur didn't have to be warned, he'd already met the man and had been treated harshly.

The two sat quietly watching Popeye saving Olive Oyl from Brutus, trying to pass the time until Shelly arrived.

Arthur kept a watchful eye on the time and the double doors leading into Ward C. When three o'clock appeared on the wall clock, he could no longer wait for Shelly. He needed to speak to her. *I'll call her cell phone.*

CHAPTER TWENTY-FIVE

He made his way to the nursing station. "I need to make a phone call."

"Arthur, you know residents aren't allowed to use the phone."

He was shocked. No one had told him. "But, you don't understand. I'm not supposed to be here."

"Now Arthur, I've heard that before. I'm only doing my job. Why don't you go back and watch television with your friend, Walter?"

"I don't want to. I want to speak with my daughter, Shelly."

The nurse had seen this behavior many times before and realized that Arthur was not going to leave before she allowed him to use the phone, which she could not permit. With her right hand, she reached under the desk and pressed the hidden emergency button, summoning immediate assistance.

The double doors swung opened and Otman stepped into Ward C. His steps pounded the floor as he approached the desk. "Is Arthur bothering you?" his voice thundered as he spoke to the nurse. After receiving a nod, he commanded. "Arthur, leave the nice nurse alone."

"All I want to do is use the telephone."

"You're not allowed to use the phones down here in this section," his voice growled with each syllable pronounced.

"Please let me use your telephone," Arthur pleaded. "I want to call my daughter. She promised me that if I didn't like it here, I didn't have to stay. Once I'm gone you won't have to listen to me anymore."

Otman did not have time for this nonsense. He motioned for another nurse to intervene before the situation escalated. He was going to put a stop to Arthur's defiance.

Arthur never saw the nurse approaching from his rear. Otman's burly fingers dug into Arthur's arms, as the nurse dabbed a cotton ball on his arm. The needle plummeted under the skin and the plunger injected tranquilizer fluid into his blood stream.

"No, stop! Don't give me any medicine," Arthur's eyes bulged at the sting the syringe inflicted.

By now, two residents had wandered up and were staring at Arthur.

Arthur's vision blurred, as his legs buckled. Otman's fingers tightened, holding him up off the floor. Arthur's legs crumpled under his body as he tried to steady himself. His head rolled from side to side as his neck muscles strained to balance the weight. Two blurred heads protruded from Otman's shoulder. Arthur squeezed his eyes closed, trying to stop the room from spinning. The urge to demand his rights drifted away. Slowly, Arthur balanced his body with his arms outstretched. Otman cautiously released his hold. Teetering from wall to wall, Arthur zigzagged down the hall.

"Give me Arthur's medical chart." Otman seized the chart from the nurse's hand. Pulling his pen out of his shirt-pocket, he increased Arthur's medication to two pills at breakfast and dinner.

"Arthur obviously needs more meds to keep him docile. The doctor warned me that one pill might not be enough to keep him tranquil throughout the day. His instructions were to increase the medication if needed." With the adjustment made to Arthur's personal file, Otman handed it back to the nurse.

Walter sat nonchalantly watching Arthur, knowing what was transpiring. He had been there and had been treated in the same manner a few times before. He knew not to intervene or he, too, would be given a sedative.

After the small crowd disbursed and Otman disappeared from Ward C, Walter made his way into the hallway finding Arthur meandering aimlessly. Putting his arm around Arthur, he said, "Come on. Why don't we go back to your room?" Walter knew the medicine would take some time to wear off, depending on the amount that was injected. From his own experience, he knew the first injection was not as potent as those that followed. He hoped Shelly was really coming to get him, but just in case she didn't, Arthur needed to be on his feet for dinner. Otherwise, he would go to bed hungry.

"Which room is yours?" he asked.

Arthur stumbled down the hallway leaning on Walter, who was becoming exhausted supporting his dead weight. "Is this your room?"

"Ye-ess."

Walter pulled him inside. "You've got to start drinking water. I found it helps to flush some of the drugs from your body. It'll give you a faster recovery time." Walter guided Arthur over to his bed. "Sit here. I'll be back." He stepped into the bathroom and found a small paper cup at the sink. After filling it with water he returned to the bed, where Arthur lay sprawled on his back. "Arthur, get up." Walter grabbed Arthur with his free hand and pulled. He slowly sat up. "Sip. It'll help cleanse the sedatives from your blood." Slurping, he emptied the first cup. Walter helped Arthur out of bed. He steadied Arthur as he shuffled over to the wall.

"Arthur, keep moving around."

The voice seemed miles away. Straining to open his heavy eyelids, his eyes fluttered, then closed again. Arthur slid onto the floor. Walter put one of Arthur's arms around his shoulder and lifted his body. Wobbly, Arthur began staggering to the other side of the room. Walter strained as he steadied Arthur, preventing him from falling again on the hard floor. He knew landing on the hard floor was a potential for broken bones.

"I'm tired. I want to lie down."

"No. You have to use your muscles. This will help circulate your blood through your kidneys which will rid your body of that medicine. Shelly is coming and we need her. Now walk!"

Walter continued to force Arthur to drink. The frequent visits to the bathroom helped to keep Arthur awake. Thirty minutes before dinner, Arthur began to emerge from his stupor. The room no longer swayed as he walked by himself. His voice no longer slurred.

With most of the sedative gone from his body, Arthur remembered Otman and the devious nurse who had jabbed him with the syringe. Arthur's eyes reddened and his breathing intensified. "How could they treat me like that?" he snapped.

"Calm down or they'll be back to stick you with a bigger syringe. Believe me; I learned the hard way. Their sedatives only become stronger and stronger, causing you to sleep longer and longer. You can't win; I've tried. I'm afraid that after the next injection, I might not wake up. Otman doesn't care how many times he sticks you or what the injection contains. The more he gives you, the easier his job becomes." Arthur stood staring at the door as if he'd pounce on the next person who entered. "Arthur! Have you been listening to me? Do you understand what they'll do to you?"

Arthur took a couple of deep breaths relaxing the best he could. It wasn't much. "Okay," he sighed, "I understand, but we're getting out of here. Shelly should be here soon."

"Let's hope so."

"Once she gets here, I'll explain everything to her and we'll get you out. The world's going to hear about this place," Arthur swore.

"You're lucky you didn't swallow your morning pills, otherwise you'd still be drugged. Remember, whatever you do, don't swallow any medicine and if you do, drink lots of water and hope it will flush it from your system."

"That reminds me," Arthur chuckled, "I still have that pill in my shoe." Reaching into his shoe, he pulled it out and flushed it down the toilet.

"Thanks for saving me," Arthur said coming out of the bathroom.

"The next thing you've got to learn is play acting. If they are to believe you're taking your medicine, which will cause you to become more like a zombie, you'll have to convince them, especially after receiving an injection. It's easy. Watch me." Walter hunched over as his face twisted and his disgusting drool appeared, oozing down his chin. With slow shuffles he moved toward the door. He stopped and stood up straight. "See, it's easy. Go ahead and try."

Arthur, bent over at the waist with his arms hanging straight down, shuffled his feet.

"That's pathetic."

"I can't do it. I don't know how to play act."

"It's easy. Start watching others as they walk and imitate them. You'll have plenty of time to get the hang of it. Your dosage of medicine shouldn't have you acting like me. As they increase your medicine, increase your acting."

Walter opened the door slightly and looked into the hallway. Not seeing anyone, he said, "I'll see you later," and slipped out.

After waiting a couple of minutes, Arthur stepped from his room. His right foot drug the floor as he emerged from his room. Sluggishly, he ambled down the hallway into the lounge. He studied an elderly woman shuffling toward the nursing desk, carrying her baby doll. Seeing the picture window from his peripheral vision he turned and looked. The cars out in the parking lot spurred him to watch for Shelly there.

He leaned on the glass. His eyes searched each row of parked vehicles, hoping to find Shelly's green Suburban. Not seeing it, he wondered where she was. He hoped she'd come soon.

"Come on Arthur. Dinner's being served." Walter was pulling on his arm.

"Go ahead without me. I'm not hungry."

"You have to eat. Shelly's flight could have been delayed. Maybe she had to stay over another night in Chicago. Who knows why she's late. Maybe her flight doesn't arrive until late tonight."

"No, she said she would be here this afternoon. She'd have known when her flight was," Arthur said, still looking out the window.

"But if her flight was canceled or delayed, she might not be back today. We'll sit close to the cafeteria's door and keep an eye out for her together."

Sounds reasonable, he thought and the two ambled toward the cafeteria. Arthur moved faster than Walter.

Sitting at the table closest to the door, they kept watching the double doors. "If she comes in, we'll see her," Walter assured him.

Arthur wasn't so sure.

CHAPTER TWENTY-SIX

In the parking lot, Shelly pulled into a visitor's space. Glad to be back, she swung the door open and leaped from the seat. Her stride was quick, but short, due to the long dress she was wearing. Inside the lobby, her high heel shoes clicked loudly on the tile floor. As she came to room number fifteen, she pushed the door open. "Hello," she said. *Who is that lady sitting in Dad's recliner?*

"Hello," the lady said, her voice sweet and soft.

"Where's my dad?" Shelly asked.

"Who?" she asked, shooting a puzzled look.

"Dad!"

"Can I help you, young lady?"

Shelly enjoyed hearing the compliment, but didn't have time to relish it. "I'm Shelly, Arthur's daughter. Is he here?"

"I don't know anyone named Arthur. Have you checked the room next to mine?" she said.

"Isn't this room fifteen?"

"Yes."

"I'm sorry to have bothered you. But I could have sworn yesterday that I asked to speak to my dad in room fifteen."

"I don't know who was here yesterday. I moved in today," she said smiling. "I can't take care of myself."

"Oh, I'm sorry to have bothered you!" Shelly said, as she stepped back into the hallway. She hurried back down the hallway toward the administration office. She looked inside the rooms that had their doors open, but she didn't see him.

Standing in front of the information window, she asked, "What room is Arthur McCullen in?"

The receptionist sitting at the desk looked up. "One minute please," and then continued writing in the journal. After a few entries, she closed the book and asked, "Now, how may I help you?"

Agitated, Shelly asked, "I'm looking for my dad, Arthur McCullen."

The woman reached for the resident directory. Thumbing through the alphabetical list, she stopped when she reached the M's. Her finger stopped at Arthur's name. Under the column for room numbers, there was no number listed, just a note that read, "Call administrator."

"Just one minute, please," she said as she drew the phone to her ear and dialed the extension. "Can you come to the front?" She laid the phone down and looked up at Shelly. "Someone will be with you shortly," and then she turned her attention back to the journal.

Shelly looked around, not knowing where the person would be coming from. She didn't have to wait long.

An administrator stepped around the corner. "Hi, I'm Paul Thornton. May I help you?"

"I'm trying to find my dad, Arthur McCullen. It seems he's been moved. I checked room fifteen where he was yesterday, but someone else is in that room."

"Oh," he said looking into the journal he held. Reading he said, "I assume you're Shelly Roble. Ma'am, you'll need to come with me to my office." He closed the journal and extended a hand, pointing in the direction of the administration office.

Shelly thought it was a strange request, but followed his gesture. As she stepped into the glassed in office, she noticed a life-size portrait of Judge Blair. The gold plate attached to the bottom of the frame was inscribed: Harrison T. Blair, President.

"My office is the last door. I'll pull Arthur's file and be right in."

The office was paneled with a dark mahogany wood. Thornton's diploma hung on the wall behind his desk and a family photo of his wife, daughter, and himself sat atop the credenza against the side wall. The carpet gave as Shelly walked to the chair in front of the desk and sat. The bookshelves were full of older, hardbound books. His coat hung on the coat rack standing in the far corner.

Paul entered a small room leaving the door open. The room was full of file cabinets. He stepped over to one and pulled open the M–N drawer. He pulled each file forward; his fingers stopped on Arthur McCullen's file, which he withdrew and then returned to his office.

The file folder lay open on Paul's desk and his eyes scanned the newly scribbled note: Arthur's a flight-risk. Moved to Ward C, wing two.

"Ms. Roble, your dad's been moved to Ward C."

"Why? Is it a better room?"

"No ma'am. Ward C is a more secure ward." He looked back into Arthur's file and continued reading: 1. Walked away from the mall and was found later. 2. Tried to walk out the front door late that same night. 3. Tried to walk out the front door at noon. 4. Later same day, walked out the front door and disappeared with a group of strangers. He was gone for hours, but later picked up.

He looked at Shelly with exasperation. "Your dad's a flight-risk. Meaning, he's tried to leave four different times. On two occasions, he did disappear for a period of time and we did not know where he was. We're responsible for your dad and he had to be moved to a secure ward."

"May I look?"

He handed her the paper. After a brief study, she looked up at the administrator and stammered, "I-I can't believe it. Dad promised to stay here. I want to see my dad." Paul didn't move. "Now!"

He stared with furrowed eyes. "May I ask what prompted you to put your dad in here to begin with?"

Shelly sat confused. "Well . . ." *maybe if I cooperate, he'll let me see Dad sooner,* ". . . during the last several weeks, Dad seemed to have had dementia and would end up getting hurt. Each time he could have been killed."

"And he continues to behave the same way. He could have been killed when he ran through cars at the mall, as he escaped. Then yesterday, he ran off to the city by boarding a city bus. He could have been mugged and killed."

She sat confused, not knowing what to believe or say. "Can't you please let me see him?"

Refusing to look her in the eyes, he looked back into the file folder. "Sorry, but he's on medication and you can't see him now."

"What!" her eyes wide open, stared at him. "Why is he on medication?"

"The medication's to calm him, so that he's more rational."

"Rational! What do you mean?"

"I'm sorry, but I can't answer that. You'll have to talk with the doctor and he's not here."

Shelly squirmed in her seat and burned with anger. "I don't care if he is under medication. I want to see my dad, NOW!" Her face glowed crimson.

"Corporate policy states that no one can see a family member who is receiving medication until the medication is regulated. Your appearance might upset him further. I can't allow it. You agreed to these conditions when you signed your dad into this facility. If you choose, you can sign a transfer-of-care form and take him home with you."

"I'll sign it!" Shelly spat, knowing her dad would be pleased that he was leaving.

Pulling the admission form to the top to read, he began glancing down the page as the phone was lifted off its cradle. "Can you bring me a transfer-of-care form?" His finger slid down the lines on the form, stopping at the line: Guardianship—Justin Roble.

A quick little rap sounded at the open door, "Sir, your form."

"We don't need it after all. But thanks."

"Shelly," Paul began, "you can't sign for his release. Justin Roble is Arthur's legal guardian, and he must sign that document."

Shelly stood up yelling, "Liar! I'm his guardian. I want to see my dad now! I'm taking him home! Justin Roble isn't his son. I'm his daughter."

The administrator lifted the phone, "I need some assistance." With an ashen face, he slid his chair backward, distancing himself from Shelly. Once an angry relative had thrown folders, books, and pens at him.

A burly man rushed in. "Hey," he yelled, "what's going on in here?"

"Mr. Otman, please escort this lady from the building. The building is now closed to all visitors," Paul's voice shakily commanded.

"Ma'am," the deep voice boomed. "You're leaving." He towered above her.

Shelly did not move until she saw his meaty hand stretching out for her. Fearing his grasp, she quickly moved. "Don't touch me," she snapped. In the doorway, she spun around, and looked Paul in his eyes and swore, "You'll be hearing from my husband," and stepped quickly out of his office. Fearing Otman, she hurried from the office and to the front doors. With a swoosh, the door opened and she hurried outside.

Otman pulled the door closed and blocked her re-entrance.

"I'm not leaving without my Dad," she hollered back at the door.

Otman crossed his arms and stood rigid in the doorway and stared at her.

Unable to withstand his sinister stare and knowing she'd never push him aside, she turned with a snap and steamed down the walkway, across the parking lot, to her Suburban. She hoped he'd be gone from his post by the time she got to the car. She fumbled for her key-chain. As her hand rummaged inside her pocketbook, she glanced in the direction of the front doors.

Otman stood staring coldly at her.

Shelly opened the driver's door and slid in. She decided to wait until Otman disappeared. Then she would return, look for her dad, and take him. She pulled her hair and wondered what kind of place she'd sent her dad to.

In the cafeteria, Arthur sat scrutinizing the different piles of puree—paper bag-brownish, military-greenish, and muddy-chocolate. He held his spoon in the paper-bag-brownish pile, and his jaw tightened. He doubted that he would be able to swallow this mush.

Walter sat watching, smiling at Arthur. Knowing his food was cooling and soon wouldn't be palatable, he laughed. "It's not bad. That brownish pile is roast beef, the greenish pile is vegetables, and I think the other pile is chocolate pie. It's really not bad. Remember, don't look at it."

Arthur scooped up a small taste and slipped it between his teeth. His tongue reluctantly touched the brown mush. "Hmm, you're right, it's not that bad." He couldn't believe it was roast beef. He wondered if the cook had added beef flavoring. The vegetables tasted like green beans, broccoli, and peas. Before trying the dessert, he glanced out the doorway, but again didn't see Shelly. Scooping into the dessert pile, he smelled it before tasting. He could smell the sugar and a little chocolate. "You're right. It's chocolate pie, but I'll never get used to the texture," he said looking at Walter with twisted lips.

After he swallowed the last spoon of dessert, a nurse appeared beside him, holding out a paper cup. "Take your medicine," she said.

Arthur took the cup and looked in. Two pills rolled to the cup's side. *Walter's right, he thought, they're planning to keep me in a stupor.* Dumping the two pills into his hand, he popped them into his mouth. They slid into his upper gum. Grabbing his glass of water, he gulped and smiled at the nurse.

Satisfied, she moved on. With the nurse's back to him, Arthur spit out the slimy pills and dropped them into his shoe.

"I've got to go back and look for Shelly," Arthur whispered. Walter had to wait for his medicine before he could leave.

Arthur hurried from the cafeteria over to the picture window in the lounge. He stood in the center of the window peering into the parking lot.

To his far left, he saw Otman trudging, apparently from the front doors of the building, down the sidewalk and out into the parking lot. His arms pumped madly as his size fifteen shoes stomped. Arthur eased backward from the window's edge and peeked around the curtain. He didn't want to be seen. *What's up with him?*

Otman stormed toward the Suburban. As he approached Shelly's vehicle, fearing what he might do, she quickly pressed the automatic lock button.

The Suburban rocked as Otman lifted the door handle. Shelly's heart raced. She wasn't leaving. His intimidation tactics were not going to make her leave until she saw her dad.

"Ma'am, roll your window down."

Shelly quickly shook her head sideways.

Otman smiled devilishly, "Scared—you'd better be. If you don't leave, I'll phone the police."

"Go ahead," shouted Shelly. "I'll be glad to explain how you're treating my dad and me."

"Ma'am, you'll not be talking with any policeman. He'll be arresting you for trespassing. This is your last warning. Get out of here!" he shouted, pulling out a cell phone and flipping it open.

Inquisitive, Arthur stretched on his tiptoes trying to see where Otman had gone.

The key turned, the vehicle roared as Shelly pressed the center of her steering wheel. HONKKKKKKK.

Arthur heard the horn blowing and tried craning his neck to see, wondering what was happening. Suddenly he saw Otman stand up. Fearing he'd be seen, he dropped off his toes and pulled back his head momentarily. Two eyes peered around the window frame.

The blasting horn and squealing tires caused Otman to jump against a parked car. "I'll be back," Shelly screamed as the Suburban screeched and backed up. Otman sucked in his belly as the outside mirror scrapped his buckle.

Again, the Suburban's tires squealed as Shelly mashed the gas pedal to the floor. The vehicle lunged forward.

Arthur's eyes widened. "Shelly," he yelled, seeing her Suburban pulling away. Jumping squarely in front of the picture window, he pounded on the glass as he screamed. "Shelly . . . I'm in here. Come back." The green Suburban drove out of sight.

Walter had faked swallowing his medicine and was shuffling out of the cafeteria when he heard Arthur's screams. "Oh no," he gasped. Forgetting to shuffle, he hurried around the corner and saw him jumping up and down screaming, pounding on the window. He was too late. To his right, two nurses ran toward Arthur. He couldn't do anything but turn and shuffle away.

Otman, standing in the parking lot, heard banging coming from one of the building's windows. His eyes narrowed and focused on each window briefly until he saw someone. "Arthur!" his roar sent birds in the woods scurrying from their perch. Angry that Shelly might have seen Arthur, he dashed inside.

Two nurses rushed to Arthur, fearing the window would be smashed. Each nurse grabbed an arm and tried pulling him away.

"Let me speak to my daughter! Let go of me," he screamed, twisting his body. The nurses' fingers tightened their grasp, digging deeper into Arthur's arms. Slowly, Arthur was dragged away from the window as Otman rushed up wheezing.

One of the nurses gasped seeing the large hypodermic needle extruding from Otman's hand. The extra cc's of sedative appeared to be dangerous. "Isn't that too high a dosage?"

The other nurse struggled to hold Arthur in her grasp. His eyes bulged at the sight of the syringe.

"No! He's a bigger man than most of our patients. It's what the doctor ordered."

Walter sat in front of the TV overhearing their conversation. Hearing "too high of a dosage," he cringed and slid down behind the backrest of the couch, hoping Otman had not noticed him. He held his breath, fearing he'd be injected with something similar.

With a quick plunge, the needle plummeted into Arthur's right arm. With the press of Otman's thumb, the narcotics gushed into Arthur's body.

"Ow! I'm going t . . ." Arthur said as the room swirled into darkness and his limp body withered to the floor.

The syringe was pulled out of Arthur's arm and handed to the overwhelmed nurse. Otman bent down and snatched Arthur off the floor. With a firm grip, he lugged the dead weight down wing two and into his bedroom. "Another troublemaker silenced," Otman mumbled as he dropped Arthur into his bed. Pivoting on his heel, he left Arthur to die in an overdosed state.

CHAPTER TWENTY-SEVEN

Shelly zigged from one lane to another in the rush-hour traffic. *How could they have put Justin as Dad's guardian?* She wondered as she passed a slow-moving car in the right-hand lane. "Get out of the fast lane," she yelled at the old man. Suddenly she felt terrible yelling at him and thought about how her dad had driven recently. "Sorry," she said pulling in front of him. She wished she had never listened to Justin's insistence that Arthur be ruled incompetent. Brake lights in front of her blazed as she reacted and stomped on the pedal.

Traffic suddenly stopped for the red-light. Impatiently waiting for the light to change, she blared out as if Justin were listening, "I can't believe it! Those idiots screwed it up. They've got you as Dad's guardian and won't allow me to bring him home. Make them change it tonight. I'm bringing Dad home!" Shelly cursed and blew the horn when no one moved for the green-light. She didn't care that someone had blocked the intersection. Finally the offending car pulled into the other lane, allowing traffic to move.

Accelerating with the traffic, Shelly swore she and Justin would return to Southern Retirement Community tonight and he would sign those papers to get her dad out. Arthur was coming home to live with them.

Walter sat stunned and speechless, having overheard the nurse's concern over the amount of narcotics used. Having witnessed another resident days before receiving an injection and dying later that night, Walter still wondered if that person had been overdosed. If Arthur had received an overdose he could easily die. Walter knew it was urgent for him to help his new friend so that they both could get out alive.

Glancing around the lounge and not seeing anyone, Walter eased out of his seat. With his head down, he shuffled in the direction of wing two. Passing a wandering resident, he kept his eye out for nurses.

His heart pounded harder and faster with each step taken. His breathing labored as he neared the doorway to Arthur's room. Nonchalantly passing the doorway, he gazed inside. Not seeing anyone inside the room, he again checked the hallway for any nurses. He saw a resident creeping past mumbling to herself. *Whew, I made it.*

"Hey!" Otman's voice rumbled loudly down the corridor. "What are you doing down this hallway? Your room is not down here. You're Arthur's friend, aren't you?" Otman thundered down the hallway.

Walter was petrified. "Huh?"

Otman grabbed Walter by his shirt collar, pulling him into Arthur's room. His voice blared, "Are you this man's friend?" Walter's head stared straight at Arthur.

Walter couldn't speak. The tightness of the collar around his neck was almost as effective as a noose. Unable to breathe, Walter hung speechless staring at his lifeless friend.

Otman jerked Walter out from Arthur's room and jostled him down the hallway. "Don't come back," the voice reverberated in Walter's ears. With his death-hold now released, Walter gasped for air and staggered away. Dazed, Walter unknowingly turned into wing one.

"Hey you," the sound reverberated as if the person were standing behind him. "Get out of that hallway. Your room isn't down wing one. Do I need to get a nurse to escort you to your room?" Trembling, Walter feared what Otman would do to him.

Heart hammering, knees knocking, Walter had to act quickly. He stared down wing one and realized he'd turned right instead of left. Quickly correcting his path, he deviated to his left and ambled into wing three. Finding his room, he slipped into its darkness.

Peering out toward the nursing desk, Walter wondered what medicine Otman had injection into Arthur. Was the injection an overdose? If not, how much would the drugs damage his brain? He knew from watching medical documentaries on television that a person's chance for survival was determined within the first few hours. If it was an overdose, the timing was critical.

CHAPTER TWENTY-EIGHT

The Suburban swayed to the right, slinging Shelly's suitcase as it swerved into the driveway. The tires squealed as she slammed the transmission into park. As the engine idled off, Shelly sprang out the vehicle's door, slamming it as she raced for the front door. Her keys jingled as she tried to insert the house key. With a twist the door swung open. "JUSTIN!" The scream echoed down the street.

Stepping inside the dark house, she wondered if he was upstairs. As the door closed, Shelly began flipping on light switches. Dashing up the stairs, she yelled, "Justin, where are you?"

Silence greeted her in every part of the house. Believing he was at work, she searched for the cordless phone. She reached for the receiver and saw a handwritten note taped to the phone. Snatching it off, she read:

Shelly, I'm flying to Atlanta to meet with a client. I'm staying at the Atlanta International Hotel at the airport. Call me when you get home.   Justin.

Shelly pounded out the hotel's phone number. The operator directed her call to Justin's room.

"Hello, Justin. I . . . ."

"No, I'm the operator. Mr. Roble isn't answering his phone. May I take a message?"

Shelly sighed gritting her teeth. "Yes! This is Shelly Roble, his wife. Please have him call me the moment he gets back in his room. It's an emergency."

"Where is he?" she shrieked as she slammed down the phone.

Watching the hallway, Walter slipped his right shoe off and then his left. Heart throbbing, he waited anxiously for his opportunity to rush to Arthur's aid. Without Arthur, his chances of ever leaving would be next to impossible. Walter eased backward into the room's darkness when he saw Otman heading to the double doors of Ward C. As Otman stepped through the doors and out of sight, Walter stepped cautiously out into the empty hallway. The cold tile floor sent chills up his back. The cold drove home Otman's threat, "Don't come back." Walter's heart raced, fearing Otman's sudden reappearance. His chest squeezed tightly creating wheezing from within. With shaking legs, Walter crept into the second wing.

Terrorized by the fear of getting caught, he dashed down the hallway and into Arthur's room. Concealed in the darkness and trembling, Walter slumped over grasping his knees, gasping for air. His head pounded mercilessly. He thought it would explode.

Easing the door closed, he hoped he was not too late. Walter could not imagine Otman allowing him to enter the room so easily.

It's a trap, panic screamed from within. *Get out now before it's too late.* Breathing slowly and deeply, reason returned and reminded him that Arthur was his only chance of ever leaving this institution alive.

Flipping the light switch on, Walter saw Arthur lying deathly still. His chest was not moving up and down. His eye lids did not twitch; it appeared as if he was in a deep sleep, or—he refused to think it—dead.

The temperature in the room seemed to be getting colder. Walter had felt the same sensations the other week when his previous roommate had passed away during the night. Had Arthur slipped into the next world?

Stepping quickly over to the bed, Walter shuddered at the thought of touching a dead person. Leaning over Arthur's face, with his ear toward Arthur's mouth, he listened for the slightest breath.

Unable to hear any breathing, Walter's heart sank with sadness. Gritting his teeth, he reached out for Arthur's wrist.

Walter snatched his fingers away from Arthur's cold wrist, fearing that he was too late.

The air in the room was still. Walter's mind screamed, *Grab Arthur's wrist or get out of here.* Once again, Walter grabbed Arthur's wrist, but this time he persevered and felt for a pulse. Hope warmed Walter's body as he felt a faint, thready pulse.

With both hands, Walter pressed firmly downward on Arthur's chest, hoping to arouse him. Then rechecking Arthur's wrist, this time the pulse was quickly definable. Walter's heart beat excitedly as the room seemed to warm.

Breathing deeply, Walter knew Arthur was a long way from being out of death's grasp. Walter began shaking Arthur's body. The arousal seemed to be working. Arthur moved some fingers and then one arm.

A smile of relief spread across Walter's face. "Arthur, wake up," he softly pleaded.

Arthur's eyes remained closed.

"Listen to me! You've got to wake up. Shelly's coming to get you out." Walter said, shaking Arthur. "I'm doing my part, but you've got to do yours. We've got to get those drugs out of your body in order for you to recover."

Arthur twitched.

Walter sensed Arthur's new insurgency to fight. "Keep fighting," he whispered.

Walter froze as his ears picked up footsteps out in the hallway. His head jerked toward the door as he heard Otman's voice.

"Don't move or say a word if you can hear me. Hold your breath if someone comes near you. Pray that they think you're dead," Walter whispered quickly. Then Walter leaped for the light switch and dove under the bed. He hoped that Otman was not looking for him. As the seconds passed and the footsteps grew louder Walter knew he was caught. Fearing for his safety, he wished he had picked up some sort of weapon for defense.

Two voices stopped outside Arthur's door. Walter's heart pounded harder. His breathing became shallower. As the door swung open, Walter's heart stopped beating. Walter's muscles tightly pulled his body into a ball. Peering from under the bed he could see Otman's large silhouette and the silhouette of a nurse he didn't recognize entering the room. *Who is she?*

Silence engulfed the room except for the footsteps on the tiled floor. The two moved toward Arthur's bed. Walter hoped he was hidden in the darkness. He tried to focus, but he could not make out either Otman or the nurse. His heart beat fiercely.

"Is he dead?" Otman sneered.

Walter's ears twitched as he listened for the answer. In the silence, Walter's ears throbbed with each pump his heart discharged. Fearing any breathing would give his presence away, he held his breath waiting for an answer.

"Well, is he or isn't he?"

"Quiet," she hissed, "I'm listening. He ought to be with those pills he took and that injection."

More seconds passed as Walter waited to hear Arthur's diagnosis. He shuddered at the thought of them giving Arthur another injection.

"Not yet," the icy voice said. "But almost."

Walter exhaled slowly. *He fooled them.*

"Good, then in the morning I can come down here with my golf cart hearse, and haul away another troublemaker."

"Someone is going to get suspicious with all of the patients who have been dying lately."

"You let me worry about that. I had to get rid of this one. I sensed trouble from him. Also, I've noticed that Walter is acting different lately. We'd better keep an eye on him," Otman said.

Walter cringed as the hair stood up on his neck and arms. *I've got to be more careful.* The threat made Walter more determined to complete his mission and revive Arthur. For now, he must remain undetected.

As they moved away from Arthur's bed, Walter's muscles tightened into knots. He did not know whom he would hit first, but he was ready. He drew his fingers into a tightly bound fist.

The silhouettes turned and pulled the door shut. Walter listened as the two mercenaries' voices faded.

"Whew," Walter exhaled the stale air. Inhaling, he tried to fend off his body's quivers. As the trembling eased, Walter cautiously crawled out from under the bed and crept over to the light switch.

The light radiated Arthur's pale face. Walter rushed back to Arthur's side.

"Arthur, it's Walter," he said while shaking Arthur's body. "Otman and that nurse have gone. Please wake up," Walter begged.

Arthur's right leg moved and then his right arm. Walter grabbed hold of his right arm and began massaging the muscle. Walter was determined to get the blood flowing through Arthur's body. After a considerable time massaging the arm muscles, he began moving the forearm, bending at the elbow to stimulate arm movement, helping the blood circulate. After the other arm was exercised, Walter began massaging Arthur's legs.

Suddenly, a hand grabbed Walter. His heart leaped into full arrhythmic beats. His chest ached. Grimacing, he waited for the harsh voice.

"W . . . Wa . . . Walter," Arthur's faint voice stammered.

Relief flooded Walter's body, but his pounding heart beat remained high, now pulsing with joy.

"Man, I thought you were a goner," Walter said as he struggled to help Arthur sit up in his bed. "You need to drink lots of water to flush those drugs out of your body. The sooner the better."

Once in the bathroom, Walter found the old paper cup and filed it with water. He held the cup as Arthur sipped the water. Dizzy, Arthur waited a minute before drinking his second cup.

Walter was relentless with the water.

After the fifth cup of water, Arthur whispered, "Walter, I need to pee."

Walter smiled. He was relieved. Arthur's movements were extremely weak and slow. Struggling, Walter carefully guided Arthur into the bathroom, avoiding crashing into anything that would draw the attention of Otman or the nurse. Finally, Arthur was seated on the toilet.

After he helped Arthur back to bed, Walter continued the onslaught of water.

Thirty minutes passed. Arthur was making the trip by himself and though his speech was still slow, he was becoming more alert.

Arthur thought about the fact that Shelly had not been allowed to see him and about how Otman had jabbed that needle into his arm. "We've got to do something to *that* monster," he whispered angrily. "It's either going to be him or us." His face flushed as his breathing intensified.

"Arthur, you'd best forget whatever you're planning and stay away from him. That man will kill us. The best thing for us to do is to get someone from outside to help. Earlier today, your medicine was a single pill and at dinner, they had upped it to two. Tomorrow, there's no telling how many pills you'll get. The dosages keep increasing. Sooner or later, you'll be given an overdose and I'll bet it's the next injection you get. Remember me telling you about Bill? He was a troublemaker and they got rid of him and they'll get rid of us also. Troublemakers are silenced. Haven't you noticed? Everyone's docile. The overdose is easily shrouded with a false cause of death explained on the death certificate. An autopsy is never performed and the real cause of death is never detected."

Arthur listened with goose-bump chills and hairs standing on end as he nodded with understanding.

Walter was glad to see him agreeing. "In the morning, they'll expect to find you dead and of course you won't be. So, you'll have to convince them that the drugs caused dementia. Don't say much and act lethargic. As you shuffle in a daze, look for someone who really is lethargic and start copying their behavior. If you're not convincing, we're not getting out of here alive."

"I've never acted before. I don't know if I can do it. I might blow it. Dang! They'll see right through me," his voice rose.

"Shhhh! Arthur, what other options do you have. Don't you want to get out of here?"

"Sure!"

"Great, then give acting your best effort. Acting demented is easy. You fooled the art teacher. Just allow yourself to intermingle with the others in this place. No one moves fast around here and copying their motions will be easy. After you've memorized some of their behaviors, the acting will become natural. Drag around a blanket, or better yet a doll."

"Not me, I'm not that crazy!"

"If you act crazy, they'll leave you alone. I've got to get back to my room before someone notices that I'm missing. See you at breakfast."

With the lights off, Walter cracked open the door. Peering out into the hallway, the lights were dim. Looking both ways and seeing no one, he eased out into the hall, his heart pounding. He feared that one of the nurses would see him and alert Otman. He didn't notice the cold tile floor, even though his feet were bare. Quickly exiting wing two, he hurried down wing three. As he neared his room, his fear began to ease and his heart rate slowed.

He breathed a sigh of relief as he closed his door. He crawled up into his bed and relaxed in the dark. Gloating and smiling, Walter closed his eyes.

—Click—

CHAPTER TWENTY-NINE

Walter's heart skipped a beat. He squinted at Otman who stood beside his bed grinning and grasping a syringe. Paralyzed, Walter lay breathless. Chills shivered up and down his exhausted body.

"Walter, where've you been?"

Walter tried to scoot across the bed, but only his hands and legs moved. Two gnarly hands had grabbed his body, pinning him into the bed. He sank into the mattress, unable to breathe. Turning, he saw a heavy-set nurse leaning over him. Her eyes told him he wasn't going anywhere. He wondered if she was the same nurse that had been plotting Arthur's demise; he hoped not.

"Were you out roaming the halls? Did you go back to Arthur's room, when I told you not to?" Otman's eyes narrowed as his behemoth hand reached out and grabbed Walter.

Walter tried to pull away numerous times, but he just couldn't free his arm from the strong grip.

His eyes widened as the large syringe fell, penetrating his biceps. "Ugh," he moaned with a wince. The sting dug down to the bone and then a cool sensation infiltrated his muscle.

Otman's thumb pressed vigorously and emptied the vial.

Fingernails dug into his skin. A cold sweat formed on his forehead as the needle was retracted. Turning his head to plea for help from the nurse, he watched the ceiling swirl above. "Help," he gasped without his lips moving. Tingles raced across his lips as his tongue, which felt swollen, lay numb.

"He'll be sedated shortly. Patients can't run wild like this one. They might hurt themselves," she said.

Walter's eyes fluttered closed and then opened momentarily. He couldn't believe this was it. *The nurse doesn't have a clue what's happening to me; or does she?*

"Sleep . . . go to sleep," Otman breathed.

Don't listen to him, Walter thought. *Don't go to sleep.* He knew time was against him. The drugs would soon overpower his body. Trying to convince them that he'd fallen asleep, he lay motionless hoping they'd leave. His breathing slowed and his chest rose and fell slightly. He felt his heart rate slowing, something he had no control over.

Otman felt Walter's muscles relaxing, and dropped his arm on the bed. Again the air in the room moved as Otman snapped, "He's sedated. Let's go." *I mean he's good as dead,* he thought smiling, not allowing the nurse to know what he'd done. Otman turned and marched triumphantly for the door.

Walter remained lifeless as Otman flipped the light switch off and closed the door.

Lying on his back, Walter struggled to open his eyes. For a moment he couldn't tell if his eyes were open or closed. It was extremely dark. Struggling to sit up, the drugs pulled him backward into bed. He rolled to the edge of the bed his head spinning. After another half roll, his feet plopped to the floor. Walter knew the drugs were swiftly racing throughout his body. There would not be much time before his body succumbed to the powerful force of the overdose.

As his feet reached the floor, his body followed, crumpling. Fearing death, struggling, he began crawling into the bathroom. His arm muscles strained as he grabbed the sink and he pulled himself up on his knees. He flipped the light switch on and darkness turned to a dull haze. Grabbing the disposable paper cup and filling it, he gulped each cup of water.

The room spun rapidly as Walter's finger muscles relaxed. The cup tumbled into the sink, splashing water over the edge as the onset of blackness slammed Walter's body to the tile floor. Water droplets showered the room.

Arthur lay on his back trying to convince himself that he needed to look for a phone and call Shelly. The darkness still caused momentary dizziness and the room occasionally would spin. The horrible sensation reminded him of how he felt moments before the boat slammed into the canal's bank. *Had drugs caused that accident?* With his mind made up to call Shelly, he sat up. The wall in front of him bent and swayed. He rubbed his eyes and the wall stopped moving.

His head throbbed as he heard Walter's warning; *Don't go out there. Wait for Shelly, she's coming.*

"I can't wait for her," he whispered back to no one.

Arthur stood and immediately careened into the bed, but miraculously didn't fall. He reached out and steadied his movements, precariously balancing as he took his first step, almost like a baby learning to walk. After teetering, Arthur braced himself at the door. Shaking off a sickening-feeling, he cracked the door open and peeked outside. He held his breath, hoping he wouldn't see anyone.

No one was in the hall as he stuck his head out from the room. Looking toward the lounge, he saw the nurse's desk and remembered seeing a phone there. It was now or never, while no one was at the desk.

Arthur pulled the door open wider and cautiously stepped out. He wondered if he'd make it. Creeping up the hallway, he steadied himself against the wall as he moved, keeping an eye out for nurses and Otman. After scanning the lounge and not seeing anyone, he hurried over to the desk, grabbed the phone and crawled under the desk. With the receiver in his hand, he listened for a dial tone. Not hearing any, he wondered which number was needed to gain an outside line. As he randomly dialed different numbers seeking an outside line, his eyes focused on a note, taped below the number pad. "No Outside Lines."

His body stiffened; he stifled a scream through his clinched jaw as his grip tightened around the phone. *Where's another phone?* Arthur hoped one of the nurses had used her cell phone and laid it on the desk, but after his head popped up for a quick glance, he knew he was out of luck.

Mabel, he thought. *If I could get to her room, I'll be able to use her phone.* His eyes widened with hope. There were no nurses around; they had to be coming back soon. He didn't have any time to waste. On his feet he headed for the double doors.

With the door approximately twenty feet away, Arthur remembered the leg bracelet and gritted his teeth anticipating the initial electrical zap. He didn't care. They'd never catch him now. Arthur bolted.

BUZZ–BUZZ–BUZZ . . . the loud buzzing noise didn't stop. The noise echoed in Arthur's ears.

Arthur froze for only a split second after the alarm sounded. He couldn't believe the leg anklet malfunctioned. He didn't get shocked. *Run! Get out of here.* He sprang forward, crashing into the doors. Staggering backward, he lunged for the doors a second time. They were locked tightly and the alarm continued to sound.

"Arthur, come on back down here. You're setting off the alarm and you're going to wake up the other residents," an audible voice was heard over the clattering alarm.

Arthur froze. He didn't know whether to hide or try ramming the doors again. Looking around, he couldn't see anyone. *Where's the voice coming from?*

Arthur cupped his hands over his ears, dulling the blaring alarm. As the noise diminished, Walter's suggestion for him to begin play acting echoed. He dreaded thinking what Otman might inject into him this time. He closed his eyes and tried to envision how that old man had walked in front of him.

A nurse's head popped out from a bedroom in wing one. "Arthur, please move away from the door. The doors automatically lock and the buzzer won't stop blaring until you've moved."

Arthur's eyes opened and he shuffled one foot forward and then the other. *So far so good.* A blank stare focused straight ahead. As he shuffled outside of the range of the leg anklet, the obnoxious noise ceased. Feeling the weight of the anklet around his leg, he remembered hearing the same sound when he entered Ward C. He didn't understand how it worked, but it had to come off.

"Thank you, Arthur." The nurse's head disappeared from the hallway back into the bedroom.

His head hung limply. He had to spend another night.

A nurse approached him from the side. "Arthur," she said kindly, as he concentrated on his new appearance. Startled, he didn't jump, but kept shuffling aimlessly. *I hope she is buying my act of senility.* "Arthur, you look tired. Why don't you go to your room and go to bed?" Something about him looked different.

She walked Arthur down wing two and at his door said, "Good night, Arthur."

He climbed into bed fully dressed. Disheartened, Arthur moaned loudly into his pillow. The muffled sound was unheard. Then a chuckle sounded. *I sure fooled her.* But the chuckle lasted only a second as reality consumed him. Exhausted, Arthur eventually fell asleep.

Ring—Ring—Ring.

Shelly slowly turned her head and looked at the clock. "Eleven-forty," she yawned. Her eyes fluttered as she tried to focus on the phone.

Ring—Ring. Shelly fumbled the phone as she lifted it. She glanced at her feet; she couldn't believe that she had fallen asleep with her shoes on. She remembered lying down and waiting for Justin's phone call.

"Hello," her voice was froggy.

"Shelly, it's me, Justin."

Her eyes opened and anger blared. "I called hours ago!"

"Sorry, but the hotel operator just gave me the message. I was at dinner when you called. I've been here for the last couple of hours."

Shelly didn't care what his excuse was. He should have called her just because he loved her and missed her. She refused to apologize. "That place . . . those people . . . ," she yelled, stammering to remember the lines she'd practiced earlier. "Those idiots have screwed up. I can't . . ."

"Shelly, calm down. Who are you talking about?"

"Those dimwits at Southern Retirement Community, that's who," she said as her face turned beet red. "I went to see Dad after I got back from Chicago and they wouldn't allow me to see him." She stomped around the room, her heart racing with hatred. "And then they told me if I didn't like the place, that I could sign for his transfer and take him home with me. Then they had the audacity to tell me that I can't take him home because your name is shown as his guardian."

"What?" he said with a smirk.

"That's right. They screwed up and put your name down. Call them tonight and tell them I'm coming to get Dad."

"Hold on Shelly. None of the administrative staff will be there at this time. I'll have to call them in the morning," he said, his voice steady.

Shelly gritted her teeth as her lips curled. "A good lawyer could make things happen tonight."

Justin shrugged his shoulders. He allowed her to vent her frustrations. "I'll call them tomorrow and then you can go get Arthur. There's nothing I can do from here."

Without saying goodbye, Shelly hung up the phone and crashed into the bed. She pulled the pillow over her head and cried. "I'm sorry, Dad," her voice muffled. Unable to get her mind off Arthur and fall asleep, she rolled out of bed and went down to the bedroom where Arthur would be staying and started cleaning the room.

CHAPTER THIRTY

Rays of sunlight filtered through the lounge window Friday morning. A few residents wandered up and down the wings, while others sat watching morning cartoons.

Light filtered through the open door of Arthur's room from the hallway. A tender warm touch nudged Arthur awake. His head ached like a hangover as he cautiously opened one eye, checking out his surroundings. Not seeing anyone, slowly he began moving his arms and then his legs, checking to see if he still could move all extremities. Thankful that the drugs hadn't damaged any muscles or joints, he breathed a sigh of relief as he relaxed on top of the ruffled sheets.

"Har–ry, good–morn–ing," Bessy screeched in a sing-song voice.

Unnerved, Arthur froze. His mouth gaped open as the loud squealing voice echoed in his ears. Arthur could see the woman they called Bessy standing at the head his bed, her hand softly tapping his shoulder.

At the nursing station, Otman leaped to his feet hearing Bessy's squeal. Dreading any undue commotion caused by one of the residents finding a dead person, he took off in a sprint toward Arthur's room.

"Morning dear," Arthur squeaked back.

Otman's long legs carried him swiftly to Arthur's room. Turning into the room, he inhaled rapidly, "Bessy get . . . "was all that he could manage. There in front of him, were Arthur and Bessy, embracing in a tight hug.

Arthur's nose twitched, smelling her unkempt hair. He couldn't distinguish whether it was soured or dirty.

Arthur peered around Bessy's hair and could see Otman's puzzled face. *Is he buying the act?* Another second passed. Otman stood motionless, evaluating the situation. Arthur, not wanting to chance what Otman was concluding, and fearing the first act was not convincing, puckered his lips together. Gritting his teeth and squinting his eyes tightly shut, their lips pressed firmly together with a loud smack. Arthur's throat muscles constricted as he fought the retching feeling rising from within his stomach. Her lips, cold and cracked with layered dry skin, seemed to prick his lips. A prune had smoother skin than her lips. Her facial muscles held her dry skin tightly in ripples.

"Yes, Bessy, I'm glad we're together again." Arthur could not believe what he was doing and saying. It was the worst kiss of his life. The desire to live was strong enough to withstand Bessy's lips. He planted another extended kiss.

"Oh, I'm so glad you still love me, Harry."

Otman was buying the act. He had hoped to find Arthur dead this morning, but this new, unexpected twist, was better than death. From the looks of it, Arthur's mind had been destroyed by the dope. Now the troublemaker was docile. Smiling, he turned around and went back to the nursing station, laughing.

"Well nurse, Arthur's much better this morning. You shouldn't have much problem from him today. He's a *new* man." Laughing out loud, his joy was uncontainable. After a brief moment, he interjected, "Arthur and Bessy are down there, loving up on each other." Laughter erupted as Otman and the nurse howled hysterically.

"You've got to be kidding," she snorted during her laughs.

Arthur shuddered at the thought of having Bessy as his new wife. Bessy was all smiles as she squeezed him. In the tight embrace, Arthur wondered if Otman's twisted mind would require them to share a room and a bed. He feared Otman was already planning their honeymoon. Wondering what would happen next, his mind unkindly joked—*what would the children look like?*—Arthur grimaced and managed a sick smile.

The smile did not last long. Arthur remembered Walter and needed to let him know he was all right. The romancing was over. He headed for the door, leaving Bessy on the edge of the bed. As he looked down the hallway, he could see Otman, laughing with the nurse.

Remembering he had to follow act one with act two in order to survive, he went back to his bed and took Bessy's hand. "Come on dear. I'm hungry. Would you like to have breakfast with me?"

"Sure, Harry. You know we always enjoy breakfast together."

Arthur helped Bessy up off the bed and out into the hallway. As they stepped out of his room, Otman looked up to see the two, shuffling his way. Watching the two carefully, Otman again began to laugh. The closer they came, the louder he laughed.

As they passed Otman, a mysterious light flashed, catching Arthur unaware. Blinded momentarily, Arthur ignored the temptation to turn around and discover the source of the flash. He continued shuffling toward the cafeteria. He tried humming to drown out Otman's horrible laughter.

The picture window came into Arthur's peripheral view. He didn't dare step over and look outside for Shelly, though he wondered when she would return today.

Bessy could smell eggs, bacon, and sausage aroma drifting into the lounge area. Tugging on Arthur's hand, she pulled him hurriedly toward the cafeteria. Bessy's gentle tugging eased Shelly from his mind.

As he entered the cafeteria, he began feeling sorry for taking advantage of Bessy. She did not deserve this humiliation. His mind wondered what Bessy's life had been like previously. *Was she a beautiful young lady? Had she been married? If so, how many children did she have?* He had not seen any come to visit her. *How old was she? Who had put her here to live out the rest of her life?*

Guiding Bessy over to an isolated table, the two sat down. "Thanks, Harry," she said and winked.

The dietitian placed two trays in front of them. Arthur could barely stomach the thought of the pureed food. The yellow pile had dark-brown flakes scattered throughout. He assumed it was eggs and bacon. The white pile with brown fragments smelled like hash-browns and he hoped the cream-colored pile wasn't oatmeal.

Bessy grabbed her spoon and without evaluating breakfast, scooped a helping of yellow puree, intermingled with lighter-brown flakes. "Yummy. Eggs and sausage," she mumbled, "my favorite."

Arthur watched as Bessy swallowed one spoonful after another. Hesitant, he scooped a spoon into the yellowish puree. Tasting, he was glad to have the eggs and bacon, bad as they were. Though the flavor was okay, his throat muscles constricted not allowing the food to slide down. *It's not that bad*, he thought trying to coax his throat into swallowing. Slowly, the muscles relaxed and he swallowed.

Arthur glanced around the room looking for Walter, who had not arrived. When he looked back at Bessy's tray, she was scraping diligently, trying to pick up the last morsel of egg.

Looking back at his tray, he lied to himself as he tried Bessy's method, scoop and swallow. Arthur quivered as the cream-color puree slid into his throat. "Oatmeal, yuck."

Arthur held his breath and gulped down the food. His tray was empty, but not like Bessy's. He wasn't licking it clean. He wondered if the puree would ever be palatable.

Otman stuck his head into the dining room, checking up on Arthur. He strode into the room, pride causing his head to stretch higher than usual. He just wanted to check up on his masterpiece.

The sight of the two eating breakfast and hearing their garbled talk left his mustache extending from ear to ear.

"Mr. Otman," the intercom blared, "please come to the nursing station. Now!"

Hearing the announcement, Arthur stiffened as his head glanced around the room for Walter.

"Mr. Otman, hurry to Walter's room," the nurse's voice blared over the intercom with panic.

Arthur cringed and his face sagged. *Why Walter's room*? He buried his head in his hands. *I hope Walter's okay.*

CHAPTER THIRTY-ONE

Rushing inside Walter's room, Otman shouted, "What's wrong?"

"He's in the bathroom," the older nurse said, motioning for him to hurry.

Otman stood in the bathroom's doorway and looked down. He growled as he saw a peachy color in Walter's face.

"I found Walter lying on the bathroom floor," the red-haired nurse said, cradling his head in her lap. "He's wet and very cold. I need your help in lifting him."

Stepping into the bathroom, Otman looked down at Walter. "Did he slip?" he asked looking at the large puddle of water on the floor.

"I don't know! He's got a weak pulse. We've got to dry him off and get him back into bed. I don't know if he's going to make it. You'd best call a doctor."

Fat chance, he thought.

"Grab his body and I'll grab his feet," the nurse said as she struggled to stand.

Seeing the wet towel lying on the floor, Otman pretended to trip on it and stumble. With a swift kick of his right leg, Otman's foot landed firmly into Walter's side.

"Ugh," air gushed from Walter's lungs.

"Careful!" the nurse shrieked as Otman's foot impaled Walter's side causing him to move an inch or two.

You're going to wish you died last night, Otman thought as he pulled his foot from Walter's body. *I'll have to up your meds*.

Walter lay shivering. His left side ached each time his lung expanded with air.

"Lift," the nurse instructed as Walter's body rose off the floor. Uric acid caused her to choke. "Stop, he's urinated all over himself."

Upon hearing those words, Otman dropped his end.

"Help me put him in the shower."

"No way. Get someone else. I'm not getting his piss on me!"

Otman washed his hands and with them still dripping, he hurriedly stepped from the bathroom and left the room.

Angry at Otman, the nurse shouted for the older nurse who was watching from outside the bathroom. Together they lifted him into the shower.

The hot water warmed Walter's body. Opening one eye, he was relieved not to see Otman. As the steam filled the bathroom and hazed the mirror, the red-haired nurse shut off the spray and undressed him.

After quickly bathing Walter, she dried him and then the two nurses carried him to his bed. There they dressed him and covered him with a blanket.

Walter lay under the blanket thankful for the warmth and glad to be alive, but unable to move.

A janitor arrived to clean up the bathroom. Unhappy to see the mess and that the nurses hadn't attempted to wipe up the water, the janitor jerked the mop head around on the floor carelessly, sloshing pine-scented cleaner against the walls. As he wrung out his mop, he wondered why either nurse hadn't used a towel to wipe the water from the floor. "It's all clean," he said, plopping the mop back into its bucket and casually walking off.

"Thank you," the other nurse said, ignoring his attitude.

Both nurses tidied up the room and they, too, left.

After eating, Arthur sat placating Bessy as she babbled. Arthur fidgeted. He was anxious to find out about Walter. *Where is he? Why did they call Otman to his room? Is he okay? Why hasn't he shown up for breakfast? Maybe Bessy and I should walk down to his room and check on him.* Deep in thought, he didn't notice the nurse walking up to Bessy.

"Bessy. It's time to take your medicine." The nurse extended her hand toward Bessy, holding the paper cup with Bessy's name on it.

Arthur swallowed hard. *Medicine!* He glanced into the cup and saw five pills in the bottom. All a different color, size, and shape. Caution blared; *Don't let Bessy swallow those pills.* Other questions raced through his mind: *Why's she taking so many? What if Walter's right about the medicine and Bessy really doesn't need all those pills? What kind of person would she be without them?*

Bessy took the cup from the nurse's hand. She lifted her water glass to take a swig. The nurse seeing Bessy following her instructions turned and walked away. As Bessy drew the pills toward her mouth, Arthur gritted his teeth, inhaled and said, "I love you Bessy." Arthur's words stopped Bessy's hand from reaching her lips with the pills. He quickly leaned into Bessy and kissed her lips. This time the kiss did not seem quite as dreadful.

Bessy forgot about her pills and sat googly-eyed in her chair with a big smile across her dry, cracked face.

With the nurse out of the room, Arthur quickly emptied Bessy's cup. He slipped the concealed pills into his shoe. Later, in his room, he would flush them down the toilet.

Just as Arthur had pulled his hand from the shoe, the nurse returned carrying another paper cup. "Arthur," she said, "here's your medicine." Reaching out for the cup, Arthur noticed someone move behind her. Hoping it was Walter, he leaned to the right, looking around her. "Oh," he said as an old heavy-set lady shuffled out into the lounge.

Arthur's fingers fumbled for the cup as he jerked his attention away from the lady. Glimpsing into the cup, five pills—all different colors and sizes—jiggled around. *Walter's right. They'll either make me docile or kill me.* Looking at Bessy, he felt sorry for her.

The nurse stood close by, waiting for Arthur to swallow the pills.

Squeezing the bottom of the paper cup with his thumb and index finger, Arthur pinched the pills and then pretended to dump them into his mouth. After seeing him swallow, she was satisfied and turned and walked away.

Before he could hide the pills, Bessy stood tugging on his hand and said, "Come on Harry. I'm ready to go." Sliding his chair away from the table, he slowly rose. Stepping toward the cafeteria's exit door, he palmed the cup tightly in his fist. As he passed the garbage can, he tossed the wadded up cup into it. Reminded by Bessy's slow movement, Arthur returned to his play acting shuffle. He muttered to himself to be more careful. Someone might notice next time.

Shuffling out the doorway, Bessy asked, "Aren't you going to hold my hand?" Arthur wondered if life could get any worse.

Reaching out for Bessy's hand, he wrapped his fingers around her soft small hand. The warmth reminded him of Laura's warm touch. He only wished she had not died. Life would be so different.

Bessy and Arthur ambled down the hall, like the other residents, going nowhere in a hurry, except he had to find out what had happened to Walter. As they passed the nursing station, he could see that Otman was gone and so were the nurses. Not knowing where they were, he feared going down wing three. He couldn't risk receiving another injection. He doubted his body had fully expelled last night's dosage.

Shuffling past the nurse's desk, Bessy tugged on Arthur's hand. "Come this way," she requested, again yanking his hand. Reluctantly, Arthur followed Bessy's lead.

Bessy led Arthur down wing one. Inhaling, Arthur caught the fragrance of roses. Arthur closed his eyes and imagined the dozen red roses that he had brought to Laura on every anniversary. A small smile eased across his lips as Laura emerged in his vision.

"In here," Bessy said tugging on Arthur's hand as she shuffled inside her room.

As Arthur stumbled into the room, Laura disappeared and was replaced by Bessy's bare walls. The smell of roses was stronger inside Bessy's room. Arthur noticed a clear vase showcasing a dozen faded roses. Stepping closer to smell them, he realized that they were silk, emitting an artificial fragrance.

Bessy tugged Arthur deeper into her room. With no windows in her room, the only light source was the fixture hanging from the ceiling. On top of the dresser drawer, a single picture portraying a couple, was perched. Curious, Arthur stepped over to have a look. He cringed. It was a picture of Bessy and himself passing the nursing station.

Arthur's face flushed as his fingers tightened into fists. *Calm down,* he subconsciously heard Walter's warning. *It's only Otman's way of evaluating your new behavior. If you react, he'll know he's been had.* Arthur exhaled and let it go.

Bessy's pink bedspread lay wrinkled across the bed. It was the only color in her small room. The walls were white and the furniture had been painted an antique white. The room seemed to be private.

"Your room's very nice," Arthur said. He watched as a smile broadened across Bessy's face, revealing her pretty white teeth. A warming sensation rose inside him.

The clock on her night-stand reminded him of what time he was to have met Walter for breakfast. He wanted to know what the emergency call to his room had been for. He hoped Walter wasn't hurt.

"Bessy, let's go for a walk."

She stood admiring their picture, touching Arthur's face. "Okay," she said turning and reaching out for his hand.

Hand in hand, Arthur led the way to the lounge, but fidgeted seeing a nurse sitting behind the nurse's desk. Unable to enter wing three, his shuffle dragged to a stop.

Bessy heard cartoons playing over on the TV and shuffled on. "Come on," she said, tugging, "let's watch TV."

Up ahead, an elderly man drifted down the third wing. Arthur wished the man were Walter. Not wanting to draw attention to himself, he shuffled behind Bessy. They found a spot on the couch where they sat hand in hand.

After more than an hour of listening to shrill cartoons and watching the nurse filling out documents and answering the phone, Arthur yawned and stretched. *Where's Shelly?*

CHAPTER THIRTY-TWO

Shelly looked at her wrist watch. "Almost nine o'clock," she muttered, as she sat holding the cordless phone wondered why Justin hadn't called with good news about her dad. She stood and walked around the couch again and into the kitchen, circling back to the couch in the family room. The carpet lay flat; she'd worn a path pacing since eating breakfast at seven o'clock. Retrieving Justin's note from yesterday, she dialed the airport hotel.

"Hello. I'm Shelly Roble and I am trying to get in touch with my husband, Justin."

"One moment, . . ." the operator said while she checked Justin's name in the guest registry. ". . . Mr. Roble checked out at eight."

"Thanks," she said, and pressed the disconnect button. *I can't believe he hasn't called me.* Without hesitation, she dialed Justin's work number.

"Hello, may I speak to Justin's secretary, Connie?" Shelly bit her fingernails waiting for her to answer.

Ring–ring . . . Ring–ring.

Shelly heard her cell phone ringing in her pocketbook. Holding the cordless phone to her ear, she hurried to the dresser where her pocketbook was. As it rang again, she pulled it from her pocketbook and held it to her ear. "Hello?"

229

"This is Connie," she heard in the other ear.

"Shelly, it's Justin," he blared.

Without thinking, she pressed the disconnect button on the cordless phone and dropped it on the dresser.

"I've been trying to reach you, but all circuits have been busy. I've talked with Southern Retirement and they will allow you to go see your dad, but you won't be able to take him home."

"Why not?" she shrieked.

"It's okay. I'll be home this afternoon and then we'll go get him. I'm flying in on Delta, Flight 252."

Shelly breathed easier, glad that Justin had worked it all out. "Okay. I'll be waiting for you. Don't be long."

"I'll call you from the airport and we can meet there."

"Thanks, I love you," Shelly said.

"Love you too," he said as they hung up.

Shelly rushed into the bathroom, showered, and was dressed in a crisp pressed shirt and slacks within ten minutes. She stood in front of the bathroom mirror drying her hair. The brush pulled at the wet knots. Before long, her hair was neatly brushed along with her teeth. The door slammed closed as she ran down the front steps to her car.

"Nurse, have you seen Arthur?" Otman inquired, holding a file folder.

"He's over there," she said pointing at the couch.

"Thanks." He hustled over to the couch, approaching from behind and pulled a syringe from his jacket pocket. Striking quickly, he grasped Arthur's left arm and his right hand plunged the syringe.

"Ouch! Why did you . . . ." Arthur moaned as the sting shot up to his arm. Turning his head to see who had grabbed him, he could vaguely make out Otman's distorted face.

Bessy turned to see what Arthur had moaned about, only to see him slumped over on the couch. "Harry, what's wrong?"

Otman rushed around the couch, sticking the syringe back into his pocket. With one swoop of his arms, Arthur was pulled off the couch. "Nothing's wrong with him. He's just sleepy. Watch your cartoons."

"Oh," Bessy said, easily distracted, turning her attention back to the TV.

Otman carried Arthur down wing two and into his room. Laying him on his bed, he pulled the sheet up to his throat. "It's a shame that you'll be asleep when your daughter comes to visit. I can't take any chances." His woolly mustache fluttered as he smiled. "Sleep tight," he said and closed the door.

Within ten minutes, Shelly pulled into a visitor's parking spot and hurried to the front door. As she stepped inside, a secretary rose from the desk behind the glass-walled office. She took short little strides like that of a toy-poodle—her legs rapidly moving back and forth, but not covering much ground—and scurried out the door and around to meet her. "You must be Shelly. I've been watching for you." Seeing a puzzled look from Shelly, she added, "I was told you drove a green Suburban."

Shelly's face relaxed as she looked down at the small woman in her late twenties.

"I'm Kathleen. Follow me," she said, leading her down the first corridor. Her ink-black hair fluttered off her shoulders as her petite arms pumped back and forth.

Pushing one of the double doors open, they entered Ward C. "I'll show you to his room. This way," she said continuing to lead Shelly to Arthur's room.

Seeing Arthur lying still, Shelly brushed past Kathleen and hurried to the bed. "Dad," she cried.

Arthur didn't move.

"Dad," she hollered, shaking him. "What's wrong with him?"

"I'm not aware of anything being wrong. He must be asleep," she said picking up his medical chart and thumbing through it.

"If he was asleep, I could arouse him. Something's wrong," Shelly said, rubbing his head. "Wake up. Please, wake up Dad."

Arthur lay motionless, not even twitching an eye.

"Get a doctor in here. Something's wrong with my dad!"

"There's no doctor here right now. Can I call a nurse?"

"Please!" Shelly pleaded, pulling his hand from the cover and holding it tight.

Kathleen pressed the button beside the bed requesting a nurse.

Otman stepped into the room. "What's the problem?"

Shelly's heart skipped a couple of beats recognizing the voice. She turned around and stared blankly at him.

Kathleen sensed the tension between them. "Is there something wrong with Arthur?" she asked.

"Not that I'm aware of," he said as he stepped closer. "He looks fine to me."

"Well, he's not waking up!" Shelly roared.

"No, he doesn't appear to be, but he should with you yelling like that. Maybe it's a combination of the medicine and his sleepiness. He wanders the hallways at all times of the night, so I'm told by the night nurses." He pulled his stethoscope out from his pocket. He placed the silvery bell on Arthur's chest and listened. "Sounds normal." And then he grabbed Arthur's wrist and counted. "His heart rate's normal too. I'll be right back and check his blood pressure."

The door swung open as Otman reentered the room pulling a small medical cart. "Excuse me," he said, stepping past Shelly. Wrapping the cuff around Arthur's biceps he squeezed the black bulb. The gage's needle fluctuated and then gave its reading. "Blood pressure one-ten over eighty-five." Looking at Shelly he continued, "He's fine. Any other questions?"

Shelly knew asking him further questions was futile and shook her head.

Otman turned and left the room.

"I don't like that man," Shelly whispered to Kathleen.

"If it makes you feel any better, neither do I."

The door swung open clunking against the door stop. Fearing Otman had heard what they had said about him, they looked up with alarm.

"Harry," Bessy said, shuffling into the room and pushing Shelly to the side so that she could get up beside Arthur. "Harry! Come back and watch TV."

Shelly's jaw dropped. "Excuse me!"

"Shelly, this is Bessy," Kathleen interrupted. "She thinks Arthur is her husband, Harry, and today he seems to believe he's Harry. These two have been going around holding hands together like they were a couple. I'll get her out of here so you can have some time with your father." She hurried around the bed and gently, but firmly squeezed Bessy's shoulders. "Come with me, Bessy," she said, turning Bessy around and leading her to the door. "I'll go watch TV with you."

Bessy seemed to forget Harry and was glad to have someone to watch TV with.

Shelly stood beside the bed, clutching Arthur's hand with one hand and rubbing his forehead with the other, wondering how he could have deteriorated so quickly. She remembered the conversation from yesterday, about the medication needing time to be regulated and wondered if his present condition was due to the drugs. "Dad, I love you," she whispered into his ear. "Please wake up and talk to me. I was going to take you home with me today, but now I'm having second thoughts seeing you lying here like this."

Arthur lay perfectly still, except for his chest rising and falling with each breath.

After watching him for half an hour, Shelly knew she had to call Justin to let him know that there wasn't any reason to meet here. Arthur needed to stay and receive professional care twenty-four hours a day.

"Bye, Dad," she said, kissing him on the cheek. "I'll come back and see you." A tear pooled in the corner of her eye. She had lost her dad. She wished she'd spent more time with him since her mother had died. She wondered if he was giving up the will to live.

She turned and ambled from the room, wiping her eyes with the back of her hand, as she stepped into the hallway. She noticed an elderly man stagger to a stop. He was less than ten feet away, looking puzzled at her. After staring for a brief second or two at him, she stepped out further into the hallway, by-passing the older gentleman.

He turned and looked behind him and then shuffled into Shelly's path. "Excuse me," he mumbled. "Are you Arthur's daughter?"

Shelly was surprised. "Yes sir, I am."

"I'm Walter," he said glancing back toward the nursing desk fearing that Otman might see him. "Thanks for helping me." Again, he scanned the area.

"I don't understand what you're talking about," Shelly said in her normal voice.

Walter's eyes widened, "Shhhh. Keep your voice down," his voice gasped as his eyes swept the hallway.

"Why?" she whispered.

"Arthur didn't tell you?"

"He's asleep. We didn't talk."

Looking up and down the corridor again, he continued. "I've got to go, but you better get your dad out of here, today." Shuffling past her, he murmured, "He's doped up." Hoping she wouldn't follow, he hurriedly scooted away.

Shelly darted a glance at Walter and then looked toward the lounge. She sensed he was watching for someone and her guess was Otman. Over at the TV sat Bessy watching the *Price is Right,* but Kathleen wasn't there. As she passed the nursing station, her strides quickened, fearing Otman would reach out and grab her. *He's doped up.* Walter's words echoed as the soles of her shoes clicked in the empty hallway. She glanced around, ready to scream if approached. Her ears rang and throbbed.

She pushed the door open from Ward C, just as Otman pushed the other double door open. They stared at each other momentarily before Shelly speed-walked away, her body shaking.

Shelly clutched her pocketbook tightly under her arm and reached inside, fumbling for the cell phone. As she reached the outside door, she pulled the phone out and began dialing Justin's cell phone. Hurrying down the sidewalk and into the parking lot, she kept looking over her shoulder fearing Otman was approaching.

Not getting an answer, Shelly dropped the phone into the purse and pulled out the key ring. The keys jingled as she pressed the remote. As the door clicked, she opened it and looked back at the building, hoping she had not been followed. "Uhhh," she wheezed. *He's watching me!*

Shelly jumped in, slammed the door closed, and locked it. Her hand shook as she cranked the car. The car lunged from the parking space and sped out of sight.

CHAPTER THIRTY-THREE

"Harry!" Bessy called with a raspy voice, sitting in front of the TV. Her head turned as her eyes scanned one side of the room to the other. "Harry?" she called louder, standing.

The few residents watching TV turned and shot her daggers. "Shhhh!"

Bessy sauntered down wing two looking in each room she passed. Halfway down the corridor, she called, "Harry, get up!"

Arthur rolled over on his back and stretched. His eyes never opened.

Her shoes swished across the floor as she scurried over to the bed. At the foot of the bed, Bessy began dragging her left hand along Arthur's foot. As her hand reached his knee, she stumbled. Unable to catch her balance, she tumbled into his bed, landing sprawled across him.

"Ump," he moaned, opening his eyes. His blurred vision focused on two large eyes.

"Hi, Harry," Bessy said.

"How'd I get here?"

She shrugged her shoulders. "I don't know."

His shocked expression faded as the wrinkles on her face seemed to disappear as he looked beyond them and deep into her green eyes.

"Hi, Bessy," he said, mesmerized by her sparkling eyes.

Bessy smiled. "Are you hungry?"

"Sure am."

"A lady came by to see you," Bessy said as they scooted off the bed.

"Shelly?"

Bessy lifted her hands in bewilderment. "Don't know." Grabbing Arthur's hand, she said, "Come on."

If it had been Shelly, I wouldn't still be here.

Before they reached the doorway, a nurse stepped into the room. Arthur froze, but Bessy continued shuffling toward the door. Bessy tugged. "Come on."

Arthur breathed a sigh of relief seeing that she wasn't holding a syringe.

"Bessy, what are you doing in Arthur's room?"

Arthur took shallow breaths. His head began to hurt as his heart rate increased. *Is she a scout for Otman?*

"I came down here to check on Harry. He's sleepy," Bessy responded.

"Bessy, this is Arthur."

"No ma'am. This is my husband, Harry," she said snuggling beside him.

Arthur studied the lady's face trying to determine exactly why or who had sent her to spy on him. His heart raced as anxiety told him to play act. "Come on dear, I'm hungry." Arthur was surprised at how easy the acting was becoming. He only hoped his mind wouldn't stray too far into this crazy world. He feared a point of no return lurked out there somewhere.

With their hands firmly grasped together, the two shuffled out into the hallway.

Bessy snuggled tightly against him as they walked. Arthur was slowly warming to her touch.

In the hallway, they ambled behind an elderly man through the lounge and then into the cafeteria.

Arthur and Bessy sat alone at a table close to the doorway. She ate like she missed eating breakfast and he tried not to analyze the three different servings of puree. He managed not to gag, but he longed for solid food.

Walter shuffled with a limp favoring his left side, his hand supporting his left ribs. Drool slipped from the left side of his mouth. Dark marks circled his eyes. His left foot scraped the floor as it dragged along.

Arthur watched with horror as Walter limped past without acknowledgment.

"Walter, why don't you sit here and eat your lunch?" the dietician said holding his tray. As he sat, she placed the tray down.

Walter smeared the puree around the plate with his fingers as finger paints.

"Oh brother! I hate to see residents digress like this," she exclaimed, briefly watching before she moved to get another tray.

With his fingers in his mouth, Walter slurped, cleaning each finger one at a time.

Arthur buried his head in his hands. He couldn't bear to watch. The thought of Otman catching Walter leaving his room last night and injecting him with drugs incited a retching feeling rising in his throat. He hoped Shelly would hurry and get him out. What was taking her so long?

Walter pushed away from the table, holding his side and stood. Shuffling past Arthur he mumbled, "Meet me later at the TV."

Arthur raised his head from his hands and smiled. Otman hadn't gotten the best of Walter.

Walter shuffled around the sofa and eased into the soft seat. Still holding his ribs, he waited for Arthur.

Arthur shuffled with a limp as his forgotten pills from breakfast jostled around in his shoe, but seeing Walter, he forgot about the pain and pulled Bessy along to the TV area. Not seeing any of the nurses or Otman, he sat beside Walter.

"You're really impressive with your acting," Arthur whispered.

Bessy's attention was focused on Sergeant yelling at Gomer Pyle.

After checking to be sure he couldn't be overheard, Walter explained, "While you were in that drug-induced sleep, Shelly came to see you. She knows you're in danger and is going to get you out. And last night, Otman was waiting in my room when I returned. He overdosed me, too." He chuckled, "And I cheated death once more."

CHAPTER THIRTY-FOUR

He's doped up! Walter's words again rattled her thoughts as she punched the keyboard, entering www.delta.com and checked the arrival time of flight 252 from Atlanta. She breathed easy, knowing Justin would be on time. To keep herself preoccupied after lunch, she finished cleaning the guest bathroom and spruced up the guest bedroom for the second time. The room smelled of Lemon Pledge.

After viewing the clock, Shelly raced to the kitchen, grabbed her pocketbook, and sprinted out the closing door. With the Suburban's tires squealing, the vehicle lurched backward out of the driveway. As the vehicle charged forward, the front bumper narrowly missed the mailbox. With few vehicles on the roadway, Shelly sped along. Frequently she looked at her watch ensuring that Justin would not be able to exit the plane without her standing at the gate to meet him.

Driving up and down the aisles of the airport's parking area, finding an empty parking place was becoming a challenge. A few vacant parking places were found on the top parking deck toward the back. Concerned about her dad and excited that he was coming to live with her, she ran down the parking garage's stairs. Two flights down, she was glad to be wearing tennis shoes. She exited the stairs out of breath and ran into the terminal. Delta's overhead arrival board displayed Justin's arrival gate.

Her leg muscles, not used to running, quivered. With approximately twenty minutes before the flight's arrival, she hurried in the direction of the gate. Her muscles stung as she moved toward gate twenty-four.

"Airline ticket please," the young women asked Shelly as she approached the security zone.

"I don't have one. I'm picking up my husband."

"You'll have to wait over there with the others who are waiting for arriving passengers."

Observing security personnel, Shelly reluctantly turned and walked over to the crowd. She looked at her watch every minute; time passed slowly. Her legs ached so much that she sat down on the floor and continued to check her watch.

Each time a group of arriving passengers appeared, the crowd tightened, anxious to greet their loved ones. Shelly waited impatiently, hoping Justin would be next.

"Delta, Flight 252 is now arriving," blared the intercom.

Shelly eased her way to the front edge of bystanders. Passengers exited the secured area. With a quick glance at each one, Shelly waited.

"This way. Follow me," the flight attendant advised an older lady. Behind them, no one could be seen.

Shelly, desperate to find Justin, ran over to the Delta counter. "Excuse me, but I was waiting for my husband, Justin Roble. Can you tell me if he was on Flight 252?"

The ticket agent's fingers rattled the keyboard's keys. Looking up, she shook her head. "No ma'am, he was not on that flight. Maybe he missed the flight."

"I must have misunderstood what he told me. Is there any way you can check and see which flight he's on?"

"No ma'am. It's against company policy for me to give out that information. Security reasons. You understand, don't you?"

Considering her options, Shelly nodded her head and slowly turned away. *What if he missed the flight or had to stay over.* She wasn't going to consider that. He couldn't stay over. He had to sign Arthur out, today. She pulled out her cell phone from her pocketbook and dialed Justin's number. Passengers hurriedly stepped around her as she stood in the center of the concourse listening to Justin's cell phone ringing.

"I'm sorry, but the cell phone you are trying to reach is unavailable," the recording announced.

Agitated, Shelly firmly pressed the numbers on her cell phone for Justin's secretary. The excessive ringing grated on her nerves. In exasperation, she pressed the off button.

Irate, she wondered what to do. *Maybe Judge Blair can help,* she thought. Angrily she punched 4-1-1. "Hold please, all operators are busy."

"RRRRR . . . ." Shelly growled as on-lookers stared at her. She watched the second hand slowly sweep the dial. After finally reaching an operator, she gave the operator Judge Blair's name. As the automated response gave her the number for the court house, she scribbled it on the only available surface, the back of her hand.

Shelly's fingers pummeled the keys. Exasperated she waited as the phone rang.

"I'm sorry, but Judge Blair's office is closed until Monday," the automated voice announced.

Shelly's body slouched in despair as she pressed the off key and dropped the cell phone haphazardly into her purse. Numbly she walked up the flight of stairs in the parking garage and across the deck to her vehicle. Once seated in her Suburban, she rested her head on the steering wheel, wondering what to do next. Her eyes were red and watering as she accepted the fact that she'd have to wait until Justin arrived before bringing her dad home.

After more than thirty minutes waiting to hear from Justin, wearied, she decided to wait at home. *Airlines, they're notorious for screwing up people's schedules.* As she pulled into traffic, the

Suburban lumbered along in the right-hand lane. Vehicles behind her hit their brakes as they encroached on her bumper. A long line of traffic accumulated behind the Suburban which was traveling around twenty miles per hour. Horns sounded as cars passed. Some drivers waved their fists at her, and swore, while some gave her the finger.

Shelly never heard the horns nor did she see the angry people. Lost in her dilemma, her tunnel-vision kept the vehicle safely in her lane. Shelly turned the steering wheel and the Suburban crept into her driveway.

Inside her house, she fell into the sofa, exhausted. Hating herself for making her dad move somewhere so wretched, and missing him terribly, *Shelly anxiously waited.*

Where's Justin? she fretted and burst into tears once again.

CHAPTER THIRTY-FIVE

"Connie," Justin said, lying in her bed, his heart racing with gratification. "It won't be long now until everything's in place. Shelly's still a problem. Did you pick up those pills?"

"Sure did," she said as she rolled out of bed. Connie bent over and picked up the bathrobe lying on the floor beside the bed and wrapped herself in it. She hurried over to her pocketbook and found the new bottle of medicine. "Here," she said as she tossed the bottle to Justin. "Make sure Shelly starts taking these pills today."

"She will," Justin answered as he pulled on his pants. "What did you get her?"

"The same drug that Arthur was taking. 'Halcion,' but in the higher dosage, .25mg. With her lower body weight, .125mg is recommended. At twice the dosage, it'll keep her in a deeper sleep."

"Halcion is perfect. It has a great side effect, known as traveler's amnesia. If she wakes up before it is eliminated from her system, she'll never remember it. I've got to be going now," Justin said as he pushed the last shirt button through the hole. He left his tie off and picked up his coat and briefcase. "I'll call you later," and he stepped out of her apartment.

Justin steered his car through traffic wondering how he would get Shelly to take the first pill. She was expecting him to take her to get her dad. He couldn't force it on her. It needed to appear as if she were depressed and was taking unprescribed medicine. *What if I . . . no that won't work. What if I stuck it in a piece of chocolate? No, she'll bite into the tablet.*

"Yesterday's Ice Cream. It's what your grandmother used to treat you with when you were a child," the radio announcement advertised. "Pick it up at your local grocery store, today."

Hmm . . . ice cream! Shelly loves ice cream. She'll never be able to refuse it. But, it'll be melted by the time I get it home. And then he smirked. *Yeah, but she'll think I'm sweet. It's the thought that counts, she'll say.*

Justin turned at the next light and headed to his right a few blocks. After a few more turns he pulled up to the old ice cream parlor. *Now, what is her favorite ice cream? Oh yeah, chocolate chip.*

"I'll take two scoops of chocolate chip, please."

"Do you want that in a cone or a cup?" the perky brunette asked.

"Cup," Justin said. He needed to blend the crushed tablet into the ice cream.

Justin closed the car door and reached for the bottle of Halcion. He slowly crushed the pill with his pen and then brushed the powder into the ice cream. He placed the container in the cup holder and then headed home.

As Justin stepped on the front porch, he looked at his watch. He was a little more than an hour late. He was glad he had caught an earlier flight so that he had time to spend with Connie.

"Shelly, I'm home," he called as he opened the front door. "Let's go pick up your dad."

Shelly leaped from the sofa. Her anger disappeared as she heard they were going to get her dad. She raced up to Justin and hugged him.

"I'm glad to see you, too," Justin said. "I'm sorry that I'm late, but I had to catch the next plane. I would have called but my cell phone was stolen."

Shelly didn't care. She grabbed her pocketbook and rushed out the door yelling, "Come on. Let's go."

"Shelly, wait a minute. I brought you your favorite ice cream, chocolate chip," he said, holding it out for her. "I bet it's a milkshake by now," and he pulled off the lid. "Yep, you'll have to almost drink it. And before we go. I've got to use the bathroom."

"Oh, okay, but hurry." Shelly reached out for the ice cream and stepped back inside. "Thanks," she said.

Justin watched as she took her first slurp. "Hey, how about a little celebration tonight after your dad's gone to bed?" he prodded as he stepped around the corner to the downstairs bath.

"Sure," Shelly answered and took another scoop of the soft ice cream. Soon she scraped the bottom of the cup for the last piece of chocolate. Justin had not finished in the bathroom. Concerned, she asked, "Are you okay?"

"Yes, but my stomach is upset from being cramped in that tiny airline seat. Give me another minute or two. How's the ice cream?"

"It was nice; thanks for thinking about me."

Justin made some appalling sounds and smiled. "I'm almost finished."

After a couple more minutes, Shelly heard the toilet flush and water splashing in the sink. She was glad to hear it. She could not wait for Arthur to be out of that terrible place. As she made her way back to the front door, her eyelids drooped. Her legs and arms felt heavy. She ignored the feelings and shouted, "Hurry up, Justin."

"I'm coming."

At the front door Justin noticed Shelly's eyes. "Are you feeling okay?" he asked, seeming sincere.

"I think so. I'm a little tired from all the excitement of bringing dad home. I'll be fine."

"Why don't you sit down for a minute?"

"No, I'm fine. I just want to go get dad."

"If you'd like, I can go and pick him up." Starting to laugh he continued, "It'll be the first time he's ever been glad to see me."

"Thanks, but I'm going."

"All right. Let's go," he said as they stepped out into the bright sunlight.

Shelly instantly began to sweat. She wobbled down the steps. Her legs trembled.

"Shelly, are you okay?"

"Yeah," she replied weakly.

Justin hurried down the steps and steadied her. "Let me help you to the car." He hoped it wouldn't be much longer until she was asleep.

Shelly leaned into him as she was helped to the car. She was glad to have Justin home. As the door opened to the BMW, she lowered herself into the seat. She felt light-headed.

Justin ambled around the back of the car. Once inside, he asked, "Shelly, are you sure you want to go? You don't look well."

Shelly closed her eyes as the dash blurred in front of her. "I'm just a little hot. I'm not leaving dad there another day. Maybe some air conditioning will make me feel better."

Justin sneered as he cranked the car and turned the air on high. *I doubt it.* He was having a hard time containing himself. He looked twice, both ways, before backing out into the street. As he shifted into drive, he saw Shelly's head deep in the headrest. Her eyes closed as she fought the effects of the drug.

Justin knew that one of the common side effects of Halcion was dizziness. He purposely sped around the corners, hoping to increase its effects.

"Where're we going?" Shelly asked, disoriented.

Justin smiled knowing that another symptom was temporary amnesia. It could occur for the duration of the drug's presence in her body. "Home."

"Uh huh."

Within minutes Justin pulled back into their driveway. "We're home."

Shelly reached for the handle and pulled, completely missing it. Again she grasped for the handle, but grabbed the armrest instead. Her coordination had deteriorated and she was completely disoriented; she fell against the door.

"Wake up, Shelly. We need to go inside."

Justin ran around the car. *I've got to call Connie and let her know that everything is going just like we planned. Who would have thought that sleeping pill would have all these great side effects?*

CHAPTER THIRTY-SIX

Arthur and Bessy sat together in the cafeteria waiting for their dinner trays to be served. Bessy sat smiling, looking at Arthur in her dreamy world, while Arthur looked away, wondering what had become of Shelly. *What's keeping her? Have they stopped her from coming to see me or is Justin keeping her away?* Abruptly his thoughts were interrupted as Otman entered the room.

He sauntered through the cafeteria, his eyes keenly evaluating each resident. Observing Arthur and Bessy together, he stepped over to where they sat. "How are Harry and Bessy?" he asked standing behind Arthur.

Arthur was not amused by the patronizing question. He had learned not to allow Otman to upset him.

"Fine," Arthur responded.

"Who's that man, Harry?"

"I don't know who he is dear. He must have just moved here." Turning to face Otman, Arthur asked, "Could you go sit someplace else? We don't want to be disturbed."

Otman was glad to see Arthur's memory had deteriorated, though he did not like the way Arthur had spoken to him. As he passed along, he jabbed his left knee into Arthur's side.

"Ugh . . . "

"Are you okay, Harry?" Bessy asked.

"Yes. Just indigestion." Arthur never acknowledged Otman, nor looked his way. Instead, Arthur's anger focused on Otman's mistreatment of the elderly. He was deep in thought when a dark shadow passed the corner of his eye. He turned and watched Walter shuffle to an empty table.

Bessy watched Arthur's eyes as they followed Walter across the room. "Who's that?" she asked.

"A friend."

"Were you fishing buddies?"

"Yeah," Arthur mumbled not knowing what to say. His eyes focused on Walter, who appeared to be in great pain.

With the dinner trays served, Arthur and Bessy sat quietly eating. Bessy glanced over at Walter's table. "Fishing! Didn't you two catch one of those big fish?" she asked rubbing her chin.

With Otman standing across the room, Arthur was concerned that Bessy's mentioning fishing would make Otman suspect that he and Walter had known each other in the past. If he thought that, he would surely kill them.

"Umm. This pie is delicious. Bessy, have you tried any yet?"

Bessy looked down at her tray. The yellowish-orange pile had not been touched. Using her spoon, she scooped up some. The moment the puree entered her mouth, the sweet peach made her mouth water. "Yummy," she murmured.

Arthur was relieved that Bessy had forgotten her question about Walter and was now devoting her whole attention to the peach puree. Dabbing her spoon into the mound, she lifted the next bite to his mouth.

A nurse walked up to Bessy's side. "Bessy," the soft voice spoke, "you need to take your medicine." Bessy reached out and took the small paper cup. Five pills jostled at the bottom.

Arthur froze as he watched Bessy grasp the cup from the nurse. *You've got to get those pills away from Bessy. But how can I stop her?*

As Bessy held the cup in her hand, Arthur quickly scooped a bite of his peach mush on his spoon. He held his breath hoping the diversion would take her mind off the pills. "Bessy, try a bite of my pie. I believe it's better than yours."

The nurse grimaced as she witnessed Bessy opening up her mouth. She turned and walked away. Two old senile people in love was too much for her to stomach.

As the nurse walked away, Arthur reached for the paper cup with his other hand. With his hand wrapped around Bessy's small hand, he gently rotated her hand upside down. The pills fell into his palm. He began slipping the pills into his shoe. At that moment, he realized he had not removed this morning's pills.

Before he had dropped the last pill in his shoe, the nurse turned to give Arthur his medicine. "Arthur, it's time to take your medicine."

Startled, the pill slipped from his fingers and softly rattled on the floor. Arthur quickly placed his foot on the rolling pill as he reached for his cup of medicine. Unobserved, he pretended to swallow the pills and the nurse continued dispensing the evening's medication. As he placed the cup on the table, he noticed Walter slowly ambling out of the cafeteria. He felt terrible for Walter.

Arthur pulled back his foot and kicked Bessy's pill across the room. He crossed his legs and began to slip the pills into his shoe. As he slipped the first pill inside he began to wonder if stopping Bessy from taking her medicine was the best choice. *What are the pills for? Is she irrational, schizophrenic, manic-depressive? Does she have a heart condition, diabetes or high blood pressure? Is one a pain killer? I hope she is not a psychopath or psychotic. If so, she could be dangerous.* A brief smile flashed as he pictured Bessy manhandling Otman. By the time he slipped the last pill into his shoe, he had become concerned. Massaging his temples, he hoped she would be rational.

Again remembering Shelly had not returned, he felt deserted. He began to wonder if she had abandoned him. If so, would he ever see her again? "Come on Bessy," said Arthur, heavy heartedly. "I want to turn in early for the evening."

Loneliness engulfed Arthur as he slowly escorted Bessy into the lounge area. The accumulation of pills began to move under the ball of his foot and his heel. Stepping on the pills, sharp pain raced up his leg. Arthur's shuffle gave way to a shuffle followed by a limp.

Seeing Otman heading his direction, Arthur feared hobbling might cause him to ask one of the nurses to have a look at his foot.

Unable to walk on the pills, Arthur began dragging his foot, like another resident he had witnessed earlier. To his surprise, Otman only laughed as he passed the two lovebirds. Arthur gritted his teeth, keeping his cool.

Bessy tugged on his arm. "Come on Harry. Please watch TV with me."

He was about to insist on returning to her room, but he saw Walter sitting on the couch, staring at the television. "Okay, but only for a little while."

Excitedly, Bessy tugged Arthur over to the couch as he tried to avoid the pain shooting up his leg. When she sat down on the couch, she glanced over at Walter. "Harry, there's your fishing buddy, Walter."

Just then, Otman reappeared. Worried she would continue talking about his fishing buddy, and afraid Otman might suspect something, Arthur pulled Bessy close to him and whispered, "Bessy, are you ready for bed?" He prayed that the diversion would cause Bessy to forget about watching television and agree to leave.

Grinning, Bessy leaned into Arthur and whispered. "Why Harry, I thought you'd never ask."

Arthur felt uneasy seeing the twinkle in Bessy's eyes.

As she stood, she looked back at Walter. Arthur could sense another question about Walter rising in her mind. Not taking any chances, Arthur sprang up off the couch, grabbed her hand and pulled her away from the television.

Eager to return to her room, Bessy began pulling Arthur down wing one. The pain in his foot was replaced by the concern that Bessy had misunderstood his request to leave. Arthur could not believe how Bessy was taking his act seriously. He feared what would happen next.

CHAPTER THIRTY-SEVEN

The moment Bessy pulled Arthur into her room, she began unbuttoning her blouse. Arthur's eyes bulged in disbelief. There was no way he was going to bed with her. If it meant passing out now rather than later in bed with Bessy, he would.

"Hey, what are the two of you doing in this room?" the deep growl boomed.

"Uhh . . ." Arthur stuttered.

"Get out. This is my room," Bessy blurted in a shrill voice, "we're married."

Arthur stood motionless, unable to speak. He was concerned with Bessy's actions, and wondered if she really needed the medicine he had kept from her to control her aggressiveness. Aware that Otman would not tolerate a disturbance, Arthur watched Otman's hands, fearing he would pull out a syringe and inject some tranquilizers into both of them.

"Oh, it's you two old lovebirds. Pardon me."

Otman snickered as he exited the room, slamming the door behind him. Concerned that he might be standing outside Bessy's room, Arthur felt trapped inside. Bessy instantly pulled her unbuttoned blouse off. Shocked, Arthur's jaw dropped as his eyes rolled to the ceiling not wanting to view Bessy as she finished undressing.

"Undress, Harry!"

Arthur did not know how to respond. He no longer wanted to be Harry.

"Harry! Come and get me," she baited. Arthur saw her slip between the twin-bed sheets wearing only her undergarments.

With Arthur's stomach tightening in knots, he knew something needed to be said quickly, but nothing seemed to be appropriate. *There is no telling what she will do if I refuse. She could burst out screaming, throw things, have an emotional breakdown, or do something else strange to cause Otman to rush back in.* His fingers fumbled with the shirt's first button. All of a sudden, pain shot through his foot, reminding him he hadn't gotten rid of the pills. *Maybe I can give her some of these pills to calm her down. I shouldn't have stopped her from taking them.*

"Harry, you're still shy," Bessy interrupted his thoughts. "Turn off the lights and come to bed." She lay patting Arthur's side of the bed.

Arthur didn't know what to do. Silence filled the room as he felt his heart pounding, realizing she expected him to climb into the twin bed with her. His stomach churned, cramping violently at the horror of climbing into her small bed. As he bent over to pull his shoes off, his face turned pale.

"Harry, what's wrong? You look sick," Bessy said sitting up.

Seizing the excuse needed, Arthur grabbed his stomach. "Bessy, I'm sorry, but I think it was something I ate."

Bessy tossed the sheets off her half-clad body and slipped out of bed. Arthur shuddered seeing Bessy coming toward him dressed in flimsy undergarments. He wished she was wearing undergarments that his grandmother would have worn. At least then she would have been fully covered.

At the touch of Bessy's cold skin hugging his neck, an icy shiver raced across his body, causing the hairs to rise. "Sex can wait," Bessy said.

Arthur gritted his teeth as his eyes squinted closed, drawing up the skin on his face. "Sex!" Arthur's throat muscles constricted.

"Harry, you're shaking. You better lie down." She pulled Arthur over to her bed and helped him sit on the edge of the bed. "Harry, slip off those pants." She reached for his waist but Arthur's hands reached his belt buckle first.

"Turn loose or else," he said as he sprung off the bed and raced to the bathroom. Each step sent sharp pains racing up his leg as the pills pressed against the sole of his foot. Stepping into the bathroom, he shut the door and grabbed the toilet just in case his stomach retched.

"Harry, stop acting shy. I have seen you in the bathroom many times."

Arthur knew she had not seen *him* without clothes on and he was hoping to keep it that way. With the pain still throbbing in his foot, he slipped off the shoe concealing the pills and quickly dumped them into the toilet and flushed. His stomach eased with relief. Feeling safe inside the bathroom, he decided to stay longer.

Knock . . . Knock . . . She softly rapped on the door.

"Do you want me to call for a nurse?"

Hope drained from his body. He could not risk Otman or that nurse administering any drugs. "No. I'm feeling better."

Remembering Bessy's demand to remove his pants and not wanting further argument, Arthur slipped off his pants, turned off the light and opened the door.

As he stepped into the room wearing his boxers, Arthur was thankful Bessy had turned off the lights. "Climb in, Harry." She patted the bed again. Arthur reluctantly slipped under the covers. Bessy used the opportunity to snuggle close to Arthur, causing him to cringe.

"Good night, Harry." Bessy leaned over on top of Arthur, kissing him on the lips. Her cold naked body pressed against him. Shivers of disgust shuddered through his body. His throat swelled as gagging reverberated. He fought the urge to return to the bathroom, fearing Bessy would call for a nurse. Swallowing hard, he tried to relax.

"Good night, Bessy," Arthur murmured wanting to quickly fall asleep. He refused to focus on his predicament. *One, two, three—* the white sheep leaped across the imaginary fence. His attentiveness to each sheep included their hooves, tails, eyes—anything to keep his thoughts off Bessy. He did not care how many sheep he had to count before he fell asleep. He was not going to allow himself to envision Bessy's body. The thought continued to cause his stomach to churn.

After a few minutes had passed, Bessy's warm breath fell into Arthur's ear, "Harry, if you wake in the middle of the night and feel better, wake me. I won't mind."

Arthur expressed a little snort, pretending he was asleep. He dared not answer her.

Bessy snuggled against him, her hot breath tormenting the hairs on the back of his neck.

Arthur could not sleep with the thought that a total stranger, old and naked, was lying next to him. He again wondered if she was insane. *What happened to the real Harry? Did she kill him? If so, does she even know she did? Is she going try and kill me in the middle of the night?* Afraid of what might happen during the night, he decided to stay awake.

In a momentary reprieve from this living nightmare, he thought of Walter and wondered how he was doing. Hopefully he would be okay in the morning.

Eventually gray sheep crossed his vision and heavy breathing replaced the quiet; the black sheep blended into the darkness.

CHAPTER THIRTY-EIGHT

Justin snuggled beside Connie in bed. "By noon Monday everything will be in place and we'll just disappear."

Connie ran her hand over Justin's hairless chest. "I can picture us lying in the sand on a sunny beach, sipping piña coladas as you rub tanning oil over my body."

"Shall I start now with that oil rub?" Justin laughed.

"I think Shelly needs her medicine."

Justin looked at the clock on the night stand. "I don't know. Maybe we should wait another hour or two."

"Are you kidding? We'll be asleep then. I'll give it to her," she said as she rolled out from under the top sheet and put on Shelly's robe.

Connie slipped into the bathroom and retrieved the bottle of pills. She shook one into her hand. *Hmm, two's better than one.* She stepped into the room that Shelly had prepared for Arthur. "Shelly, wake up. It's time for your medicine. Open up and swallow," Connie instructed as she pushed two pills between Shelly's lips. Then she picked up the glass of water on top of the night stand. "Here you go; take a sip."

Shelly struggled to wake up. Her puffy eyes strained unsuccessfully to focus. She gagged as she swallowed. Water ran down both sides of her mouth and splashed on the sheet, and her head hit the pillow.

She'll sleep real good tonight.

Connie returned to the master bedroom. Her eyes sparkled in the candle-lit room. Justin sat up in bed and next to him was a silver tray with a bottle of white wine and two long-stemmed glasses. Justin had arranged crackers and slices of cheese on the rest of the tray.

"Wow, a picnic at midnight. How romantic."

"How's our guest?"

"Fine. I gave her two tablets."

"Two!" Justin said and almost toppled the bottle of wine. "Is that safe?"

"Relax. It's only .5mg. That's the maximum recommended. We will be able to sleep late tomorrow morning before she'll need her next dose."

"I'll bet she won't need it until tomorrow afternoon," he said, looking happy as he filled both glasses.

Connie untied the robe and let it slip off her shoulders and slipped back into bed. Justin handed her a glass. The two glasses met together in an unspoken toast. Smiling at each other, they sipped their wine and ate cheese and crackers.

Justin looked at Connie. He reached out and took her glass and the tray and set them on the floor. She smiled. "My thoughts exactly. Finally, we're together. It's been worth the long wait."

CHAPTER THIRTY-NINE

"RAPE—RAPE!" echoed off the white walls.

Arthur stiffened as the shrill scream echoed in his ears. His dream world shattered as he jolted, sitting up in bed. "Bessy's crazy!" Arthur gasped, rubbing his eyes. Confused, his eyes narrowed on the lady standing pressed against the wall, wrapped in a sheet. Arthur wondered where Bessy was and who this was. He turned his head left and right looking for Bessy, but didn't see her.

"Help!" the woman screamed again, easing toward the door.

"Stop screaming," Arthur whispered. Her hair, a matted mess—kinked and knotted—stood away from her head. She vaguely looked like Bessy, but her skin was less wrinkled and appeared softer and younger. His concentration moved to the door knob she was fixing to grab. "I didn't rape you. We're in danger."

Her eyes were wide with fright.

"Bessy," Arthur breathed. Now that he was certain of who she was.

Puzzled at this man calling her by name, she pulled the bed sheet snugly against her body as air rushed into her lungs. "I wake up in bed with you. I don't have a stitch of clothes on, and you expect me to believe you didn't rape me."

"Yes, I'm telling the truth; please give me a chance to explain." He marveled at Bessy's appearance. *How could she change that much overnight? But what happened to her memory? Why doesn't she recognize me?* "Please don't yell," he pleaded again. "I'm Arthur McCullen. Last night, you dragged me to . . ." Arthur glanced at the door as if he was expecting someone. "Trust me. We're in trouble. Someone's going to come bursting through that door and investigate your screams." Arthur's gaze was on the door as he spoke rapidly. "If we don't act like people in a nursing home, no telling what they'll do to both of us."

"A nursing home? What do . . ." Bessy's face cringed as her head tilted to the side with disbelief.

". . . When the door opens, don't talk. Let me do all the. . . ."

The door swung open, slamming into the wall. Otman's enormous body filled the doorway.

Bessy felt exposed and pulled the sheet tighter. She eased down the wall, away from the strange man. His intrusive stares caused her to shiver. More afraid of this man who just entered than Arthur, Bessy remained quiet.

Observing the situation, Otman began to smirk. "Harry, you devil you. Have you been naughty? Did you do what I think the two of you did?" Laughing with a devious snort, he turned around. The air in the room vibrated as the door was firmly pulled closed.

"You'd better hurry and explain why my clothes were off this morning and why you are standing in your boxer shorts."

"Keep whispering, otherwise that man might hear you. If he finds out we are not under the influence of drugs, we'll be in great danger."

Bessy's eyes warned Arthur that she wasn't trusting a thing he said. There was much he needed to explain, hopefully he could do that to her satisfaction before it was too late.

With an impulsive look back at Bessy, Arthur was astonished at how the absence of drugs from Bessy's body had revealed a different person. Bessy was still shooting daggers, so reluctantly

Arthur twisted his body around. "Please get dressed and then we can talk," Arthur instructed. "I can explain everything. If you listen to what's going on and you still don't believe me, then you can yell for help."

"All right, explain," Bessy spoke, unable to keep the distrust out of her voice. Keeping an eye on the stranger, her eyes darted back and forth searching the room for her clothes. "Where are my clothes?" she snapped.

"Some are on the floor," Arthur pointed to Bessy's blouse and skirt strewn where she had dropped them last night in her haste to get to bed. "And the rest are on that dresser."

Staring at the faded, wrinkled clothes, she shook her head adamantly. "Those are not my clothes."

"Well, those are the ones you wore yesterday and the day before. Try them on and I guarantee they'll fit."

Cringing, wrapped in the top sheet, Bessy waddled to the blouse and reluctantly bent down. Gingerly she touched the disgusting blouse. "This isn't mine!"

Arthur nodded, "Slip it on. You'll see that it fits."

"I think not!"

"Well, I don't believe you want to wear that sheet all day."

Reluctantly Bessy stepped over to the mid-length skirt, lying crumpled on the floor. Then she moved to the dresser, where she stared at the old worn-out panties and bra. She gritted her teeth as she picked up both pieces. "How disgusting!"

Waiting for Bessy to dress, Arthur tried to contemplate where to begin explaining Bessy's situation. He couldn't get over how bright her face and eyes appeared.

"If you look while I'm dressing, I'll scream," Bessy warned.

"I promise not to look," Arthur answered with exasperation as he closed his eyes.

Bessy was adamant that she was not going to wear those soiled smelly undergarments, so she looked through the dresser for some clean ones. They didn't look any better, but at least they were clean. She found a clean but wrinkled gray shirt, and a pair of faded black slacks, crumpled in the bottom drawer. "These aren't mine either," she mumbled to herself.

She slowly released the sheet, which fell around her ankles. Wincing, she reluctantly pulled on the undergarments, pants, and then the blouse. "Okay, you may turn around and begin explaining," she said, as the last button slipped through the hole.

Arthur's face turned red realizing he was standing in his boxer shorts. "May I put on my pants, please?"

"I swear nothing happened last night," he said as he hopped on one leg and pushed his foot into the leg hole. "I'm Arthur McCullen. You believe I'm Harry, your husband."

"My husband?" Bessy said. "I don't think so. I don't even know you."

"We're not married."

"I'm confused," she shook her head with disbelief.

Arthur had never witnessed a person on drugs; he didn't know how the chemical substance could make a person appear aged. Her face was now relaxed. The harsh wrinkles had softened. Her voice seemed more relaxed, like a younger woman. Her movements were quicker.

"I'm telling the truth," Arthur continued explaining. "I don't know anything about you other than your first name is Bessy. You were in this nursing home before I arrived."

"I'm where?" Bessy interrupted, standing rigid.

"You're at Southern Retirement Community, in West Palm Beach, Florida. I don't know how you got here, but my son-in-law had me committed through the court system."

"I'm leaving." Bessy turned, moving toward the door.

"Wait!" Unable to finish snapping his pants, he held them together and rushed toward the door. "You can't leave." Arthur's fingers pressed the snap into place. "If you try, Otman, that terrible man you just met, will inject you with drugs. Lately, he's been trying to overdose some of his patients, me in particular."

Bessy backed away from Arthur and the door, having seen Otman she believed that he was capable of anything. Her eyes were wide open.

"Don't panic," Arthur said, trying to encourage her. "My daughter Shelly is supposed to be coming to get me out of here. She came once, but Otman drugged me so I couldn't talk to her. She can get you out, too. We just have to be patient and pretend that we really belong in here. If Otman or his nurses suspect something different, they'll do something terrible to us."

"But why? What did I do? I can't remember anything." Bessy sat on the bed.

With frequent glances at Bessy, Arthur could not stop admiring her charm. He stepped over to where his shirt lay on the floor. With his right hand swooping to the floor, he snatched it up and began putting his arms through each hole. "Breakfast is being served. We'd better get down to the cafeteria."

"Not until you explain further."

"All right. First of all, this is your room. Last night while you were on drugs, you pulled me into your room and tried to seduce me."

"I did not!"

"Before the door was closed, you were unbuttoning your blouse. And in bed. . ." Arthur stopped his explanation. He figured telling her the whole story was nonproductive. "But nothing happened. I swear! You fell asleep and so did I. Then this morning you woke up and didn't remember who I was—and here we are."

Arthur stepped over to Bessy. "Listen, if we miss breakfast, we'll draw attention to ourselves. We cannot risk that. Please trust me a little longer. I don't know any more about you than you know about me. But if we are going to survive, for now, we must trust each other."

"Bessy, you look like you don't believe me. If you want to find out more about this place and yourself, then you'll have to act like nothing has changed. Just follow my lead and watch the other people here. If you act like them, the staff will leave you alone. As you walk down the hall, always shuffle and amble along. Never get in a hurry."

Arthur reached out and grabbed Bessy's hand. "Come on. We need to be in the cafeteria now."

Bessy jerked her hand away from his. "I'm not going to hold a stranger's hand!"

"Bessy," Arthur said, annoyed, "you started this so called husband and wife arrangement. You must act the part or Otman will suspect something. Just give it a little time; you'll see I'm telling the truth. I might do something you won't like, but I promise never to mistreat you. If you have to close your eyes and grit out the moment, please do it. That's how I get through the tough times."

Again, Arthur reached out and took Bessy's hand. Reluctantly she decided to trust him for a few minutes. As they ambled down the hall, Arthur whispered, "Your name is Bessy. I'm your husband, Harry. All the nurses here know your story and are playing along with our actions."

Bessy took long strides almost pulling Arthur along. "Bessy," Arthur whispered, "slow down, you must shuffle like me. This is how you moved yesterday. The staff will notice the change." Bessy began shuffling as they passed the nurse's desk. Arthur gritted his teeth as they passed Otman.

"Hey Harry. Did you know what to do with her last night?"

Bessy turned looking at Otman. Arthur could see her lips separating. He could not let her speak. "Bessy, I love you," he spoke loudly. "Shh," he whispered as he pretended to kiss her. Their lips never touched.

Bessy lowered her head as she felt Arthur's breath blowing on her lips.

"Shh," Arthur whispered again.

Not understanding what was happening, but disliking Otman, she shuffled along. "Thanks," she could not remember the name she was to call him, "and I love you," she added trying to be convincing.

The two continued on their way to breakfast. "I'm sorry, I forgot your name," she whispered.

"Harry," he said in a low voice.

As they stepped into the cafeteria, Bessy looked at her new surroundings. "Harry, I want to sit over there, by the window," she said, pulling him to the table where the sun was shining. Bessy admired the puffy clouds floating across the brilliant blue sky. Her eyes followed a sparrow diving past the window.

Arthur scanned the small patio. He had never stopped to admire its quaintness. His gaze was interrupted as their breakfast trays were placed in front of them.

"Harry, or whoever you are," the soft voice drifted into Arthur's ears. "Please finish explaining," she requested, staring at the three piles of mush on her plate. "What's this?"

Preoccupied, Arthur shrugged his shoulders. "What's what?"

"This stuff on my plate."

Smiling, Arthur turned his attention to Bessy. "That's pureed food. They serve it so that no one will choke on their food, especially for those with no teeth."

Bessy picked up her spoon, while Arthur watched. Slowly she scooped up a small portion and smelled. She wrinkled her nose and said, "It smells like eggs."

"That's what I tell myself and then I eat it quickly."

Bessy brought the spoon up to her lips and tasted. "It does taste like eggs," and then she put the rest into her mouth.

Arthur watched as she gagged. He smiled as he remembered the first time he had tried the puree. "Swallow quickly. That's what I do. You'll eventually get used to the texture. I'm still learning to tolerate it." And then he scooped up the yellowish puree and swallowed.

Bessy gagged two more times, once as she tried the oatmeal, and again trying another bite of eggs. "How long did you say it will take to get used to this?"

Arthur smiled, "Not too long."

As she lifted her last bite, she asked, "What else can you explain to me?"

"I can't think of much more to explain right now. I'm sure I'll think of something later, but until I do, how about telling me your last name?"

Bessy closed her eyes as she searched her mind. Opening her eyes, she shook her head, "I can't remember."

When they had almost finished eating, a female nurse stepped up to their table. "Bessy, it's time to take your medicine."

Arthur's body stiffened.

CHAPTER FORTY

Bessy looked at the nurse, puzzled.

"Bessy, you take these pills every morning. Please take and swallow them," the nurse instructed, her patience waning.

Arthur sat paralyzed. He did not want Bessy to swallow any medicine. He'd forgotten to explain the do's and don'ts about taking medicine. He had to stop her from swallowing the pills or else Bessy would revert back to her old self. He was beginning to enjoy her charm.

Bessy's eyes glanced over at Arthur as she waited for her next clue.

"Dear, let me help you take your medicine." Arthur reached out for the small paper cup holding the capsules. The nurse smiled and allowed him to take the cup.

"Thank you, Arthur, for helping." After giving the cup to Arthur, she turned to walk away.

"Here you go, Bessy. Open your mouth," he said and then mouthed the words. "Act like you are swallowing the pills." With the pills concealed in the palm of Arthur's hand, he pretended to drop the five pills into her mouth.

Bessy gulped as she faked swallowing.

"Sorry," Arthur mouthed, "I forgot to warn you. I'll explain later." Scratching at his ankle, he stuffed the pills inside his shoe. Sitting straight in his seat, Arthur noticed Walter ambling around in the cafeteria. His gait was short and slow. He continued ambling up one side of the tables, then back down the other side.

"Here's your medicine Arthur, I mean Harry." The nurse held out the cup for him to take. Arthur pretended to swallow the pills and the nurse left.

Arthur's heart sank wondering if Walter was really hurt. "Bessy, I'm finished eating." He pushed his breakfast tray away. "I'd like to leave now."

"I'm almost finished, dear."

Arthur twitched in his seat. Ignoring Bessy, he stood to leave, but Bessy grabbed his hand and pulled him down. "Not yet. I'm eating."

"Bessy, there isn't any food left on your plate."

"How's my acting?" she whispered, her eyes glittering brightly.

Arthur was relieved and smiled. "Nice," he muttered.

Standing to leave, Arthur grimaced as Walter shuffled slowly back into the cafeteria, heading straight at him.

"Come on," Bessy said, pulling at Arthur's hand trying to leave.

With all employees gone from the cafeteria, Walter hurried over to Arthur. "I'm feeling better today. I've had to up my acting," he whispered. "I'm planning to rest most of the day in my room. I'll talk with you later." Walter turned and ambled from the cafeteria.

Down wing one, Bessy and Arthur sat on the edge of Bessy's bed.

"Okay, Arthur, I mean Harry—whoever you are," smiling, she continued, "I'd like to hear more about this place, you, me, and why that nurse called you Arthur."

"Okay. My name is Arthur McCullen. I operated my own heating and air-conditioning business for years, until I retired seven years ago. But, please don't call me Arthur. That name will get us killed." Arthur paused, mesmerized by Bessy's younger appearance.

"Yessss," Bessy said teasing as she noticed Arthur gazing into her eyes.

272

"Oh, I'm . . ." Arthur sheepishly eased his gaze away from Bessy. "I did not mean to uhh. . . ."

"No harm done," Bessy attempted to cover her smile, but a small grin emerged. *He certainly is charming.* "So, I'm to call you Harry. Continue."

". . . and I ended up here, locked away, against my will. The employees working in this section believe our minds are no longer functioning properly. You know, Alzheimer patients or something like that. For our safety, we have to continue making them believe our minds are gone. There is one employee, Otman, who seems to be keeping an eye on me. If he suspects that my mind is functioning properly, he'll inject me with drugs. Two nights ago, he injected me with an overdose of tranquilizers and tried to kill me. I don't trust him. He'll do it again and now you are at risk, too."

Bessy leaned away from Arthur like he had a disease, no longer smiling. "Why me?"

"I don't know, other than you're with me." The air in the room seemed to chill as he spoke of the unknown danger. "We just have to be careful," his voice lowered as he looked at the door, "just until Shelly comes to get us."

Bessy eased over next to Arthur. She quivered.

Feeling the bed shaking and Bessy beside him, Arthur reached his arm around her and pulled them snugly together. Realizing what he had done, he instantly withdrew his arm.

"Oh, I don't mind," said Bessy earnestly, feeling protected. "You said we're married," she smiled. "Didn't you?"

Arthur grinned as he quickly replaced his arm around Bessy.

Relaxed, feeling safe, Bessy teased, "And we slept together?"

"No," Arthur blushed, "not like you're implying. We just *slept* together—well, you made me—I promise to sleep in my bed tonight."

Bessy smiled as Arthur continued to blush. "We'll see. It might be very dangerous for us to split up," she teased. "Anything else that I'm to be blamed for?"

"No . . ." Arthur mumbled, rubbing his head. "Well, I believe that's it. No, come to think about it," Arthur smirked, ". . . I'm to be blamed for our kissing."

"You took advantage of me!"

"It was an innocent kiss. I was only trying to save us from Otman."

"That's understandable," Bessy said with delight.

"It is . . ." Arthur stopped short. At first he had not wanted to kiss her withered lips, but now her lips were plump and reddish.

"Well . . . I had to." Lifting his chest, Arthur felt heroic. Either the room was getting hot or he was. "You were about to take some medicine and I had to create a diversion. So while I kissed you, I slipped the pills away from you. The kiss must have startled you. You forgot about your medicine."

"I did?" Bessy tried not to show her smile. There was something about Arthur that seemed to warm her. After all, he was somewhat attractive. "Do you plan to continue kissing me?"

"Well," embarrassed, Arthur hesitated in answering her question.

"Is that a yes or no?"

"Actually, the first kiss happened in my bedroom after Otman injected me with an overdose. Walter helped flush the drugs from my body. He told me to act like the other residents and Otman would leave me alone. So, when you came into my room screeching a sing-song, 'Har-ry, good–morn–ing,' you drew Otman's attention and he came charging into my room. So, I pretended to be your husband. He was not buying my act and that's when I kissed you." Arthur held his breath wondering what Bessy's response would be.

"So, is that a yes . . . or no?" Bessy held her breath, anticipating a yes.

"Come to think about it," Arthur grinned, "we've been kissing almost since we met. You smacked me with a wet one, just minutes after I arrived." Arthur thought about how he had wiped away her slobber and decided not to tell *everything*.

Seeing Arthur's flushed cheeks, she grinned and answered her own question, "Sounds like kisses, pecks, smooches, and smacks are compulsive and inescapable."

Arthur laughed, "If you put it that way, I'll do *my* part."

"And I'll do my part." Bessy paused briefly, "Now, tell me who I am."

"I don't know. I have only been here a few days. You sought me out asking, 'Harry is that you?' That's all I know about you. I was hoping you could tell me something about yourself."

Bessy sat quietly searching answers. "I'm sorry, but the only person that I seem to know is you."

"And remember the guy that bumped into me as we left breakfast, his name is Walter. Otman tried to overdose him too," Arthur said.

Arthur was glad to be snuggling with Bessy. He just wished they were anywhere other than here at Southern Retirement Community.

Bessy enjoyed Arthur's presence. She liked this stranger who made her smile. He was exciting, daring, protective, and handsome for his age. He still had all of his teeth. She just smiled, but her face soon clouded. *Who am I and how did I get here?*

CHAPTER FORTY-ONE

Otman hurried from the lobby, into the corridor, past the cafeteria, and stepped into a private office. Janet, twenty-eight, was anxiously waiting in her small office for her job evaluation and the possibility of a promotion. Her black hair, cut below the ears, exposed her thick neck. At five foot eight inches, her body swamped the chair. She was a highly trusted employee. A young nurse, with high ambitions and a high degree of loyalty, she had built the trust of her supervisors. She followed instructions perfectly. She was eager to please the administrators. Not married and with no boyfriend, her long hours at work exemplified her ambition of making supervisor of nurses by the time she was thirty. She did everything asked, without questions.

Otman sat down in the wooden chair across the desk from Janet and held his yellow pad. With a quick turn of the top sheet, he began. "Janet, we have a position that has just become available. It's a job promotion. Your supervisors believe that you can do the job. I have been given the responsibility to verify whether or not you're qualified. I'll need to ask you a few questions."

"First question, do you follow instructions given to you by your supervisors?" He already knew the answer, but not trusting others, he wanted to verify for himself.

Janet, who took work seriously, was sitting up straight, paying full attention to every word spoken. "Yes, sir. I believe if a supervisor gives instruction for a particular task to be completed, then by all means available, I should complete that task."

Otman was pleased with his first impression of Janet. Her answer and attitude were perfect for the job at hand.

"Next question, Janet. Do you second guess your supervisor's directions?"

"No, sir. I believe my supervisor is only following his or her job specification, which has been handed down by his or her supervisor. A chain of command should never be second guessed. It's just like the military. Everyone is given a specific job to do and when someone fails to complete the given job, it just makes the tasks for the others harder. Someone else must pick up the uncompleted task."

Otman's mind was made up. Janet was a team player.

"Janet, if you'll excuse me for a minute, I'll be right back."

Janet waited eagerly for his decision and he soon returned.

"Janet, you have been promoted to Nurse Supervisor in Ward C. If you live up to your work ethics, you'll go far within this organization. Here is your new company identification badge."

Janet held the badge, looked at her picture, and read the inscription. "Janet Baldwin, Nurse Supervisor, Ward C." She beamed as she read her new title one more time. "I won't disappoint you," she said looking at him. *One more promotion and I'll be supervisor of all nurses.*

Janet's composure and confidence assured Otman that he'd chosen the right person. "Remember our motto, 'We Give Professional Services.' In Ward C we expect the residents to be watched to prevent accidents. It's our responsibility to insure that each resident takes his or her meds correctly. Accurate medical records must be kept on each resident. Housekeeping and maintenance are very important with the elderly. They prevent accidents. And remember to give each resident the care and services that provide the best quality of life. I want you to begin today. Don't worry about any paper work or job tasks today, just familiarize yourself with those who work in Ward C and the residents. Janet, I'm expecting great things from you. I know you can do the job. Don't let me down and congratulations." He stuck out his hand and shook hers. He knew the residents would never push her around.

"Thank you, Mr. Otman. You can count on me. When it comes to service, I'm a zealot," she said.

Janet pulled off her old badge and proudly attached her new identification.

"Oh, one last thing. I demand strict confidentiality."

"Yes sir."

"Good, because in Ward C, you'll be asked many questions about the residents by visitors and if that person isn't their guardian and you answer them, you have breached patient/client privileges. The State of Florida could revoke your nursing license. And if a lawsuit is filed, it will be costly for both you and this corporation. You don't want to lose your license and your job. If someone asks you a medical question, refer them to the administration office. That way you'll never be accused."

Janet stood listening and remembered how her nursing teachers had drilled this into her.

"You're free to go," he said, while entering notes into Janet's personnel file.

Janet charged out of the room, head held high.

CHAPTER FORTY-TWO

The double doors swung open and Janet stepped inside Ward C. She stood tall and looked around her new surroundings. Many of the residents were huddled around the TV. A few ambled in the hallways and one older woman shuffled past her heading for the double doors.

"Excuse me," Janet said, catching the woman's arm and stopping her. "Where are you going?"

The woman stared back at her with a puzzled look. "Ow, you're hurting me."

"I'm Janet, the new Nurse Supervisor," she said as she released her tight grip. "Why don't we find a place in front of the TV?"

The woman smiled and then joined the others who were watching as Gilligan dropped a coconut on the Skipper's head. Bessy was glued to the show laughing along with the others.

Arthur had grown bored. *I wonder what's keeping Shelly. Something's got to be wrong or she would have been here by now and gotten me out of this awful place.* He looked around the room, trying to figure a way out. He became nervous as he noticed a shadow ease up to the sitting area and stand motionless over the group. Arthur resisted the temptation to turn and see who it was.

As Janet looked at each of the residents, she noticed something different about two of them, the man and the woman who were sitting close together. She couldn't quite put her finger on what made them stand out from the others, but something was different. She made her way over to the desk to begin looking through the folders on each resident. There, she began to familiarize herself with each person's medications and conditions.

Arthur sensed that the person behind him had moved on. He peered over the top of the sofa so that he could see who had been standing there. He noticed a new nurse sitting at the desk shuffling through folders. He turned back around, not wanting to draw attention to himself. *Who is she and what is she searching for?*

From time to time Janet would look up and watch what was going on in the room and then return to her folders.

"How's it going?"

Janet was startled. She hadn't heard Otman approach. "Fine. I'm looking over the patients' folders. It won't be long before I can put names with faces."

Arthur recognized Otman's voice and cringed. *Great, what's he up to?*

Otman looked at the desk and shifted folders around until he found Arthur's folder. "I've got a minute. Let me introduce you to one of them." He opened Arthur's file and handed it to her.

Arthur heard his name mentioned and wondered what to do. His eyes locked on the TV, but he listened as Otman yelled, "Arthur."

Otman stepped over to the sitting area. Janet followed. "That's Arthur," he said pointing.

Arthur didn't flinch, but kept his eyes on the show.

"Arthur!"

Again, Arthur remained in control.

Bessy wanted to look, but knowing that Otman was the one causing all of the commotion, she felt she should ignore it and did.

Otman turned to Janet and explained. "I forgot. He thinks he's Harry, Bessy's husband." Instantly he turned around and looked at Arthur. "Harry," he barked.

This time residents simultaneously said, "Shhh!" Arthur looked up at him and then back at the TV.

Otman stepped away from the sitting room and motioned for Janet to follow. He reached for Walter's file and said, "I don't have time to introduce you to Walter right now, but you'll probably find him in his room, resting. He's not doing very well. Go down there later and introduce yourself to him. Oh, and also look at the file on Bessy."

"Keep an eye on Arthur, Bessy, and Walter," Arthur heard Mr. Otman's instructions. He wondered why Janet had been brought in. He had to warn Walter.

An hour had passed and Arthur had not moved off the couch. Bessy did not know what to do. She waited for Arthur to make a move. He had snuggled against her and appeared to be absorbed in Seinfield.

Janet continued to sit at the desk taking notes and kept an eye on both Arthur and Bessy. She had noticed something different about their eyes. Most residents' eyes appeared hazed as if they didn't know where or what they were doing. Theirs were not. She assumed with their daily drug consumption, their eyes should not be clear. She was going to impress Mr. Otman on her first day.

Janet crept around the couch without anyone noticing her. "Harry," she said, hoping to catch him not recognizing the name he went by.

Arthur nuzzled against Bessy laughing at Kramer.

"Arthur!" she said, knowing that he'd respond.

"Shhh!" someone hissed as they watched Kramer tip-toe into Seinfeld's room. Arthur never looked up at her, but watched as Kramer opened the refrigerator door.

Bessy pulled his hand into her lap and held it with both hands. She didn't know what to do. Her fingers quivered.

Angered at not being responded to, Janet grabbed Arthur's shoulders and began shaking his body. "Look at me when I call your name."

Arthur looked at the bridge of Janet's nose trying to avoid direct eye contact. She stopped shaking him.

Knowing that she hadn't trapped Arthur, she let go and walked away. She decided to try something else and headed down wing three.

Arthur watched fearing she was headed to Walter's room. He wished he'd had time to warn Walter about Janet. All he could do was sit and hope that Walter didn't fall for anything she threw his way. Unconcerned about Seinfeld, he kept glancing at wing three wondering what was happening.

In about ten minutes, Janet marched from wing three. Arthur bit his lip to keep from smiling as he wondered what Walter had done to cause her to become enraged. He could sense she hadn't given up on her quest to gather information on the three of them. Round two would start soon.

Janet shot a couple of cold glances over toward Arthur and Bessy knowing it was a matter of time before she uncovered the mystery. She was determined to prove to Mr. Otman that he had chosen the right person by promoting her. Because he had warned her that the three seemed to be acting strangely, especially Arthur and Walter, she sensed that Arthur was trouble and was determined to catch him.

Arthur felt Janet's stares. Feeling uncomfortable, he asked Bessy if she minded leaving the lounge and going back to her room; she quickly agreed. As they stepped into wing one, the hairs on his neck tingled. He knew Janet was watching everything they did.

"What's wrong?" Bessy asked closing the door to her room.

"Janet," he replied.

"Don't let her get to you. We're smarter than she is," Bessy said grinning.

Suddenly the door swung open and Bessy's grin disappeared.

Janet rushed inside. "Whose room is this?"

"Mine," Bessy said puffing up and putting her hands on Janet trying to push her out of the room. "Get out!"

"Stop that Bessy," she snapped trying to free Bessy's hands from her chest. "Arthur, get out of Bessy's room."

Arthur turned away from her and climbed into the bed.

"Arthur!" she demanded, "Get out of Bessy's bed."

Otman, who was about to enter Ward C, heard Janet's ranting and burst through the double doors rushing inside. *Janet's caught Arthur,* he told himself as residents looked down wing one. "Get out of the way," he shouted as he rushed past. Stepping inside the room gasping for air he demanded, "What's the problem?"

"Arthur's in Bessy's bed," she said, pointing to Arthur stretched out with his hands behind his head and eyes closed.

"Get out!" Bessy shouted stamping her foot at Janet. "Now!"

"Calm down," Otman shouted holding up both hands as if he were separating a cat fight. "Come on Janet, let's leave them alone and step outside for a moment."

Janet, red faced, followed him into the hallway leaving the door ajar. He stopped a few feet from the door. "Bessy's mind's gone. You'll never make any sense to her."

"Are you sure?" she answered.

"Definitely. She's been looking for her husband for years and she thinks Arthur is Harry," he said smiling.

Arthur heard Otman's mumbled explanation and wanting to hear everything, crept over to the door to listen.

"Bessy's crazy, but like I said before, I have my doubts about Arthur. I'm not convinced that he's really demented. Keep an eye out for him and Walter. If you see any normal behavior, let me know." Otman rubbed his forehead and began to grin. As he thought, the grin expanded hideously. "You know Janet, you might have come upon the right solution. We might need to separate Bessy from Arthur. Give me tonight to think what I should do and tomorrow I'll come back for her. If he's pulled the wool over my eyes, I'm fixing to snatch it away," he said watching Bessy's door.

Arthur gulped as his eyes grew large. *What would Otman do to Bessy?* He didn't want to imagine. *That man will stop at nothing. Shelly, where are you?*

CHAPTER FORTY-THREE

Walter spent most of the day in his room resting except for the visit by Janet and the light stretching exercises he had done earlier. As he lay in bed, he wondered how much longer both Arthur and he would survive. With Arthur still locked up and with Shelly apparently unable to remove Arthur from this institution, he feared they didn't have many days left. It was almost dinner and he was feeling better, but his ribs remained sore to the touch. He didn't care. He had conceived an idea for escape, had massaged it, and now had the perfect plan for tomorrow. He couldn't wait to tell Arthur. Sunday afternoons brought many visitors.

Arthur and Bessy stayed the rest of the afternoon in her bedroom. Arthur told stories of Shelly growing up, like the time she tried to make pancakes for him at the age of seven and how the box had slipped from her fingers and hit the floor, casting a cloud of pancake mix into the air. But Bessy had no memory and could not share stories of her identity. Arthur knew the drugs had stolen those memories and wondered if with time she would regain her past. She was enjoying listening to Arthur's stories, but she wished she could remember some of her own.

"I'll tell you more about my life after dinner. I'm hungry," Arthur said as he helped Bessy off the bed.

"So am I," she said scooting off the bed.

She's charming, he thought as she stood beside the bed. He grinned as he watched her shuffle to the door, keeping up the act.

In the lounge area, Janet watched as they shuffled past the desk. She sensed that Bessy wasn't as crazy as Otman thought. She was going to follow them to the cafeteria and keep a close eye on them.

Walter sat alone at the window. As Arthur entered the cafeteria, Walter gave a slight nod of his head.

Arthur was glad to know Walter was all right. Not wanting to draw attention, he and Bessy sat across the room at a table of ladies. As Janet entered the room, Arthur nonchalantly nudged Bessy and nodded toward the door.

"Thanks," Bessy mumbled and took a drink of water.

Arthur gagged on the first bite of pureed mush.

Janet heard and stared at him.

Bessy froze momentarily and then scooped a spoon of brownish puree and swallowed.

Arthur knew he was being watched and coughed, spraying puree onto the table.

That's disgusting, Janet thought and turned away to look at Walter.

Arthur longed to chew a piece of steak as he lifted another spoon to his mouth holding his breath.

Janet walked from one table to the next trying to familiarize herself with the other residents, but her main focus was on Arthur. He was the one Otman specifically said to watch. Something about Arthur seemed to grate at her. She knew from looking at the residents' records that he was the youngest man in Ward C. His stature and eyes were not like the others. As she watched she'd tell herself, *patient . . . just be patient and he'll make a mistake.*

Arthur kept his eyes downcast. With his peripheral vision, he kept track of her every move. He wished she'd leave.

At the window, Walter sat patiently wanting to tell Arthur his plans about tomorrow's escape. As Janet walked by the table, he pushed his fingers through the greenish puree—vegetables—and then licked the food from his fingers, never acknowledging the lady in the white coat.

Janet sneered, wondering what was going through his mind, if anything. As the residents ate, she kept walking from table to table watching the three in particular. When their plates had a small amount of food left, she stepped from the room. After a brief absence she returned and in her hand she carried three paper cups with individual names written along the bottom: Arthur, Bessy, and Walter.

"Arthur," Janet said, approaching the table. Without any acknowledgment, she nudged him on the shoulder. "Here's your medicine," she said pulling one pill from the cup.

Arthur reached up for the cup and to his surprise, she dropped a single pill into his hand. He couldn't believe she was going to give him one pill at a time. Ignoring her, he scooped up a bite of the greenish puree and put it in his mouth.

"Swallow your pill," Janet demanded, pushing the spoon from his mouth.

With the pill in his left hand and the water glass in his right hand, he lifted the glass for a drink. The back wash turned the water a dull green instantly.

Janet cringed. "Gross!" she said as her eyes twitched.

He popped the first pill into his mouth and acted like he was chasing it down with the murky water, but spit it into the green muck.

Janet smirked as she watched him *swallow* each pill individually. He wasn't going to pull anything over on her. "Open your mouth," she said after he swallowed his last pill. Reaching into her jacket pocket, she pulled out a tongue depressor and examined his mouth. Satisfied he had not hidden the pills in his mouth, she put his empty pill cup on the table.

Bessy assumed he hadn't swallowed the pills, but wondered how he could have completed this sleight of hand.

Janet turned around and said, "Bessy, here's your medicine."

With a puppy-eyed look, Bessy turned eagerly and looked at Janet, who was holding the cup of five pills. She reached out and took the pill cup. Slowly she turned around, noticing that she was being watched, and lethargically lifted the water glass. Then her head tilted forward and rested the cup on her lower lip; next she raised her head and the cup. She followed it with a glass of water and swallowed.

Arthur, aghast at seeing the cup emptying into her mouth, hoped that he could get her to the bathroom in time to throw them up, before they could take effect.

Janet knew that they had taken their medicine. It would hold them through the night. Satisfied, she scampered over to Walter. "Here," she said, giving him his cup. As he took the cup, she looked back at Arthur with apprehension. *If he's really taking the pills then why don't his eyes show it?*

Walter quickly dumped the pills into his hand and into his lap, before she turned around. As she turned around, Walter pulled the paper cup from his mouth and gulped.

Janet snapped her head around and walked over to the doorway. There she watched the residents as they left.

Walter was disappointed knowing he'd have to wait until later to tell Arthur his plan. He slowly rose and ambled—dragging a foot—past Janet.

Bessy stood and pulled on Arthur's hand. "Come on. I'm tired."

Arthur rose quickly. If Bessy had swallowed those pills, she needed to get them out of her stomach.

"Slow down," she mumbled.

They held hands as they shuffled past Janet.

Janet watched Arthur and Bessy until they were out of sight, down wing one.

CHAPTER FORTY-FOUR

"Hurry Bessy, we need to get to your room, so you can throw up those pills."

"Slow down, it's okay. I didn't swallow them."

"What! But I saw you."

"No, I poked a hole in the bottom of my cup. I've got them in my hand," opening her hand slightly, she showed him.

"You sure fooled Janet—and me too."

Arthur stayed with her until the lights in the hallway dimmed for the night and he felt it was safe to leave Bessy's room.

"Good night," Arthur said as he stepped toward the door.

"Wait," Bessy exclaimed.

Arthur stopped and turned around.

"I'd like to take a shower. Would you mind keeping watch while I bathe?"

"Sure," he said.

Bessy stepped into the bathroom and shut the door.

Arthur sat on the corner of the bed. The soft sounds of the spraying water caused him to lean back in the bed. He hadn't seen her cleaned up and wondered what she'd look like when she stepped from the bathroom. Glancing at the bedroom door and then to the bathroom door, he was glad to be alone. A tickle of excitement stirred within him.

Concerned with his appearance, he scooted off the bed and stepped over to the dresser mirror. Analyzing his reflection, he shuddered at the thought of not having had a shower himself. He rubbed through his stubbled face and unkempt hair. He patted at his hair, trying to press it into place, but it was no use. As he licked his finger, hoping to wet the hair into place, the bathroom door swung open.

Bessy emerged wearing a tightly wrapped towel. "I forgot to take clean clothes with me," she said.

Arthur stood shell shocked. Her skin, a light tan and smooth, looked soft and beautiful—he had not seen a woman like that since his wife died. His heart raced with excitement.

"Are you okay?" Bessy asked jokingly, but concerned.

"I'm sorry," he said, turning and looking away.

Bessy beamed as she hurried over to where he stood, brushing against him. "Excuse me, please. I need to get my clothes out of one of these drawers."

"Oh," he said, feeling the warmth of her body and taking another glance at her before moving. He could smell the rose scent on her body. His heart raced.

She opened the top drawer, but did not like anything there. Opening the next drawer, she quickly pushed it closed too. Then, she hesitantly pulled open the bottom drawer. Cringing, she pushed it closed and started with the next row of drawers. But she found all of those drawers to be empty. With a little shudder, she pulled open the first drawer again. "Whose are these? They're disgusting," she murmured pushing garments aside. At the bottom of the drawer was the newest looking nightgown. A few years old and the least frayed. Withdrawing it, she held it up to herself.

"That'll look good on you," Arthur said.

"Thanks." Bessy stepped back into the bathroom and closed the door. The towel dropped to the floor. Gently, she slipped the nightgown over her head and brushed out the wrinkles. With a quick glance in the mirror, she was satisfied and stepped out into the bedroom.

Arthur stood in silent awe. Before he could make a fool of himself, he stepped to the bedroom door. "I'll see you in the morning."

"Wait!" Bessy pleaded as she hurried to his side. Her lips pressed against his lips.

"What's that for?" Arthur asked, pleasantly surprised.

"Um . . ." Bessy stuttered. "Oh that was a spontaneous diversion. I thought I should practice just in case, you know." Bessy bit her lower lip, trying not to show delight.

"Sure," Arthur smiled. "In case Otman and Janet need a little convincing." When he turned to leave, Bessy grabbed his arm.

"Wait," she said as her mind searched for her next words. "Didn't you say earlier that if we were to survive, we needed to stay together?"

"Well . . . yes, something like that." Arthur's eyebrows rose. "And what are you proposing?"

Bessy shyly lowered her eyes. "If you leave me alone tonight, won't I be in danger?"

Arthur's heart beat with excitement. "Well, I hadn't thought about that, but now that you mentioned it," he knew she was right, "yes, maybe I should stay."

Raising her eyes and looking at Arthur's exuberant face, she tugged on his hand. "Stay."

Arthur could hardly breathe, as his chest pounded. "I can't," he wheezed remembering the image in the mirror. "I've got to go back to my room. I need a shower."

"Don't be silly," she said gleaming. "You can use my shower and I'll share my bed with you again."

Arthur hurried into the bathroom, closing the door.

Bessy giggled. "Isn't he adorable?"

The hot water sprayed on his face as steam billowed inside the shower. The steam and hot water quickly relaxed Arthur and his breathing returned to normal. As his fingers lathered the shampoo into his hair, he heard the bathroom door open. The shower curtain screened their identity.

Water hissed from the sink faucet.

Pulling the edge of the curtain back, he could see Bessy standing at the sink, washing something. Easing the shower curtain back into place, he moved away from it against the cold tile wall. "Uh, Bessy," he said.

"Yes," she answered, "I'll just be a minute. I promise not to look," she said smiling, having already looked.

Modestly, he watched both edges of the curtain while he washed the soap from his hair, his heart once again pounding.

In the hazed mirror, Bessy watched as Arthur's silhouette bent over and washed his legs.

As the water rinsed the soap from his body, he wondered how much longer she'd be before leaving. "Are you almost finished?" he asked.

"Almost. Do you need me to wash your back?" she asked knowing he'd refuse.

"No!" he snapped, hoping the reply didn't come across negatively.

With the water spraying off his back, he carefully pulled the edge of the curtain back. "Uh," he gasped, as the curtain fell back into place. Bessy was looking at him. *How could she? She promised not to look.*

"I'm done," she said pulling the door closed behind her.

When he pulled the curtain back, he saw his wet clothes hanging across the towel holders. He couldn't believe she'd washed his clothes. Pulling the curtain around his body, he breathed, "Bessy!"

"Yes," she answered opening the door with a grin.

"What am I going to wear? You've washed my clothes."

"They'll be dry in the morning. Keep the big towel dry and wrap yourself in it. It'll look like a bath robe. You can sleep in it, can't you?"

Arthur didn't have a choice. It was either wear the towel or nothing and he wasn't doing the latter. "Okay," he sighed, still holding the curtain tightly around his body.

"Do you mind?" she said teasing. "You could wear something of mine."

"No, thank you."

Bessy stood in the doorway watching him.

"A little privacy?"

"Just pretend I'm not here," she said grinning from ear to ear. She wondered in her previous life if she had teased like this.

"Please," Arthur begged.

"Oh, all right." Smiling, she turned and closed the door.

Arthur hurriedly stepped out of the shower and dried himself off before she returned. Once dry he wrapped the large towel around his body. He felt strange, clothed with a towel, and hesitated to open the bathroom door. *What if the towel falls off?* His hand froze; he couldn't open the door.

The door swung open. "What's taking you so long?" Bessy's eyes quickly glanced at his attire. "Nice," she teased.

The room was dark. The only light in the room was coming from the bathroom.

"Come on," Bessy said, reached for his hand and pulled him into the bedroom.

Arthur's other hand kept a tight grip on the towel.

"You're so cute wrapped in that towel," she said, wanting to pat his butt.

Arthur eased into bed; one hand held the top of the towel tight, while his other hand held the bottom down, so not to expose himself.

Bessy stepped back to the bathroom and pulled the door closed. A small amount of light emitted into the bedroom. She slipped between the sheets and leaned over Arthur. "Goodnight," she said, and kissed him on the lips. "Just practicing."

"Good night." Arthur held tightly to the towel hoping it would not slip off during the night. As he lay motionless and with closed eyes, he reflected on Bessy's changed appearance. It was amazing what drugs did to the human body. He shuddered at the thought of Bessy being given an injection like Walter and he had received.

Drugs! Suddenly he opened his eyes and the darkness seemed to momentarily swirl. *Drugs cause people to do things that they wouldn't generally do: like standing up in a boat before it stopped on the canal's bank; putting a car into drive inside a garage; attempting to fix a gas leak without first ventilating the room; cutting down a large tree without help; or, breaking out a window pane with an elbow. How did Justin drug me? Whatever drug he used, it caused me to use poor judgment.* Arthur fell asleep trying to figure out how he had been drugged.

Bessy lay in bed staring at the dark ceiling. Her cheeks sagged as she tried to recollect her past. *How can I not remember my past? Who am I? Where is home?* As she searched for some clue, her hand inadvertently fell against Arthur's side. "Uh," she breathed and then started to remove her hand. Before she did, she changed her mind and left her hand at his side. The distraction sent wonderful images through her mind of the day's activities. Thinking about their last kiss, she fell asleep.

Walter lay in bed, rolling from one side to the other wondering who this new nurse was and where she had come from. He hadn't seen her before and didn't like the way she kept a watch on them. Sensing it was more Arthur, than Bessy or himself, he didn't dare sneak out from his room tonight. He'd risk telling Arthur his plan at breakfast. After rehearsing his escape numerous times, his eyes slowly closed. Soon he was asleep.

CHAPTER FORTY-FIVE

In the morning, the door opened from the bathroom. Its bright light shown in Arthur's face, waking him. Bessy stood in the doorway. Her face glowed and highlighted her beautiful cheeks and nose. Her captivating green eyes held Arthur spellbound. He quickly felt for the towel, making sure he was properly covered. He was glad to know he was.

"Good morning," she said with delight.

"Good morning." Arthur smiled, feeling wonderful. "That's the best night's sleep I've had since being locked up."

"Are you taking me out for breakfast?" Bessy teased.

"Sure," Arthur answered springing off the bed holding the towel tight around his body. In the bathroom he found his clean clothes, dry; and with a quick glance at Bessy, he pulled the bathroom door closed. Arthur lifted the clothes off the towel rack and hurriedly dressed before she *accidentally* opened the door on him. Dressed, he stood at the sink and splashed water into his face and then patted his hair down into place. Ready for the day, he opened the door and greeted her with a tight hug.

"Don't you look bright and cheerful this morning," Bessy said squeezing him.

"Oh no," Arthur breathed. His jaw dropped as he stared at her. "Look at us. We look like visitors."

Bessy hurried over to the mirror above the dresser. Her eyes scanned from her head down to her knees. "You're right."

Arthur pulled his shirt tail out and ruffed up his hair. He glanced into the mirror.

"You've got to do better than that," Bessy said as she started to pull off her blouse. "Don't look," she teased, but he had already turned away from her. She proceeded to take the blouse off and then began wadding it up and ringing it. She held it tightly twisted and then shook out the blouse. With all the wrinkles it appeared as if she had slept in it. "Take off your clothes and wad them up. It helps."

Redressed and standing in front of the mirror, their appearances looked similar to yesterday's except the clothes were cleaner and lacked body odor.

"Hopefully no one will notice," Arthur said as he put an arm around her. "We'd best go to breakfast before someone comes looking for us."

As they walked into the cafeteria, Arthur saw Walter already eating his breakfast. Arthur led Bessy over to the table behind where Walter was sitting. With his back to Walter, Arthur sat down with Bessy beside him. Soon, their breakfast trays were placed before them. His upper lip curled at the thought of another pureed meal.

Walter glanced around the cafeteria, insuring that no employees were looking his way. With all the staff out of the room, Walter leaned backward. "Arthur," he whispered, "meet me in the men's bathroom after you eat."

"Okay."

Bessy agreed to wait for Arthur in the cafeteria. Arthur watched Walter leaving as he shoveled a bite of egg into his mouth. "I'll be right back," he mumbled, leaning against Bessy.

Arthur pushed the bathroom door open. Walter held his index finger up to his lips. Then he flushed a toilet. As the water gushed out and the door closed, he whispered, "Talk softly." Turning on a faucet, he began.

"Arthur . . ." Walter stared. "You look different today."

"Does it show? I've cleaned up."

"It's not that noticeable, I guess. It won't matter in an hour anyway. I've figured a way out of here. Today's Sunday. That means visitors after lunch. And it's Otman's day off. The added number of people scurrying around should help conceal our absence. I've noticed Bessy is not wearing an anklet like we are. If you can coach her to open the doors out of Ward C, they won't lock as we approach. Trust me, there's going to be mass confusion in Ward C. While the staff is dealing with them, all we have to do is slip out of the building, through the front door, cross the parking lot, and we'll be in the woods. They'll never catch us after that. Once away from here, we can call Shelly to pick us up."

"Bessy's feigning dementia like we are," Arthur grinned, as the water continued to splash into the sink. "I did as you taught me. I kept her from swallowing those pills. When she woke yesterday morning, her mind was miraculously clear again, although she doesn't remember her past. She wants out of here, too. She'll do anything to help."

Janet punched the time clock as she entered the employees' entrance. Checking her mail box for her daily instructions, she found a patient psychiatric evaluation form and a note attached from Mr. Otman:

Janet, I want you to get Bessy first thing this morning and take her into the office. There, complete her yearly evaluation. Be thorough in your questioning. If you finish before I arrive, keep her there. I'm taking care of some business and I'll meet you there when I'm through. Otman.

Janet picked up the form, slipped it in a folder and grabbed her coffee mug. Hot steam swirled from the mug as she left the nurses' lounge. Sipping coffee, she walked toward Ward C. The double doors swung open and she strolled up to the nurse's desk in the lounge. Looking around and not seeing anyone, she looked at her watch realizing the residents were eating breakfast.

With the folder tucked under her arm, she stepped into the cafeteria. Scanning the room, she saw that Bessy was sitting alone. Janet trudged over to her. "Bessy, will you come with me?" she asked, looking down her pudgy nose.

The voice was distinct. Suspiciously, Bessy turned and looked. Bessy knew not to go, but what else could she do? She had to find some way to stall. Arthur had warned that they should stay together. With a quick glance at the door, she wondered where he was. She did not know how to react or respond this time. She wished Arthur would return and help her.

Janet, eager to complete her first assignment, pulled on Bessy's chair, dragging her away from the table.

Remembering Arthur speaking about diversion tactics, she remembered he was in the bathroom. "I've got to pee," she said standing, holding her pants.

"Sure. Come on."

Bessy shuffled slower than usual hoping Arthur would appear. Slowly she pulled open the ladies' bathroom door and shuffled inside. *What do I do now?*

CHAPTER FORTY-SIX

Inside the men's room water continued to splash in the sink. "Walter, give me a minute before leaving, then meet me in Bessy's room. I'll have explained everything to her and we'll be ready to leave."

"Take your time. We can't leave before the chaos begins." Walter grinned. "You'll know when it's time."

Arthur meandered back to the cafeteria. His heart sank when he didn't see Bessy sitting at their table. He wondered if she had grown tired of waiting for him and had returned to her bedroom. Shuffling quickly, he headed off to wing one.

Janet was anxious to begin Bessy's evaluation. She wanted it completed before Mr. Otman arrived. She knew making a good first impression would be a lasting impression. "Let's go, Bessy," she demanded, banging on the stall. She wasn't going to disappoint him.

Walter waited for what seemed to be a long time, then he eased the door open and saw Bessy with that new nurse, Janet, exiting the ladies' bathroom. Bessy was visibly upset. Peering out from the bathroom door, he watched as Bessy was ushered into the office across from the bathroom.

Fearing their planned escape was in serious jeopardy, he hurried to warn Arthur. When he entered the cafeteria, Arthur was nowhere to be found. He hurried down to Bessy's room.

Arthur was concerned when he looked in the room. It was empty. "Bessy," he called, rushing to check out the bathroom. *Where is she?*

Arthur heard footsteps approaching from behind and hoping it was Bessy, turned around. Walter was shuffling swiftly toward him. He could tell by the expression on Walter's face that something was wrong. *Bessy?* His stomach felt queasy.

Walter grabbed Arthur and pushed him back into Bessy's room. Walter wheezed. "Arthur, that new nurse has taken Bessy to her office."

Arthur's body shuddered with anger. Adrenalin pumping, he dashed for the door.

"Wait!" Walter yelled, hoping to stop him before he got both of them into trouble.

"Let's go," Arthur said, motioning for him to follow.

"Wait," Walter pleaded, "it hasn't started yet."

Arthur looked perplexed. "What?"

"When I left the cafeteria to meet you in the bathroom, the nurse, who was carrying the morning medication, put down the tray in order to help one of the residents who had fallen. When she turned her back, it was too big of a temptation. To help our escape, I mixed up a few of the residents' pills."

Arthur saw a grin on Walter's face and knew that more than a few of the residents had received the wrong medication.

"We have to wait a little longer before the medicine has time to take effect." Walter said.

Arthur paced back and forth, sat on the bed, and paced some more. *Why did Janet take Bessy? I've got to find her.* He didn't know how long he had waited, but he had waited long enough. Just then, he heard the piercing scream.

"Ahhhhhh!" Rang throughout the hallway.

Arthur exploded off the bed. "Is that Bessy?"

"No, but chaos has just begun."

"Put me down," a lady's voice screamed.

"That sounds like one of the nurses," Arthur said.

"Yep, have a look," Walter said as he stepped out from the room.

Arthur followed and saw an elderly man slowly dragging a nurse across the lounge floor.

Walter screamed. "Help meeeeeee! They're coming to get me! No! Stop! Don't hurt me!" His hands swung wildly through the air.

Arthur grabbed hold of Walter, "What's wrong?"

Walter grinned wildly. "Come on Arthur. Everybody's medications' been mixed up. Act like the rest of us."

"Ahhhhhh!" The scream echoed down the hallway again.

"What," Arthur yelled over the lady's scream.

"It'll take hours before this place is back to normal," Walter said.

CHAPTER FORTY-SEVEN

Otman drove into the rear parking lot, between Ward B and Ward C. He climbed out of his car as a black hearse backed up to the double doors. *He's a little early,* he thought and grinned. *I'm going to need a little extra time.*

The driver of the hearse, a pudgy man, got out and opened the rear doors. Otman approached him. "It might be a little while before Mr. McCullen's body is released."

"Fine, I'll wait in the car," the driver said. He shut the rear doors and enjoyed the air-conditioning blowing in his face.

Otman slipped into his office, using the back door. He picked up the phone and dialed Janet. "This is Otman. Is Bessy still with you? . . . Good, take your time. I'll be there later. Keep her occupied till I arrive."

Otman retrieved a vile full of clear, refrigerated liquid and then pulled a syringe out of his desk drawer. After preparing the lethal dose, he pulled on a white coat and dropped the syringe into his pocket. He left the locked office and climbed on the golf cart that he used as a hearse.

Arthur laughed, "I can't believe you got away with that."

"Me either," Walter joined in.

"Come on," Arthur yelled, "We've got to go rescue Bessy."

"Not yet," Walter insisted. "There's not enough confusion in this place to hide our escape."

"Bugs! Bugs! Bugs!"

Arthur and Walter looked down the hallway to see an elderly woman yelling and swatting the air. She dashed over to the wall and slammed her hand against it with a bang. "I killed one," she said grinning as she slapped the wall with her other hand. "I got another bug." Her head spun as she watched the floor. Suddenly both of her legs began rapidly pumping up and down as her feet stomped the floor. "Help me! There are hundreds of bugs crawling everywhere."

Arthur felt sorry for the woman.

"Ahhhhh! They're all over me," she screamed.

A woman in her eighties, who had a hunched-over back, shuffled along and headed toward wing two, yelling, "I'm not! No! No, I'm not!"

A nurse heard the commotion and ran into the hallway to help. Elmer stepped in front of her and grabbed her. "Owww! Stop pulling on my shirt."

"Come on dear. Stop playing hard to get. It's you and me, together at last," Elmer said, with a toothless grin.

"What!" She snapped.

"We're made for each other. Take off your clothes."

"What!" The nurse gasped as she realized that Elmer was naked.

"Yes, my dear. I've waited a long time for you."

"I wonder what kind of pills they had him on to suppress his sexual desire?" Arthur asked.

"Elmer! You need your medicine," she yelled as she pushed Elmer away and ran back into Dorothy's room and held the door closed. *What's happening to these people?*

Elmer stood at the door and pounded on it. "Open up sweetheart." He tried to push the door open. It rattled, but did not open.

Arthur and Walter laughed knowing that the nurse would not be leaving that room anytime soon.

"Get them off of me. Get them off. Help me! They're killing me!" the woman screamed as she rolled on the floor, trying to kill the bugs.

The last nurse on the ward, stood shell-shocked, wondering where the other nurses were. She looked around the lounge area and wondered who to help first. *Oh, there are so many of them and only one of me.* There on the floor was an eighty-plus year-old woman who looked like she had just fallen asleep. She did not appear to be hurt. Another lady stood in front of the TV changing stations, screaming for help. She too did not appear to be in any physical trouble. But, the woman that was rolling on the floor screaming, seemed to be in great distress. Forgetting about the others for now, she rushed to her aid.

"What's on you Ms. Juliana? I don't see anything at all," the nurse said as she got down on her knees searching for what was attacking the woman.

"They're bugs, big bugs. Help Me!" and her arms flailed across her body.

"Stop, you're going to hurt yourself," the nurse said.

"Aaaaaa!" Jose screamed rushing to help Juliana. With a loud thud the nurse slammed into the hard floor, unconscious.

Jose rose and stood over Juliana triumphantly. "You're safe Ms. Juliana. Nothing will hurt you now." He helped her up off the floor and they walked away.

"That-a-boy Jose. That's the last nurse. We're free now," Walter said. "Who would have guessed mixing up small little pills could have caused such behavior changes and wreaked this much havoc."

"No one is going to stop us now," Arthur said.

Otman steered the golf cart hearse straight at the obscured double doors. The front bumper pushed open the doors, causing them to slam into the wall.

The ruckus caused Arthur and Walter to turn instantly. "Otman!" they said together, and headed back for Bessy's room.

The tires hissed as the hearse rolled across the tiled floor. Otman had a big grin on his face. He looked straight at them.

"He's coming for us," Walter said as he glanced around the room for some sort of weapon. He didn't find anything.

"Over here," Arthur said as he stepped to the head of Bessy's bed and pushed the headboard away from the wall. *I sure wish Shelly would walk through that door right now.*

Walter had just moved between the bed and the wall when the hearse rolled to a stop outside the room. Footsteps approached the door. "Arthur, I mean Harry," Otman called as he stepped into the room.

Arthur held his breath as he watched Otman standing just inside the doorway.

Walter stood there shaking, knowing they were moments away from death. He had never seen Otman driving the golf cart hearse unless someone was dead.

"There you two are. I see that neither of you have been taking your medicine." He took a step inside the doorway. "Walter, you may leave now. A nurse will come by your room and take care of you later."

Walter didn't move.

Sweat beaded up on Arthur's forehead.

Otman grinned as he looked at Arthur. "Harry," he laughed, "you finally get your wish; you get to leave today."

Arthur's hands trembled. He grabbed the headboard hoping Otman wouldn't notice. He had to appear confident.

"What's wrong? You scared?" Otman stuck his hand into the pocket of his jacket and pulled out the syringe. He pointed the needle into the air and depressed the plunger until a small amount of liquid squirted airborne.

Arthur elbowed Walter. "Grab the bed," he mumbled. He wanted to fight—not withstanding the fact that he was outweighed by a hundred or so pounds.

Walter followed Arthur's lead even though he didn't know what Arthur had planned. He didn't think they would be able to keep the bed between Otman and themselves; he would just climb on the bed and grab them.

"Arthur?" Otman said. His skepticism had been right; Arthur was faking his senility. He was glad that Bessy was out of the room. She'd never know what happened to her *Harry*. The muscles in Otman's face tightened and his teeth gnashed as he realized that he had been played for a fool.

"Push," Arthur yelled.

The metal bedpost scraped across the hard floor, emitting an awful screeching sound.

Otman looked at the bed and smiled. He held out his free hand as the bed approached.

Arthur's feet dug in with each push. His jaw tightened.

Otman's hand slipped off the footboard and the metal bed frame hit him at knee level.

Arthur and Walter grunted as they continued to push the bed. Shivers ran up their necks as crunching cartilage stretched, cracked, and popped as Otman's knee buckled.

"Ughhh," Otman moaned, as he hit the floor.

The bed didn't stop. It slammed into his torso, knocking the air out of him. Otman's body continued its backward fall. The bed's momentum continued. With his torso almost flat on the hard floor, the bottom of the bed frame rammed into his forehead.

Arthur and Walter stared at Otman who was lying unconscious under the bed's frame.

"Is he dead?" Walter asked, backing away from the bed, afraid Otman would wake up any moment and lash out at them. With his anger, he'd kill them where they stood.

Arthur saw a pair of scissors lying on the floor beside Otman's jacket. He picked it up and cut off his ankle bracelet. Walter stuck his leg out, and soon booth bracelets were on the floor.

"Come on," Arthur said. "We've got to get Bessy and get out of here." He jumped in the driver's seat of the golf cart and grabbed the steering wheel.

Walter climbed in beside Arthur. The wheels screeched as Arthur stomped on the gas. His legs quivered. The cart swung around and headed for the lounge.

Walter pointed toward an office door. "That's where she took Bessy."

Arthur had to jam the brakes and turn the steering wheel as he approached a woman standing beside the empty nurse's desk. Her finger was shaking in thin air over the top of the desk. "No, I'm not. No. No. No."

Arthur turned the golf cart toward the office. In a moment, they were rolling to a stop outside the door. Walter jumped off while they were still moving and ran for the door. He twisted the knob. "It's locked," he shouted.

Arthur pressed the pedal and pointed the front end of the cart toward the door. The bumper smashed into the door. The knob clanked on the floor and the door swung open.

Walter entered first. He grabbed Janet.

Bessy jumped up and helped Walter hold Janet down.

Arthur rushed in and grabbed the telephone and dialed Shelly's number.

Shelly lay in bed. A dull ringing throbbed deep in her ears. She rolled her head toward the constant ringing. Her head pounded. The ringing continued. She reached for the receiver, jostled it and knocked it to the carpet.

"Hello, . . ."Arthur said, waiting for a response.

Silence

"Hello. "That's strange," he said, as he disconnected and then re-dialed Shelly's number. This time, Arthur got a busy signal and hung up. "That's weird." Arthur sensed something was wrong.

"What's wrong?" Bessy and Walter said in unison.

"No one answered the first time I called. When I called back, it was busy."

Arthur yanked the cord from the phone and pulled it out from the wall. He stepped over to Janet and used it to bind her wrists and feet.

"Let's get out of here before security shows up," Walter said. He jumped on the golf cart and backed up.

"My hero," Bessy teased, as Arthur grabbed her hand.

Out of the corner of Arthur's eye, he saw a file folder lying on the desk. He turned to look at it. The name read: Elizabeth "Bessy" Tillman. He snatched it off the desk and stuck it under his shirt.

Bessy and Arthur jumped on the back of the cart. "Hang on," Walter said. He headed for the far double doors where Otman had entered. No one was going to know they had left until it was too late.

A woman stood beside the TV. "Shut up. Shut up. Shut up," she shouted continuously.

Arthur grinned. "She must have been the oldest sister."

Bessy nodded.

Walter rammed the doors like Otman had, and drove into the dark hallway. To his right were another set of double doors and sunlight seeped past the edges of the door. The golf cart stopped and he jumped off and peered out the door. A black hearse was waiting outside.

Arthur and Bessy stepped up and looked out, too.

"What are we going to do?" Bessy asked"

Arthur quickly formulated a plan.

Walter and Bessy sneaked out the door and down behind the hearse.

Arthur came jogging out of the building and up to the driver's door. The engine was running and the driver was leaning back in the seat, relaxed. Arthur tapped on the glass window. When the man opened the door, cool air met Arthur.

"Mr. Otman needs help with the dead man and asked if you could assist him." He hoped that this was something that the man was accustomed to doing.

As Arthur and the funeral home employee moved down the side of the hearse, Bessy and Walter moved up to the front of the hearse. As Arthur and the driver stepped inside the building, Walter ran to the driver's door and jumped in.

Bessy ran to the back and pulled herself in.

Walter pressed the brake and snatched the transmission into drive and waited. He didn't have to wait long.

Arthur ran out and jumped into the back with Bessy. "Go, go," he shouted.

Walter jammed the gas and the car lunged forward. The back tires squealed as the car sped away. The back door was snatched out of Arthur's hand before he had closed it. The door swung wildly behind.

Arthur grabbed hold of Bessy, trying to keep her from tumbling out the open door.

When Walter slammed on the brakes at the first stop sign, the door slammed shut. Hearing the pounding noise from the rear, he assumed it was the funeral employee trying to recover his stolen vehicle.

The hearse accelerated as the back end slid around the corner. Walter was amazed how well the hearse responded. He had imagined hearses as heavy and slow vehicles.

"Slow down, Walter. You're going to get us killed," Bessy screamed, the irony lost on her. It had been a long time since she had been in a vehicle.

Walter changed lanes to pass a pickup truck, then veered back into the previous lane as he passed a slower moving vehicle. With traffic spread out, the hearse continued effortlessly on its exodus.

Winding through the semi-busy streets, Bessy rolled over, kissing Arthur. His chest beat with excitement as the kiss lingered. But, the hard surface that they were lying on soon ended any romance. Arthur led the way, crawling slowly to the front

312

seat. They climbed over the seat and buckled up. He felt the folder under his shirt. He pulled it out and opened it. The first page had Bessy's personal information. When Bessy saw her name, she leaned in and together they tried to figure out who she was.

Name: Elizabeth "Bessy" Tillman
Address: 750 Royal Palm Way

"Wow," Arthur murmured. He knew the location to be an exclusive neighborhood.

DOB: 7-20-1941

Bessy's thumb hid the year. She was too late. Arthur had already seen it and knew how old she was.

Arthur smiled.

Tires squalled as Walter yelled, "Hang on."

All three bodies leaned hard to the left, squeezing Walter against the door. "Sorry. I misjudged the curve. It's been a while since I've driven."

"Walter, we're going to 750 Royal Palm Way."

"Why?" Walter asked.

"That's my address!" Bessy replied, looking out the window and wondering if they were close to her house.

Arthur gave Walter instructions on where to turn. As they got closer to Bessy's house, Arthur grew anxious. He had to know more about Bessy.

"There's the house," Arthur pointed and the hearse slowed.

Bessy leaned forward peering out the front windshield and exclaimed, "That house is mine? It's enormous!"

The three stared at the two story Mediterranean masterpiece. An eight-foot wrought-iron fence skirted the estate and double gates leading into the estate stood open. The St. Augustine grass was immaculate, freshly clipped at three inches. The asphalt driveway, neatly edged, circled in front of the house and eased around behind to the three-car garage.

The hearse eased down the road beside the fence as they continued to admire Bessy's house. "I don't recognize my house. May I walk up to the front door and look inside? It could trigger my memory."

"I don't think that would be a good idea," Walter cautioned.

"What if we come back later tonight?" Bessy pleaded.

Arthur wondered if it would be okay. He really wanted to know more about her and if this would trigger her memory, then he was all for her having that look later.

"Walter, we need to come back tonight and let Bessy look around. That is, if no one's home. The neighbors are far enough away that she would be hidden in the dark," Arthur said as he felt Bessy leaning closer against him.

Walter reluctantly agreed. "Okay, but for now, we need to hide this hearse. It looks suspicious and if a cop spots us, he'll recognize it."

Walter found an abandoned dirt driveway miles away and backed into it in case they had to make a quick get away. There, they relaxed and sat watching the evening sky showcasing its brilliant orange, salmon, red, and pink.

CHAPTER FORTY-EIGHT

"Justin!" Connie shouted as she stood beside Shelly. Her eyes were glued to the telephone receiver lying on the floor.

Shelly snorted as her eyes fluttered open. She closed her eyes against the bright light.

"What?" he answered running into the bedroom. He sucked in another breath of air. "What's wrong?"

Connie pointed to the floor. "Look! She tried to call someone."

"You don't know that. Maybe she knocked it off in her sleep."

"And maybe she tried to call someone. We can't take that chance," Connie fumed. She bent down and picked up the receiver and placed it back in its cradle and looked at Shelly.

Ring—Ring . . . Ring—Ring.

Connie jumped. "I told you she's called someone."

Justin looked and shook his head. "You're jumping to conclusions," he said reaching for the phone.

Shelly gave a couple of snorts as she breathed hard. Her body was sprawled on the disheveled sheets.

"Hello!" Justin looked at Connie and waited for a reply.

"Justin," the deep voice said.

"Who's this?" Justin answered without giving his name, just in case he needed to say I'm sorry you have the wrong number.

"This is Mr. Otman."

"I can barely hear you."

"Sorry, I'm in the emergency room. I've been trying to call you. Has anyone notified you that Arthur's escaped?"

"He escaped! When!"

Connie grew nervous as she listened.

Shelly's face relaxed, almost as if she had cracked a smile.

"A few hours ago."

Justin wanted the details but knew he didn't have time to listen for the explanation. "Thanks for the call." Justin dropped the phone back into its cradle. "You might be right about Shelly calling someone. Arthur's escaped. They might be planning to meet."

"I told you so," Connie cried out. "What are we going to do?"

Justin stood rubbing his temples. Then he began to pace beside the bed. "Maybe we should spend the night at your apartment tonight, just in case Arthur comes here."

"Why don't we just leave town?" Connie snapped. Her body trembled. "I don't want to get caught and go to jail."

"We can't leave. The paper work's not completed. I'll have to ask for a favor tomorrow. Let's hope it's granted. Give her the drugs and come on," he shouted as he ran from the room. He rushed into his bedroom and grabbed his suitcase. He quickly threw clothes into it.

Connie stood beside the night stand holding the bottle of medicine. As the bottle tilted, all the pills rolled into her palm. She counted nine tablets. "Hmm," she thought as she looked over at Shelly. "Two pills didn't work. Hmmm," she said and grinned. She looked back at the bottle and read the typed instructions. "Not to exceed two tablets. To be taken at bedtime," she read aloud. "Oh really?" and she dropped six tablets back into the bottle. "She won't be making any phone calls tonight," she said as she yanked the cord from the wall and grinned. Connie forced open Shelly's mouth. Never fully awake, Shelly swallowed the pills.

Justin closed the suitcase and lugged it to the door where Connie stood pleading, "Hurry up."

"Let's go. If anyone asks about Shelly, I'll tell them she got depressed and that I could no longer live with her. Come on."

The BMW eased off in the dark.

CHAPTER FORTY-NINE

As the night darkened and the moon had not yet risen in the sky, Walter pulled the hearse back on the street and drove back to 750 Royal Palm Way. As the hearse slowed in front of Bessy's house, Arthur opened the door and waited for the vehicle to come to a complete stop. He and Bessy jumped out and ran across the street. Standing beside the wrought-iron fence, she peered into the dark night air. All she saw was a large silhouette of the house.

Desiring a closer look, she hurriedly walked beside the fence and entered through the driveway's open gates. Arthur reluctantly followed. He feared they would become trapped.

Walter ran up to Arthur, "We can't leave the hearse beside the road. Someone will see it and call the police. I'll drive around the block and then come back and pick you up. Don't take long."

The hearse quietly eased down the wide boulevard.

Arthur looked up and down the street. Not seeing any cars approaching, he followed Bessy, who had not waited for him. He berated himself. *Why are you here? You're going to get caught.*

Catching up with Bessy, he could hear her whispering, "Come on, Arthur."

They carefully made their way up the slow rising steps to the porch. No one appeared to be at home.

Arthur tapped on the front door, hoping he wouldn't hear a dog barking.

Standing on the front porch, Bessy strained to see inside as she peered through a windowpane. Darkness obscured any identifiable object.

Bessy reached for the door knob and twisted. The door was locked. She could vividly picture a hidden key, behind one of the large flower pots, on either side of the door. She blindly reached behind the one on the right and metal tinkled. Her hand froze.

She picked the key up and slid it into the key hole. Bessy held her breath and twisted the key. The door swung open.

"Bessy!" Arthur gasped. He could see a small red blinking light flashing. "The house has a security system. We've got to get out of here."

Bessy casually walked over to the keypad and punched some numbers. The light blinked green.

Arthur let out a long sigh and then asked. "How did you know the security code?"

"I don't know," she said, shrugging her shoulders. "Come on."

Bessy seemed to know her way around the house in the dark. She ambled through the foyer without turning any lights on. Arthur followed close behind.

Walter had completed his first drive around the exclusive neighborhood. Not seeing his two companions, he decided to make another pass.

Having made their way up the marble spiraling staircase, Bessy led him down the wide hall and through a doorway. The darkness sent chills racing throughout Arthur's body. His heart beat faster with each step. Suddenly, he stiffened as a dim light arched across the room.

Bessy had found a flashlight and was searching the room. A king size, early American canopy bed graced the wooden floor. She was standing on an elaborate Persian rug.

"Turn the light off before someone sees it and calls the police," he begged as he bent over trying to keep from being illuminated from the beam of light.

The beam darted across the room, flickering on the white walls. She searched for any pictures that might help her identify who her family and friends were. Not seeing any, the beam of light stopped, revealing an old plantation desk, ten feet tall. Bessy pulled out the chair and sat down. Opening drawers, she rummaged through each, trying to discover something about her previous life. Sadly, she pushed each drawer closed. Without saying a word, she sat wondering where to look next.

"Come on. I want to go downstairs to see what I can find."

Bessy brushed against Arthur as the flashlight flickered and the light mysteriously disappeared.

Squeak.

Giggling, Bessy and Arthur landed on the soft bed, her lips pressed firmly against his.

"What . . ." Arthur was interrupted by another lingering kiss.

"I just wanted to remember what my bed felt like."

"Now that's what I call a spontaneous diversion," Arthur replied while savoring the moment.

"Arthur, this bed feels wonderful. Do you think we could just sleep here tonight?" she giggled.

"That would be great, but I don't think it will fit in the hearse." Laughing, he rolled out of bed. "Walter's waiting, we better go."

Reluctantly Bessy led the way back downstairs. She stood motionless in the living room, as the beam of light illuminated an almost life-size portrait hanging above the fireplace mantel.

Arthur could not believe how beautiful Bessy was in the portrait, painted when she was a young woman. Her hair was styled with curls that hung inches below her shoulders. The gown was a luxurious green, accentuating her eyes. Diamonds dazzled her delicate neck. The spaghetti straps graced her smooth tanned skin.

The grandfather clock's deep chimes struck eleven.

"We have to leave before someone comes home," Arthur said with great apprehension.

Bessy was disappointed that she hadn't learned anything about her past. She dismissed his comment; something seemed to be drawing her down the wide hallway. Shiny flashes of light flickered from the far room as the light beam disappeared into the hall's depths.

As Bessy passed the next room, she briefly shined the light into the room. The beam slowly arched across the cherry panel walls.

"Wow," Arthur uttered. An ornate bookcase rose from the floor to the ceiling. In front of it was an enormous mahogany desk. A couch lined one wall and above it was a picture of a Hatteras extended-deck yacht.

The old question of who Bessy was reappeared in Arthur's mind. He knew she had lived an aristocrat's life sometime before.

Bessy continued down the hall. At its end she stepped into the next room, the beam of light revealed a stainless steel double-door Sub-Zero refrigerator. The sight of the refrigerator reminded her that they hadn't eaten in quite a while.

"Food," Bessy said holding one door open.

"Yum, real food!" Arthur said ogling the treasure laden shelves. "No more puree for me." He snatched a banana off the counter, peeled it and consumed it.

After inspecting the Kentucky Fried Chicken box—two breasts, a leg and thigh, biscuits and coleslaw—she found a plastic shopping bag lying on the counter and dropped it in. "Our to-go-box," she said grinning.

Arthur grabbed a handful of apples and tossed them into the bag and closed the door. "We'd better get out of here," and he grabbed the bunch of bananas.

"This should tide us over for the night," said Bessy.

On the counter beside the refrigerator was a case of bottled water. Arthur put the bananas on top of the case and picked it up.

Passing the center island, Bessy reached above the marble counter top and opened the cherry cabinets on the right-hand side of the sink. There in the corner was a bulky key ring. Grabbing the keys, she hurried to a closed door that dwarfed her. As the door swung opened, the beam from the flashlight illuminated a candy-apple red metallic Eldorado Cadillac. Smiling, Bessy ran around the front of the car, her finger caressing the fender as she approached the driver's door. She tossed the bag of food into the back seat and sat in the driver's seat. The key slipped into the ignition and the garage door opened.

Arthur's heart pounded, fearing a neighbor would notify the authorities and they would soon be caught. He threw the bottled water and bananas into the back seat, and jumped into the passenger's seat.

Walter had finished circling the neighborhood again. He was becoming alarmed. They had been gone too long. This time he did not dare stop. The black hearse began its left-hand turn, for another round, when suddenly he heard a car's engine racing. His eyes scanned the darkness for the source of the approaching sound.

Instantly a car's silhouette appeared in front of him. Closing his eyes and gritting his teeth, he jammed the brakes. The hearse rocked violently, barely missing the Cadillac.

Opening his eyes, Walter gulped. Someone stood beside the hearse. He was caught.

"Roll down your window."

Recognizing Arthur, Walter shouted, "You scared the crap out of me."

"Let's abandon the hearse. Follow us." Arthur ran back to the car and lunged into the passenger seat.

Bessy was smiling at the smooth ride and the ease with which the Eldorado turned. The two vehicles disappeared. Five miles away, Bessy turned down a dark road.

Walter, in a hurry to ditch the hearse, drove sporadically off the road and into a thicket of bushes. The red taillights vanished as Walter shut off the hearse. He squeezed between the door frame and front seat, and slipped into the back seat of the Cadillac. The car sped away into the night and the three were safe for the moment.

Without any money, tired, and with no place to sleep, Bessy drove a couple more miles before she turned the Eldorado onto an abandoned dirt road and parked it under some low-lying branches. She pulled out the bag of fruit and the leftover chicken and biscuits.

Walter smelled the fried chicken. "I'll take a drumstick if you've got one."

Bessy reached in the box, "You're in luck," and passed it to him.

Arthur broke out the water and gave each a bottle.

Everyone was hungry. Not a word was heard as they gulped down the feast.

After eating, Arthur reclined his seat, and closed his eyes. He contemplated calling Shelly, but quickly dismissed that thought, fearing the cops were watching her place. He was glad to be free.

CHAPTER FIFTY

The shiny red Eldorado lay hidden under a cloak of darkness and branches. Arthur squirmed trying to get comfortable. Above the trees, stars twinkled brightly in the black velvet sky. Arthur wondered how they would survive without money. He knew his old bank account contained plenty of money for the three of them to live comfortably the rest of their lives, if only it hadn't been stolen. He hated Justin.

Arthur looked out the window and could see a bright star through the dense foliage. As it twinkled, he remembered as a boy finding the first star and making a wish. *I wish I had my money.*

The star's twinkle mesmerized Arthur. He sat on top of a horse riding with other men. Their long coattails flapped behind them. Small clouds of dust rose as the horses' hooves dug into the dirt road. The strangers rode through town and stopped at the bank. With synchronized movement they all dismounted. Two stood guard outside while Arthur and the others pulled their pistols and entered.

Arthur walked to the teller counter; his spurs clanged. Silence filled the bank's lobby. "Fill up that sack with all your money," he demanded. He quivered and quickly shoved the money into the sack. They fled out the front door as two customers watched, their hands still in the air.

With quick kicks, the horses thundered off, leaving a large cloud of dust and a hail of bullets behind. Arthur's trigger finger twitched with each imaginary pop.

The twinkling star reappeared as a cloud floated away. Its brightness caused Arthur to blink. His fantasy disappeared.

A devious smile spread across his face. He laughed at the thought of walking into West Palm Beach Bank and demanding money. After all, it was his.

During the night, Arthur's mind stayed active playing different scenarios of ways to make a withdrawal from his bank.

A ray of sunlight pierced the front windshield, flickered across Bessy's face, awaking her.

Arthur smiled as their eyes focused on each other. "Good morning," Arthur whispered.

"Good morning," Bessy smiled.

"Do you know where West Palm Beach Bank is on US 1?" Arthur asked softly, trying not to wake up Walter.

"No," Bessy said wondering why he wanted to know.

By the sun's position in the sky, Arthur sensed it was close to nine o'clock. "I'll show you."

Bessy didn't like the gleam in Arthur's eyes. "What are you thinking?"

"I'd like to withdraw my money from my bank." Arthur did not want to tell her his real intentions. She'd object. "It's early and there shouldn't be many people there." He smiled. He hadn't told her that Justin had taken his money.

Walter was still sleeping in the back seat when Bessy cranked the Eldorado and pulled out of their hiding place.

"Turn right," Arthur said. He was amazed at her driving skills. *How could someone remember how to drive and not remember anything else?*

On the center console lay a pair of sunglasses. Arthur nonchalantly put them on.

Bessy slowed, turned on her blinker, and pulled into the parking lot. Arthur noticed the blue handicap decal swaying from the mirror.

"Park here," Arthur said pointing to the first handicap space, "and keep the car running. Walter's asleep in the back. Don't wake him." Arthur stepped out of the Cadillac. He saw a baseball cap in the back seat and grabbed it before he shut the door. The cap, pulled down to the sunglass's top rim, fit perfectly.

Arthur walked up to the front door, opened it, and stepped in and around the security guard. Arthur cringed seeing the pistol against the guard's hip. Glad that there were no customers in the lobby, Arthur started toward one of the tellers.

You're going to get caught. Don't do it! Arthur's conscience pleaded.

Arthur stopped and turned toward the deposit slip counter. He began to wheeze. His hand trembled and his heart pounded as he picked up a deposit slip off the counter. *Maybe I should leave. This isn't a good idea.*

"Excuse me, sir."

Arthur froze. The security guard stood beside him.

"Sir, are you all right?" the guard asked.

"Well . . ." Arthur froze seeing the guard's right-hand beside the gun. "I . . . I've Parkinson's d-disease. My hands s-shake aw-f-fully." He wondered if a person with Parkinson's stuttered as they talked.

The guard put his hand on Arthur's shoulder, "Take your time, sir."

"W-Would you go outside and ask my wife to c-come inside, please?"

"Yes sir, I'd be glad to."

As the guard stepped outside, Arthur quickly moved to the closest teller. "Give me my money and don't do anything stupid."

The teller could see the guard outside, through the glass doors. Unprotected, she feared she'd be shot and killed. She opened the cash drawer and shoved money into a cloth sack. "Please don't hurt me," she begged as she pushed it across the counter.

Arthur grabbed the bag, stuffed it under his shirt, and ran for the front door. *I'm glad I don't have to jump on a horse,* he smiled until he saw Bessy getting out of the Cadillac.

Arthur immediately began shuffling. "Dear, I don't feel well. Can we go home?"

Bessy was befuddled. Her eyes questioned Arthur's statement, but climbed back into the seat. "Sure?" *What's wrong with him? He was fine a minute ago.*

The guard stepped up to Arthur and helped him into the car.

"Thank you for your help," Arthur said.

"Any time," the guard said smiling as he closed the door.

"Hurry! Get out of here," Arthur pleaded, locking the doors manually before the automatic switch had time to engage.

As the Eldorado backed up, a teller ran outside screaming, "Help, we've been robbed!"

The Cadillac lunged forward as Bessy read the lady's lips. "Stop that car!" The engine roared. The tires squealed as the car accelerated out of the parking lot and around the corner.

"What's the hurry?" Walter was groggy as he sat up and rubbed his eyes.

"Arthur, what was that lady screaming?" Bessy asked, her hands shaking.

"They would not give me my money. So, I demanded that teller give me my money."

"You . . . You robbed them?" Walter shouted.

"Not exactly."

"You did so. You robbed that bank?" Walter's eyes appeared as if they'd pop out any minute. "Great, now we have the police looking for us, too. What were you thinking?"

"We need money to live on," Arthur said.

Bessy tuned everything out except driving. Suddenly, a city police car appeared in front of her. Its blue lights flashed wildly and headed straight for her. She gripped the steering wheel fearing the cop would force her to stop.

Walter braced himself as he watched the rapidly approaching cruiser.

Bessy held her breath as the arching strobe lights and the wailing siren, intensified. The police car zoomed past and the Eldorado swayed as it collided with the turbulent air. Bessy exhaled and relaxed the grip on the steering wheel. She watched the police vehicle disappear in the rearview mirror.

Arthur sat in the front seat counting his withdrawal. "I can't believe it. I only got forty-three thousand, one hundred and fifty-seven dollars. That's not enough! We'll have to make another stop."

Bessy zoomed around another vehicle and through a yellow signal light as she sped west, out of town.

Walter sat straight up. "No way. We were lucky to get away last time. Bessy, keep driving."

Walter feared they were going to make one more withdrawal.

CHAPTER FIFTY-ONE

"Connie," Justin said with his cell phone pressed into his ear as he sat outside Judge Conlin's office. His secretary was busy typing at her computer trying to ignore his unwelcome stares. He fidgeted as air-conditioning blew down his neck, which added to the chill in the room.

"Justin," Connie spoke through gritted teeth in a low but firm voice. She looked around to make sure no one was approaching. She had sat at her desk all morning trying to appear busy, even though the computer had not been turned on. The desk's top remained spotless except for a legal pad. Lines laced the page, creating a big black blob. "Every time the phone rings, I jump. Aren't you through yet?" She sat scribbling another line on the page.

"No. The judge is still in a hearing." He lowered his voice and added, "I need you to go over to the house," he glanced at his watch again. "Shelly needs . . ." He was afraid to say any more over the phone.

"I'm not going over there by myself."

"You have to," Justin fumed under his breath.

"I'm not. What if someone is over there? What if the cops are there?"

"If you see any cops, don't stop. Call me immediately. If Arthur's there, he won't know who you are. Just tell him you have the wrong house. Shelly won't be up and moving around. You've got the house key in your drawer; take it with you and if no one is there, let yourself in. Now hurry. I hope to be through soon."

"But, . . ." the phone went dead.

Justin hung up as the judge's door opened. Three men stepped from the judge's chamber. The secretary looked up and smiled. "Have a good day."

The phone buzzed on the secretary's desk. "Julie, send Mr. Roble in."

Julie bit her lip as she resisted being rude to Justin who was still staring at her. "You may now go in."

Justin smiled as he passed her desk. "Thank you." He pulled the door closed.

Connie fumed as she walked from the law office to her car. "This is the last time I'm doing it." Her face grew brighter red.

As she approached Justin's house, Connie eased her foot off the gas. Up ahead the street was empty. *So far so good.* As the car slowed and coasted to a stop, it appeared as if the house were deserted. Cautiously, she pulled into the driveway. Her eyes quickly scanned the windows facing the street. They were empty.

As Connie knocked on the front door, her heart raced, hoping no one would answer. When no one did, she lifted the key to the door. Her hand shook and the key jangled as it slipped into the hole. The door creaked open. "Hello! Anyone home?" She held her breath. Silence drifted through the house.

Her body trembled and her heart pounded as she stepped inside and closed the door. She tried to suppress the anxiety by taking a couple of deep breaths. She hurried to the bedroom where Shelly lay.

Shelly's eyes fluttered as the overhead light came on.

"It's time for your medicine," Connie said as she stepped over to the bed.

As the bottle of sleeping pills tilted, six pills dumped into Connie's palm. Connie lifted Shelly up. Shelly's head pitched and the room spun. Connie forced open Shelly's mouth and dropped in three pills. She picked up the glass of water and held it up to Shelly's lips. "Drink." Connie looked at the three remaining pills. *I'm not coming back to do this again.* She forced the other three pills in.

"Good night," Connie said and turned out the light.

She hurried to her car and returned to work. She watched the clock. *Hurry up Justin,* she kept repeating silently to herself.

"It's done," Justin whooped as he stepped up to Connie's desk almost two hours later. "All the paperwork's done and delivered. I have the airline tickets. We're flying out . . ."

"Where have you been? I've been sitting here going nuts," Connie blurted.

"I've been tying up all loose ends. Come on. Our plane leaves in a few hours. We're flying to Switzerland . . ." Justin said.

"But you said we were going to the Caribbean. You promised I could swim every day."

"And then we'll catch another plane to Bali."

Connie smiled. "Bali!" Her eyes widened along with her smile. "Let's go."

They stopped off at Connie's apartment to pick up their luggage and then they were off to Palm Beach International Airport. At the airport Justin drove up one aisle and down the next looking for a parking place.

"I'm glad we're leaving today," Connie said as she looked at herself in the mirror on the visor. She brushed at her hair with her hand. "We'd have to get more drugs for Shelly if we were staying here tonight."

"What?" Justin wheezed and glanced at her. "There were six tablets yesterday when we left."

"Yeah and now there's none," Connie said smiling into the mirror.

"You gave her all six!" The BMW skidded to a stop.

"She gulped them all down."

"Connie! That's an overdose." He remembered what the pharmacist had advised when he picked up Arthur's medication. "We've got to do something to help her. I'm not a killer."

"I'm not a killer either. You should have told me what the pharmacist said." The smile slid into a smirk. She never did like Shelly.

Justin spun the steering wheel and began to turn the car around.

"What are you doing? You can't help her now. It's too late. The pills have been in her system for more than three hours. She's beyond help."

Justin saw an empty parking space and the car swerved into it. Perspiration formed on his forehead. "I can't believe it," he fumed looking at the car in front of him. "Hopefully we'll get out of here before someone finds her. Let's hope Arthur stays away from that house." Justin turned off the car and left the keys in the ignition and popped the trunk open.

Connie watched as Justin got out. "You forgot the keys."

Justin looked at her and smirked. "With the keys left in the ignition, it won't be long till it's stolen." He pulled out a small pin knife and pricked his finger. Blood dripped from his fingertip and landed on the driver's seat and carpet. After he smeared blood on the steering wheel and door panel, he squeezed his finger to stop the flow of blood. He asked Connie to pull out the band-aid from his shirt pocket. It was quickly wrapped around his finger. As they were pulling their luggage to the terminal, Justin said, "Sooner or later the cops will find the stolen vehicle and when they do, they'll find the blood and that poor fool will be questioned for hours about my whereabouts. The cops will suspect foul play and charge him with murder. They'll never find my body."

They disappeared into the airport terminal.

CHAPTER FIFTY-TWO

Bessy slowed the Cadillac and merged with the flow of traffic. With no blue lights in her rearview mirror, she relaxed. Cold air blew from the vents.

"We've got to make one final withdrawal and it has to be from the main bank, downtown. They have the most money," Arthur said, enjoying the cold air blowing in his face.

"That's too risky," Walter snapped.

"We can't hit all the branches; we'd get caught. Cops will be everywhere." With a long sigh, he continued, "You know, with one more withdrawal, we'll be set for life."

"Forget being set for life. We'll be sent away for life." Walter closed his eyes.

Up ahead, Bessy saw the street leading to her house.

She wanted one last look, so she steered the car into the exclusive neighborhood. Lavish mansions appeared on both sides of the street. Driveways snaked across their immaculately groomed lawns. Decorative iron fences surrounded each property.

The Eldorado slowed as Bessy gazed dreamily at her Mediterranean style house. *I wish I could remember.*

Out in the circular driveway was a black one-ton, dual-rear-wheel, Chevrolet truck. Attached to the four-door truck was a shiny black, Donzi 30ZF with twin-300 Mercury outboard engines. An aluminum triple-axle trailer cradled the thirty-foot boat.

"Wow, look at that boat. It wasn't there last night," Arthur said. He wished they had looked through the drawers last night and found out who lived there.

Walter did not share the same sentiments about the boat. He got seasick on them.

"Let's get out of here. The cops are looking for a red Eldorado. We need to hide. It's easy to spot this one," Walter said. *He wished they were heading out of town. How would they ever escape now with the cops looking for them? I can't believe we're going to rob another bank. It's just a matter of time before I'm locked up again.*

Bessy drove back to their hiding spot. She leaned over and gave Arthur a kiss and then reclined her seat.

Walter was tired of being cramped in the back seat, but it felt better than sitting in Ward C. He tried to make himself comfortable and relax.

Arthur closed his eyes. He hoped Bessy would continue to surprise him with her spontaneous kisses. His thoughts turned from her to the bank. He couldn't believe they were going to have to try another bank.

The car pitched as Bessy quickly sat up. She jingled the keys. "Look, two new GM keys and a keyless entry remote. I bet these keys fit that black truck in my driveway."

"Great thinking, Bessy," Walter said.

"What luck. With the speed of that boat, we could be in the Bahamas within one hour. Let's hope those keys work." Arthur said.

Walter suddenly didn't feel well. He rubbed his stomach. "I get seasick if the waves are big."

"Walter, do we have any other options?" Bessy asked.

"I was hoping so, but I guess not."

"If you get sick, it'll only be for an hour. You can endure an hour of seasickness for freedom, can't you?" Bessy asked.

Walter held his stomach. "Sure," he breathed hoping the Atlantic would be calm. He had heard of horror stories about waves in the Gulf Stream that resembled elephants on the horizon.

Bessie separated the GM keys and pulled out onto the street. Bessy handed Arthur the new keys and the remote.

"Wow, keys to my new truck," and Arthur laughed. "Thanks, Bessy."

As they pulled up, Arthur looked around the yard and at the mansion. It appeared to be deserted. He climbed out and ran through the open gates. Sweat ran down his back and his heart pounded. He kept glancing at the front door, expecting someone to come out at any moment. He lifted the remote and pressed the unlock button. He heard a click, grabbed the door handle, and jumped in. Black exhaust erupted from the tail pipe as the diesel engine rumbled to life. The truck and boat lumbered forward.

Up ahead, Arthur could see the Cadillac disappearing. They were to meet out of town at their hideout.

As the black truck eased to a stop along the right-of-way, Bessy and Walter emerged from the underbrush. "Walter," Bessy hollered, "throw the money in the boat."

The sack of money made a thud as it landed inside near the back of the boat.

.

CHAPTER FIFTY-THREE

The traffic was moderate on the four-lane highway. Arthur was becoming concerned as traffic zoomed past them. The truck labored pulling its heavy load. *We'll never out run the cops in this.*

"Maybe we should unhitch the boat," Arthur suggested. "It'll only slow us down."

"We can't get rid of it, how will we get to the Bahamas? You said we would be there in one hour," asked Bessy.

Arthur smiled at Bessy. "You're right. We'll keep it."

Walter couldn't believe he was going to rob a bank. The more he thought about it, the more he fidgeted and pulled at his fingernails. He had never done anything this dangerous. He hoped it was true that police didn't shoot at unarmed suspects.

Arthur removed the dark sunglasses and handed them to Walter. "People won't be able to see what you're looking at." He kept the cap for himself.

Seeing the bank's sign, Arthur applied brakes. He waited for the oncoming traffic to pass before making the turn. While waiting, he looked into the parking lot and noticed low hanging branches.

"We'll never make it under those low hanging branches. Any suggestions?"

"I have one," Bessy said. "I'll drive the truck up and down the street while you two go inside. As I pass by you can jump in. It'll be a quicker get-away."

"Sounds risky," Walter warned. "I say we skip this bank and leave the country now, before we get caught. We can sell the boat in the Bahamas before flying out."

"We can't sell it. We don't have the title," Arthur said as he found a place to switch drivers.

Walter sighed. Arthur wanted *his* money and *he* wanted to flee the country.

Bessy slid across the seat while Arthur ran around the truck and climbed in.

"Let's go," she said as the truck began to move.

As they came up to the bank, Bessy applied the brakes slowing the truck to a stop. Arthur and Walter immediately leaped out.

Arthur's body no longer trembled with the thought of taking his money. Each stride he took built confidence within him. It was, after all, his money.

Walter, angry and scared, stepped inside first. Arthur followed right behind him. The guard turned and watched them enter.

Walter froze.

Arthur stepped around the guard before he realized Walter wasn't with him.

The guard looked suspiciously at Walter. His hand inched toward his pistol.

Realizing what was happening, Arthur quickly jabbed his knuckle into the man's back. "Freeze!"

The guard didn't move.

The tellers stared in disbelief.

"Don't do anything stupid. Drop the gun on the floor," Arthur instructed the guard. The gun hit the floor. "Now kick it away from us." The gun went scooting across the floor and stopped against the far wall.

"Walter, go get my money!"

Walter hurried over to a teller and demanded, "We are here to withdraw Arthur's money. Now fill up the sacks!"

With the guard's hands in the air, the teller remembered her training. She slowly deposited stacks of bills into a sack. As she filled the sack, she pulled a crisp stack of twenty dollar bills out from the back of the drawer. Carefully she placed the stack on top. She nervously held out the sack.

Something about her movements, her eyes or something about her face, sent a warning to Arthur. He shouted, "Something's wrong."

Walter hesitated and withdrew his hand. "Please open the bag and show me the money."

With a horrified expression on her face, she slowly opened the sack.

Poof!

An aerosol of red smoke was released into the air, covering the young lady, the counter and the sack of money.

The terrorized teller broke down and cried, "Please don't hurt me!"

Walter remembered hearing that banks used dye-packs to spray bank robbers and to mark the cash. He wanted to flee, but it was too late. He was now a bank robber and fleeing without Arthur's money would cause them to rob another bank. He took a deep breath and walked to the next teller.

Through clenched teeth, he instructed the middle-age woman to fill up a clean sack with money, without any dye.

As she obeyed, Walter hollered instructions for the other tellers to do likewise.

The guard remained motionless. Arthur kept glancing out the door for Bessy and the truck.

After the woman showed Walter that the sack was free of dye, she pushed it across the counter to Walter. "Thank you for banking with us," the dysfunctional middle-age woman said, horror stricken. "Would you like a lollipop?"

"Don't mind if I do," Walter chuckled and grabbed several.

Before each teller handed him her sack of money, she was instructed to open the sack and rummage her hands deep inside.

Satisfied that the sacks were dye-free, Walter picked them up and rushed over to Arthur. The weight of the money caused his stressed-out muscles to atrophy. He juggled the sacks.

"L . . let's get out of here." One bag slipped out of his arms, and tumbled to the floor.

Arthur hoped that Walter would be able to make it safely to the truck. With his right hand still stuck into the security guard's back, he reached out and grabbed the remaining bags from Walter.

Walter bent over and picked up the lone bag at his feet.

"Everyone, turn around and look at the back wall," Arthur's voice boomed. "You," nudging the security guard, "drop your pants to the floor and put your hands high into the air."

The man unsnapped his pants and let go. Arthur eased backward, step by step toward the door, keeping watch over the employees. He hoped the guard wouldn't turn around and see he didn't have a gun.

Walter squeezed the sack of money and ran for the door. "No-o-o," Walter gasped looking out the glass door. "The truck just rolled past."

Arthur heard Walter wheezing. He knew Walter was not far from losing control. "We're going to make it. Don't worry," he said calmly. Walter looked awful. "Step outside and watch for the truck. I'll stay inside the building and keep an eye on everyone." He hoped the fresh air would calm Walter.

Standing outside in the fresh air, Walter's nerves continued to unravel. *You're going to get caught,* his inner voice warned.

Cars zoomed past, but no black truck. "Hurry up," he continued to mumble while he waited.

"It's coming. It's coming. The truck's coming." Sprinting, Walter did not wait for Arthur. His legs rapidly pumped as the money bag swung wildly.

"I mean it, don't anyone move!" Arthur commanded.

344

Arthur lugged the heavy sacks, his legs straining, his running slowed. Each step became more laborious.

Walter threw the sack of money over the boat's side and ran to the front door of the truck.

"Go - go," he yelled as he opened the door.

"Where's Arthur?" Bessy shrieked.

"He's coming. G-o-o-o!"

CHAPTER FIFTY-FOUR

Up ahead flashing lights darted wildly.

Bessy looked in her outside mirrors and could see a patrol car pull out on the four-lane boulevard, four blocks behind. The engine roared as she stepped on the gas. Thick black exhaust bellowed from the tailpipe.

"No," Arthur gasped. "WAIT!" his voice demanded, but Bessy never heard.

Arthur's lungs heaved. Air rushed in and out rapidly as he chased the truck. With the truck slowly pulling ahead, the boat and trailer were now beside him. As the boat began to pass, Arthur grunted loudly, tossing the bags of money. Up, over the side of the boat they flew. Soft thuds could be heard as the bags landed on the fiberglass flooring.

The dive platform was now beside Arthur. He stretched out his hands, leaped and barely grasped it with his fingertips. His throat was dry and scratchy as he gasped for air. *Am I having a heart attack?* His ears throbbed, blocking out the patrol car's siren, two blocks behind.

"Where's Arthur?" Bessy demanded.

"He's somewhere. Keep going," Walter screamed, leaning forward looking in the rearview mirror.

Bessy's attention was quickly diverted. A patrol car was heading straight at her.

"Hang on," Bessy warned.

Walter looked up in horror. "Bessy, you're not planning on ramming that patrol car, are you?"

The truck did not change directions or slow down. Its engine growled as the gas pedal lay on the floor. They were moments away from a head-on collision.

Walter closed his eyes. His hands braced the dashboard as the truck swerved, and its tires screeched.

The boat and trailer swerved violently, snapping instantly behind the truck as it came out of the turn.

Whoosh.

The patrol car zoomed past Arthur's head.

The trailer's tires hummed as the speed of the truck increased. Arthur's muscles throbbed as he tightened his grip on the dive platform.

Bessy wondered if they would make the curve ahead. She pressed the brakes.

The police cars were almost upon them.

Arthur wondered if they would start shooting; he did not want to be hit. The pavement rushed beneath him. With one hand he reached up and grabbed the boat's transom and climbed over. As he lifted his left leg, the truck and boat suddenly decelerated. He held on for dear life as his body's momentum tugged forward. One by one his fingers slipped off the fiberglass side and he tumbled. He slammed into the captain's chair; it stopped his forward motion. The trailer chased the truck around the curve as tires screeched across the pavement.

Cars veered out of the path, and skidded to the edge of the pavement.

Arthur lay in the floor and massaged his throbbing elbow. He was glad to be alive. After catching his breath, he pulled himself up and held onto the steering wheel.

"I see Arthur," Walter exclaimed.

"Where is he?" demanded Bessy as she gripped the steering wheel and looked into her rear view mirror. All she saw was a large boat.

"He's in the boat."

Looking in the side rearview mirror for a split second, Bessy relaxed and smiled. She could see him. Now all she had to do was lose the patrol cars.

Arthur knew that Bessy would never lose the two patrol cars behind the boat without help. Seeing a large ice chest, he picked it up and heaved it overboard.

The ice chest crashed into the pavement, its lid separating, sliding away from the tumbling bottom.

One patrol car swerved, but its front right tire ran over the chest and crunched into many pieces, scattering fragments along the roadside. Arthur watched as one tire quickly went flat. "Yes," he yelled, as he clapped his hands.

With one patrol car left, Arthur looked for something else to toss out from the boat.

The trailer started to slide as the truck went into another turn. The tires again squealed and Arthur hunched down on the floor.

The Chevy truck shook violently. Walter grabbed the dash and the door handle keeping him from being thrashed around.

Bessy fingers squeezed the steering wheel as they entered the turn. Shock emitted from her face. "Ohhhhh," she mumbled as the truck slid and skidded around the bend.

"Watch out!" Walter yelled as they approached upon a slow-moving car.

"Ohhhhhh!" Bessy moaned and jerked the truck into the other lane. The truck swerved sporadically.

The boat and trailer swerved.

Creeeeeeeeeek, the tongue of the trailer moaned.

Bessy spun the wheel in the opposite direction trying to get the truck back under control. The truck shuddered and skidded again.

The cop car was gaining on the trailer.

The boat quaked. Arthur remained crouched on the floor and held on. His body tossed one direction and then another.

Walter grabbed the dashboard and pushed. He was inching closer and closer to it.

The boat and trailer fish-tailed behind the truck. Layers of tread were ripped off.

Arthur felt the boat lean to the right. The trailer's right tire disintegrated.

The truck swerved again.

Creeeek—Craaack—POW!

The tongue of the trailer fell to the pavement. The boat rocked violently as the trailer began to spin. Arthur held his breath and closed his eyes.

"Oh No!" Bessy gasped. She saw in the rearview mirror, the boat separate from the trailer and skid behind them. "ARTHUR!" she squealed and jammed the brakes. "Walter, what do we do?"

The cop car rammed the trailer causing it to spin, flip, and teeter then become lodged under the car spraying sparks into the air.

Walter looked behind. His mind went blank. He didn't know what to do.

The truck moved erratically. Bessy kept her feet on the brakes.

The whites of Walter's eyes grew. "Go! Go! The boat's coming at us!"

Bessy stomped on the gas. The boat slid up to the back bumper and tapped it.

"Hit your brakes Bessy," Walter yelled.

Bessy held her foot on the brakes until the truck and the boat had stopped.

Two officers jumped out of their vehicle and realized there was nothing they could do.

Arthur grabbed the bags of money and heaved them overboard. He climbed down and picked up the money. Walter had the door open as he ran up. Arthur tossed the money inside and jumped in.

Off in the distance they could hear sirens.

"Go Bessy," Arthur and Walter yelled.
The truck became lost in the traffic, as the sirens faded.

CHAPTER FIFTY-FIVE

Up ahead of them a red light had stopped traffic. Bessy, Arthur, and Walter sat nervously waiting for the light to change. On the side of a brick building a billboard read: Palm Yacht Club, Next Right.

Bessy studied the sign. Large yachts were docked along piers, row after row. She thought she had seen the sign before. The light turned green and traffic moved. As they were in the intersection, Bessy turned. A sign beside the road warned: Dead End.

Walter looked at Bessy in shock. "Why did you turn? This is a dead end. We shouldn't have come this way."

Arthur was thinking the same thing. They would be trapped if a cop saw them.

Bessy looked ahead at the marina entrance. The entrance gate was open. "I think I know where I am," Bessy said with apprehension.

That got Arthur's attention. He sat up and looked around. *Maybe this will trigger her memory. Maybe she'll remember who she is.*

The truck rolled across a speed-hump as they entered the marina. Out in front of them were large yachts. "I've been here," Bessy mumbled. Her heart beat with excitement. Her eyes darted in all directions.

"I have a yacht here," Bessy said. "I wonder which one it is?"

Arthur and Walter scanned the boats.

The truck stopped and Bessy jumped out. Her eyes squinted in the bright sunlight.

"There it is," she said pointing.

Arthur looked at the end of the dock. There was the Hatteras he had seen in the picture that was hanging in Bessy's study.

"Wow," Walter said in disbelief. "Now that's a yacht."

Bessy, anxious to walk down to her yacht, left the truck in the middle of the road. Arthur grabbed the sacks of money and followed. Walter quickly moved the truck and parked it at the far end of the lot, in the bushes.

Bessy walked up the aluminum gangplank with her large key ring in her hands. She moved the keys around the ring until she found what she hoped was the right one. She slipped it in and turned. She pulled the door open and she stepped inside. Dry cool air and a hint of roses greeted her.

Walter stood on the dock mesmerized by the yacht and wondered who Bessy really was.

Arthur's senses strained as he listened, wondering if someone was on board. He was relieved not to hear any sounds.

Bessy motioned for them to come in and they did. They stood inside the pilot helm.

Walter eased the door closed. "This boat's unbelievable," he said looking at all the navigational instruments.

Bessy had a feeling that the engine keys were kept somewhere close by. At the bottom of the first drawer she opened, she found two keys. She quickly inserted each key. "They fit," she exclaimed. "We'll stay here until dark. Then we can slip out without anyone knowing we have left the country." Bessy beamed. "I love this boat. Wow, I've finally remembered something about myself."

Walter's excitement faded as he realized big yachts did not zip across the water like speed boats. "How long will it take us to get to the Bahamas?"

"Not long. Somewhere between three and five hours depending on sea conditions," Bessy said. "With this boat, we can cruise the Caribbean Islands and become lost forever. We'll each have our own stateroom."

Walter held his stomach. *Three to five hours? That's a long time.* He stepped out of the helm area, past the galley and into the salon. *Wow!* There was a leaded-glass dining table with four chairs. A white leather couch and two matching reclining chairs, sat atop plush navy-blue carpet. In front of him, along the window, was a plasma TV. He plopped down on the white leather couch and stretched out.

Bessy locked the door and led Arthur down tight spiral stairs into the sleeping quarters. At the bottom was a small sitting area with two chairs and a small built-in desk.

Bessy stepped to her left. "Come on," she said, grabbing his hand.

Arthur had hoped for a tour, but had to settle for a quick glace around. Forward was a small stateroom in the bow of the boat. All he saw were bunk beds before he was pulled around the corner. After passing two more staterooms and a long hallway, he followed Bessy into the owner's suite.

Bessy pulled Arthur toward the queen size bed. It was positioned in the center of the room. Its bedspread was sprinkled with sea life. The walls and furniture, a rich mahogany wood, stood as if they had just been polished. She pulled him into bed and smiled as she gave Arthur a kiss, a peck, a smooch, and a smack. "It's compulsive," Bessy said, her eyes gleaming, as she slipped out of bed.

"And inescapable," Arthur added with a smile as he watched Bessy close the door.

CHAPTER FIFTY-SIX

Walter's eyes strained to see through the darkness. He was amazed at how well he slept on the leather couch. Feeling refreshed, he sat up and wondered where Arthur and Bessy had gone. He crept along the window back to the front of the boat to where he had left them. Looking out the window, the marina looked deserted except for the lights shining down on the docks. "Bessie, Arthur, where are you?" Walter's voice echoed. He stood watching the floodlight shimmering off the calm water.

Arthur opened his eyes having heard Walter's call. A dim light glowed through the port-hole window. "Bessy, wake up."

Bessy moved slowly, rubbing her eyes. "What is it?"

"It's time to leave. Walter's calling us."

Arthur opened the door and stuck his head out into the hallway. "Walter, we'll be right up."

Arthur's eyes squinted as the stateroom's light was turned on.

"Turn off the light," Arthur demanded. "Someone will see us."

"We have to have lights on. Otherwise, we'll look suspicious. It's the law; all boats underway must have their running lights on. It allows other boaters to know our location and our course of movement."

"Yeah, you're right. Sorry, I'm just edgy." The hallway was dim. He was glad she had left the cabin light on. At the bottom of the stairs, he could see Walter standing at the top looking out the window.

Arthur and Walter stood in the pilot house watching Bessy studying the many gauges and levers. Her hand ran across the different switches. It was apparent that she was trying to recall the sequences of operating the yacht. "Can we do anything to help?" Arthur asked.

"No. Give me another minute or two and I'll be ready." Bessy mumbled as she twisted the starboard engine key.

The diesel engine sputtered as it cranked. Soon the chattering calmed. Twisting the other key, the port engine cranked. It too settled out and idled smoothly.

"Bring aboard the gang-plank and untie us," Bessy instructed as she climbed the steps to the flybridge.

Arthur and Walter stepped out on the deck. Walter went to the bow and untied the lines. Arthur pulled the gang-plank aboard and secured it. Then he made his way to the yacht's stern and untied the lines from the pilings.

Bessy was now on the flybridge sitting in the captain's chair. She looked behind her and kept her hands on both throttles. The navigational lights—red, green, and white—beamed brightly. The boat eased out of the slip.

As Walter climbed up to the flybridge he heard the VHF radio broadcasting the marine weather, "Seven to twelve knots, wind from the southeast. Seas—two to three feet." He hoped the winds would remain light.

The boat glided through the calm waters of the Intracoastal Waterway. Unable to locate any other boat's navigational lights, Arthur relaxed. The Hatteras soon passed the last buoy heading east, away from West Palm Beach inlet. The bow sliced through the water, rising and falling moderately in the three-foot seas.

Arthur sat on the edge of his chair scanning the horizon for other boats. With no boats visible, he leaned back in his chair and got comfortable. They had made it.

Bessy engaged the autopilot and released the steering wheel. She held her head into the breeze, breathing the cool sea air. "Isn't this nice?" she said as she slumped backward into her seat.

Walter sat with the wind in his face, relieved that he didn't feel seasick.

"I'm hungry," Bessy said as she stood. "The boat's on autopilot. You won't need to do anything except keep a look out for those two large ships," she said as she pointed to the radar screen. "I'm going down to the galley. I bet I can find us something to eat." She climbed down the steps and disappeared.

Walter did not feel like eating. He was afraid it would come back up.

Arthur looked at the radar screen—the two ships were miles away.

The lights from the city slowly disappeared as an orangish, half-moon appeared above the dark horizon. Walter had begun to relax. He was no longer concerned with becoming sick or being caught, and a smile eased across his face.

The boat sliced through the water at eighteen knots, rising and falling gently now on two-and-a-half foot waves. The stars lit up the sky.

"Hungry anyone?" Bessy said, her head rising above the ladder.

"Sure," said Arthur as he quickly stood to help with the tray of food and bottled water.

"I can't believe you found food," said Walter, now a little hungry.

"The cabinets are loaded with non-perishables. There's plenty of bottled water and canned drinks." Bessy opened the bags of Ruffles, Chips Ahoy, and pretzels. Grabbing a hand full of chocolate chip cookies and a bottle, she sat in the captain's seat. While eating, she kept watch over the boat's instruments.

The boat was performing perfectly. With the radar scanning forty-eight miles, two new blips appeared on opposite edges of the radar screen. Bessy realized one was an island in the Bahamas and assumed the other blip was another yacht heading the same direction. It was too far away to worry about. Finished eating, Bessy leaned back in her chair and relaxed. Another twenty minutes passed with the late night weighing heavily on her eyelids. Her head nodded, another few minutes passed and she was sound asleep.

Arthur leisurely scanned the horizon, looking at the many stars. A light jostled above the western horizon. Uncertain as to what the light was, he decided to have a look at the radar screen.

Overhead in the darkness a strobe light flashed. The aircraft raced to the Bahamas. Walter wished they were on that airplane. He was not much of a boater even in calm seas and could not wait to get on land.

The green screen blinked with every revolution the radar's open array antenna circled. Ten miles ahead was the first Bahamian island they would pass. A blip on their radar screen indicated a faster boat was behind them.

Concerned, he shook Bessy. "Wake up. There's a fast boat approaching from behind. What should we do?" Even though he had operated small boats all his life, he had never operated a yacht and its many gadgets and dials were overwhelming. He didn't want to break anything.

Groggy, Bessy opened one eye and then the other. She strained to focus. "Everything's fine. He'll pass us on either side. He's just riding in our wake. It's smoother there."

The seas had calmed and were now less than two feet. Walter watched the water in the bottle. It had little movement. He felt fine.

Bessy studied the radar screen. Again the blip indicated the distance between the two boats was rapidly closing. Another ten minutes and they would be overtaken.

"Let's head for that island," Bessy commented, feeling a little uneasy that the boat had not started its arch around them. She twisted the dial on the autopilot and the boat turned ten degrees to their left. "Just in case the boater doesn't see us. They'll continue on a straight course." She then turned on the VHF radio. She hoped to hear the other boat, stating its intentions as to which side it planned to pass.

Five minutes passed and Bessy grew more concerned. The boat behind them appeared to have turned their way and was heading straight at them. Bessy pushed the engine throttles forward. The boat's speed increased five knots. She kept an eye on the radar screen.

Arthur had turned around and was watching the boat. Its navigational lights were bright and high above the water.

Screech . . . Crackle. The speaker on the radio squawked. "This is the United States Coast Guard. Acknowledge your name and the name of your vessel," the voice demanded.

Crackle . . . "This is the United States Coast Guard. The ship heading east into Bahamian waters, please acknowledge your name and the name of your vessel."

CHAPTER FIFTY-SEVEN

"Don't respond. Pretend that your radio is not on or broken," Arthur advised. "Bahamian water is generally shallow. Continue heading straight for that island. That Coast Guard cutter draws more water than this boat. He can't follow us there."

Bessy held the course straight for the island. She tried pushing the throttles forward, but they were already maxed out. Her major concern now was for the unseen underwater coral. If they hit one, it would be over.

Suddenly, an intense flood light illuminated their boat as rotary blades thundered above. The blinding light radiated the flybridge. Hurricane force winds pelted their bodies, causing their hair to whip wildly.

"This is the United States Coast Guard. Please bring your boat to a stop, immediately," the P.A. speaker blared.

The three huddled together motionless. They tightly squeezed their eyes shut protecting them from the brilliant light.

Bessy fumbled blindly for the twin throttles and pulled them back. The boat began slowing. Their hearts sank knowing they were going to jail or worse, back to Southern Retirement Community.

Their boat bobbed on the waves as they waited further instructions.

"We have to do something," Walter's jittery voice broke. Raising his trembling hands above his eyes, he cupped them shielding his eyes from the light and wind. Squinting, he saw a small skiff heading toward them with four Coast Guardsmen aboard. "Bessy! There's a skiff approaching from behind. Put the boat in reverse and ram it. It'll give us a diversion. While they are rescuing their fellow Coast Guardsmen, we can make our get-a-way."

"NO," Bessy snapped as she pressed both engines' kill buttons. The twin diesel engines rumbled to a halt. "They're the U.S. Coast Guard. It would be instant death for us. They'd blow us out of the water. Act calm and let me do the talking."

The rotor blades continued to thunder overhead. The down-force pelted the deck, swirling trash around the flybridge.

"This is the United States Coast Guard calling the captain of the vessel below, identify yourself."

"This is Bessy Tillman. I am the captain of Anchors Away."

The Coast Guard cutter now hid in the darkness, its navigational lights no longer showing. It waited a couple hundred yards behind. Its large fifty millimeter gun, zeroed in on their vessel.

"Anchors Away, there are four Coast Guard officers waiting to board your vessel from the stern. Do they have permission to board, captain?"

"Yes, sir."

"Do not make any sudden movements," the PA speaker squawked.

Clunking sounds emitted from the vessel's aft as a wave pushed the skiff into the dive platform.

Their hearts sank with disbelief that they had almost made their escape. Faint footsteps could now be heard on the deck.

Walter's stomach began to feel queasy.

Their hearts pounded as two officers suddenly appeared with pistols drawn.

"How many people are on board?" the commanding officer, a lieutenant, yelled loud enough to be heard over the noise of the helicopter.

"Three," Bessy replied, holding three fingers up.

"Please stay in sight while two officers inspect below. . . ."

The rotary blades thunder-clapped while they waited anxiously on the flybridge.

"Sir, there is no one below," his radio blared.

"Ms. Tillman, whose boat is this?"

"Mine."

"I'll need to see some identification and the boat's documentation. This boat has been reported as stolen."

Bessy froze. "It—uh—it was?" she uttered surprised. Not knowing what to show the officer, she rubbed her forehead thinking. "Please follow me, sir."

The lieutenant followed, then Arthur, Walter and the other officer, whose gun was now pointed at the floor, brought up the rear.

Descending the steps to the pilot helm, the intense light diminished as did the rotor noise. Bessy suddenly remembered that her passport had always been kept in the boat's safe. "Will my passport do?" she excitedly asked, hoping the documentation was with it.

"Yes ma'am, that will verify who you are, but I'll need to see the boat's documentation."

Bessy led the lieutenant and one other guardsman down the spiral steps into the small sitting room. She pulled out a cane-back chair, sat, and moved books off the shelf, revealing a small hidden safe.

Click-click-click emanated as the combination was dialed. Clunk. The door swung open. Bessy began pulling papers out from the safe. There in her hand was an official government document. She smiled as she read, United States of America, Department of Homeland Security, United States Coast Guard, National Vessel Documentation Center, Certificate of

Documentation. Her eyes scanned down the page and there in the middle she read the words, Owner's Name: Elizabeth Tillman. She thumbed through the other documents. An uncertain feeling crept into her stomach. She didn't see her passport.

"I promise, the last time I saw my passport, it was in here."

"I have to see something that proves you are Bessy Tillman," the officer said.

Arthur and Walter remained upstairs in the pilot house wondering if Bessy had found what she needed. The other two guardsmen, whose hands hovered close to their automatic pistols, stood guard.

She reached back into the safe, desperately. *Who would have removed it? Maybe I'm not remembering correctly.*

Her fingers dragged across the safe's bottom. Hope surged as she felt a small ridge in the floor of the safe. Frantically peering inside, she made out a small booklet. She slowly lifted. Crackling sounded as it tore free from the bottom. Pulling the mysterious booklet out, the words "United States Passport" appeared.

Bessy breathed a large sigh and smiled as she handed the officer her passport.

The passport opened and Bessy's picture appeared.

"Ms. Tillman, I apologize for the wrong information we've received. There must have been some sort of a mix up. You're free to go."

With the Coast Guardsmen off her boat, Bessy started the engines. Again underway, the engines hummed as the boat sliced across the waves on its original heading. The island that they had headed for was now off their left.

They watched as the cutter turned on its navigational lights. The boat slowly turned around and its white stern light faded.

"That was close," Arthur breathed.

"Too close," Bessy said as she tried to calm her shaking body.

"Bessy, you were great back there." Walter was ecstatic with her quick thinking.

Easing back into their seats relaxing, all were smiling, knowing they were free at last.

"Captain," the radio operator on the United States Coast Guard cutter announced, rushing into the pilot house. "We've just received these faxed photos from the Florida Department of Law Enforcement. They're notifying us to be on watch for three residents from the Southern Retirement Community." Laughing, he handed the photos to the captain and added, "Can't imagine us finding three old people out here, huh Captain?"

CHAPTER FIFTY-EIGHT

The captain reached out, grabbed the pictures, and laughed. "Did you say they were Olympic swimmers?" Viewing the first picture and then the second he could hardly contain himself, "These two men are old!" Holding the last picture, he added, reading her name, "Bessy Tillman, she's a haggard old woman." His laughter rumbled inside the bridge.

"Captain, did I understand you to say Bessy Tillman?" The boarding lieutenant stammered, as his face froze rigidly stiff. "May I see her picture?"

The captain and others in the room stopped laughing.

The lieutenant chuckled as he viewed the photo, "If these ladies are the same, then the one I met has had plastic surgery. She's much younger and much more attractive."

"How many Bessy Tillmans can there be, lieutenant? Take a look at the two other photos," the captain ordered as he handed the other photos to him.

The lieutenant's jaw dropped as he scrutinized the first photograph. Quickly, he grabbed the next photograph and pulled it into view. "Captain! These are the two men who are on Anchors Away."

"Turn the cutter around," the captain ordered. "Notify Florida Department of Law Enforcement we have located the three from Southern Retirement Community and are in pursuit."

"Yes, Captain," the helmsman replied and spun the wheel to his right.

"Attention," the intercom blared with the captain's voice. "Everyone report to your post. We're in pursuit of three residents from a nursing home."

The captain put the mic down. "Careful, they're old and dangerous, I mean—breakable," and laugher erupted inside the pilot house.

Before the cutter had completed its one-hundred-and-eighty-degree turnaround, the pilot house door slammed open. The radio operator bolted inside. "Captain," he gasped for oxygen, "those three are considered dangerous and wanted for bank robbery."

"Now hear this," the intercom blared. Everyone stood motionless listening. "Full alert. Repeat, full alert. The three are considered armed and dangerous," the captain shouted. His eyes strained as he looked for the Hatteras in the dark. "Don't take any chances."

"Request backup from our helicopter," the captain snapped as he looked at the radar's green screen. "There's the boat," he pointed with his finger.

"WATCH OUT!" Walter yelled.

The Coast Guard cutter swooshed alongside them.

"Stop your engines," the cutter's PA speaker blared as a U.S. Coast Guardsman stood aiming the fifty caliber machine gun at them. "The three of you are under arrest. Put your hands into the air."

Bessy shut off the engines and the three stood with their hands high in the air. With their eyes tightly closed, they stood motionless, held captive by the light's intensity. They listened with dread as their captors' boots clattered on the fiberglass deck.

Suddenly, they were pushed to the deck as guardsmen subdued them.

"You're hurting me," Bessy moaned.

Arthur cringed as the handcuffs snapped tightly around his wrists.

Walter groaned as a knee was put in his back, pinning him to the deck.

Following instructions, one by one they were led to the back of the boat and helped down the ladder to the dive platform. A skiff jostled in the water waiting for their arrival.

Standing on the dive platform, Walter thrashed his body backward hoping to land in the water for an escape, but the guardsman's grip was unbreakable. With one quick snatch, Walter landed in the bottom of the skiff.

On board the cutter, they were escorted below deck to the brig. Their handcuffs remained snug around their wrists. Sitting in the small cell, the hum of the engines reverberated. Arthur's head hung down, his eyes clouded with moisture. He feared what awaited them.

As she looked at Arthur, Bessy's heart ached. "Arthur, you brought us this far. I believe in you. With a little more initiative we'll be free and will never go back to Southern Retirement Community. Please don't give up now."

Hearing Bessy's encouragement and remembering the excitement that she had brought back into his life, he lifted his head. Now with a weak smile on his face he looked at Bessy and then Walter. "Don't say anything to the cops. We have to be careful. We've been tricked before. We'll communicate between our attorneys."

"I can't afford an attorney," Walter griped.

Sitting straight in his seat, Arthur's shoulders lifted. "The court will appoint one for you. Between three attorneys we should be able to demonstrate to the judge our unjust imprisonment at Southern Retirement Community." He hated attorneys and he wondered what kind they'd get—probably ones straight out of college with little or no experience. He hoped out of three attorneys, one would be sharp. "Remember, whatever happens, communicate through our attorneys and we'll be able to stand strong."

Within four hours of their capture, the three were ushered off the cutter and were standing on the city docks of West Palm Beach. Seagulls squawked spiraling above the flood lights.

As a gentle sea breeze blew, a police van skidded to a stop at the end of the dock. Arthur, Walter, and Bessy were quickly ushered off the dock and into the awaiting van, then whisked away like criminals.

CHAPTER FIFTY-NINE

Shelly squirmed in her bed. Her arms and legs seemed heavy and didn't respond to instruction. Her heart raced as someone pounded on the front door. She tried to lift her head from the bed but some foreign force seemed to press her firmly in bed. Her neck muscles strained.

At the sound of a loud bang downstairs, her eyes opened wide. *Someone's in the house.* Her heart throbbed. *Get up!* she commanded herself. Unable, she pushed herself to the edge of the bed and one leg fell to the floor like lead and then the other. Slowly, she pushed herself off the bed. Her legs ached. She could not lift them to walk. Dragging one leg behind the other, she forced her way to the bedroom door. She slammed it shut and locked it.

She heard footsteps on the stairs and then in the hallway. *Oh no! They know I'm in here.* She gasped silently and pressed her body up against the door hoping the extra weight would hold the door closed if they tried to open it.

Suddenly the door jiggled. Shelly held her breath as silence filled the room. She could hear her heartbeat in both ears.

"I know you're in there," the intruder said.

"Go away," her voice faded, realizing it was Otman.

"I'll go away as soon as you open up. I've never lost a patient and Arthur's not going to be my first one. I know he's in there. Open up or I'll kick the door down. Either way, I'll get Arthur."

"He's not here." She couldn't understand why she was so tired and weak.

"All right, I'm coming in," he shouted.

The door quaked violently. Shelly stumbled away. With the next kick, the door swung open.

Shelly's heart pounded as Otman stepped into the room. "Where is he?"

She tried to move but her legs seemed petrified. Even her toes would not wiggle. Her chest pounded as her lungs rasped. *I can't breathe. I'm going to die.*

Otman took a step toward her. "Arthur!" he yelled as he looked around the room.

The next few seconds seemed like an eternity. The only noise Shelly heard was her heart pounding; she thought she would pass out. *You've got to fight,* she told herself. *Don't give up.*

"So, you want to play hardball. Okay."

Shelly wheezed and took a step backward before Otman had his hands on her.

"Now tell me where he is," he said as his grip tightened.

As pressure intensified on her biceps, moisture began to pool in her eyes. "Leave me alone."

"As soon as I have Arthur," he snarled and pushed her to the floor.

Shelly had no time to scream. Her body recoiled off the carpet. She feared what he would do after discovering that Arthur was not there. She knew her body was weak but had enough energy for one last attempt to be rid of him. Her lungs burned as she inhaled. Her body ached. Tears washed over her eyelids. *Just a little more*, she coached herself and then her lungs were full. She closed her eyes and prayed the neighbors would hear.

"Ahhhhhhhhhhh!" she screamed.

Shelly's eyes opened. Her heart pounded as her echo ricocheted around the room. Her eyes strained as she looked into the darkness. *Where is he?* Her eyes darted around the room. Her ears strained as she listened for the slightest sound. She knew he was somewhere. It would only be seconds before he pounced on her again. He was tormenting her. Her nose twitched and her throat constricted. *What's that awful smell?* She cupped her hand to her mouth and tried not to breathe as her heart raced. Her body demanded oxygen and she had to breathe. She inhaled through her mouth and hoped she wouldn't be sick. *Was Otman really here? Was that a nightmare?* She put her hand down on the carpet to push herself up. It was wet, gooey, and sticky. *Vomit!* She quickly withdrew her hand and placed it on her other side and pushed herself slowly into a sitting position. She rubbed her throbbing neck. *Where am I?* She felt tired and sore. Her stomach growled. As her eyes slowly focused, she realized she was in the guest bedroom. Dizziness swept over her. She leaned against the bed waiting for her head to clear.

CHAPTER SIXTY

Downtown, at the police headquarters, Arthur, Bessy, and Walter were escorted through the back door and ushered into the booking room. Inside the locked room, an officer removed their handcuffs. They stretched and massaged their sore shoulder muscles. Then, one by one their fingerprints were taken. Walter's fingers cracked as his prints were lifted from his fingers. Bessy stood at the sink scrubbing her fingers, trying to remove the sticky black ink. Arthur was last.

Next, the officer led them over to the mug shot camera. Arthur was positioned behind the white line on the floor. As he held his criminal number across his chest, a light instantaneously flashed.

With two more flashes their identities were locked inside a computer, intermingled among criminals.

Arthur looked at the phone. He knew he got one phone call, and he wanted it to be Shelly, but was afraid it would be wasted. *Is she mad at me? It seems like the last few days she hasn't wanted to talk to me. Last time I called, she didn't speak. Is she okay?* Arthur rubbed at his tired eyes and continued to think: *What if Justin answers the phone and doesn't let her talk to me? I'll have wasted my only phone call.*

Since neither Bessy nor Walter had anyone to call, they anxiously waited for Arthur to phone his daughter. They wanted someone they could trust to know how they had been treated before it was too late.

"Arthur, please call Shelly. There isn't anyone else to call," Walter pleaded while Bessy nodded.

Arthur knew Walter was right, but what would Justin do if he found out first. He was confused. He held his breath and dialed Shelly's number.

Shelly opened her eyes as she heard the phone ringing. The room spun as she tried to get up off the floor. Unable to lift her body, she crawled over to the night stand to get the phone. She felt across the top; the phone was missing. She moved her hand up the base of the lamp and turned the switch. The light illuminated the room, causing her to squint. Her eyes slowly adjusted to the brightness. *Where's the phone?*

Shelly tried to stand, but her legs wobbled. As the phone rang again, she crawled out into the hallway and headed down to her bedroom. The ringing stopped, but Shelly continued. She had caller I.D. and wanted to know who had called. She hoped it was Arthur.

Inside her bedroom, she pulled herself up to the phone. The overhead light allowed her to read the caller I.D. box; West Palm Beach Police Department. She breathed a sigh of relief. She was glad to know it had been a wrong number.

Shelly gagged as she smelled the odor her body emitted. She knew the carpet in the guest room had to be cleaned. She pulled herself up using the night stand and the bed. Her legs quivered. Slowly her legs strengthened and she took a small step alongside the bed. With growing confidence she stepped to the door. She used the wall in the hallway to steady her way. As she stepped into the guest room, she covered her nose. The odor saturated the room. With self determination, she made her way into the bathroom and found carpet cleaner, tissues, and air freshener.

Kneeling down on the carpet, she looked at the vomit. Her nose twitched. It was clear liquid except for six small, blueish-gray blotches that bled into the mass. She wiped at the mound

378

with a hand full of tissue. A small residue remained. She blotted it up and flushed the tissue down the toilet. She returned and sprayed carpet cleaner on the stain and air-freshener liberally into the air. She noticed a folder lying on the night stand and hurried over to pick it up. She stopped as she heard a crunching noise from under her foot. A transparent orange medicine bottle lay shattered on the floor.

Curiosity about the folder kept her moving. She picked it up and slowly opened the cover. She read the top page: Dissolution of Marriage. "What?" she gasped as she read the document and saw her name along with Justin's. Her eyes focused on the date. *What's today's date?* She made her way back to her bedroom for a calendar, but realized that she didn't know what day it was. *How long have I been asleep?* She grabbed her laptop and turned it on. As the arrow covered the time, she gasped. *Tuesday? What happened to Friday, Saturday, Sunday, and Monday?*

She scanned the documents to see when the judge had signed off on the divorce. *Yesterday? Did I sign these documents?* She looked at her signature. It appeared to be hers.

When did I sign these documents? Shelly read the date. *That's impossible. That's the day I signed Dad's guardianship papers.* Shelly slowly sat down on the bed. *Justin hid these documents in between Dad's.* She fumed as she flipped the pages until she found how their assets were to be split, then she breathed easier. The judge had given her the house, the Suburban, and the BMW. Justin got the rest and she knew it wasn't much. *What a loser.* Happy, she went into the bathroom and drew hot water into the whirlpool. As the tub filled, she showered quickly in the separate shower. She wanted to soak in clean water.

Shelly eased beneath the hot water. Her mind raced over the documents she had read. "No!" she sputtered and sat up. *I'll never be able to repay all those loans. The bank will foreclose and I'll lose everything.* She pressed the switch on the whirlpool and bubbles drowned out thoughts of Justin.

"Try phoning Shelly again," Bessy said. She knew it wouldn't be long before they would be transferred to the county jail.

The officer allowed Arthur to try again.

Arthur held the phone and listened to the ringing. He didn't know why Shelly wasn't answering. It was late at night and she should be home sleeping.

The jets thrashed bubbles into Shelly's body. Her once aching muscles now were relaxed and she felt better.

The phone in the bedroom continued to ring, but with the water splashing around her ears, she didn't hear it.

"Something's wrong! Justin has done something. I can feel it," he said as his jaw tightened. "No one's answering. We're on our own."

Bessy and Walter slumped in their seats.

"What now?" Bessy asked.

"We're doomed," Walter said, shaking his head. He cradled his head between his hands.

"Don't give up. We'll think of something," Arthur said. He hoped something would come to mind. He wished he'd never met Justin.

The metal door squeaked as it opened. "It's time for you to go. The van is here to transport you to the county jail." The guard secured the handcuffs and led the way.

CHAPTER SIXTY-ONE

Massive floodlights lit up the county jail. The van stopped outside the gated fence as they watched it open. Dawn rose on the horizon painting a pinkish mural among the clouds. A sickening feeling swept over them. With no plans and no one notified of their arrest, their hearts sank as they watched the gates close. Arthur looked around and saw the tall barbed-wire fences surrounding them. There was no escaping this time. They could never scale those fences. They were in for a long haul and it didn't look very promising.

The van door swung open. They stepped out and were led into the building. Bessy was directed through a door on the left. She turned and looked at Arthur. "Don't forget me," she said as a tear ran down her cheek.

"I'll never forget you," Arthur said. "It'll all turn out fine." He wished he could hug her one last time.

Bessy disappeared behind the closing door.

Arthur wondered if it really would turn out all right. He and Walter walked down a cold concrete hallway and through another door. He knew they were about to be frisked down like all criminals. From the looks of the outside perimeter, the institution was huge. He wondered how far apart their cells would be.

"Don't give up," Arthur said. Walter was ushered through the door first.

Walter's lip curled with a forced smile. "Right!" The guard smiled at the sarcasm. He knew they weren't going anywhere. At their age they would never see parole.

After being searched, Arthur pulled on his newly acquired cotton jumpsuit. It fit loosely. He was surprised at how comfortable it felt. He had always imaged clothing like burlap cloth, itchy and stiff. Dressed, he asked if he could make his phone call.

Reluctantly the guard handed him the phone. "Not too long," he snarled. He wanted to go back to sleep.

Shelly's skin was shriveled and the water, now warm, was no longer enjoyable. A flicker of sunlight dashed through the bathroom window. She would have forgotten about time except her stomach growled constantly telling her it was past time to eat. Stepping from the tub, she grabbed a towel and began to dry. Looking in the mirror as she buffed her back, she noticed her stomach. It looked trimmer. She turned sideways and smiled. She had lost pounds and now realized why her stomach was growling.

The phone rang. With the towel wrapped around her, she walked into the bedroom and picked up the phone.

"Hello?" she answered inquisitively, having noticed the caller I.D. indicating Palm Beach County Jail.

"Shelly, it's Dad."

"Dad," she shouted. Her heart leaped with joy. "Where are you?"

Arthur drew a deep breath. "I'm in the county jail."

Her heart sank. She dropped to the bed. "What? . . . Why? . . . Are you okay?"

"I'm fine but it's a long story. I need you to get me a good attorney. Justin stole all my money."

She bit her lip, "Dad, Justin took my money too, and he maxed out my credit cards. I can't hire you an attorney." She felt terrible. "I'm sorry," she said as her chin quivered. She took a deep breath. She couldn't speak.

Arthur could tell by the change in her voice that she was about to lose control. "Don't worry. We'll be given attorneys by the court. Everything will be fine. I've been charged with bank robbery, but it's not like that."

"Bank robbery!" she said as her head snapped up. "Dad, you'd never rob a bank. What happened?"

The guard looked at Arthur with disgust and pointed to the clock on the wall.

"Well," Arthur hesitated for a moment wondering if he should give her the whole story.

Shelly swallowed hard as she listened to his explanation of two bank withdrawals, the harrowing escape, and the capture. "Dad, you could have been killed." She froze when she heard the same words that were said weeks ago, which started the whole mess.

"I'm coming to see you," she said and finally took a breath.

"I don't think you'd be allowed to visit this early."

The guard who stood listening, shook his head. "Visitation begins at ten-thirty. She can stay for one hour."

"Are there any other times?" Arthur asked.

Arthur thought as the guard told him the times. "Shelly you might as well go to work. You can visit in the evenings after five-fifteen."

She started to argue, but Arthur cut her off.

"Okay, I'll see you at six." She knew the hours would creep by.

"Shelly, I've got to go. See you then," Arthur said as the guard gave him the look that told him his call was over. He followed him through the steel door and down the hallway until they came to a cell.

Inside, Walter sprung off the bed when he saw Arthur on the other side of the steel wall.

Arthur stepped inside and the door was slammed shut. He cringed at the sound.

"At least they put us together," Walter said.

"Yeah, I hope Bessy's okay by herself," Arthur smiled. "I finally spoke with Shelly and she's coming to see me at six."

"You finally got her? That's great."

As Shelly hung up the phone, she noticed something on the far side of the bed. She stepped over to investigate. Her mother's silver tray and two wine goblets. A couple of broken crackers and dried up cheese crumbs were piled to one side. *Who's been here?*

She shivered, at the thought of Justin bringing another woman into her bedroom. *Who shared the other glass? Connie? Was she here? Did I dream it? I thought I saw her.* She could tell from the disheveled bed that he had slept with someone. That explained why she woke up in the other room. *How could I have slept through that? Why didn't I hear them?*

She remembered seeing the broken plastic bottle on the floor in the other bedroom. Shelly maneuvered down the hallway and into the room. She scooped up the broken plastic, stretched out the label, and read; Shelly Roble. Halcion. Take at bedtime. *No wonder I felt so bad. They drugged me!*

CHAPTER SIXTY-TWO

As Shelly backed out of the driveway on the way to work, she realized that the BMW wasn't there. It was missing and Justin had to be driving it.

Shelly slipped in the back door at work; she didn't want to have to answer any questions. As soon as she reached her desk she made a call.

"Good morning," the police officer said. "This is West Palm Beach Police Department."

"Hello, um I'd like to report a missing vehicle." She was hoping to get back at Justin for ignoring the judge's ruling.

"One moment please. I'll put you through to that department."

Shelly gave the detective all the information on the car and suggested Justin might be driving it. *I'd like to be there when they handcuff him.*

The stacks of papers on her desk seemed to pile higher as the morning went along. She knew the work had to be completed, but her mind couldn't shake Justin's devious actions. She ate lunch at her desk, trying to catch up. Her progress slowed as she thought about Halcion. She gave in to her curiosity and accessed the Internet. With a few key strokes, she found it.

"A sleeping pill!" she mumbled and continued reading: Comes in two different strength tablets. The white tablet is .125mg and

385

the gray/blue is .25mg. Maximum recommended dosage, .5mg. She leaned back in her chair and thought about the broken bottle and the six bluish-gray blotches in the vomit. She gasped and covered her mouth. *He tried to kill me.* Her body began to tremble. She continued to read: Common side effects are sleepiness, drowsiness, difficulty with coordination, dizziness, and lightheadedness. Do not take if planning to drive or operate machinery. Hand-eye coordination can be affected. *Those are the same symptoms that Dad complained about.* Shelly sat rigid. *The mysterious pieces finally make sense. Justin set us up, drugged us, and has taken everything.*

"Is Shelly Roble in? I need to speak with her," a man's voice drifted over the partitioned offices.

She quickly cleared the computer screen. Shelly watched as a police officer stepped inside her cubicle. She rose and held out her hand, "I'm Shelly Roble."

"I'm Officer Newberry, a detective with the West Palm Beach Police Department."

"Please have a seat."

"Mrs. Roble, this might be hard for you but we found your BMW. We had to chase it down on Interstate 95, but we finally intercepted it and arrested the driver."

Shelly smiled. She wished she could have seen Justin's face when they slapped the handcuffs on him.

"We need you to come down to the station and verify that it's your vehicle. We didn't find Mr. Roble. The man that was driving your car was a young man in his twenties."

Shelly was surprised.

The detective followed Shelly to the police station, where he led her to the compound lot. There in a row of parked vehicles was her BMW.

After Shelly identified the vehicle, the officer escorted her inside and into a small room. "Have a seat Mrs. Roble," he said and motioned to the empty seat. "We have a few questions to ask, then you'll be free to go."

Shelly nodded her head. "Okay." She sat down facing the mirrored window.

"We found blood inside the car." He watched waiting for Shelly's reaction, but she did not show any.

"Mrs. Roble, is there something going on between you and Mr. Roble that I'm not aware of?"

Shelly sat nodding her head ever so slightly. "Yes, sir. We just got a divorce."

The room grew quiet. The detective watched Shelly's body language. She seemed distant and cold toward Justin. "Do you know where Justin is?"

"No," Shelly answered shaking her head.

"When was the last time you saw Justin?"

"Friday."

"How long has the BMW been missing?"

"I don't know. I noticed it missing this morning."

The detective scribbled in his small notebook. "What have you done since Friday?"

"I slept."

"Slept," the detective stopped writing and looked at her closely.

"I think Justin tried to kill me. He gave me an overdose."

His eyebrow rose. *She's good. I wonder what else she'll claim?* Then he turned in his seat and looked into the mirrored glass and rolled his eyes. He didn't believe her story. If someone had tried to kill her, she would have reported it. *This is going to be interesting.* "Do you have anyone that can vouch for your whereabouts since Friday?"

"No! I told you, I was drugged."

"Do you take drugs on a regular basis?"

"No! Why are you asking me these questions?"

"Have you filed a complaint against Justin for trying to give you an overdose?"

"No, I can't prove it."

"But you've made the accusation."

Shelly squirmed in her seat.

The detective smirked, knowing he had her. *Look at her twitching. Just got a divorce. She's mad at him. Blood in his car. He's missing. She did it. She killed him.*

Shelly didn't like the look in the detective's eyes. *What is he thinking?*

"Why aren't you out there looking for Justin? I woke up from a near overdose and found divorce papers on my night stand. The court signed off on our divorce Monday."

He stood. It was intimidation time. "Why do you think Justin tried to kill you? You must have some kind of proof."

Shelly looked down at the table, leaned her face in her hands, and rubbed her eyes.

"You can't prove it because it didn't happen," he shouted.

Suddenly the door swung open and a woman entered. "Newberry," his supervisor called and motioned to him. "Excuse us a minute, Mrs. Roble." The two stepped out of the room, closing the door behind them. "Calm down. We don't have any proof Justin's been killed. We don't even know if the blood belongs to him."

"Yeah, but look at her. She's guilty. Anyone can tell that."

"She might be. You haven't read her her rights. Whatever she admits to can't be used in a court of law."

"She got a divorce yesterday and today he's missing. Blood was found in his BMW. I bet it's his. This is a classic example of domestic violence and she took it upon herself to get even. Give me a little longer. I'll read her her rights. She'll crack."

"Take it easy with her. Don't screw it up," she said, pointing a finger at him.

"I won't." He opened the door and stepped inside. He stood in front of Shelly. "Mrs. Roble, you have the right to remain silent. You have the right to have legal counsel represent you. Anything you say can be used in a court of law. Do you understand your rights?"

"What!" Shelly's eyes widened. "What are you charging me with?"

"Nothing at this time, but you need to be aware of your rights," he said, sending her a suspicious look. "Do you understand your rights?"

"Yes," Shelly said nodding her head.

"Do you want your lawyer present?"

"I'm not guilty of anything. He's the one that tried to kill me," she paused, wiping her nose.

He snickered to himself.

"Aren't you going to write that down?" Shelly's face reddened.

"What did you get in your settlement?"

"The house, the Suburban, and the BMW."

"And what did the judge give to your husband?"

"Not much," and she smiled. She watched as Newberry's eyebrows raised and then realized what she just said wasn't making her look like the victim, but the villain. "I'm not answering any more questions without a lawyer present," she said as she leaned back in the chair and crossed her arms.

Newberry knew the confrontation was over for now. "Okay," he said. He knew there wasn't enough evidence to charge her with a crime, especially since Justin's body hadn't been found and the blood analysis hadn't been completed.

"You're free to go for now, but we'll be wanting to ask you more questions later. Don't leave town."

Shelly didn't say a word. Her body trembled as she stood. She hurried out of the room and down the hallway.

Newberry watched her as she left. *I think she killed him and drove his car to the airport to make it look like he caught a flight out.*

Once in her car Shelly leaned over the steering wheel and cried. *They have it all wrong. I'm the victim.*

CHAPTER SIXTY-THREE

The afternoon sun shown through the clouds as Arthur and Walter sat in their cell wondering what would happen next.

The cold steely door creaked as a guard entered. "Mr. Walter Clemmons. Please follow me."

Walter laid his empty plate down and rose. "Where am I going?" he asked as he stepped out from his cell.

"Straight ahead," the officer instructed.

Walter reluctantly followed as he moved from one hallway to the next and then entered a private room.

"Mr. Clemmons, please have a seat. Your attorney will be in to speak with you shortly." The guard closed the door as he stepped into the hallway. The door's lock clicked and silence spread across the private holding room.

Walter wondered what kind of attorney he would end up with.

Finally the door swung open and a young man wearing a polyester pinstripe suit stepped into the private room. His unscathed, plastic-leather briefcase plopped down on the table. Walter wondered if this was his first day on the job.

"Mr. Clemmons, my name is Hector Rodriguez. The court has appointed me to be your attorney."

Walter closed his eyes and slumped down in his seat.

"Mr. Clemmons, are you all right?"

Walter shook his head in disbelief. *He's just a kid. I'm doomed.* "No, I'm not fine. I'm in shock." Walter never looked up.

"Do I need to call for a doctor?"

Fearing what a doctor might inject into his body, he quickly asserted, "No thank you."

"Well that's good. I'm here as your court-appointed attorney. I have read the police report and to be frankly honest, we are going to have an uphill battle on our hands to convince a jury of your innocence."

"Excuse me, but you seem to already believe I'm guilty. I have two problems here. First, I was wrongly put into Southern Retirement Community against my wishes by Judge Blair. He's crooked. And second . . ."

"Hold on. I can't do anything about your incarceration into Southern Retirement. The only issue that I'm allowed to deal with is this crime spree that you and your two partners went on. Now what was the second problem?"

"Your age. How long have you been practicing law? Have you ever handled a case like mine?"

"Don't let my youthful appearance mislead you. I can assure you, Mr. Clemmons . . ." he said turning to look at his notes. He couldn't believe the Public Defender's office had assigned him a bank robber. He'd only handled petty theft cases during the last month—his first month on the job, ". . . I'm a fully qualified attorney. Like all practicing attorneys in Florida, I passed the Florida Bar Exam. Now, I suggest we plea bargain."

"Plea bargain, no way. That would mean a death sentence for me. They'll send me back to Southern Retirement Community. Otman will be waiting for me. Do you know who the judge is that will hear my case?"

"A judge has not been assigned, yet. The prosecution is hoping that you'll plea bargain."

"No way. I want a new lawyer—one that will believe in me."

"Sorry. The legal system does not work like that. You can fire me and represent yourself, but the courts will not give you a new lawyer without a sound reason. At this time, you don't have a justifiable excuse to ask for a different lawyer. Do you want me to stay or leave?"

Sitting in a separate holding room, Arthur waited for his attorney. He doubted the competency of any attorney, especially a court-appointed one.

The door swung open and a man appearing to be about a foot shorter than himself squeezed through the door.

"Hello, Mr. McCullen. I'm Fred Schulte, your court-appointed attorney."

Arthur stared in unbelief. The older man, heavy set, whose clothes—pinstriped suit, vertical striped shirt, and zigzag striped tie—overshadowed his wiry and oily hair. He obviously did not care about his first impression. Arthur assumed the attorney had tenure and was waiting for retirement and was not interested in his defense. Whatever the path of least resistance was, that was the path he seemed to be pursuing. Reluctantly, Arthur knew he had to give the man a chance.

"Can you help me?" Arthur bluntly asked.

"Yes, that's why I'm here."

"Good. You need to be the head counsel for the three of us. With you leading the other attorneys. . . ."

"Whoa, hold on. What do you mean the three of us?" Fred asked.

"Bessy, Walter, and myself. The three of us need your help."

"Whoa! The court appointed me to be your attorney. Are Bessy and Walter the other bank robbers?"

"We didn't rob any bank. It's a long story."

"Whoa," Fred said glancing down at Arthur's file folder. "The police report says you did rob a bank and that's why I'm here. I can't do anything for Bessy and Walter. They have their own attorneys."

"And you need to orchestrate our cases. I'm not a bank robber. I withdrew *my* money that I had on deposit at that bank. We've got to present our case together. It's the only way we'll win."

"Whoa," Fred said holding up his hands. "I can't promise that, but I'll get in contact with their attorneys and find out what they are planning."

"Great," said Arthur feeling better about standing before the judge. "And how's Bessy?"

"I guess she's fine. Now, back to the issue of your charges; you need to know that the evidence is strongly against the three of you. With your background, the court has offered a plea bargain. The court knows you need twenty-four hour supervision. By pleading, they have agreed to send you back to live at Southern Retirement Community. It saves them the expense of a trial and you won't have to spend your time in a courtroom."

"No way! I'm fighting this. I just withdrew my money. I didn't take anything that was not mine. It's my only chance to rectify the injustice I've received."

"So you're saying you want to go to court." Fred's eyes glanced at Arthur with disbelief.

"That's right."

"You'll lose. There are videos of you robbing two different banks. You can't win. Accept their offer and it'll all be over."

"No, thank you."

"I'll see what I can do," Fred said exhausted, shaking his head in disbelief. The evidence was convincing. "I'll call you later," Fred breathed and stood to leave. The guard opened the door and he ambled down the hallway, shoulders drooped, with the file folder under his arm.

Walter was lying in his bed as Arthur entered the cell.

"My attorney understands our position," Arthur said as the door clanged shut. "He's going to set up communication between our attorneys. We'll be able to plan our strategy for our defense."

"Great, you get the good attorney," Walter grunted, sitting up on the bed. "My attorney believes I'm guilty and wants me to accept a plea bargain. And I told him no way."

Arthur sat on the edge of his bed. Something started to gnaw inside him. "My attorney suggested the same." Arthur wondered if the district attorney had already met with their attorneys and had offered all the same deal.

"Don't accept the offer," Arthur said standing. "We have nothing to lose by going to court. The worst we can get is to be sent back to Southern Retirement Community. If we go to court, at least we'll be able to tell of the horrors there."

Walter's eyes shown brightly. "You're right. You're a genius. A jury will hear our testimony." He jumped up. With a clenched fist he added, "Watch out Otman, we're going to get you." Walter walked over to the metal door and looked out. "I'm glad they denied me bail. I would have run." Walter smiled and turned to look at Arthur. "I can't wait to see his face when we testify." Laughing he added, "I couldn't have afforded bail anyway."

Shelly stepped through the metal detector inside Palm Beach County Jail and into the visitor's room. "Dad," Shelly said as she rushed up to Arthur.

Arthur held out his arms as they met. "It's good to see you," he said as he hugged. After a long embrace, Arthur led her over to a table where they sat and caught up. "The court appointed me an attorney. I think he'll do a good job. All we can do now is wait for the trial."

"Dad, you've been right about Justin," Shelly said, as she looked down at the table. "He set us both up and took everything we had. He used a drug called Halcion, a sleeping pill, to manipulate us. It causes many symptoms: Lightheadedness, dizziness, blurred vision, and coordination problems."

"That's exactly what I had. That explains all of my accidents."

Arthur told Shelly all about Bessy, Walter, Otman, and the Southern Retirement Community. The hour passed quickly and soon it was time for Shelly to leave. The guard escorted Arthur back to his cell, where he filled in Walter about what had been happening to Shelly.

As the night progressed, Arthur lay in bed wondering how Bessy was. He hoped she was safe. He became depressed thinking of her all alone in a distant cell.

The days passed as their court date grew near. Neither attorney visited his client. Their law offices always accepted their collect calls, but they reported that the lawyer was out of town. Each day Shelly came to visit her dad, but instead of telling her the truth, Arthur would fabricate another story about what their attorneys were planning. He didn't want Shelly to worry.

Arthur sat dejected in his cell. Walter was unable to cheer him. Something nagged within that Bessy, alone, was not faring as well.

"And I thought our lawyers would try to put our case together collectively. I can't believe they haven't kept in contact with us," Arthur snarled, lying in bed.

"I guess we're on our own," Walter said, looking over at Arthur. "But remember what you said. We have nothing to lose. We get to tell people how we've been mistreated."

Arthur smiled. "Thanks for the reminder." Sitting up, he started thinking of what he'd tell.

Two days before the trial, Arthur had finally gotten an appointment with his attorney. Sitting in a private room, he waited. His attorney was late.

Finally Fred came straggling in. His shirt tail hung out, as did his wiry hair. The tie hung loosened around his neck and his eyes drooped.

"Why haven't you contacted me?" Arthur yelled.

"Hello Arthur. Sorry that I'm late, but I've been haggling with the D.A. I'm here to work out a plea bargain. If you plead insanity, I can get the charges against you dropped. I told them you'd never go for it."

Arthur sighed and clinched his jaw. Fred appeared to have been run over by the D.A. and wasn't in the mood to be harassed. Arthur ignored the question and asked, "How's Bessy?"

"I don't know," he snapped. "Her attorney hasn't returned my phone call. I need to know your answer."

"You already know my answer. I'm not insane and will not agree to it. I want my day in court. I'm not guilty. I've told you it was my money. Now get out there and put my case together." Arthur stood up and banged on the door. "Guard, take me back to my cell."

Back in his cell, Arthur paced the floor wondering what the D.A. was preparing against them.

Walter sat on his bed cradling his head with both hands. He too had been offered the same deal. He had left an hour ago without answering his attorney. "We better make our plans. Our attorneys believe we're guilty."

"I hope Bessy hasn't accepted any plea bargain," Arthur said sitting on the bed.

"What are you going to do when court starts, or are you planning some sort of escape? If so, count me in," Walter probed.

"I don't know other than telling how we got sent there and how they treat the residents. I hope something will spark my thoughts and soon." Arthur stretched out on the bed, staring at the ceiling. His thoughts soon evaporated and exhaustion overcame him.

Arthur woke early, worrying about his trial beginning the next morning. He could not believe that his attorney had not found out how Bessy was.

Having reached his attorney's secretary, he grimaced, listening to her harsh voice over the telephone. "Listen, Fred is preparing for a trial tomorrow and you can't disturb him."

"I'm Arthur. That's why I'm calling, to discuses how Fred is planning my defense."

"I don't care who you are," the voice blared from the receiver. "He's very busy and you cannot speak with him. Good day," and a loud clunk sounded. Arthur's collect calls were repeatedly rejected. He wondered what kind of defense his attorney would present. A poor one, he imagined.

Walter spoke briefly with his attorney, only to hear the same offer. "No thanks," and he slammed the phone down. "What's with him?" he snapped.

Shelly promised that she would be in court the next day.

Apprehension intensified as the hours passed. "What do you think Otman will do to us when they send us back to Southern Retirement Community?"

"I'm hoping that the judge will send us to prison. We'll be treated better there," Arthur vented. "I wish I knew how Bessy was." He dreaded the thought of never seeing her again. She was the first woman he had allowed himself to care about since Laura had died. In fact he had come to care about her a great deal. The kisses were no longer diversions, but had developed into passionate symbols of their love for each other. *If we had spent a little more time with each other, I would have asked her to marry me.*

Angered, Arthur sprang off the bed. "You know, somehow I'm going to fight them," he brooded, pacing the floor. "And I'm going to beat them. I promise."

That night neither Arthur nor Walter could sleep. They both tossed from side to side, as different scenarios played out in their minds as to how the next day would develop: *Was an escape possible as they were being transported to the courthouse? If not, how could they get a fair trial? What would their judge be like—was he fair and would he listen to how they had been unjustly institutionalized? How would they present the evidence?*

Arthur prayed that they would get a compassionate jury.

They finally sat up and discussed their defense.

First, they were unjustly stripped of their power-of-attorney by Judge Blair. Second, some of the staff at Southern Retirement Community had tried to kill them and many other residents had died under their care. Third, they did not rob West Palm Beach

Bank, but Arthur had only made withdrawals from his bank account that he had worked hard for and trusted the bank to safeguard for him.

They feared the first statement would fall on deaf ears. Judges rarely ruled against another judge. They were all fraternal brothers. They tended to defend each other.

But if freedom was not attainable, then at least the issue about Southern Retirement Community would be addressed. And if they could not get their freedom back, then the robbery did not matter. They were already ruled incompetent and couldn't make rational decisions for themselves.

"We're doomed," Walter said. Chills tingled his spine.

CHAPTER SIXTY-FOUR

"Get up. You're due in court today," the guard shouted.

Arthur and Walter got dressed and breakfast was served. Chewing a sausage link, Arthur wondered what dinner would be like—pureed or solid.

Walter's fork quivered as he lifted a bite of egg to his mouth. He tried to calm himself, but it was useless. Before the fork reached his mouth, most of the egg had fallen back on his plate.

Shortly after they brushed their teeth, a guard stepped into their cell and placed chains around their wrists and ankles. Then they were ushered down the hall and to the awaiting prisoners' transportation van.

At the courthouse, Arthur and Walter were whisked upstairs to a holding cell, where their restraints were removed. Anxiety weighed heavily upon them, causing their stomachs to be unsettled.

Arthur paced back and forth in the small holding room. "Hey Walter, if at any time during our trial you believe the situation is heading south, plead guilty to bank robbery. Hopefully they'll send us to prison. We'll have rights there."

"Good idea," answered Walter.

After a few minutes of waiting, a guard appeared and instructed Walter to step from the cell.

Not knowing if they would be tried separately or together, the two wished each other good luck and Walter disappeared down the hallway.

Arthur sat waiting nervously. An eerie quiet filled the cell. His heart pounded with the anticipation of telling the judge and jury about how his money had been stolen from him, and how he had been drugged and institutionalized against his wishes. He knew it was a clear-cut case, even if his attorney did not prepare with him prior to the trial.

Soon the bailiff returned for Arthur and ushered him into the courtroom. Those in attendance watched as he walked across the floor.

Arthur scanned the room. The prosecutor sat at one table. Bessy sat at a different table with her attorney and Walter sat beyond her, at a third table, with his attorney. Arthur's attorney sat at the last table beyond Walter's. He was glad to see that they would all be tried together, but he had hoped to be seated with Bessy and Walter in order to speak with one another during their trial. It appeared the judge intentionally split them up so there would not be any conferring between them.

"Hi Bessy," Arthur whispered and his heart fluttered as he passed in front of her table.

Bessy eyes looked straight ahead, glazed over.

Passing Walter's table, Arthur asked mouthing the words, "Is Bessy okay?"

Walter shook his head slowly, back and forth.

Arthur's head lowered as grief overwhelmed him. Inhaling deeply, his gait slowed as he followed the bailiff to his table. He glanced out into the audience and saw Shelly sitting in the front row. As he approached his table, his attorney stood and greeted him.

Arthur turned and looked at Shelly.

A tear slid down her cheek. "I love you," she mouthed.

Arthur quickly turned away with water pooling in his eyes. He knew that he had to be strong in court in order to have any chance of winning his freedom.

The courtroom waited with anticipation for the judge.

At nine o'clock, the door opened as the bailiff entered. "All rise. The Honorable Harrison T. Blair presiding."

"Judge Blair!" Arthur mumbled through clenched teeth.

The judge's black robe fluttered behind him as he walked up the steps to the bench.

Arthur shot a quick glance at Walter. Fear shown in their eyes.

When the judge was seated behind the bench, the bailiff notified the courtroom, "Please be seated."

The judge acknowledged the four attorneys sitting at different tables. They in return greeted him with smiles and pleasant formalities.

Walter sat slumped over the table with his head cradled in his hands, wondering how anything could help now.

Seeing Judge Blair, Arthur's hate for the man magnified. Arthur sensed something sinister. The judge seemed very cozy with all the attorneys present in the room, including his.

"Is there any business that needs to be brought before the court at this time?"

"Your Honor," Arthur's attorney, Fred, rose from his seat and spoke, "My client, Arthur McCullen, pleads insanity." Turning to Arthur, he mouthed, "It's for your own good."

Shelly sat mortified, *Why did he plead insanity? He should have told me,* she breathed silently.

Arthur jumped to his feet and yelled, "No sir, I'm not pleading insanity!" Arthur looked at his attorney. "You're fired! I'll represent myself."

Lost in his thoughts, Walter's head jerked off the palms of his hands as he heard Arthur firing his attorney. Quickly glancing over at Arthur, he wondered what he had missed.

Bessy sat staring at Judge Blair as if everything in the courtroom was normal, unaware that anyone was upset.

"Order in this courtroom," the judge demanded. "Sit down."

The courtroom's large double doors creaked as they swung open. Otman strolled into the courtroom. In his right hand a black bag hung at his side. "Excuse me," he said softly as he inched his way onto a bench.

Arthur turned his head to see who had entered, causing the commotion. Gasping, he watched Otman sit seven rows behind Shelly. He could see bruising on Otman's forehead under his hairline.

Otman's eyes connected with Arthur's eyes. A venomous grin spread across Otman's face.

"Mr. McCullen . . . Mr. McCullen!" Startled, Arthur twisted his head around looking back at Judge Blair. "I'm not sure that I can allow you to represent yourself. Another court has taken away your power-of-attorney."

"Sir, you were that judge in that other court and Justin Roble, my son-in-law, deceived you into giving him my rights. Since then, he has emptied my bank account. Please sir, give me my rights back."

"I'll consider it and will give a ruling, tomorrow. Until then, you must keep your court-appointed lawyer. Let's seat a jury please."

The day dragged on as the attorneys collaborated amongst themselves, cleverly picking certain jurors and dismissing others. The judge seemed to know many of the potential jurists and excused them from serving, expecting their votes in the future.

In the middle of the afternoon the judge seated the six jurors—four ladies and two men—and two alternates—a man and a woman. "Be back here tomorrow at nine o'clock," the judge ordered.

Bessy was quickly ushered out of the courtroom before Arthur or Walter could speak to her.

Arthur leaned back and patted Shelly's hand, "It'll be okay." *I hope I'm right.*

The guard stepped up to Arthur and separated them. "Let's go, Mr. McCullen; I have to get you downstairs to transportation."

As Arthur was led to the courtroom's side door, he speculated that if his power-of-attorney was reinstated, there were items he might need. Stopping, he turned, "Shelly, please bring your laptop and cell phone tomorrow." She nodded and he turned and disappeared into the hallway.

Riding in the van back to the jail, Walter sat shaking. "We're in big trouble," he groaned. "With Blair as our judge, our arguments about what happened to us at Southern Retirement Community are useless and the jury will never believe we withdrew your money. They'll say we are bank robbers. We're never going to be free now." He hung his head and neither said another word for the rest of the trip.

That night Arthur and Walter could not sleep. Late into the night, Arthur blurted, "Walter, Bessy looked different. They've drugged her, or do you think that she's acting and doesn't know how to respond in court?"

"Let's hope she's acting, but I doubt it."

The next morning, Arthur's grim demeanor fled as he entered the courtroom and saw Shelly sitting on the front row. A smile spread across his face but quickly vanished, when he focused on Otman, grinning evilly, one row behind her. Arthur's body quivered.

Court started promptly at nine o'clock as Judge Blair took his seat at the bench. The jurors' seats remained empty as the judge opened a file folder.

Bessy sat glassy-eyed, staring at the judge.

Walter's fingers rapped on the table as he steamed, hating the judge.

"We have some matters that need to be addressed before the jurors are seated," Judge Blair began. "Mr. McCullen, I'll reinstate your power-of-attorney. Do you still wish to fire your attorney and represent yourself?"

Arthur stood beside the defense table. He could sense the judge was up to something. "Yes, Your Honor, I do."

Judge Blair shook his head in disbelief.

Arthur's attorney closed his notebook. Staring at Arthur, he whispered, "I hope you hang yourself."

Staring back, he spoke gritting his teeth, "If I hang myself, the noose won't be as tight as your knot."

Arthur felt wonderful being in control.

"Let's proceed. Please seat the jurors."

Mr. Douglas, the prosecuting attorney stood. "I call to the witness stand, Arthur McCullen."

Raising his right hand, Arthur swore to tell the whole truth and nothing but the truth and then sat in the witness seat.

"Mr. McCullen, on Monday morning, the day after you stole a hearse from Memory Funeral Home, could you tell the jury where and what you were doing?"

"Well, I'm not sure how to answer your question. I need a clarification from the judge before I can answer your question. May I ask him?"

Mr. Douglas was anxious to hear what nonsense Arthur would ask the judge. "Please do."

"Your Honor, was my power-of-attorney reinstated back on the day it was taken away from me, or was it reinstated effective today?"

"Mr. McCullen, why do you care when I reinstated your power-of-attorney?"

"Well, if I didn't have the capability to think what I was doing before today, then I can't be held responsible for my actions. Can I?"

"I see your point, Mr. McCullen. Obviously you're a proud man and would like to have your personal records cleared. They won't indicate that you were temporarily unable to care for yourself. I don't blame you. I realize that I was duped into believing you were a danger to yourself. Mr. McCullen, your records are officially changed. The court finds that you have always had a sound mind."

"Thank you, Your Honor. Would you please restate your question, Mr. Douglas." Arthur smiled.

Mr. Douglas smiled back. "Mr. McCullen, would you please tell the court where you were Monday morning when West Palm Beach Bank was robbed?"

"I was with Bessy and Walter. Do you want a minute-by-minute description of what I did and where I went?"

"That won't be necessary. I will be more specific with my questioning."

"On the Monday morning in question, were you at West Palm Beach Bank?"

"Yes sir."

"Did you rob West Palm Beach Bank?"

"No sir."

"Harry!" Bessy called out.

The heads in the jury box turned and watched her.

Arthur froze. His head spun, looking beyond Walter, who also had turned his head and was looking at Bessy. Her beauty had faded. Her skin was pale, tight, and drawn. Arthur realized that she had in fact been drugged again. He now recognized Bessy's blank stare, it was the same she had when on drugs at Southern Retirement Community. His eyes narrowed on Otman.

Otman's eyes were honed on Arthur. "You're next," he slowly mouthed, pointing his index finger toward Arthur.

"Harry, is that you?" Bessy's voice boomed again, catching the courtroom by surprise.

The man in the jury box that was sitting on the middle front seat smirked wondering who she was calling.

Bessy's shrill scream sent chills throughout Arthur's body. Arthur whipped his head around, looking back at Bessy.

Arthur was unable to answer her. If he responded, the jury would believe he should be locked up at Southern Retirement Community. Horror overwhelmed him. He had lost Bessy. She was the best thing that had come into his life since Laura. His eyes watered; he gritted his teeth and fought the emotions.

Walter sat slouched in his chair, having seen Otman's intimidating stares. He was certain Bessy was not acting.

The chair screeched away from the table. Bessy stood, slammed her hand down on the table yelling, "Look at me Harry when I'm speaking to you!"

Arthur looked, but said nothing.

The two ladies sitting beside each other on the back row as jurors glanced at each other. "I hope she's okay," one said.

Silence engulfed the courtroom.

Judge Blair pounded his gavel. "Order in this court room. Ma'am, if you don't sit down and remain quiet, I will have the bailiff remove you from this courtroom."

Bessy darted from her table.

The bailiff bolted from his seat toward her.

Arthur sat in the witness seat motionless. He dared not respond to her pleas.

Walter swallowed the lump that was forming in his throat.

"Harry, why did you . . ."

The bailiff tackled Bessy, knocking her to the floor.

The jurors watched in surprise.

Standing, the judge ordered, "Mr. Otman, please sedate this woman and then remove her from my courtroom."

Arthur cringed.

"Harr . . ." Bessy's mouth was covered by the bailiff's large hand.

Otman pulled a large syringe from the black bag, trotted past Arthur and whispered, "Why didn't you help her Harry? Coward!" Sneering, he grasped Bessy by the arm and plunged the needle into her skin.

Bessy's limp body lay on the courtroom floor. Otman easily lifted her. Carrying Bessy past Arthur, he muttered, "You're next."

Arthur was paralyzed. His mind raced for some answer.

"This court is adjourned until tomorrow morning."

The judge, obviously shaken by the events, quickly stood and left the courtroom.

Arthur and Walter were led back to the holding cell until the police transport vehicle could be brought to the courthouse.

While the two sat, hours passed without a word spoken. Each feared his outcome. Arthur finally persuaded the deputy to allow him access to the telephone because he was now his own attorney.

"Shelly, this is Dad. I need your help. A strange sensation just came over me. It's almost five o'clock and the courthouse will be closing. Can you hurry back down there and see who owns the property at 750 Royal Palm Way?"

Unable to make sense of Arthur's request, but wanting to help, Shelly placed the cell phone down in the passenger's seat, slowed her Suburban and turned around. She sped through traffic, passing one vehicle after another. The afternoon traffic was heavy, but with a little luck, she could make it.

Break lights engaged. Vehicles stopped. Shelly's temper erupted. Furious, she leaned on her horn. Three cars in front, an elderly woman was trying to make a right-hand turn from the middle lane.

More horns blew, but the old lady seemed unaffected. She continued to wait until a vehicle finally stopped and allowed her to make the turn.

Even after she had turned, the traffic remained at a standstill. The signal had changed to red.

Shelly's heart beat faster. *Will I make it in time?* she kept asking herself.

When the light turned green, the two cars in front of her took off. They seemed to be in more of a hurry than she was.

The Suburban swayed as it turned into the courthouse parking lot.

Sighing loudly, Shelly jumped from her vehicle and raced for the front door. Looking at her wrist watch, she realized she had ten minutes before closing. *Whew, I made it.* She ran up the steps, through the double doors, and down the hallway to the records department. Huffing and puffing, she grabbed the door knob and twisted. The door knob did not turn. It was locked.

Her heart pounded. Peering through the door's glass window, the clock on the wall indicated five-o-five. Looking back at her watch, the hands still indicated four-fifty. Realizing her battery was dead, she began banging on the door.

"We are closed," a voice from inside the room sounded. "Come back tomorrow."

"Please help me. It'll only take one minute. I just need to find out who owns the property at 750 Royal Palm Way."

"Look on our web page. You can access that information yourself."

"Thanks." Shelly couldn't believe that she could have gotten the information from home to start with.

With the five o'clock traffic bumper to bumper, Shelly relaxed and waited patiently as the traffic moved slowly along.

Once home, Shelly logged onto the Internet. Her heart raced with anticipation wondering what Arthur had suspected and what she would discover.

Chapter Sixty-Five

Shelly bit on the end of her pen as she watched the monitor. For some reason the Internet was slower than usual. With a sudden imprint, the web page appeared. Shelly stopped biting her pen and leaned forward reading line by line.

Appraised Value: $2,350,000.00

Property Owner: Elizabeth Tillman given by deed from William Tillman

Address: 750 Royal Palm Way

William Tillman - Husband or Dad? Why does Dad need this information? Shelly printed out the information, folded the paper and stuck it into her purse.

The next morning Shelly was up early, anxious to inform her dad that Bessy Tillman owned the property in question.

Arriving early, Shelly sat on the front row fidgeting, waiting for Arthur to be ushered into the courtroom. At eight-forty-five, Arthur was brought into the courtroom, along with Bessy and Walter.

Bessy sat beside her attorney. Her eyes stared blankly toward the ceiling. Her face was drawn into tighter wrinkles, her bloodshot eyes strained to focus. The drugs had reclaimed Bessy's beauty.

"Is Harry going to be here today?" she blurted loudly, looking at the man seated beside her. Her court-appointed attorney, in exasperation, rapped his fingers on his briefcase and wondered why he always represented demented people.

Arthur wanted to rush to Bessy's side, but knew it would be too risky. *Otman's increased her medicine. He's going to kill her. Oh, please Bessy, don't die.*

Walter watched Arthur wondering if Arthur would hold together. He knew someone was trying to get at Arthur and they were doing a good job by using Bessy. Looking between Arthur and Bessy, he feared he would be the one that now had to present the facts. He did not know if he could do it.

Arthur stared at Bessy. He needed to get her to stop taking the medicine, but then remembered that Otman had injected her the day before and was keeping her sedated. He did not know what to do. Heartbroken, Arthur looked away.

The courtroom seemed to grow colder as the minutes passed. Arthur sat alone feeling deserted. He wished he could talk with Walter or Bessy. He needed some encouragement. Court was soon to begin and he had lost what to say. Southern Retirement Community seemed closer to a reality now.

"Dad," Shelly whispered, interrupting Arthur's self-pity.

Arthur leaned backward.

"Dad, Bessy Tillman's name shows on the deed to the property you have asked about. A William Tillman deeded the property to her. I hope that's the information you wanted to hear."

It was minutes past nine o'clock and the judge had not entered the courtroom. Small talk was heard throughout the room.

"All rise. The Honorable Judge Harrison T. Blair presiding," the bailiff said, holding open the door for the judge.

The courtroom became silent as all rose, watching the judge enter and sit down at the bench.

The state prosecutor, Mr. Douglas stood, "Your Honor, if it pleases the court, I would like to call Mr. Walter Clemmons to the stand. Mr. McCullen seems to be a hostile witness. Therefore some groundwork must be laid out before I can question him further."

"I object, Your Honor," Walter's defense lawyer demanded.

"Overruled."

Walter looked over at Arthur with great puzzlement. "What are they up to?" Walter mouthed.

Arthur shrugged his shoulders.

Walter hesitated to follow Mr. Douglas' directive, but knew there was nothing he could do. Slowly he sat down in the witness box.

Standing only inches away from Walter, Mr. Douglas stood stoically, intimidating the witness.

Walter had never given his testimony. He sat trembling in the witness seat. Mr. Douglas noticed and began with his most direct question.

"Mr. Clemmons. Is this you in this photograph?" Mr. Douglas handed him the picture.

Looking at the photo, Walter could see his face clearly standing at the center counter where the deposit slips were kept at West Palm Beach Bank's downtown location. His mouth quivered as he tried answering the question, but no sound was forthcoming.

"Please repeat your answer. The court could not hear you," the judge asked.

Walter's chest, tightened, "Yes, sir."

Encroaching tightly into Walter's airspace, the prosecutor grinned, "Now what does this picture show that you were doing at the bank?"

Walter stiffened in his seat. *Careful how you answer*, he warned himself. His chest constricted; he was unable to breathe. He searched for an acceptable answer. He knew if he answered the question truthfully, he would be convicted of a crime. Then the judge would send him to a state mental hospital immediately, where he would spend the rest of his life, locked up under the influence of administered drugs. If he said he did not remember, the state would tell the jurors he had run away from Southern Retirement Community and then send him back to Ward C for his own safety and the safety of others as they could see from the photograph. He knew that would only mean death by overdose.

"Your Honor, I need some help here," Mr. Douglas requested.

"Answer the question, Mr. Clemmons," the judge ordered.

Needing to buy additional time so that he could come up with an answer, Walter decided to try Arthur's approach. "Your Honor, are you going to reinstate my mental capacity like you did Mr. McCullen's yesterday?"

"Absolutely not. You have not provided me with any reasonable doubt for any wrong done to you."

Walter realized he was next to be injected with zombie drugs, like Bessy. Otman's evil eyes penetrated him. He was not going to give the court any information that they could use against Arthur. He knew Arthur was his only chance left to be set free.

Drool began running down Walter's face. His head twitched. His hands grabbed his shirt, ripping it open. Buttons flew throughout the courtroom, bouncing everywhere. Without fear, he took off one of his shoes and threw it at the judge.

"What's Walter doing?" Arthur gasped.

"Ow." The shoe landed squarely on the judge's neck. A red welt rose immediately.

The jurors sat stunned.

Walter looked over at Arthur and smiled.

The bailiff responded immediately, pulling Walter from the witness seat to the floor.

"Bailiff, remove Mr. Clemmons from the courtroom. Mr. Otman, please assist the Bailiff and return Mr. Clemmons to Southern Retirement Community promptly where he can receive his needed medication. Everyone has witnessed how unstable he is."

Arthur sat in his seat, scared. He was now alone to fight for the three of them. With the corrupt judge, he knew there was only a short period of time left before his doom.

The bailiff pulled Walter toward the door. Walter gave an honorable fight, kicking and yelling as he slowly shuffled, slowing the judge's orders, smiling at his disruptiveness.

Otman rose from his seat holding a hypodermic needle.

"Harry, stop that this instant," Bessy stood yelling.

The jurors turned and looked at Bessy.

The bailiff and Walter froze in their steps.

"Here we go again," the man on the second row said to his fellow jurors.

Arthur's heart raced as he jerked his head around and looked at Bessy. He didn't understand why he was being scolded.

"Stop that Harry. I mean it," she slammed her hand down on the defense desk, her teeth clenched.

Arthur's eyes widened as his jaw dropped. Bessy was not looking at him, but at the judge. He wondered how many drugs she had been given. She was crazy.

"Bailiff, get her out of my courtroom," Judge Blair thundered.

The courtroom broke out in loud chittering, with everyone asking what was transpiring.

The bailiff did not know what to do. He was given two orders to follow and decided to accomplish both at once.

Walter realized this was his only chance to further confuse the judge and just maybe, escape. Feeling the bailiffs' grip easing, Walter snatched his arm free and bolted for the door. As he took his second step, the big hand grabbed his arm again.

"Harry!" Bessy screamed, as she shuffled toward the bench.

"Bailiff, help!" the judge roared, backing away from the bench.

The jurors looked at each other wondering what they should do.

Wheeling around on his heel, the bailiff realized the peril facing the judge. He released Walter and darted toward Bessy.

Otman leapt over the railing which separated the audience from the court proceedings and rushed to the judge's defense.

Mr. Douglas also rushed toward Bessy, trying to protect the judge.

"I'm glad I was picked as a juror," the man on the first row said to the man behind him.

"I've never heard of anything like this happening in a courtroom," the man replied, leaning forward.

As the mayhem unfolded, Arthur slid his chair backward to the railing. "Shelly, quick give me your laptop and cell phone. Hurry."

Shelly pulled her laptop from its carrying case and handed it to Arthur. Reaching into her pocketbook, she pulled out her phone.

Arthur quickly took the phone and plugged it into the laptop. With the power switch activated, the processor crunched through its startup procedures.

Walter darted out the side door. He was appreciative of Bessy's sacrifice, allowing him to escape.

"Look, that one's fleeing," the woman alternate juror said, as the door closed.

"Stop, you're hurting me," Bessy screamed.

"Uhhhh!" the lady juror sitting beside the man on the front row gasped.

The laptop had finished its boot-up procedure and Arthur pressed the Internet button. The modem started its dialing process.

Arthur looked up. His heart ached. The bailiff was sitting on Bessy, fastening handcuffs around her wrists. Mr. Douglas held her head down on the floor, by a handful of her hair. Arthur envisioned hitting the two with his chair, but knew that would only lead to his being thrown out of the courtroom and his eventual demise.

Shelly watched in horror.

Kneeling on the floor beside Bessy, Mr. Douglas noticed Arthur using a laptop. He wanted desperately to get over there and see what Arthur was up to, but was detained, assisting the judge. He expected a ruling in his favor during the trial.

With his fingers gliding over the keyboard, Arthur searched the Internet for the State of Florida's web page. With a click of the laptop's enter-button, he was into the State's web page. Surfing quickly from page to page, Arthur heard the judge's seat squeaking as he sat back at the bench.

Mr. Douglas stood, brushing dust and lint off his pressed suit, looking directly at Arthur.

The keys clattered. Arthur hit the enter key.

The prosecutor stepped hurriedly toward Arthur.

Hurry, Arthur whispered toward the laptop. He did not want Mr. Douglas to see what he was searching for. Hopefully, it would be a surprise.

The courtroom was filled with commotion. The jurors wondered what would happen next.

"Order in this courtroom!" Judge Blair banged the gavel. "Order!"

With a blink, the screen filled with information.

The bailiff scooped Bessy up off the floor and handed her to Otman, who grasped her and carried her to the back doors. Her mouth had been taped closed. Her eyes were red and teary.

All jurors' eyes watched Bessy being carried off.

Arthur could not look at her. He continued to read the information on the laptop's screen.

The courtroom quieted as Otman stepped out of the courtroom.

Mr. Douglas stepped to the table and moved around its side to have a look at what Arthur was reading.

Out of the corner of Arthur's eye he could see Mr. Douglas rounding the table.

Click — Arthur's finger pressed the sleep button. The screen went black as Mr. Douglas maneuvered behind him. He could only hope the information had not been read.

"We're going to take a fifteen minute recess, then the court will reconvene," said the judge.

After the judge stepped out of the courtroom, chatter erupted from the people remaining.

Arthur stepped to the railing where Shelly stood.

Mr. Douglas watched Arthur. He knew something was up and did not want any surprises, not with this case unfolding the way it was. This trial should soon be over.

Arthur noticed the beady eyes honed on him and did not want to be heard. With a quick surge, he wrapped his arms around Shelly. "Call the media. The newspapers, radios and any television stations. Tell them there is a corrupt judge and he is about to be identified. They don't want to be the only media missing the latest breaking news. Hurry."

Realizing that Shelly's cell phone was in his hand, Arthur called out, "Shelly!"

Stopping, she turned around.

"Here's your phone and laptop."

Shelly hurried out the double doors.

Mr. Douglas sensed something was up and moved to follow her.

Not wanting him to interfere with her phone calls, Arthur stepped in front of Mr. Douglas. Every time he moved one way or the other to go around, Arthur moved the same direction.

"Get out of my way," Mr. Douglas grabbed Arthur and shoved him aside.

Arthur smiled, walked back to his table, sat down and waited.

The bailiff stepped over to where Arthur was and kept an eye on him.

Mr. Douglas ran out into the hall.

CHAPTER SIXTY-SIX

Arthur sat staring at the clock on the wall. With the passing of each minute, his heart rate increased and his breath quickened. *Where's Shelly? Why hasn't Mr. Douglas returned?*

With one minute remaining before the judge's return, Mr. Douglas stepped into the courtroom and sat at his table.

Otman returned to the courtroom smiling. He bounced toward the front row, sitting where Shelly had been sitting throughout the trial. Leaning forward he breathed, "Arthur, you're next," as he tapped on the black bag.

Arthur stiffened in his seat, listening to the debaucher's laugh. Trying to distance himself from Otman's voice, Arthur leaned as far forward on the table as possible. *Don't listen to him.*

"All rise. The Honorable Harrison T. Blair presiding."

"Please be seated."

"Mr. Rodriguez," Judge Blair began, "your client has been found to be incompetent by this court. Therefore, when he is caught, he will be returned to Southern Retirement Community where he will spend the rest of his life. You are dismissed as his attorney."

While Mr. Rodriguez gathered up his papers and placed them in his briefcase, the jury waited anxiously wondering what would transpire next.

"Mr. Douglas, will you call your next witness," the judge requested.

Rising to his feet, Mr. Douglas spoke, "I call Arthur McCullen to the stand."

Arthur turned to look at the back doors of the courtroom. *Where's Shelly?*

The doors remained closed.

Arthur needed her now. She had the laptop. He slowly rose to his feet, trying to stall the court's proceedings. Each stride was short and slow. He could see the judge's patience growing thin with his behavior. But he did not care.

"Mr. McCullen, please move faster to the witness seat. If you need help, I'll instruct the bailiff to assist you."

Arthur ignored the judge's comment.

Judge Blair motioned for the bailiff to assist Arthur.

With two swift steps taken, the bailiff grabbed Arthur's arms, lifted him off the ground and positioned him on the witness seat.

Mr. Douglas grinned at Arthur's treatment.

"Mr. McCullen, yesterday you told the court that you were at the West Palm Beach Bank and demanded money. Now today we heard Mr. Clemmons identify himself, standing next to you. We know you held the bank guard hostage, detaining him from protecting the bank, while you and Mr. Clemmons robbed it. Now I want to present you with a new exhibit, photograph number two. It shows you fleeing with sacks of money from the bank. Now are you going to deny that this is you fleeing the bank."

"I need to ask questions to clarify what you said."

"Mr. McCullen," Judge Blair interrupted, "you cannot ask questions. That is the prosecutor's responsibility. You must answer his questions."

"Mr. Douglas, when did Walter, I mean, Mr. Clemmons . . ."

"Mr. McCullen, you are not allowed to ask any questions. Now is that clear? Answer Mr. Douglas' question," the judge snorted.

Arthur glanced where Shelly had been previously sitting. Otman held the black bag up so that Arthur would see. Arthur quickly looked away. He wasn't going to be intimidated.

Arthur scanned the room for Shelly. She was still missing. Glancing at the double doors, wishing they would open, his heart sank with despair. "Where is she?" he asked under his breath.

Arthur asked Mr. Douglas to repeat his question and the court reporter read back the question.

Arthur sat on the edge of his seat and listened closely to the question being asked, knowing Judge Blair would not tolerate further delay from him. As he listened to the question, his mind searched for what he had agreed to earlier. Unable to remember the exact words spoken, he sided with the prosecutor, reasoning that he would never make an untruthful statement in front of the judge.

Arthur inhaled, "No . . ."

The courtroom doors jostled open with a loud commotion following. All eyes turned toward the back of the courtroom to see who was entering.

All three men in the jury smiled. With today's earlier surprises, they watched eagerly, wondering what would happen next.

Shelly entered, followed by a television camera crew and two newspaper reporters.

Judge Blair was startled; his eyes searched those who entered.

Mr. Douglas watched dumbfounded as the group walked to the front.

Leading the way, Shelly eased into the second row, sitting behind Otman. The media eased into the third bench.

"May we continue, Your Honor?" Mr. Douglas pleaded.

"Mr. McCullen, answer the question," the judge ordered.

"I would like to show the court a web page I saved earlier today."

"No, you may not, Mr. McCullen!" the judge snapped. "You are only allowed to answer the questions asked."

421

Arthur did not listen to Judge Blair's outburst. His eyes were locked with Shelly's eyes, pleading for her to understand his encrypted speech.

Shelly did not fully understand his message, but understood that he needed her to turn on the computer. She opened the laptop as the judge thundered.

"Mr. McCullen, I have warned you for the last time. . . ."

Shelly was startled as she lifted the lid of the laptop. Her finger inadvertently brushed the space key.

The laptop hummed as the screen flickered on, revealing Arthur's last page he had downloaded. Shelly smiled. Arthur had put her laptop into sleep mode.

". . . . One more outburst and you'll be unable to testify in this courtroom."

Arthur stared at Judge Blair, listening with contempt.

As Shelly read the screen, the journalist behind her looked over her shoulder and read.

"Harry!" Shelly yelled as she stood.

Otman turned, looked, and shot daggers at her.

The television camera crew saw Shelly standing, unsure of what might happen next, the cameraman pressed the power button on the camera and began recording.

Arthur watched Judge Blair's reaction. He sat motionless.

The jurors quickly turned and watched Shelly.

"Harry is short for Harrison," Shelly continued. "This marriage license, a public document, indicates Harrison T. Blair is married to Bessy Tillman."

"Bailiff, remove that lady, NOW!" Judge Blair bellowed.

As the bailiff stormed toward Shelly, Arthur stood, pointing his finger at Judge Blair. "This man built Southern Retirement Community in order to lock up his wife by drugging her, so that he could take her money. He stole . . ."

"Bailiff, remove Mr. McCullen this moment!" the judge yelled, his face turned a deep red.

The bailiff stopped in his tracks, looking to see who he should remove first.

"Judge Blair is a wicked person. He allowed my son-in-law to steal my money from the West Palm Beach Bank. This man sat as the officiating judge in both of my cases. If this man did this to me, how many others were robbed and unjustly locked away? This man needs to be arrested."

The men in the jury watched with exhilaration. "I can't believe we're getting paid to watch this," the man on the second row whispered to the man in front of him.

Judge Blair stood, his chair slammed into the back wall, and he scrambled toward the witness box.

"West Palm Beach Bank was started by William Tillman, Bessy's dad," a newspaper reporter shouted. "It was willed to Ms. Bessy when he died. Judge Blair is the president of that bank."

Arthur turned to watch the judge coming down the steps toward him.

The reporter stood demanding answers, "Judge Blair, did you put Bessy Tillman in Southern Retirement Community to take control of her dad's bank and steal her money?"

The bailiff with many questions of his own, responded to the judge's movements. With thunderous footsteps, he raced toward the witness seat.

Arthur was fifty pounds lighter than the judge and years older.

The judge leapt toward Arthur.

The jurors rushed to the back of their boxed-in seats. Fear emanated from their faces.

One of the newspaper writers angered by what he had heard, dropped his pad and pen as he led the others to the witness seat to assist Arthur.

Arthur turned to flee from the witness box, but the witness chair blocked his exit. The chair quickly rolled to the box's right side. Arthur stepped out from the box as the judge's body appeared in the corner of his eye.

With a quick dart to his right, Arthur softened the judge's blow, as the two toppled to the floor. The bailiff had reached out and grabbed Arthur's body, keeping him from crashing hard.

The large newspaper reporter was next to arrive. His massive hands grabbed the judge's black robe, jerking the judge off Arthur.

Judge Blair's balled fist swung, contacting the newspaper reporter's head. The judge's other fist was arching through the air, but stopped inches from contact.

The bailiff held the arm firmly in both hands.

The large newspaper reporter shook off the blow he had received, reached up behind the judge and grabbed the black collar. The judge's body bowed backward, as his body slammed to the floor.

The bailiff pulled out his stun gun and applied a quick blast of electricity. Judge Blair's muscles instantly turned to gelatin.

With a quick jerk, the judge's body rolled over to his stomach as his arms were snatched behind his back. Two clicks echoed in the courtroom as the handcuffs secured Judge Blair. Then, he was led from the courtroom, having been read his rights.

The bright lights from the camera crew followed the judge's expulsion.

The jurors had hesitantly returned to their seats not knowing what they should do.

Otman nonchalantly stood and crept silently out of the courtroom's back doors.

Some news media were on their cell phones reporting the latest breaking news to their supervisors.

Shelly ran up to her dad and flung her arms around him. "Thank goodness you're all right."

After a few minutes a different bailiff entered the courtroom. "Order in the courtroom."

The noisy courtroom quickly became silent as everyone stopped what they were doing and turned their attention to the bailiff.

"All rise. Judge Joseph Ruben presiding."

The judge sat and directed his attention toward Arthur. "Mr. McCullen, you are released on your own recognizance if you promise not to flee overnight and if you agree to appear back here in this courtroom, tomorrow morning. This case has not been dismissed. There are still serious charges pending against you."

Arthur agreed and asked permission to meet the judge in his chambers, immediately after the court adjourned.

Arthur's joy was apparent as he passed Mr. Douglas, who was sitting shell-shocked. Arthur and Shelly sat in the judge's secretary's office, waiting for the judge to finish interviewing the bailiff.

"Good luck, Mr. McCullen," the bailiff spoke as he exited the judge's chambers.

"Thanks for your help, bailiff."

"Don't mention it; I was glad to help."

Judge Ruben invited Arthur and Shelly into his chambers and asked what he might do for them.

Arthur explained that Bessy was not dangerous and that she was at great risk staying at Southern Retirement Community due to unscrupulous employees who were doping her and had killed others. He asked that Bessy be released into Shelly's care overnight. He promised that she would also appear in the courtroom tomorrow.

After receiving permission to take Bessy to Shelly's for the night, Arthur then explained how Justin, his son-in-law, and Judge Blair had teamed up to deliberately steal his life's savings.

Judge Ruben listened intently as Arthur explained that Walter and Bessy had also been wrongly institutionalized.

CHAPTER SIXTY-SEVEN

Arthur grasped the judge's orders tightly in his hand.

Excited to have Arthur back, Shelly glowed as she wove in and out of traffic speeding to rescue Bessy. As they drove up to Southern Retirement Community, a deputy was waiting for them. The deputy led the way into the facility.

The frightened receptionist was glad he was not there to arrest her and quickly told them Bessy was back in Ward C in her old room.

Arthur bolted down the hallway and through the double doors into Ward C.

Otman saw Arthur and rushed toward him, but suddenly stopped when the deputy entered the room.

Arthur flashed the court order and Otman begrudgingly led Arthur, Shelly, and the deputy to Bessy's room.

A nurse appeared at Bessy's room with a wheelchair.

"Bessy, I'm here to take you home. You'll never have to spend another night here," Arthur said, tenderly lifting Bessy from her bed, mesmerized by her soft touch. He wanted to hold her forever.

"Arthur," Bessy said as her eyes strained to recognize him.

"Mr. Otman," the deputy's deep voice boomed, "I have a warrant for your arrest." With Otman's hands cuffed behind him, the deputy read him his rights.

Arthur and Shelly were elated as they witnessed Otman being pushed into the backseat of the deputy's vehicle, while they freely made their way to the Suburban. It was unfortunate for Otman that his already bruised head hit the roof of the car as he was forced in.

Bessy did not seem to know what had transpired, except that she was leaving.

With an arrest warrant out for Justin Roble, Shelly felt wonderful driving home. She knew sooner or later he would be arrested and brought back for trial.

At Shelly's house, Bessy was given much water to drink. The intoxicating drugs would soon be gone. By midnight, she was almost normal.

After waking from a short night's sleep, Bessy asked if she might use Shelly's telephone. The second telephone conversation did not last long and soon they were on their way. As they entered the courtroom, Walter ran up to Arthur and Bessy. The three embraced for a long time.

Walter explained that he had seen the previous evening's news and learned of Judge Blair's arrest. He had called and spoken with the news reporter covering the courtroom drama and had been advised to be at the courthouse at nine o'clock this morning.

People pressed tightly inside the courtroom wanting a chance to witness what would happen to Arthur who had become an overnight hero. News media intermingled in the crowded courtroom. Bright lights illuminated the large airy room. Legal pads lay in many laps waiting to be filled with the final outcome from yesterday's startling courtroom drama.

When Judge Ruben entered the courtroom, silence promptly spread across the entire crowd.

The jury box sat empty.

"Mr. McCullen, Mr. Clemmons, and Ms. Tillman, I am glad to see the three of you here today. It is my privilege to inform you that as of today, all of your rights have been reinstated. The bank's testimony is that there were no bank robberies, but only a customer withdrawing his money. The charges against the three of you have been dismissed."

Judge Ruben smiled as he declared. "The three of you are free to go."

The audience broke out with loud cheering as strobes instantaneously flashed and brightened the courtroom.

Shelly ran up to the three and gave a group embrace.

"Ms. Tillman," the judge called as he walked up to the defense table. "Here are your divorce papers. Mr. Blair signed them this morning."

"Ladies and gentlemen, may I have your attention?" the judge's voice proclaimed. "Quiet, please."

"Arthur wants to speak." The judge looked at Bessy and winked.

Bessy beamed with a huge smile back at the judge.

"I do?" Arthur questioned, as he looked at the judge and then Bessy. He remembered Bessy having made a secret phone call earlier that morning and wondered if this had anything to do with it.

Bessy's eyes glowed, looking at Arthur. She shyly raised her eye brows.

"Oh! Yes, I do!" Arthur beamed, "Bessy, will you marry . . . ?"

Before he had finished speaking the final word, "YES," resonated inside the courtroom.

"I just happen to have a marriage license with me," Judge Ruben said, winking at Bessy.

Cheers and laughter erupted from the audience. Shelly nodded, sending her approval. The crowd quickly found a seat to watch the ceremony.

The judge pulled out the license from a folder he held under his arm and placed it on the table. All blank lines had been previously filled in, with the exception of two. The blank lines needed two signatures. Bessy and Arthur quickly signed the license.

"Bessy, do you take this man to be your lawfully wedded husband?"

"I do," Bessy eagerly replied jumping in Arthur's arms, not waiting for further instructions, and — KISSED — the groom.

Laughter filled the audience, as the kiss lingered and the judge's voice boomed, "I now pronounce you husband and wife. You've already kissed the bride."

"Congratulations!" Walter said wondering if they had really gotten married. Then the three friends embraced.

The double door swung open as a caterer rushed in carrying a three-tiered wedding cake, enough to share with all of their guests.

After Bessy and Arthur experienced the usual cake in the face routine and met the crowd, they said their goodbyes. A white limousine whisked them away from the courthouse. Bessy had thought of everything.

Anchors Away—the sixty-foot Hatteras, eased backward, out from the docks. Bessy and Arthur leaned back in the puffy white chairs, sitting on top of the flybridge. Their honeymoon cruise to the Bahamas had begun.

ELLIOT FICTION

For Additional Information Contact

Elliot Fiction
P. O. Box 277
St. Marks, Florida   32355
http://elliotfiction.com

The sequel is being written now. Look for it in the upcoming year.

Thank you for reading this book. We welcome your comments. Please email us at sales@elliotfiction.com.